Praise for Gary McMahon

"*The Concrete Grove* is a tense, ghoulish, creeping horror guaranteed to give you recurring nightmares! Brilliant characterisation, economic prose and with genius control of building tension, the climax of *The Concrete Grove* will leave you reeling! There's a new wave of brilliant horror writers – and McMahon's right there at the top of them."

– Andy Remic, author of *Kell's Legend*

"Gary McMahon is one of the finest of a new breed of horror writers. His work combines spare, elegant writing with an acute sense of the growing desperation felt by those having to deal with the crime and crumbling infrastructure of our urban centers. Illuminating these themes with a visionary's sense of the supernatural makes *The Concrete Grove* one exciting read."

– Steve Rasnic Tem, author of *Deadfall Hotel*

"Gary McMahon is a spellbinding storyteller. *The Concrete Grove* is as feverish and unnerving as it is gripping: a bleak orchard of humanity where you hardly dare to look at what dark things hang gleaming and winking in the branches of the trees."

– Graham Joyce, author of *The Silent Land*

"*The Concrete Grove* is an outstanding mix of urban horror and dark fantasy, hints of King's *The Dark Tower* series, hints of Holdstock's pagan fantasy but ⟨...⟩ as the ⟨...⟩es."

Also by Gary McMahon

Hungry Hearts
Pretty Little Dead Things
The Concrete Grove
Dead Bad Things

SILENT VOICES

GARY McMAHON

SOLARIS

First published 2012 by Solaris
an imprint of Rebellion Publishing Ltd,
Riverside House, Osney Mead,
Oxford, OX2 0ES, UK

www.solarisbooks.com

UK ISBN: 978 1 907992 78 0
US USBN: 978 1 907992 79 7

Copyright © 2012 Gary McMahon

Map artwork by Pye Parr

10 9 8 7 6 5 4 3 2 1

A CIP catalogue record for this book is available from the
British Library.

Designed & typeset by Rebellion Publishing

Printed in the US

For Charlie, my Best Boy:
I can't wait to see what kind
of man you grow up to be

Acknowledgments

Thanks always to Emily and Charlie for giving me a reason to fight; to Ross and Katarzyna Warren for checking and correcting my pitiful attempts at the Polish language; to John Probert for the medical advice regarding stab wounds; to Michael Wilson, Jim McLeod, Jason Baki, Colin Leslie and many other kind reviewers and bloggers who supported the first *Concrete Grove* book; to Mark West (again) for his interest and enthusiasm; and finally huge thanks must go to John Roome for some sound advice given at a time when it mattered.

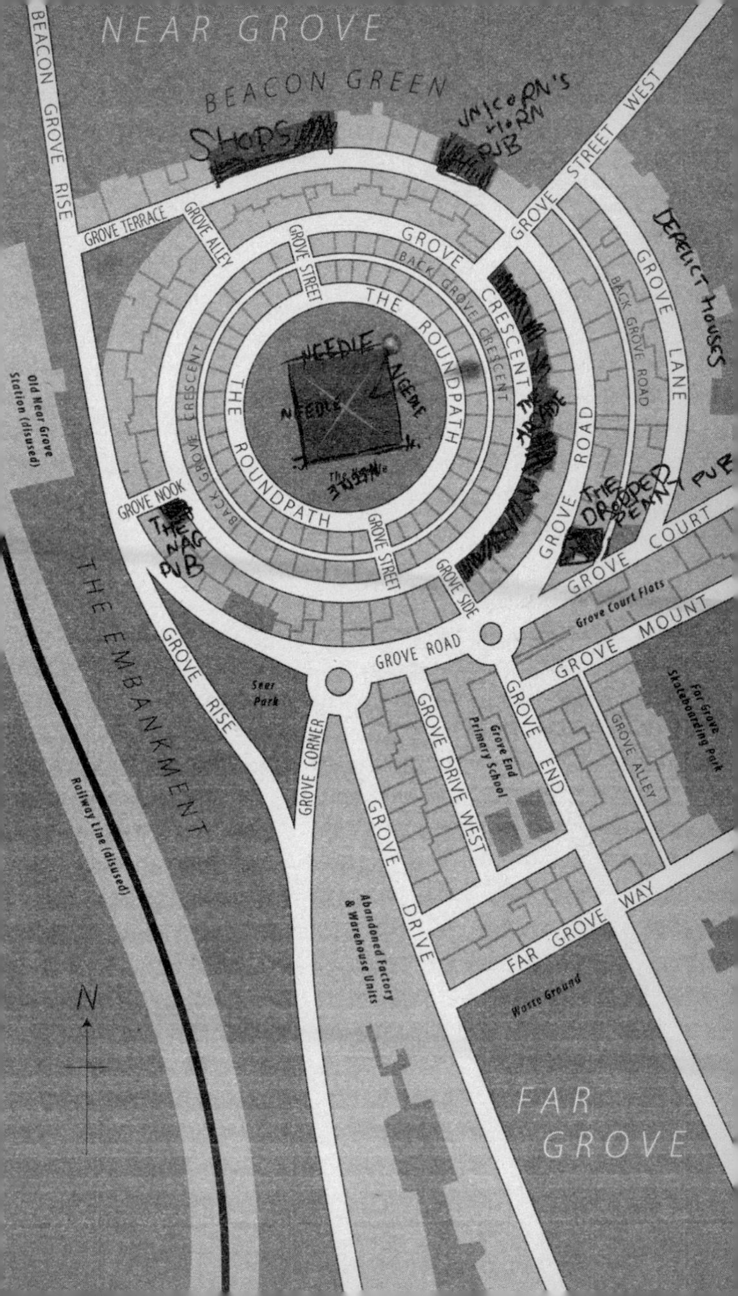
NEAR GROVE
BEACON GREEN
BEACON GROVE RISE
SHOPS
UNICORN'S HORN PUB
GROVE STREET WEST
GROVE TERRACE
GROVE ALLEY
GROVE STREET
GROVE CRESCENT
BACK GROVE CRESCENT
THE ROUNDPATH
NEEDLE
DERELICT HOUSES
GROVE LANE
BACK GROVE ROAD
GROVE ROAD
THE ARCADE
THE DROPPED PENNY PUB
GROVE COURT
Old Near Grove Station (disused)
GROVE NOOK
THE NAG PUB
GROVE SIDE
Grove Court Flats
GROVE MOUNT
THE EMBANKMENT
GROVE RISE
Seer Park
GROVE CORNER
GROVE DRIVE WEST
Grove End Primary School
GROVE END
Far Grove Skateboarding Park
Railway Line (disused)
GROVE DRIVE
Abandoned Factory & Warehouse Units
FAR GROVE WAY
Waste Ground
N
FAR GROVE

"The rest is silence."

– *Hamlet*, Act 5 scene 2
by William Shakespeare

"Humpty Dumpty sat on a wall,
Humpty Dumpty had a great fall.
All the king's horses and all the king's men
Couldn't put Humpty together again."

– Old English Nursery Rhyme (circa 1811)

TWENTY YEARS AGO, WHEN THE WORLD WAS SO MUCH SMALLER...

THE SUN IS a bronze penny hanging motionless in the sky as the boys toil beneath its hazy glare, laughing and sweating and having fun. The kind of fun that they will never have again, once they go beyond a certain age: kid fun, all happiness and innocence and mercifully free of the sharp edges adults develop, even in their play.

It's been a long day for the Three Amigos – a typical English summer day, filled with running and play-fighting and sweet, long bike rides along the old railway line that runs along the bottom of the Embankment, with the gang pretending they are on their way to somewhere special – a place other than this one, with its embittered people and grey concrete promises.

But now, late in the afternoon, the bikes have been put away and the three boys are planning to build something in the trees at the north edge of Beacon Green, just up the hill from the old Near Grove railway station: a high platform, the beginnings of a proposed tree house.

Marty brought back the necessary tools from the drawers in the garage when he returned from a tense lunch with his perpetually warring parents, and Brendan stayed behind while the others returned home to eat so that he could gather enough wood for the project. Brendan never goes home for lunch: his father is dead and his mother drinks too much, even during the day. *Especially* during the day. Simon, the third member of the group, often feels guilty that he never invites his friend home for a meal, but the tension between his own parents is too uncomfortable to inflict upon anyone else. They are going through a 'bad spell'; that's what they call it, as if it's the result of some kind of dark magic. As far as he can tell, he once told Brendan, their entire marriage is a bad spell – one that's been going on since before he was born.

"Get that bit over there," says Marty, the muscle of the gang. He points towards the splintered remains of a timber pallet and waits for the other two to walk over, drag it from where it lies half-hidden under the bushes, and then carry it over to the site of their construction project.

"Jesus, it's heavy." Brendan is very thin; his elbow bones jut out like twigs and his face always looks starved.

"Yeah, but that's because you're a wimp." Simon laughs at his friend and gives a tug on his end of the wooden pallet, causing Brendan to stumble. Brendan sticks out his tongue; it is a child's riposte, lacking sophistication even for a ten-year-old.

"Come on, then. Let's get this thing built!" Marty is standing with one foot resting on the mouldy trunk of a fallen tree. He has his hands on his hips, and he pouts as if he is waiting to be kissed. To the other boys, he looks strangely alluring: like an asexual being that's been trapped somewhere between childhood and the great unexplored country of adulthood. A tree nymph or a woodland elf: some mythical being from a story book, rather than the streets of a northeastern council estate.

"Yes, Miss!" Brendan's voice carries through the silent trees, disturbing a ground-dwelling bird or a small mammal from its hiding place. The animal darts through the undergrowth, rustling the leaves and branches, as Brendan and Simon let loose with a brace of laughter.

Marty shakes his head and slowly lets his arms drop to his sides, abandoning the pose. "Piss off!" he shouts, much too late to salvage his dignity.

The boys fall quiet for a while, occupied by the simple task of sorting out pieces of wood. They discard ruined, shattered pieces of timber and form a pile of decent material that can be re-used. The sun moves slowly down the sky, tracing the day's journey towards early evening. The sky seems to shimmer above the scene, like the underside of a distant body of water.

Brendan stops for a rest. He walks across to the nearest tree and sits down at the base of its trunk, retrieving a can of pop from his jacket, which lies grubby and creased on the ground. He opens the tab and drinks deeply, his eyes closed and his head tilted upwards. His fringe falls back to reveal a forehead pocked with livid acne and absently he scratches his thigh with his free hand. It's a displacement trick he learned long ago – scratch another part of your body rather than the place you really want to scratch, and pretend that you've eased the discomfort.

Brendan opens his eyes as he lowers the can, scanning for a moment the green expanse of Beacon Green which lies beyond the line of the trees. He narrows his eyes, leaning forward with an intent look on his face. He licks his lips, stray droplets of pop making them sticky and sweet. Close to his position, gouged into the bole of the nearest tree, someone has used a penknife to write a single nonsense word: *Loculus*.

Brendan studies the hand-carved word. It means nothing to him, yet something inside him stirs. The spotty skin on his back crawls, as if tiny feet are walking between his shoulder blades. His forehead begins to itch.

His eyes widen. He has seen something, some kind of movement, way behind the carved tree; an image that he believes does not belong here. He begins to stand but pauses partway to his feet, staring at a point beyond the trees. What was it? Did he even see anything at all, or is he just tired?

Staring in wonder, he watches a tall, dark figure as it passes between the final row of trees, taking short, dainty strides – almost skipping along – and facing forward. The figure is wearing a long black overcoat that reaches down to its ankles. On its head is perched a strange black cap – like a flattened top hat, but with a wider, floppier brim. Beneath the hat is a sort of black snood or cowl that falls down the back of the head, protecting the rear of the neck.

Brendan wants to call out to his friends, but something has robbed him of his voice. He crouches there, with one hand pressed flat against the base of the nearest tree, supporting him, and the other still gripping the empty pop can. He watches the figure as it passes from tree to tree, visible for seconds at a time as it dances gaily between the broad dark trunks.

The figure is either hideously deformed or wearing some kind of mask. The bone-white face is pinched forward and outward to form a long beak with a sharpened end. The large, bulbous eyes look like swimming goggles, but with black frames and lenses.

The figure is terrifying. Fear has taken Brendan's voice, and only when he realises this does he regain the ability to communicate.

"Lads!" He turns and glances towards his friends, and then back again to where he saw the figure. It has stopped and turned towards him in the short time when his attention was elsewhere; he feels its gaze, even through the absurd goggles. There is a thin walking stick in the figure's yellow-gloved right hand, and it raises it, like a weapon or a magician's wand, pointing it in Brendan's direction. The other hand, also covered by a dull yellow glove, makes abstract shapes and patterns in the air, the fingers moving in intricate contortions, as if they are tying knots out of nothing. He knows that he should not be able to pick out such minor details at this distance, but somehow he can. It is as if the figure has grown more vital in his perspective, like an embossed image standing proud from a flat background. The effect is disorienting: he feels sick, his head begins to pound; his eyes water as the figure looms in his vision, drawing closer and increasing in definition without taking even a single step towards him. It must be an optical illusion... a trick of the light.

Then he begins to hear the clicking sound, like fingers snapping along to some otherworldly tune.

Brendan opens his mouth, but no words come out. He stares at the figure, at the way its coat flaps about the thin body even though there is no wind to cause the motion; the way the material bulges and rises slightly in front, as if a rogue gust is trapped under there, between the figure's long, thin legs. Then, one by one, what looks like several additional limbs seem to emerge from beneath the hem of the coat, their small, bare, two-toed feet kicking and flapping as they descend awkwardly to the ground.

"Quick, lads! Come here!" His voice sounds raw, as if his throat has been damaged, his mouth parched. But at least he has found the strength to speak.

He glances away and then back again. The figure is no longer there. A beam of sunlight blazes in the spot between the trees where the figure had stood, making the air look as if it has caught fire. The two trees that had framed the figure seem to bend fractionally outwards, making the space bigger than before and straining beneath the pressure of reality.

"What's up?" Simon is standing beside him, reaching down to help him complete the journey from sitting to standing. "You look like you've seen a ghost."

Brendan turns his head and stares at his friend, at his wide, amused eyes. He feels the small pimples on his forehead tighten; the larger ones clustered across his back and shoulders begin to pop, covering his flesh in a warm, sticky excretion. He doesn't quite know if he's still afraid or simply relieved that he was just seeing things out there, beyond the trees.

Should he be glad that his imagination is creating phantoms, or should he be afraid that it has done so to fill some kind of gap in his brain?

"I think I did," he says, shaking now, unable to hold back either a scream or a laugh – he's not sure which – for much longer. "A ghost... or a monster."

PART ONE

LEARNING TO SPEAK

"Sometimes you have to go back just so you can move forward."

– Simon Ridley

CHAPTER ONE

SIMON RIDLEY SAT at the window and stared out at the seething darkness of King's Cross. His torso was bare; he'd spilled some wine on his shirt earlier, when he'd been preparing a late dinner, and it was warm enough in the flat that he had not bothered to put on a clean one. The July sky was clear and the thin, fragile clouds drifted like skeins of semen in bathwater.

The room was dark, too. He had not turned on the lights. The dinner he'd made sat cold and untouched in a bowl on the kitchen counter, the pasta stiffening and the tomato and garlic sauce congealing like old blood. He rubbed his face with his hands, and realised that he needed a shave. His head felt emptied, hollowed out.

A creased, padded manila envelope lay on the dining table before him, and he tried his best not to look again at the printed handwriting. The package had been posted here, to his home address, rather than the office, and it had arrived after he'd left for work. So he'd only seen it when he got back a few hours ago, after leaving the office early because of the overnight car journey he had scheduled.

The book sat next to the discarded packaging, the outer edges of the cover slightly blackened, perhaps by fire. The title was illegible, the author unknown.

But he knew what the book was. Once, a long time ago, it had belonged to Simon. He had owned it in another lifetime.

The book was called *Extreme Boot Camp Workout* by Alex 'Brawler' Mahler. It had once belonged to Simon's father, a man who enjoyed keeping fit more than he liked spending time with his family. Simon had lost track of the book years ago, when he left home to come to London. But now it was here, back in his hands.

A helicopter hummed past his window, miles away but still visible in the crisp evening sky. Simon turned his head and watched it go by, reminded of something he had seen or been told of a long time ago but could not quite grasp with any level of clarity right now – something to do with hummingbirds.

He reached out and touched the other item that had been inside the envelope along with the book: a single immature acorn, its shell caught in the process of darkening from green to brown. Carved roughly into the shell were his initials: SR. His fingers traced the letters, and then he pulled his hand away, as if he were afraid to touch the thing for much longer than a few seconds.

His laptop sat open on the table, its screen the only bright spot in the room. The web browser displayed an article from the *Northumbria Times* newspaper. It was old news, from before Christmas. November, to be exact: almost nine months ago. He couldn't even remember what he'd been doing back then. Lately his life seemed to be running away from him, leaving him with vague, unsubstantial memories of business meetings and social events, deals and parties and random encounters with people who held little interest for him.

The article was about a fire on a housing estate in Northumberland which the locals called the Concrete Grove. Simon had grown up there, and left as soon as he was old enough to get out on his own. But despite him not setting foot back there in the best part of fifteen years, the place had never really left him.

You can take the boy out of the Grove...

According to the reporter a small gym owned by a local gangster had been set alight, and the fire had killed two people: the owner, Monty Bright, and one of his associates, a man called Terry Bison. Both men's bodies had been so badly disfigured in the fire that they could only be identified by partial tattoos and dental records. The second man had also been identified by his prosthetic arm.

A few columns down the page, printed as an unrelated side bar, there was mention of unidentified birds gathering over the local landmark known as the Needle. The old tower block – derelict for decades – seemed to have been the focal point for the congregation of tiny birds on the night of the blaze. Hundreds of them had hovered around the tip of the tower, remaining there for half an hour, and then disappeared once the blaze was under control. It was reported as a natural phenomenon, a weird bit of local colour.

A hard copy of both of these articles had been included in the envelope, along with the book. Their headlines were crudely circled in red pen by whoever had sent him the package. Simon had no idea why anyone would send him these now, so many months after the fire in the report. The postmark on the front of the envelope showed that it had been sent from the northeast. It didn't take much to put the clues together and realise that someone from the Grove had sent him the information. Probably the same person who regularly sent him clippings from the local rag, leaflets taken from the Tourist Information Centre, and countless other pieces of seemingly random information. He'd been receiving this stuff for years. Even when he moved house – which was often – the anonymous sender somehow managed to track him down.

But none of this information was random – not really. It was all connected by geography.

Simon reached out and grabbed his mouse, double-clicking on the left button and opening a shortcut on his computer desktop. The icon was a link to an online server, where he stored all the information he collectively termed the Concrete Warehouse.

The rented space on the server acted as a depository for anything that he felt might be linked to his old home town – things he'd been sent by his nameless informant, information he'd gathered himself. He also had copies of everything on a portable hard drive that he kept hidden in a drawer of his desk back at the office. He had been updating these files for years, since he moved away from the area to live in the capital. The files weren't exhaustive; he had probably missed a lot of things, mostly due to his inability to afford a decent computer until his business concerns had begun to do well. Before that, he'd done what he could, storing information when he was able. Only when he was in a position to buy good equipment had he switched to the server.

If asked, he would struggle to give a reason for doing this. It just felt right. He thought it was a thing he should do, an interest he should maintain. It was also for these vague reasons that he'd kept an eye out for the names of his old friends on the estate, particularly the two boys he'd shared his childhood with. The boys he had never made contact with since leaving the Grove. Only one of those names had proved fruitful, and he'd kept tabs on its owner for quite some time. The other name was as good as lost.

Simon ran his hand across the roughened cover of the book. It felt calloused, like old skin. He turned back to the window and stared out at the night. He picked up the book and opened it, thumbing through the pages at random. Scrawls and scribbles; doodles and diagrams. A page from an old A-Z map was pasted over the centre pages, and the word 'Loculus' was written in black pen and underlined several times on the back page; other words had been written, too, the handwriting different for almost every one.

He turned to page twenty-nine and stared at the words he knew he'd find there. His own handwriting, years out of date, looked like a fake, a forgery. But he had written the words himself, just after the single biggest event of his life. This single sentence was the reason he knew the book was the same one he had owned when he was ten years old.

The Concrete Grove is a doorway to Creation

He had never known what the phrase meant, but it had been in his head when he and his friends had emerged from the derelict tower block that morning, battered and bruised and covered in filth. Like a message in a bottle, it was meant for him: a warning, a declaration of war, a reminder from his childhood self that he could never escape the shadows of his past.

He shut his eyes and closed the book, placing the palm of his hand across the cover, as if trying to hide it from view. He felt like crying, but he wasn't sure why. Sorrow grasped him, squeezing him tight.

"I need a drink," he said. He was already feeling light-headed, two Martinis to the wind, and he had a long way to drive later. But he no longer wanted to drink alone; he needed company, even if it was the company of strangers.

Making a decision, Simon put on a T-shirt and checked his reflection in the mirror. Then he grabbed his coat, shrugging it on as he crossed to the door of the penthouse flat, went out onto the private landing and pressed the button for the lift. He watched the lift lights flash on and off as he waited, showing the elevator climbing through the floors. He experienced the absurd notion that somebody was in the lift, coming to meet him.

The lift doors opened, and after only a slight pause he stepped inside the empty chamber, hitting the button for the ground floor. Nobody else got on during the downward journey. It was late – the other tenants in the building were either entertaining at home, enjoying a quiet Friday evening in, or out and about in the pubs and clubs of the capital. He had picked this apartment block specially, because none of his neighbours was aged over thirty-five and they were all well-heeled executive types, with busy social lives. This was a young place, a vibrant environment, and the endless activity in the rooms and corridors helped him not to dwell on the past – or, at least, the parts of the past that he could remember with any real clarity.

Simon felt his mobile phone vibrating in his inside jacket pocket. He retrieved the phone and glanced at the screen. Natasha was trying to call him. He made no move to answer the call. He didn't want to see her, not tonight. He needed to clear his head, not muddy it by having to deal with her demands and recriminations. Things had been strained lately, because of his fuzzy plans to return to the estate of his youth, and the fact that he had not invited her along for the ride had irked her, making her angry and paranoid. For reasons of her own, Natasha was unable to fully trust any man.

"Sorry, darling," he muttered, and put the handset back in his pocket. Before he reached the ground floor, the vibrations ceased. Then, as if on cue, the lift doors opened. Simon stepped out into the lobby and walked towards the main doors. Norman, the aged security guard, was sitting at the front desk reading a slim paperback and ignoring the flickering bank of CCTV monitors to his left.

"Going back out, then?" He smiled and lowered his book.

"Yeah, I fancied a few pints. I couldn't settle up there on my own... not tonight." Simon liked the old man. He had a good face: all lines and creases, but with sharp bones underneath.

The security guard smiled and nodded, as if they were sharing a private joke. "Enjoy," he said, and raised a hand, palm open, fingers splayed. "Have one for me, would you?" He made a slow fist, the sight of which set off tremors inside Simon's mind.

"You bet. See you later, Norm." Simon went through the sliding doors and stepped out onto the footpath, aware of an obscure fear dogging his heels. The night was warm; there was no breeze. It was going to be a hot summer. Part of him was glad that he'd be in the milder climate of Northumberland, while the rest of him was beginning to yearn for London before he'd even stepped outside her borders.

London, he thought, *becomes a part of you. It slips under your skin without you knowing, and before long you ache at even the thought of leaving.*

He headed southwest, in the direction of Caledonian Road, where his friend Mike owned a small bar called The Halo. An odd place, never quite full but rarely what would be called empty, and the rough-edged clientele made for an interesting and varied bunch. Simon felt safe there; he found himself drinking at The Halo more and more these days, as if it offered something he craved but could never quite identify.

Cranes dotted the skyline, rearing against the darkness like strange prehistoric beasts. The area was being renovated, cleaned up and made into a tourist-friendly location: the word was that the Borough of London wanted King's Cross to be a destination itself rather than simply a way station for weary travellers on their way to somewhere else. The old porn shops and stripper bars were slowly being forced out of business, and in their place had sprouted chain sandwich bars and coffee shops. Simon knew this was a good thing, and that it could only raise the profile of the area, but he would miss the seediness he had always associated with the streets around the station.

The Halo was situated on the corner of Caledonian and All Saints Street – a street name he'd always found amusingly inappropriate. The windows bled light, and music and the buzz of conversation drifted from the open doorway. The jukebox was playing Bowie, which meant that Mike was back behind the bar after his trip to Dublin.

Simon walked into the bar, feeling a sensation of belonging. Mike was the closest thing he had to a real friend, and he was glad that he'd get the chance to say goodbye. He wasn't sure why this was important, but he knew that it was.

"Hey, Simon! Good to see you." Mike started pulling a pint of Guinness. By the time Simon reached his usual stool at the bar, the glass was being put down on the scarred bar top to settle.

"How was Dublin?"

Mike shook his head. His tousled blond hair was a mess, as usual, and his blue eyes glistened. "Not bad. The stag couldn't hold his drink, the best man was pick-pocketed by a stripper, and half of us ended up going for an Indian meal instead of to the nightclub." He smiled. "I think I must be getting old."

"You and me both, brother. That Guinness settled yet?"

Mike topped up the glass and pushed it towards Simon, his eyes scanning the bar. It wasn't packed, but there were enough customers in there to keep him busy, especially if they all wanted serving at once. Robert, a tall, thin transvestite who drank there every night, stood by the jukebox idly flicking through the playlist. He turned and nodded at Simon, then returned his attention to the music.

"On your own tonight?" Simon took a sip of his drink, closed his eyes and savoured the cold iron taste on his tongue. It wasn't the best pint of Guinness to be found in London, but it was good enough.

"The girl's meant to be here, but she hasn't arrived yet. I haven't even had a call to tell me she's running late." 'The girl' was a short, dark-haired Goth named Betty who helped out at The Halo three or four nights a week, and more often when the place got busy. Mike had a crush on her but had never got up the nerve to make a move.

"She'll be here. She can't keep away from you, man." Simon grinned.

"Fuck you, rich boy." Mike grabbed a rag and started wiping down the bar. He moved away for a moment to serve three middle-aged men double whiskies, and then returned to stand opposite Simon.

"I'm going away, mate." Simon put down his glass. "Tonight."

"Prison? I told you not to shag that girl – she only looked about twelve."

Simon stared at his friend. "I'm serious. I might be gone... for a while."

"Is anything wrong? Can I help?" Mike leaned across the bar, falling short of grabbing Simon's arm but clearly thinking about it.

"No, no. It's nothing like that. No trouble. Just some stuff from my past that I need to confront." Simon tried to smile but he didn't quite manage a convincing attempt. "I'm going home."

"Northumberland? I thought you'd turned your back on that place for good. Didn't think you'd ever go back." Mike's eyes were hard, like chips of ice. He was worried, and that made Simon feel sad. It was nice to have someone who cared, but in truth he'd always found this kind of close personal attachment difficult to deal with.

"Nor did I, but sometimes you have to go back just so you can move forward."

"Ah, Confucius say, 'you pretentious prick'."

Simon laughed; the moment was broken. The tension vanished.

"What about Natasha?" Mike raised one eyebrow. It was a comical gesture, but hidden behind it was a serious question.

"I don't know. I really don't. One minute I can't get enough of her, the next I wish she'd just leave me alone."

"Nice problem to have, that. A Russian supermodel hassling you for sex."

"Please. I know I sound like a complete tosser, but seriously it isn't as neat and tidy as it sounds."

"But is it as good as it looks?" Mike threw the rag at Simon, and then stalked the length of the bar to serve a heavily tattooed young woman in a low-cut vest top. He took longer than was necessary, revelling in the attention, and Simon smiled as the woman wrote something down – probably her telephone number – on a piece of paper before handing it to him, smiling, and walking away. When she sat back down at her table, her friends let out a muted cheer.

"Jesus, mate," said Simon, when Mike returned to his spot behind the bar. "I've seen you do that with at least two or three women a week ever since I've known you, and still you're too scared to ask Betty out on a date."

"Tell me about it," said Mike, shaking his head. "I'm an idiot. But what can I do? The girl brings out my inner awkward teenager."

Simon had almost finished his pint. He drained the glass, listening to the comforting throb of noise in the bar. "Do me a favour?" he said, finally. "Keep an eye out for Natasha while I'm away. I don't know how long I'll be gone or what'll happen while I'm there, but I'd like to know that someone I trust has her back."

Mike nodded. "It goes without saying, mate. When she and all her model friends decide to pop in here for a few pints of bitter, I'll make sure she keeps her hands out of Robert's fishnets."

"I'm serious. I have a bad feeling, a *weird* feeling about things. Just let me know if you hear anything. Or even if you don't hear anything and just have a suspicion that something's wrong. Just call me. You have my number, so use it."

Mike nodded. "Okay, man. Don't get so heavy."

"Sorry. Things on my mind; I'm under a lot of pressure."

"Yeah, it must be tough being a millionaire."

A few minutes later, after exchanging several more insults and shaking hands, the two men parted. Simon left The Halo, feeling as if he were leaving a part of himself behind, lost in the beer-smelling shadows. He glanced over his shoulder as he walked out the door, and saw Mike staring at him, a strange expression on his face. When he realised that he'd been spotted, Mike did not smile; he did nothing but raise one hand in farewell.

Simon gave the thumbs-up sign and stepped out into the night, wishing that he could turn back and order another drink, then another, and another, until he was more drunk than he'd ever been in his life. But even then, he knew, he would be unable to cut the shackles and let himself loose from the ties that bound him, the invisible chains and ropes connecting him to a past he could barely even remember.

CHAPTER TWO

SIMON LIKED TO drive at night, especially if he was going a long way. The darkness soothed him, and he had trouble sleeping anyway so the constant motion of the motorway held a strange kind of appeal. Less traffic meant that he could open up the engine and get where he was going a lot quicker than during the day, and most of the night traffic was made up of long-distance heavy-goods vehicles, hauling God-knew-what to God-knew-where, so he got to sit in the fast lane and cruise past them all.

It took him a while to get out of London, but he made good time along the A1. By the time he passed Scotch Corner and the road turned into the A1(M) it was almost two in the morning. The dual carriageway was deserted; there weren't even vans and trucks on this stretch of road. He felt sober now. Parts of the road were badly lit, so he drove through entire stretches of darkness, glancing at the flat black fields and the occasional stunted buildings.

He began to crave coffee, so decided to stop at an all-night service station with an annexe that was done up like an American diner from the 1950s. Chrome sides, signs proclaiming *24-Hour Eats!* and a large pool of yellow light in which were parked a few cars and a motorbike.

Simon sat in the car until the song playing on the radio ended. It was one of his favourites: 'No Alarms', by Radiohead. When the song faded he reached out and turned off the engine. Silence rushed in to swallow the retreating sound.

He got out of the car and walked across the gravel car park, feeling oddly exposed in all that open space. He glimpsed a man sitting in the window seat of the diner, drinking Coke directly from the bottle and reading from a Kindle. There was a crash helmet on the table next to him; this must be the owner of the Kawasaki he'd parked next to. Simon paused at the door and looked up. The moon seemed impossibly distant, and the sky was sharp and clear, as if it were waiting to be filled. All the Hollywood alien invasion films he'd ever seen started with a sky like this one.

He grinned to himself and went inside the diner.

A skinny woman with dyed blonde hair stood behind the counter. She could have been anywhere between thirty-five and sixty. Her hair was dry, like straw, and the lines around her eyes and her mouth were as deep as stab wounds.

"Evening," she said as Simon bellied up to the counter, grabbed a stool and settled in. "What can I get you?"

"I'll have a coffee, thanks. No milk. No sugar." He smiled at her and took out his phone, checked it for text messages. There was one from Natasha, just as he'd expected. He opened the message and read it: *miss u already. call me when u can. x.* He fucking hated it when she used text-speak. Simon was the kind of person who properly punctuated his texts, even to the point of using semicolons. He deleted the message and placed the phone on the counter.

"One coffee," said the woman behind the counter. "No milk. No sugar."

"Thanks," he said, and grabbed the cup. It was almost too hot to hold. "That's lovely."

"Anything else?"

He took a sip, burning his lips. "Lovely," he said again. "Yes, I suppose I could use a bite to eat. Do you have a sandwich, or something?"

"Whatever you like, love. We serve food 24-hours here. Hot and cold. Sweet and savoury."

"How about a tuna salad baguette?"

"Speciality of the house." She winked, and it was a grotesque sight. The eyelid moved slowly, as if it had been damaged. The motion reminded Simon of a faulty roller blind going down over a dirty window.

"Thanks," he said, and spun around on his stool.

The motorcyclist in the window seat was still absorbed in his Kindle. A young couple sat at a table by the toilet door, holding hands across the tablecloth. They were staring into each other's eyes but not saying much. The woman had been crying; her cheeks were grubby from the tears. The man was biting his bottom lip.

Further along the counter from where Simon was perched, an older man sat staring at his hands as they made knots on the countertop. He looked like he was puzzling over an intense riddle. He kept frowning, shaking his head, and then frowning again.

These places at night, Simon knew from experience, attracted only the lost and the lonely. Long after all the normal travellers – the families and the truckers and the salespeople – had got wherever it was they were headed, these troubled souls remained on the open road, and they were drawn here like moths to a guttering flame.

The woman brought out his baguette. It looked surprisingly good.

On the counter, his phone began to vibrate. Simon picked it up and looked at the screen. It was another text from Natasha. She was either out late with her modelling clan or sitting up unable to sleep and thinking about him. He supposed that Mike was right; he *was* in an enviable position. He was a rich man and had a Russian underwear model pestering him to settle down and make their relationship more stable. If he detached himself from his life, and examined it all like an outsider, it seemed perfect. But in reality, nothing had ever been perfect for him. Since his youth, Simon had felt dogged by something. Whatever good things happened, he was always expecting the other shoe to drop, or waiting for the hammer to fall... he only ever acknowledged the dark cloud to every silver lining. It was as if he were tainted by darkness, and where other people saw the connections in human relationships, all he ever saw were the cracks.

He switched off the phone and considered throwing it in the bin, severing all ties. He wasn't sure why this urge came upon him, but he felt that it might be something to do with the surroundings and a hell of a lot more to do with the fact that he was going home.

Not for the first time, Simon admitted to himself that he was more comfortable in places like this diner, among people like these, than he was in his penthouse flat sharing space with his girlfriend. All his life he'd felt cast adrift, untethered, as if the normal rules of society did not concern him. He only ever felt at ease when he was in transition, between destinations; he only ever sought companionship from those who would not hang around for long. The single constant in his life was that there were no constants; he held to no routine and followed his whims as if they were sent to guide him.

He ate half of his sandwich, paid the bill, and got up from his seat, ready once again to answer the call of the road. Lights flared in the distance, and he couldn't tell if they were approaching or moving away. As he drove the car past the diner's windows, the woman behind the counter stared at him. She lifted a hand, as if to wave, and then looked at the hand as it hung in the air, unmoving. Her expression was troubled; she didn't know why she had begun the gesture. By the time she worked out what to do with her hand, Simon was leaving the diner behind him to rejoin the dark stretch of dual carriageway.

The rest of the journey unfurled just as smoothly. Before long, Simon found himself driving past the familiar landscape of Birtley and Low Eighton before Antony Gormley's Angel of the North statue reared majestically into view.

Simon felt a vague tugging sensation inside his chest as he watched the statue rise above him, as if the hill upon which it stood were slowly lifting away from the earth. The Angel was a massive, imposing structure, twenty metres tall and fifty across the wings. The blank face of the statue gazed impassively, overseeing the region like some cold, emotionless deity.

Simon pulled over into a lay-by and parked the car facing the hill. He switched off the engine and stared through the windscreen, feeling strangely attracted to the controversial structure. He remembered the uproar when it was first conceived; how a lot of people had spoken out about the faux rusted effect on the metal figure, and complained at the waste of the million pounds it had cost to create and erect. But now, all these years later, the figure had become an icon, an emblem of the northeast. Simon had always thought the Angel an unsettling sight. Its straight, razor-edge wings, the rigid stance, and the suggestion of the figure looking on in disdain... it was as creepy as it was compelling. He wasn't sure if he loved the thing or loathed it.

"So I guess this means I'm home," he whispered, staring at the Angel. The dark sky offered a dramatic backdrop, and the thin clouds and the distant stars seemed to retreat from the figure, afraid to get too close. As Simon watched, he was overcome by the sensation that the hulking figure was just about to move, that it was going to turn its massive rusty head and gaze down at him, judging him unworthy of entry into the land where he had been born, the place where his forefathers had set down their roots and carved out a life for themselves. He became convinced that the two-hundred-tonne metal figure was poised to shift, tilt, and then perhaps tear its feet from the concrete foundations in order to chase him, crush him, and finally send him back into the bosom of the earth from which he had sprung...

He shook his head, smiling. "Jesus. I must be going mad." He gripped the steering wheel, clenching his fingers around it. He left the car, not bothering to lock it, and entered the site of the statue. He climbed the hill, feeling drowsy yet energised, as if the air up here were fresher and cleaner than that on the road.

When he drew level with the elevated feet of the Angel, he reached down and touched the rough metal. He expected to feel something – anything: a shudder along his spine, an itching at the back of his neck – but nothing happened. He remained unmoved. The feelings he'd experienced back at the car, whatever they meant, had deserted him, and all they left behind was a curious emptiness.

"You don't want me, do you? I've come home, and you don't even care."

The Angel did not respond.

Simon sat down between its feet and stared at the sky. There was no light yet visible at the edge of the horizon, and for a moment he felt that he might never see daylight again, that he was trapped inside some endless night, populated by lonely waitresses and heavy metal sculptures. Then, sighing, he got to his feet and walked back down the hill to the car, feeling as if the giant figure had slowly twisted at the waist to watch him depart. He paused, stood still, suddenly too afraid to turn back and take a look. Then, allowing the feeling to pour through him and out the other side, he finally glanced behind him. The Angel had not moved.

"Of course not," he whispered, trying and failing to smile. He hurried the rest of the way to the car, and once he was inside he locked the doors before starting the engine.

He'd be home soon. In half an hour he'd reach Morpeth. From there it was less than twenty minutes to the Concrete Grove, where God knew what was waiting for him.

The Angel receded in his rear-view mirror as he drove further north. It did not move, nor did it register his departure. It was just a hunk of metal parts. A grim angel of broken promises standing at the border of a land whose dreams had always been dark and restless.

CHAPTER THREE

BRENDAN WAS DOING the hourly rounds. His lower back ached from sitting in his chair and he was feeling sorry for himself because of the way Jane had been acting earlier that evening, but the work had to be done. The work *always* had to be done.

He walked one more circuit of the Needle, feeling the rash across his shoulders bristle as he stepped into the tower block's night-time shadow, and then turned back towards the squat, modular grey shell of the Portakabin that served as the on-site security station. The stars looked impossibly tiny in the black night sky, and the moon hung there like a polished silver coin left underwater: vague, almost ghostly.

Brendan heard a sound behind him, coming from the tower block. He turned, waving his torch at waist level so that the beam skittered across the base of the structure. Nothing moved. He saw rampant weeds hugging the concrete, debris and litter on the uneven ground, and a lot of building material that had been dumped over the years when previous refurbishment or development projects had been abandoned.

The sound came again. This time it was louder, and he thought that he might be able to pinpoint its source. One of the ground floor windows – the ones with steel security shutters over them. Several of the shutters had been replaced when the site was shored up and the perimeter fence erected, but others had been randomly removed. He wasn't sure why; it seemed a silly thing to do, especially in this rough and rundown area, where putting up a barrier was tantamount to an invitation to break and enter for the local street kids.

"Hello?" He felt stupid saying it, but what else could he have called?

There was no reply.

Brendan walked slowly towards the Needle, his torch beam slicing through the darkness to illuminate parts of the whole: a sealed door, a barred window, a cracked wall, a plastic bin leaning against a pile of bricks.

"This is private property. I'm legally obliged to remove you from the premises." More empty words. He wished that he had a dog with him, but the security firm wouldn't pay for him to do the dog-handling training, even though he'd asked them countless times. When he'd asked for a partner to accompany him on the night shift, his boss had just laughed and told him to "man up" and "grow a pair."

They were real investors in people, Nightjar Security Services...

Hearing nothing but the late-night urban lullaby of barking dogs, distant voices and revving engines, Brendan moved closer to the side of the building. He flashed his torch across the wall, looking for an aperture by which someone might have gained entrance to the place. The graffiti was illuminated briefly: swear words and sex words and obscure gang tags sprayed in blood-red paint. None of the security shutters had been interfered with; everything seemed secure. He walked along the wall, then turned and advanced along the side of the Needle. He did another complete circuit before finally coming to a halt beside the main doors.

Brendan stepped forward and tried the handle. He wasn't expecting the door to open, so when it did he simply stood there, staring at his hand as it pulled the door wide.

"Shit," he muttered, wondering if he had forgotten to lock it.

Now that he'd discovered the way in, he knew that he couldn't walk away without inspecting the interior of the building. He didn't like it in there. Apart from the fact that it was a spooky old building, and he was alone here at night, there was the part of his past that he never liked to think about. The time when he and two of his friends had come here, and everything since had turned sour.

Everything.

Sometimes he felt that whatever had happened to them that night had stained his life, each day that followed becoming steadily darker as a direct result of them coming here, to the Needle. And the end point, the final blackness, lay just up ahead, at the end of his days, waiting for him like an open mouth.

Brendan's throat was dry. He tried to swallow but it was difficult.

There came another sound from deep inside the building: a short, sharp impact, like something being thrown against the wall.

"Shit." He said it louder this time, but the curse brought with it little bravado. Brendan was scared, and there was no way of ignoring that fear. So instead he embraced it, tried to take strength from his terror. For a second he could even pretend that it was working.

Brendan had been inside the Needle many times since the childhood experience that even now he struggled to remember; he had fought long and hard to conquer his fear of the place, and had finally arrived at a state of compromise. He was physically able to enter the tower block, but he would never feel truly at ease within its walls: his psyche began to tremble whenever he walked there, and he knew the footsteps he heard echoing around him as he did so were not necessarily his own.

Brendan pushed through the main doors, feeling as if he were taking a step backwards through time, drawing close to an event that he could never quite grasp and claim as his own. A soft breeze stroked his cheek; dust drifted in the dimness; tiny sounds seemed to move towards him from all sides.

"If you don't get the hell out of here, I'm calling the police. There's a fast response time. They'll be here before you can even get past me to the door." He tried to sound brave, to make his words seem fierce, but all he felt was small and lonely, like a little boy trying to act like a TV tough guy. He didn't even have his two-way radio; he'd left it back in the security cabin.

More sounds emanated from the depths of the building. There was definitely someone else in there, moving around on the ground floor. He tightened his grip on the torch, the only weapon in his possession. It was heavy, rubber-coated, and once, on another job, he'd knocked someone unconscious with a blow to the head. He'd been trained in subduing an opponent, but wasn't what anyone would call a natural fighter. He knew some basic technique, but that was all. If he came up against a hard man who knew what he was doing, then Brendan would have no chance.

He peered into the dimness, trying to make out shapes. There was evidence of someone staying here: an armchair, a row of old television sets, all turned to face the wall, several heaps of what looked like clothing, a burst mattress, the remains of a kebab and its wrapper scattered across the floor. The walls, when he flashed the torch beam across them, were covered with graffiti: gang tags and obscure band names, phone numbers that you could call if you wanted a blowjob. The air smelled of hops and old cannabis fumes. The floor was covered with all kinds of loose material, and for a moment he caught a whiff of what smelled like shit.

He stared at the doorway ahead of him, and it was only after the figure crossed the space from left to right that he realised he'd seen someone.

Brendan twitched in shock; a delayed reaction, a strange little side-step because his body was unsure how to react. "I'm armed!" He gripped the torch even tighter, hoping that he would not have to use it – or if he did, that he managed to get in the first blow and it was hard enough to count.

The figure crossed the doorway again, a dark silhouette moving this time from right to left. It moved with a staggering gait, as if whoever it was had been drinking heavily.

It's a doper, he thought. *He's stoned and doesn't know where he is.*

He relaxed slightly, more sure of himself now that he could put a name to his fear. Drug users had been known to break into the Needle to shoot up or smoke crack; kids sometimes came here to fuck; once or twice the most desperate transients had even popped in for a night's sleep.

"Show yourself. Come into the main space here, and I'll escort you off the premises. If you do not comply, I will be forced to call for police back-up and you will be arrested." He thought that he sounded like some sad old rent-a-cop: a pathetic character in a shitty movie. "This is private property. You are trespassing."

The figure stumbled back into view. It was thin, unsteady on its feet, and had now turned to face the doorway.

"That's right. Just come through here and we can sort this out the easy way."

Brendan flicked his wrist to bring the torch beam around, so that he might highlight the figure. The man stood framed in the doorway, his clothes dirty and ragged, his hands clutching the shattered wooden frame, and his face a white featureless mass hovering above his narrow shoulders.

"Shit." Brendan stepped backwards, almost tripping on a pile of something directly behind him. "What the fuck?" The torch beam danced across the walls, striping the figure as it advanced through the doorway and into what used to be the main entrance hall, but was now just a vast space filled with junk.

The man moved slowly. His arms hung loosely at his sides. His bloated white head was rigid, locked facing forward. He had no eyes. No mouth. Just a tattered white mask, an image from a nightmare...

...and then Brendan realised that the man's face was bandaged. He was limping; he wasn't drunk or stoned, but injured. He dragged his feet across the filthy floor, twisting his hips awkwardly and moving towards the sound of Brendan's voice.

"Are you okay, mate?" Brendan no longer felt threatened. The man was unwell. He had clearly come here to hide his infirmities away from the world. Cursed with his own medical condition, this was a reaction Brendan could understand – he empathised with the man's desire to hide, to lock himself away from a mocking world.

He remembered the names he'd been called at school: *Rashback, Beam-Me-Up-Spotty, Dot-to-Dot*... and a hundred more, each worse than the last. The skin across his shoulders and the top of his back cried out in sympathy; his pain reached out to this other man's agonies, like a hand across a chasm.

The man with the bandaged face made a low, soft sound, somewhere between a cry and a sigh.

"It's okay, mate. I won't hurt you. Come on; let's get you out of here. I have food and drink back at the cabin."

The man reached out a hand and it flailed in the air like a damaged bird.

Brendan grabbed the hand and tugged, helping the man across the detritus-covered floor. Close up, the bandages were surprisingly clean. They looked fresh, as if they'd been recently applied. Somebody somewhere was looking after this man, and they were making sure he kept his dressings clean. That was something, at least; it meant that he wasn't completely alone in the world. There was someone to tend to his most basic needs, to treat him like a human being.

Brendan guided the man towards the door, feeling invisible eyes upon him as he turned his back on the interior of the Needle. He always felt this way, as if the building itself were watching him, waiting for him to slip up. He'd overcome his surface fears, but other terrors ran deeper, caught in the blood and the marrow. Some terrors could never be beaten, no matter how hard you fought against them.

"Come on, mate," he said, as they left the building and returned to the relative safety of the night. "I'll put the kettle on and we can have a little chat. Have you been living here?"

The man allowed himself to be led but he did not reply. He walked in silence, unable or unwilling to communicate. His hand was limp; the fingers felt boneless. His lumbering steps carried him wherever he was taken, and he acquiesced without as much as a whimper of protest.

Just as they reached the security cabin, Brendan heard the sound of a car engine as it cut out and tyres simultaneously coming to a halt on the gravel beyond the hoardings. He stopped, patted his companion on the arm, and left him there as he approached the front gate to the compound. Who was this so late at night? Drug dealers, using the place for their transactions? He stood at the gate and peered through the railings. There was a black 4x4 parked a few yards away where it had driven off the edge of Grove Street to stop just outside the pool of street light, and someone sat behind the wheel staring at the tower block. All he could see was the dark outline of a man or a slim, mannish woman: short hair, square chin, sunken patches where eyes should be.

Brendan turned on his torch and pointed it at the vehicle, trying to illuminate the person inside. The figure moved quickly, as if panicked, and the engine started up again. The tyres spun on the gravel, and the vehicle reversed at speed, heading towards the southern edge of Grove Crescent.

Some terrors, he thought again for no apparent reason, *can never be beaten.*

CHAPTER FOUR

"WHAT HAPPENED TO you?" Brendan was making tea. The camping kettle had boiled on the small portable gas-powered hob, and he'd poured it into two large mugs along with some long-life milk and teabags. He stirred the cups, waiting for the milky water to turn dark, and then he scooped out the bags and dumped them into the plastic carrier bag he used to collect his rubbish.

His guest sat at the small table in silence, staring at the wall.

"I know you, don't I? I've seen you before." Brendan picked up the mugs and carried them to the table. He placed one in front of the bandaged man and sat down in the plastic chair opposite. The furniture in the security cabin wasn't exactly comfortable, but it was practical.

The man didn't move. He just sat there. The bandages were wrapped tightly around his head and there were slits left for his eyes, nose and mouth. What little skin was visible looked raw and shiny, like badly healed scar tissue.

Scars.

That was it. Brendan suddenly knew who this was sitting in his cabin.

"You're Banjo, aren't you?"

The man twitched slightly at the sound of his

name. He tilted his head sideways and glanced at Brendan, as if he'd suddenly realised that he was not alone.

"You're the junkie... sorry, the bloke who escaped from the fire at that gym on Grove Street. I read about it in the papers. That loan shark Monty Bright and his mate died. You were seen in the area before the fire started, and everybody said you must have started it."

Banjo's eyes were shining. He looked like he might be crying.

"Did you? Was it you that started the fire?" Brendan remembered the news reports of Banjo scratching off his own face in the street, and his subsequent disappearance from hospital. Because of an eyewitness stating that Banjo was back in the Grove on the night of the fire, it was assumed that he'd been the one who burned down the gym, and that he had run from the scene when the sirens started.

Banjo turned his head away, glancing at the far wall. He couldn't make eye contact; there was something he didn't want to communicate.

"It's okay, man. Let's just get some hot tea down you. And a sandwich. Do you like ham and cheese?" He stood and crossed the room, retrieving his lunchbox from the bench near the window. He took out a small cling-filmed package, unpeeled the wrapping, and handed Banjo a sandwich. "There you go. Here – have them both." He took out the second sandwich and handed it to his guest.

Banjo grabbed the food and began to stuff it into his mouth, without any consideration for manners.

Brendan wondered when the guy had last eaten. It looked like it must have been days ago. "Here," he said. "Have it all. There's an apple in there, and a chocolate bar. Take it."

Banjo took the lunchbox, glanced into it, and smiled at Brendan. His mouth, beneath the dressings, was twisted, but Brendan got the gist. He knew he was being thanked.

He watched Banjo eat, trying to discern the extent of his wounds through the bandages. He thought again of the news reports at the time – statements about a local drug addict trying to tear off his own face with his bare hands. Apparently he'd had some kind of seizure, and suffered brain damage as a result. When he walked out of the hospital, the police had issued an announcement that he wasn't dangerous, but the public should be wary of approaching him. His mind had snapped.

"Jesus," he muttered, watching as Banjo bit the apple in half with a single lunge of his jaws. He ate the lot: even the core. "You must be starving."

He made another two cups of tea and sat back down, smiling. "You're safe here. It's okay; I won't call the police. You're not doing any harm, or causing any damage. I know that." Brendan knew he was a soft touch; his wife, Jane, never missed an opportunity to tell him this. But better to be soft than hard as stone, like a lot of the other people he knew around here. If he could help someone out, he would. It was in his nature. He was, he supposed, a caring sort of person.

"So, what are we going to do with you, then? I mean, I can't keep you here – in the hut. I'd get fired."

Banjo was still eating. There was apple juice on his chin.

"Fucking hell, mate. You're like a child. You should really be somewhere that people can help you." Brendan felt such a wave of pity and compassion that he thought he might get up and hug the man. But he got himself under control and simply sat and stared, wishing that he could do something practical. When he was a kid, he'd been the most selfish little shit imaginable, but as an adult, he felt such empathy for those who suffered. He supposed it was something to do with that time when he and his friends had been taken. That's what everybody had said: they'd been snatched. But the truth was that none of them could remember; all they knew was that they'd been building a tree house one Friday evening, and then they'd come staggering out of the Needle the following Monday morning, scratched and bloody and aching.

He didn't like to think too hard about that time, but he knew that it was impossible to erase it completely from his mind. That weekend was part of him; it was a piece of his personal history. Sometimes, in the early hours, when he couldn't sleep and Jane lay snoring beside him, he'd try to grab hold of the images inside his head. Something about a white mask with a beak, screams, shadows... and trees. Of all the things that came to him in the night, this image of huge oak trees was the strangest.

Massive oaks, all set out in a rough circle, with Brendan and his two best friends in the world sitting in the centre of that circle. Screaming.

But that was all he could hang on to before the images faded. However hard he tried, focusing intently on the pictures in his head, they still faded away. Perhaps it was for the best. The doctors had told his parents at the time that the boys had been 'interfered with', that someone had torn their anuses and mauled their genitalia. They'd been sexually abused. And none of them could remember a thing about it.

Brendan, Simon and Marty: not one single reliable memory between them. Brendan retained nothing but fuzzy mental pictures... soft-focus images from a dimly recalled film.

Banjo suddenly got to his feet, pushing away from the table and sending the chair scraping across the floor. The noise disturbed Brendan, pulling him from his thoughts. He glanced over at the bandaged man, and tried to smile in a reassuring way. "It's okay, mate. Nobody can hurt you here."

Banjo's eyes blinked rapidly. He turned his head briskly from left to right, as if searching for something.

That was when Brendan heard the noise. It was a faint clicking, like someone shuffling a deck of cards or flicking the pages of a new glossy book. It sounded like it was coming from just outside the window. Brendan got up and crossed the room, all of a sudden afraid of the sound. It connected somehow with his vague memories of that night twenty years ago. The mind pictures stirred, like embers raked into a pit, and the clicking noise set them flaring up again into weak flames.

He'd heard the noise, or one very much like it, before. Back then; during that lost weekend.

"Clickety..." The word came out of his mouth before he was even aware of speaking it out loud. He stopped, turned, and looked at Banjo. The other man was backing away, moving towards the door. His hands were raised in front of him in a protective gesture, as if he thought Brendan might attack him.

"No," said Brendan. "It's okay. Just a noise. Out there, in the dark. It's probably something blowing in the wind... a bit of sheet metal or something."

Banjo shook his bandaged head. He'd reached the door now, and his back was pressed against it. Giving one final, vigorous shake of the head, he spun around, opened the door, and ran outside. The door swung slowly closed, and Brendan watched the slim, shattered figure of the junkie as he pelted towards the Needle.

The clicking sound had stopped. Outside, there was no wind. The night was calm.

"Clickety," said Brendan again, but he had no idea what it meant. "Clickety."

He walked over to the door, pulled it tight to the frame, and locked himself inside the cabin. He would not make another circuit of the site tonight, and he certainly wouldn't be going anywhere near that damned tower block. Something had spooked him, and it was more than the noise, more than the word he'd uttered three times now. Perhaps it was the same unimaginable thing that had scared his guest enough to run back inside the ruined walls of the Needle, that somehow made him feel safe there?

Perhaps it was something they should all be afraid of; the whole estate, and everyone who lived here. Maybe it was a sign that something was coming. Something from the past: something that had always been there, biding its time and waiting for the right moment to return to finish what was started twenty years ago, when three boys had lost a slice of their lives and emerged at the other side bloodied, abused, and bearing much more than physical scars.

Brendan looked down at his feet and saw the large acorn on the floor. It was at the side of the door, as if Banjo had dropped it as he ran out of the cabin. The acorn was turned over onto its side, and roughly three inches long by an inch broad. The seed shell was turning brown but the acorn had not yet fully matured; it was still set firmly in its cupule.

Bending down to pick it up, he noticed some kind of markings on the acorn. When he examined it closely, he saw that there seemed to be two letters cut into the meat of the seed: B.C.

He felt dizzy, so straightened up, still clutching the acorn.

His name: Brendan Cole. Somebody – perhaps Banjo, perhaps someone else – had etched his initials into the acorn. The work was clumsy, childlike, but there was no doubt that the scratches were meant to stand for his name.

He pocketed the acorn, turned back towards the window and looked out into the darkness. His reflection stared back at him from the black glass. He looked thin, pale; a ghost of himself. The thought unsettled him even more, so he turned away. He was clenching his fist around the acorn inside his pocket. For some reason this disturbed him, so he took his hand out of his pocket and stared at his fingers. They were fine. Had he really expected them to be tainted in some way?

Brendan sat back down at the table and drank the rest of his tea. It was cold now, but he barely even cared. The rash on his back was burning. It felt like someone had laid a hot iron between his shoulder blades and pressed down on the handle, applying as much pressure as they could.

He couldn't wait to get home and take off his shirt, have Jane apply a soothing balm to his pustules and cysts, and then go to bed and chase sleep so that he might put this strange night behind him.

CHAPTER FIVE

THE SUN WAS shining when Simon woke up late the following morning. Pale fingers of daylight reached for him through the window, clutching through the space between the curtains he'd neglected to close when he arrived at the flat last night.

He was sprawled face-down on top of the bed sheets, with his legs dangling off the side of the bed and his hands and forearms jammed under the pillows. His neck ached. His mouth tasted stale and salty, as if from the residue of bad takeaway food. He pushed himself off the mattress and stood before the full-length mirror, struggling to open his eyes. He had not slept long; after driving back from the Needle he remembered drinking a large whisky and then stumbling to bed.

He scratched his head and cupped his balls. Then, yawning, he headed towards the bedroom door, and went through into the bathroom. He brushed his teeth – twice, to remove that terrible taste – and sat down on the toilet. The seat was too small. He'd owned the flat for almost ten years, a bolt hole he'd never used until now, but had felt like a lodger as soon as he stepped inside. This was not his home. These unknown rooms did not readily accept his shape within their walls; the flat seemed to fight against his presence.

He flushed the toilet and took a long shower, trying to wash away the layers of exhaustion. Last night he'd driven right up to the hoarding that surrounded the Needle, parked the car, and stared at the portion of the old tower block that was visible above the timber boards. He knew the place well, but mostly from his dreams. He hadn't set foot inside there for two decades – not since he and his friends had emerged from the building into early morning sunlight, blinking and stumbling as they walked hand-in-hand away from the centre of the estate.

The blood had stopped flowing, the scars had healed, but the damage done to their minds had sent shockwaves into their future – a future that had too quickly become the present. Even now, all these years later, he was afraid of cramped spaces and hated the way early evening shadows moved lazily in a dim room. The sound of rustling – bushes, leaves, even papers disturbed by a breeze through an open window – brought him out in gooseflesh.

He wondered how his friends had managed for all this time, living in the shadow of that building, and the darkness it generated. How had they survived the rest of their lives after the puzzling, nightmarish thing that may or may not have happened to them all?

Simon had built fragile barriers of wealth and success; his business deals and property developments formed a vulnerable defence against the blackness that he sensed radiating from this place like ripples on a pond. He had escaped, leaving the Grove when he was only sixteen; this distance alone had prevented the ripples from reaching him. But his friends had stayed behind, like ancient guardians or gatekeepers: holders of the flame. What coping mechanisms had they erected to protect themselves from the lack of memories, the lacuna in their recollections from that long-lost childhood weekend?

Once he was dressed, Simon made a cup of instant coffee. Black. There was no milk in the fridge; he'd forgotten to take some from his fridge back in London or pick some up at a service station last night, on his way here, even though he'd remembered to bring the whisky. He would need to go to the local supermarket for supplies, later, once he'd come to terms with being back here, right at the heart of his broken past.

After the coffee, he ate some stale biscuits he found in his briefcase, and then left the flat and checked the rental car hadn't been broken into. The doors were secure; nobody had tampered with them. The alarm had not sounded during the night, but still, it paid to be sure.

Simon left the car where it was, parked at the kerb in a narrow lay-by, and walked west along Grove Road, tracing the perimeter of the circular streets at the core of the estate. Even this place, he noted, looked okay when the sun was shining. The sky was clear; the glare was powerful enough that he put on his shades, and the clouds were high and thin and wispy. Yet still, beneath the scene, he was aware of the darkness twitching.

Passing the north end of the old Grove End Primary School, he glanced through the railings. He'd gone to that school, had spent his infant years playing and dreaming inside its gates. He could not remember what he'd learned there, other than how to survive, but suspected that the lessons had served him well.

Last night, after he'd made his abortive drive-by of the Needle, Simon had attempted to explore the area around it and reacquaint himself with the streets he'd once known. But after years away from the estate, the Grove made him nervous. The sounds of revving motorcycle engines from the direction of Beacon Green, the loud voices carried on the night-time breeze, the barking of dogs, the intermittent wail of a car or a house alarm from one of the streets adjacent to the Arcade – these had all set his nerves on edge. So, instead, he'd retreated inside the flat and locked the door, watching the estate through the windows as he slowly unpacked the few clothes and belongings he'd brought along with him.

Now, during daylight hours, the threat was a lot less apparent. Yet still, as he walked the streets, Simon felt like a stranger, an interloper. He'd been away too long to consider himself a native, and he knew that if he tried to pass himself off as one they'd smell it on him like shit on the soles of their shoes. The people who lived in the Grove were insular; they had their own defences. There were good folks here, people simply trying to get on with their lives, but also a high proportion of scroungers and criminals. The trick was to recognise which was which and make sure you moved in the right circles.

So he walked with his shoulders hunched, and kept glancing over his shoulder. He didn't want any trouble. Not here, not now. He'd paid his dues to this damned estate years ago, and he refused to allow it to take anything more from him than it had already stolen...

Brendan Cole lived in a small three-bedroom, semi-detached council house overlooking the Embankment. They were all the same, these properties: identical dwellings built for identikit families. Even the gardens looked similar, with their overgrown lawns, wild borders, and children's bikes and scooters and trampolines littering the space like the detritus from a rowdy street party.

Simon crossed the road and stood in the bus stop adjacent to Seer Park, an old patch of ground that had once boasted new swings, a slide and a roundabout, but now had become a dumping ground for empty beer cans and fast food wrappers. The remains of the swings – a buckled, rusty tubular steel frame – looked more like a hangman's gibbet than a plaything. He leaned against the clear PVC panel, squinting through the marker-pen mural of ancient graffiti, and watched the house.

He tried to remember what had been here before the bus shelter, and an image of an old-fashioned red telephone box came to mind. He'd used it to speak to girls so that his parents couldn't overhear his conversations, and had once even phoned emergency services to report a traffic accident he'd witnessed from the same box.

After about twenty minutes, a woman with dirty-blonde hair pulled back into a severe ponytail – what he'd heard referred to as a 'council-estate facelift' – emerged from the front door. She was wearing white running shoes, baggy grey sweatpants and a voluminous purple sweatshirt with the words

'Will Dance for Money' printed across the front. She carried a large sports bag to the silver Citroen people-carrier parked on the drive, opened the boot, and placed the bag inside. She jogged back to the front door, closed and locked it, and then climbed into the car and started the engine.

Simon knew her. It was Jane Fell – Jane Cole, now – the girl he used to go out with, back in the day. A twinge of what might have been guilt or simply regret tugged at his guts. He knew that he'd done wrong by the young girl he had left behind, but he was glad that the woman she'd grown into had found someone to settle down with – even if it was one of his best friends.

He watched her from the bus shelter as she sat in the car fiddling with the dashboard stereo, looking for a song she liked. She used to be beautiful, but now she looked tired, worn out. She was old before her time. He knew that the Coles had kids, twins: a boy and a girl. He also knew that she worked part-time in a Pound Shop in Near Grove, just to help out with the bills. Her hair was a dull shade of yellow rather than the pure blonde it had once been. She was carrying two, maybe three, extra stone of weight. He guessed that she was going to the gym or a dancing class – which would explain the obscure slogan on her sweatshirt. He wished that he could walk over there, open the car door, and say hello. Just say hello to the girl he'd once loved, who was now trapped inside the body of a woman who looked too exhausted to even care.

Smiling – presumably she'd found the right song – she pulled out of the drive and turned left, heading back the way he'd come. Simon huddled inside the bus shelter, tilting his head down but still managing to keep track of her as she passed him by.

For a moment he felt stranded there, caught in a moment between the past and the present, but once the car had turned the corner and vanished from sight he was able to shake the feeling and break free. She was no longer the girl he had known. She had a life now, a family. He had his own story, too, and it was a tale of success and hard work, of money and models and penthouse apartments. They were both different people, now; they were not the kids they had once been. All that had changed, it was gone.

He turned his attention back to the house. The bedroom curtains were open wide, which meant that Brendan must be up and about. Simon checked his watch. It was 1:30 PM. Perhaps, like him, Brendan had trouble sleeping. Maybe he sat up drinking after his night shifts, trying to quieten his demons.

Simon left the relative safety of the bus shelter and walked across to the house. He stood on the pavement outside, feeling exposed, trying to see through the net curtains strung like giant grey cobwebs across the ground floor windows. He could not make anything out: the place might even be empty.

"Here we go," he said, blowing air through his lips.

Simon walked through the gate and along the front path, took one hand out of his jacket pocket and knocked on the door. Then, impatient to get this over with, he rang the door buzzer. Through the etched glass panel, he watched a blurry shape appear at the far end of the hallway, grow closer, and finally reach out to open the door. He almost ran away then; his instinct was to bolt, to get the hell out of there and never come back. But he put his hands back in his pockets and stood his ground, remembering that they used to be friends. Best friends. He tried to focus on that fact more than any other, because it might just stop the man who was now opening the door from punching him in the face and kicking him into the street.

The man – short, with thinning fair hair, watery eyes and a nervous grin – opened the door and took a step back into the hallway.

"Hello, Brendan," said Simon, tensing against a potential blow.

"Simon Ridley? Is it really you, Simon?" The nervous grin became a smile, and then faded, dropping from his face like a sheet pulled away from a corpse. His eyes narrowed; his cheeks tightened. "What the *fuck* are you doing here?"

"Yeah," said Simon. "It's good to see you, too."

Brendan's mouth was hanging open, his lower jaw slack and immobile. Simon had only ever seen this expression in films, and the sight of it now, in real life, was almost enough to make him laugh out loud. But he didn't. He kept it all inside, because he didn't want to alienate his old friend before they'd even had a chance to talk. He didn't want to push too hard. "It's been a long time," he said, smiling. "Too long..."

Brendan seemed to compose himself; he shook his head, smiled, and took a step forward, onto the doorstep. "I suppose you'd better come in. We don't want to stand talking out here. I'll get us a couple of beers from the fridge." He opened the door wide, turned away, and walked along the hall.

"Okay," said Simon. He entered the house and closed the door behind him. He followed his host into the kitchen, where Brendan was leaning into the fridge to pull out two cans of bitter.

"Is this okay? I don't drink anything stronger for breakfast." He winked. It was a purely instinctive action, and the quip was probably one he'd used a hundred times before, but the very fact that he was able to make light of the situation made Simon relax.

"That's fine," said Simon. "Thanks." He reached out and took a can, popped the ring pull and dropped it into the bin by the back door. The kitchen was small and neat, with modern silver appliances, a pine breakfast bar, and varnished wooden cabinets. "Nice place."

Brendan took a long swallow from his can, burped quietly, and then looked around the kitchen. "It's okay, I suppose. Probably a lot different from your millionaire's mansion, though." He saluted Simon with his beer can.

Simon shook his head. "I live in a small flat. I have a tiny kitchen, two cramped bedrooms, and a view of grungy London streets. It's hardly Buckingham Palace."

"And a mattress stuffed with fifty pound notes, no doubt." Brendan winked to show that he was joking. "Come on through. We can talk in the living room."

The other downstairs room was twice the size of the kitchen, and dominated by a huge flat-screen television with cables streaming out of the back to connect the set to three separate games consoles. The Mario Brothers were paused mid-leap on the screen, their legs flickering, as if they were desperate to start moving again. There were framed landscape prints on the walls and family photographs on the mantelpiece, and the room contained too much furniture. A pine bureau was pushed up against the party wall, a bookcase stood packed with ornaments, and a pair of leather sofas and matching recliner armchair were gathered around a coffee table in the centre of the floor.

Brendan sat down on one sofa, so Simon took the other. They stared at each other at an angle. Suddenly Simon forgot why he'd come here. He'd run out of things to say before he had even said anything. He'd lost his bearings, and forgotten where the door was. The room was a box with a sealed lid. The net curtains at the window were opaque; he could see nothing of the outside world through them. They were spider-webs blocking his view.

He opened his mouth and said the first thing that came to mind: "How's the new job?"

Brendan put down his can on the shelf by his arm. "How do you know I just got a new job?"

"Because you're working for me. Well, specifically, I contracted the company you work for to keep an eye on one of my investments." The room returned to its proper dimensions. Sunlight brightened at the window.

"Nightjar Security Services? Why them? Why us?"

"Because it's the company you work for."

A silence threatened to overwhelm the two men. They drank from their cans simultaneously, arms rising and falling in syncopation. Brendan crushed his can in his fist. The sound – a loud creaking – made Simon think of something that he couldn't quite grasp. It sat there, the image, crouched in the shadows at the back of his eyes, waiting to be seen.

"Why are you here?" Brendan's voice was low, almost a whisper. He put his empty can on the floor by his feet. "After all these years. Why have you come back?" He reached up and scratched the back of his neck, wincing as he moved his hand back and forth across the same spot. "What's left for you here?"

Simon finished his own drink. "Any chance of another?"

Brendan nodded. He stood up, picked up his own can and grabbed the one from Simon's outstretched hand, and went through into the kitchen.

Simon rubbed his cheeks. His hands felt dry, dusty. Was he doing the right thing by coming here? Did he even know what the hell he was doing?

"Here." Brendan was standing next to him. Simon had not even heard him come back into the room.

"Cheers." he took the can, opened it, and drank. His head felt light, as if he were on the way to getting pissed. One can of weak bitter and he was already dizzy. It was pathetic.

"So?" Brendan looked at the television screen, frowning at the Mario Brothers, as if he'd only just noticed them. He grabbed a remote control from the floor and turned off the set.

"I got all your little gifts." Simon sat forward and took off his jacket, setting it down next to him. He was suddenly hot. The air was heavy.

"What are you on about?" Brendan sat back on the sofa, stretching out his legs. "I haven't sent you a thing. I don't even know your address – just that you live in some swanky gaff in London. Why the hell would I send you anything, man? You walked out of here and never looked back. You didn't even say goodbye. Not to me, or to Marty, or to–" He stopped himself from saying his wife's name, gritted his teeth, exhaled. "Not to anyone."

"I know, and I'm sorry. I should have at least spoken to you before I left, but it all happened so quickly. My mum died, my dad moved to Whitby to be with his psycho older brother, and the only other option I had was to run away. I couldn't stay here..." He didn't want to complete the thought.

"We did. None of us had a choice."

"You all had a choice – *we* all did. Nobody forced you to stay here."

Brendan didn't respond. He looked at his can, staring at the rim, into the small dark hole.

"Listen, I didn't come here to stir up bad feelings. I've come to apologise for leaving things the way I did, and for not keeping in touch."

Brendan sighed. The sound was too loud; it seemed faked. "What did you mean about gifts? What am I supposed to have been sending you? Letter bombs?"

Simon put one hand on his jacket. He squeezed the leather. "The newspaper clippings, the emails. The little reminders of what's been happening here for all these years, while I've been away."

"Sorry, mate." Brendan pursed his lips. "No, that wasn't me. I'd tell you if it was. I've had other things on my mind, like trying to raise a family, keep a roof over our heads, and hold down a shitty job. You know – crap like that." He crushed his second can. "Another?" He lifted the can to eye level and jiggled it, a small challenge.

"No, thanks. I haven't eaten properly since last night. I'll be pissed if I have another."

Brendan shrugged. "Please yerself. All the more for me, then."

"So it wasn't you? You didn't send me any of those things?" Simon stared at the other man, into his eyes, looking for deceit.

"Why the fuck would I bother? Who the fuck are you, anyway, you self-centred prick? Do you think that all the time you've been away all I've done is think about you, collect things, and then post them to you? Get real, man. This might come as a bit of a shock, but you're not the centre of the universe. You never were."

Simon pushed his hand into his jacket pocket, fumbled around for what he was looking for, and then withdrew his hand, the fingers clasped around an object. "So," he said, reaching out towards Brendan. "You didn't send me this, either?"

Brendan looked at the acorn sitting on Simon's palm. His face went slack, like the blood had suddenly run from his head and into his feet. He was pale; his eyes began to water.

"Did you?" Simon didn't break eye contact.

"No," said Brendan, standing. "No, I didn't." He went back through to the kitchen and returned with yet another can of beer. This one he drank quicker, as if he were trying his best to get drunk.

"What's wrong?" Simon closed his hand over the acorn. "You look like you've just seen a ghost." It sounded like something he'd said before, a hundred years ago.

Brendan lowered his can and stared at Simon. "A ghost or a monster..."

Simon's chest tightened. He squeezed his fist around the acorn. A sense of *déjà vu* came upon him, and he felt ten years old again, standing in the shade of the trees on Beacon Green. His cheeks were warm and wet; he was crying and he didn't know why. He quickly wiped the tears away with the back of his hand.

Brendan was standing at the centre of the room, the backs of his knees pressed against the coffee table. It looked as if that was the only thing stopping him from swaying.

"Maybe I will have another drink," said Simon. The world tipped back onto its axis and the muscles in Simon's chest slackened, allowing him to breathe again.

"No," said Brendan, shaking his head. He took a step forward, away from the coffee table, and his legs almost buckled. He staggered slightly, a man in need of support, and then moved across the room and grabbed the wall. "No, I think you need to leave."

"We have to talk, mate." Simon stood and made a move towards his old friend, but then thought better of it. He stood there, watching and waiting, wishing that he knew what to do. "Please. I have something I need to run by you – it's important. It might help us all. Me, you... Marty: the three of us, the Amigos. Remember that? The Three Amigos? It's what we called ourselves back then, when this fucking place was the whole wide world. Our club. Our gang. The Three Amigos."

Brendan closed his eyes. He was scratching at the top of his back with his free hand. His lips formed a tight line; his entire body was tensed, rigid.

Simon persisted: "Seriously. This might be the thing we've all needed for twenty years. Maybe even a way out, a way back, a way beyond whatever it is that none of us can remember."

"I can't, not now." Brendan opened his eyes. His shoulders were hunched, as if he were in pain. He spoke through gritted teeth. "Give me your number. I'll call you later – we can meet for a pint before I have to go to work. We'll talk then. I'll listen to what you have to say. No promises. But I'll listen..."

Simon grabbed his jacket, took a pen from the coffee table, and wrote down his mobile number on a till receipt from the petrol station last night. "You promise you'll listen?"

Brendan nodded. He was still in pain. "For old times' sake," he said, and opened the living room door: it was as clear a signal to leave as a person could possibly give.

Simon set down the till receipt with the scrawled number on the arm of the chair and left the room. He didn't look back, just in case he spoiled things. He didn't want Brendan to change his mind. He needed the chance to speak – even if it was just for 'old times' sake'.

He wanted to try and put things right for them all.

CHAPTER SIX

BRENDAN WAS ALREADY on his sixth beer by the time Jane got home. He was sitting at the breakfast bar, staring at the wall, and trying to keep his mind blank. Drinking; just drinking, and not thinking about anything at all. Afternoon sunlight streamed through the window, but it didn't quite reach him. He stared at the patches of brightness as they crawled slowly across the kitchen floor.

"Don't tell me you've been sitting here drinking all day." Jane hefted a couple of shopping bags and put them on the breakfast bar beside him. "Well?"

"No," he said. "Not all of it... I slept a bit this morning, and then I had a visitor."

"Was it that freeloading idiot Mark Maginn again? I hope you didn't lend him any money. This shopping doesn't come cheap, you know." She started to unpack the shopping bags, placing the tins in the cupboard above the sink and the fresh stuff in the fridge.

Brendan watched her in silence. Then, feeling the need to break into the moment, he spoke again. "No, it wasn't Mark Maginn. Not this time. It was someone else – somebody I haven't seen for a long time."

Jane had her back to him so he couldn't see her face. Her chunky arms were raised above her head as she shoved two boxes of cereal – the twins' favourite – into the cupboard alongside the tins of beans and spaghetti hoops. Her hair was still sweaty from her dancing class. She loved to dance; it made her feel young again. She'd told him this once, as they lay in each other's arms after making love. Brendan couldn't remember when it was. Nor could he remember the last time they'd made love.

"It was Simon Ridley."

Jane stopped moving. Her hands were still inside the cupboard, pushing a cereal box through the blockage of tin cans. She was standing on her tiptoes. She paused there, unmoving, and the cereal box dropped from the cupboard and fell onto the floor. It made a rattling noise, like someone shaking a bag of bones.

"He's come back. He says he wants to speak to me about something important."

Jane started moving again. She bent over and picked up the cereal box. Brendan stared at her backside. It was bigger and wider than when they'd first met, but it was still one of her best features. She was a beautiful woman, his wife. He used to tell her that all the time, but he hadn't for years, now.

"I said I'd meet him later." Brendan drained his can, belched. "Pass me another beer, would you?"

Without objection, Jane crossed to the fridge and took out two beers. She opened both cans, passed him one, and poured the contents of the other into a tall glass. She took a sip, paused, and then took another, bigger mouthful. "Fucking hell," she said.

Brendan did not respond. He hadn't heard her swear since the cat was run over in the road by a boy racer last summer. She didn't like expletives; she was proud of her broad vocabulary.

"Fucking hell," she said again.

Brendan could not tell if she were smiling or grimacing. He decided that he'd rather not know. Sometimes it was safer to play dumb – often, it saved your marriage.

"What did he want?" She walked over to where he was sitting, placed one of her hands over one of his. She squeezed. Her fingers were cold from the beer glass. "Is he back for good? I can't imagine that. Isn't he rich now, some kind of property investor?"

"Yeah. He's loaded. From what he told me, I think he might have bought the Needle." Admitting this out loud, in the bright light of day, Brendan realised that it didn't sound quite as crazy as it had when Simon had alluded to the fact earlier.

"Why would he buy that old place... especially after what happened to you all there? I mean, what's he trying to prove?" Jane sat down. She moved her hand away.

"Maybe he bought it *because* of what happened to us. Perhaps he wants to try and remember." He stared at her face, her hard blue eyes, her sunken cheeks, and the once-knife-sharp bone structure still visible through her sagging face. Her hair needed dyeing again; the roots were showing.

"Do you think he *has* remembered? That might be what he wants to talk to you about. I bet he's spent a fortune on posh psychiatrists and dug up the memories of what happened that weekend, and he wants to throw it all in your face, have his Jeremy Kyle moment in the spotlight." The bitterness behind her words was astonishing. Brendan hadn't realised she hated Simon Ridley this much.

"I doubt it," he said, lowering his head so that she

couldn't look into his eyes and see the hurt there. "I think he might be planning to renovate the bastard, turn it into apartments or something." He looked up.

Jane grinned. "Ha! Right. Like anyone would buy a nice apartment in the middle of the Grove. He's not that stupid – he can't be if he's made his fortune down south." She shook her head and took another mouthful of beer. "So, are you going to meet him?" Her eyes were hard again. The smile had vanished.

"I thought I should. If only to hear what he has to say. I'll let him buy me a beer and talk out of his arse for a while, and then I'll go to work and forget about it." He wondered if she could tell that he was lying. Jane knew him better than anyone – even better than he knew himself. She'd been finishing his thoughts and ending his sentences since they'd first got together. So, yes, she knew that he was lying. Of course she did.

"Just be careful." She touched his hand again, but this time tenderly. "Don't let him push you too hard, or talk you into anything you don't want to do."

Brendan flipped over his hand on the breakfast bar so that it was palm-up, and then he held her fingers. "We're not ten years old anymore, pet. I'm an adult. I can't be talked into anything against my will."

"Only by me," she said, smiling again.

"Only by you," he agreed, squeezing, squeezing, and wishing that he never had to let go.

"Listen, I have to finish putting this shopping away, and then it'll be time to pick up the twins." Jane stood, gulped down the last of her beer, and put the glass in the sink.

"Do you want me to go for them? I don't mind."

She turned to him, the sunlight catching in her dyed hair. "No, it's okay. You didn't sleep much this morning, did you?"

He shook his head.

"I'll go. You have a shower and put on your good jeans. We don't want Simon-bastard-Ridley thinking we're a couple of scruffs now, do we?" She turned away quickly, but still he saw the smile drop away from her face; and the way her eyes went distant, as if she were staring inward, at a place that he could never go to, no matter how close they were as a couple or how much love they shared. It was a place that she kept secret; somewhere she went when she needed to, her own private store of memories that she would never open up to let him see.

Brendan stood and left the room, leaving her there with her face to the wall as she rearranged the food in the cupboard. He knew that he should go to her, turn her around, and hug her, perhaps even tell her that he loved her and he always would. But there was something in the way: Simon, and all the things he represented. He'd never been a man who could talk freely about his feelings, and right now that reticence was worse than ever. There was so much he could have said – *should* have said – but none of it would come. He kept it all inside.

He went upstairs and undressed in the bathroom. His body ached. He felt older than his years. Staring at himself in the mirror, he saw a small man with too much loose flesh around his middle; a beer belly hanging down over his waist. Thin arms. Pale skin. Thinning hair, pale as straw. When he'd looked at Simon earlier that day, he'd seen a man who spent a lot of time in the gym, dressed in expensive clothes, and ate good food. The two of them could not be more different, and yet back then, when they'd been children, they had been like brothers.

Sometimes memories acted like a wedge, coming between people and pushing them apart. Time broke your heart and skinned you alive. It was a madman with a flensing knife, grinning as he stalked you from behind, drawing incrementally closer to his prey with each passing moment.

The shower was hot; the water prickled his scalp, burned the tops of his shoulders and sent a shiver of pain down the back of his neck. The spots and buboes across his back and shoulders at first flared up, and then the hot water began to soothe them. It drew out the sting of pain, made him feel for a moment that he wasn't suffering from this dreadful acne, that his flesh was fine and unblemished instead of ravaged by infection.

Brendan reached over his shoulder and gently patted the wounds. They were always wet; they never seemed to dry out. But this time, under the shower jet, it was a clean wetness. The water washed away the vile yellowish ichors which had bled from the burst pustules and crusted over the top like a fine honeycombed layer of cinder toffee. The skin around the infected areas felt smooth and clean. Brendan closed his eyes and pretended that he was healed. That he was normal and healthy, that he was like Simon Ridley.

Sometimes he was certain that the damaged flesh could hear his thoughts, that it knew exactly what he was thinking, and it was displeased. The response would be a massive flare-up, where the blisters would rise, and burst, and bleed... sometimes it felt like he were being punished, but he had no idea what his crime might have been, or when he was supposed to have committed it. He tried to be a good man. His only vices were alcohol and self-pity.

Just as he was dabbing himself dry with a towel – one of the ones only he was allowed to use, because they got dirty quickly from his back – Jane knocked on the bathroom door.

"Are you decent?"

"Never," he said, rubbing his leg with the towel.

"Well, I'm coming in anyway, so you'd better put that weapon away." She was smiling as she pushed open the door and walked into the small, cramped room. "Here, let me." She took the towel from his hands and finished drying him off. "They look a bit better than they did this morning," she said, standing behind him as he leaned against the shower glass.

"They always look better just after a shower. They'll be clogged and clotted again in an hour." He closed his eyes and wished that he didn't need his wife to do this. He knew Simon didn't have open sores on his back; his skin would be toned and tanned. It would be flawless.

Jane hung up the towel on the hook and moved to the sink, where she opened the door of the cabinet on the wall – the one that was mounted too high for the kids to reach. She pushed a few bottles of pills and mouthwash out of the way and then brought out the tub of benzoyl peroxide ointment. "Here we go," she said, smiling at him in the mirror. The smile lit up her face, but it didn't touch her eyes. She washed her hands with disinfectant soap, using her elbows to turn off the taps, just like Brendan had seen actors do in Saturday night hospital dramas. Then she walked back over to where he was leaning against the bathtub, his forearms resting on the edge of the tub and his knees pressed into the cool tiled floor.

"I'm sorry," he said, wishing that things could be different – that she didn't have to do this for him.

"Don't be silly." Her hands were shockingly cold – the lotion was smooth and clammy against his inflamed skin.

Brendan closed his eyes. He pretended that there was a stranger tending to his needs, and not his wife. He often did this; imagined that she didn't have to see his wounds. He wished that someone else could do this in her place.

"You're right. They're really bad today, babe. The worst I've seen them for a while, now that they're dry. I'll try to be as gentle as I can, but you're probably going to feel some discomfort."

He nodded. He kept his eyes closed, hoping it would help stop the tears from falling. He winced, his entire body tensing and stiffening, bit his bottom lip, and bent his head forward over the bath.

"Sorry... God, this is bad. Most of them have popped. The rest of them are filled with fluid. I'll try to be gentle."

"How can you do this? How can you do it and still love me?" Immediately, he wished he hadn't said the words.

"Don't be stupid." Her voice was hard, sharp. "I love you no matter what. You know I do. Why should this change anything?" Her hands moved over the infected area slowly and gently, sparing him more pain. She was good at this; she'd had a lot of practice. "I'll always love you, whatever happens..."

You wouldn't have had to do this for him – for Simon fucking Ridley. The thought hurt him. It was like a knife stirring around inside his skull.

"Feeling any better?" Her hands... they were magical.

"Yes. Thanks." *No. No, I feel worse. I feel like a bastard, a hideous monster, for having you do this. I wish it could be different. I wish I was different...* "That's much better."

Afterwards, Jane stood up without saying anything more. She brushed the back of his neck with her lips, a small show of affection. Then she went to the sink and washed her hands again, put away the lotion. "I'll go and get the twins from school," she said, leaving the bathroom. "I won't be long."

She hid it well, but he could sense the revulsion behind her words. Despite what she said, and how she acted, he knew that she secretly hated him for what she was forced to do. He could smell it on her, like a strange spice. The resentment, the bitterness, the regret that she'd ever become involved with him and his loathsome flesh. It was all compressed inside her, held in by the cage of her bones: some day, he knew, it would come spilling out and everything would change.

Brendan went into the bedroom and started to get dressed. He picked out the newest pair of trousers he owned: a pair of black chinos Jane had bought him last Christmas. Then he selected his best shirt, the grey one with the fake Lacoste emblem on the breast pocket. The front door slammed shut as he buttoned the shirt. His hands trembled.

Perhaps she'll take the kids and never come back. Maybe Simon will take her away and show her a better life... better than this one, anyway.

Why did he do this to himself? It was a form of flagellation, a self-imposed punishment for crimes he had not even committed. He knew that in reality Simon would want nothing to do with Jane, not now. Their time was past. He probably spent his time shagging models and B-movie actresses, so why the hell would he want to take a faded, washed-up ex-beauty from the old estate to his bed?

He instantly regretted thinking of Jane in those terms. She was still beautiful, despite the hard times they'd gone through. She still shone; was always the light of his life. Her beauty was a counterbalance to his ugliness.

Trying to distract his mind, he thought again of the acorn Simon had shown him during his visit. He'd feigned ignorance, trying to make out that he had no idea what the acorn meant or who might have sent it to his old friend, but the truth was that he had more of a clue than he'd let on. He wasn't quite sure why he'd been so reticent to speak, but it had seemed like the right thing to remain silent, to keep a secret.

Brendan walked over to the fitted wardrobes, pulled a sturdy wooden box from under the bed and moved it in front of the wardrobe doors, and then stood on the box. The timber joints creaked, but the box held, as it always did.

He reached up and opened one of the small doors at the top of the wardrobe, near the ceiling. Behind the doors was one long storage space, stretching the entire length of the unit. Jane never used the space; it was Brendan's little hidey-hole, where he kept his stash. She pretended that the doors were not there, and ignored the things which lay behind them. It was not her concern; she refused to even acknowledge what he kept there.

He moved a stack of imported bondage magazines out of the way, and slipped his hand behind a box set of hardcore fetish DVDs imported from Amsterdam. There was a moment of panic when he couldn't find what he was looking for, but then his questing fingers closed on the acorn. He paused for a moment, unsure. It felt bigger than before, when he'd stashed it here, but that couldn't be right. Acorns didn't continue to grow when they'd fallen from the tree. Did they?

He gripped the seed and pulled it out into the open. He was right; it *was* bigger. Much bigger... almost twice the size it had been when Banjo had left it for him.

Brendan closed the door, shutting away his pornography. He promised himself a treat this weekend, when Jane took the twins to her sister's for tea. That new DVD set had not even been opened; it was still in the cellophane wrapping.

He stepped down off the wooden box and backed away from the wardrobe doors, towards the bed. When the backs of his knees met the mattress he sat down heavily, acorn held to his chest, eyes closed, mind floating somewhere else. He thought that he heard the wind soughing through treetops, the soft rustle of undergrowth, and the sound of distant singing... and then, from somewhere far away, a clicking sound began to draw closer. It was still a long way off, that sound, but it was approaching steadily, and whatever was making it would be with him soon. The sound both scared him and put him at ease. It was a contradiction, a paradox, and although he wanted nothing more than to see the owner of what he was already thinking of as a strange voice, he also wished that it would turn away and leave him alone.

Brendan did not know what he wanted, but he was certain that he didn't want this, whatever the hell it was. But he was sure that the owner of the arrhythmic, clicking voice wanted him... and for a moment he felt sure that that he had encountered it once before, perhaps a long time ago.

He looked down at his hands, drew them away from his chest. They opened like pale pink flowers, without him having to control them. He stared at the oak bud. Although the acorn had almost doubled in size, the carved initials had remained their original size. The two letters – a B and a C – looked tiny now, but they were still legible on the side of the seed.

The acorn felt warm and soft, like a small, living animal. It twitched in his hand, pulsing slightly – growing again, even as he watched. Then it was once again still and dead, just a discarded seed from an old tree, a small piece of nature's detritus.

But for a moment there, as he'd held the acorn, Brendan had begun to think that it was alive, and it was reaching out to him.

Or that *something* was.

CHAPTER SEVEN

SIMON HAD BEEN in a lot of pubs that were worse than The Dropped Penny, and had mixed with clientele even rougher around the edges than those currently surrounding him, drinking their pints and their shots and watching the world through rheumy, alcohol-blurred eyes. Back when he'd still lived on the estate, the pub had a reputation as being an old man's drinking den – the haunt of ancient crones and wizened old blaggers who spent their days winding down towards the grave. It had always been a hotbed of gossip, the place you came to find out who had double-crossed whom, which bloke was sleeping with his neighbour's wife, what the latest drug of choice might be on the streets of the Grove.

Brendan had called him thirty minutes ago, asking him where he wanted to meet up. The Dropped Penny had been the natural choice; a hotbed of street-level information, the place seemed tailor-made for this kind of meeting. And what kind was that, he asked himself as he sipped his pint? Was it just two old friends catching up after twenty years, or something more? What was the real reason behind them coming here, to this shabby little boozer that probably should have been pulled down years ago?

Simon stared at himself in the mirrors behind the bar. He looked tired, pale and gaunt. His hair was a mess and his cheeks were hollow. He had not been sleeping well, not since receiving the acorn. London seemed a million miles away, or part of another existence altogether. Right now, he felt that he'd stepped back into a cloudy past that had not changed, while out in the world everything about him had altered dramatically.

He had been shopping at the Tesco Express in Near Grove when he'd taken Brendan's call. He'd gone straight to the checkout, paid for his meagre provisions, and then returned to the flat to unpack the bags. He didn't have time for a shower or a coffee; he left the flat and came straight here, where the only reasonable thing to do was buy a drink.

An old man brushed up against him and leaned across the bar, interrupting his thoughts. "Pint of bitter," he mumbled to the skinny barmaid. She was standing against the wall reading a fat, dog-eared paperback with a water-damaged front cover. Most of the title had been rubbed off – something about kicking a hornet's nest. The barmaid glanced up from the page, nodded, and pushed away from the wall like a swimmer moving away from the shore. She put her book down on the bar and pulled a pint, her thin, hard forearms tensing as she tugged on the pump.

"Ta, petal," said the old man, leering as he handed her a five pound note. She sighed, shook her head, and gave him his change.

"Stupid old fart," she said to herself, as she picked up her book and drifted back to her spot against the wall.

Simon laughed, but she didn't even acknowledge him. He coughed lightly, dipped his lips to his glass, and looked around at the rest of the drinkers.

The Dropped Penny had not changed a bit since he'd last been here. Even the faces looked the same, only older, more worn and wrinkled. It had never seemed to get too busy back when Simon used to sneak in for an under-age drink, nor was it ever empty. Always roughly the same number of punters, drinking quietly, chatting in low voices, and watching the world from over the rim of a dirty glass.

He saw Brendan enter the pub, watching him in the mirrored wall. His old friend looked twitchy, on edge. His eyes were rimmed with red, as if he'd already been drinking heavily. Or perhaps he was simply deprived of sleep, like Simon.

He was just about to turn around when Brendan saw him. A look of regret – or was it sadness? – crossed his face, and then he walked towards the bar.

"What can I get you?" Simon smiled. It took some effort, but it was the least he could do. He had to try and get the man on-side.

"Pint of Landlord. It's good in here."

"It certainly is," said Simon, nodding towards the remains of his own drink. "Two Landlords, please," he called to the barmaid, who was lost in her book.

The woman looked up, sighed, and trudged to the bar to pour the drinks.

"If it isn't too much trouble, that is." Simon smiled.

"Don't get smart with me, son, or I'll bar you." She did not return the smile.

"The old Ridley charm... it never fails." He turned to Brendan and winked.

Despite himself, Brendan smiled. "I remember you could charm the pants off a nun... an old nun, with a smelly crotch and poor personal hygiene."

"Thanks, mate," said Simon, handing Brendan a pint. "You always knew how to make me feel better about myself."

"Let's sit down. There's a table over here." Brendan moved away from the bar and sat at a table near the window, more relaxed now that he had a drink in his hand. He took a long swallow with his eyes closed, and then placed the pint glass on a soggy beermat but kept hold of it, as if he were afraid that someone might try to take it away.

"Shall we start again?" Simon sat down opposite him.

"What do you mean?" Brendan hunched his shoulders, and winced, as if he was experiencing mild pain.

"I don't think I handled our reunion very well when I came to your place. I barrelled right in like a bull, ignoring all the pleasantries."

Brendan shrugged. "Aye. Whatever. It doesn't matter." He took another swig of his drink, draining the glass to the half-way point.

"But it does matter. These things do matter, don't they? We were best friends. We haven't seen each other for twenty years. And what do I do? I charge into your house and demand answers to questions I barely even understand. I was out of order. I'm sorry."

Brendan shrugged again. He looked uneasy. "No harm done. Want another?" He drained his glass and stood, moving towards the bar without waiting for an answer.

Simon watched him as he ordered two more pints of bitter, sharing a quiet joke – no doubt at Simon's expense – with the barmaid. They seemed familiar; he wondered if she was an ex-girlfriend, or part of a crowd Brendan had hung around with after Simon had left the estate. He realised that he knew little of his friend's life history. He'd known him as a child, and less so as a teenager, but was now meeting him for the first time as an adult.

"Thanks," he said as Brendan sat back down and slid a glass across the table. "So. How have you been?"

Brendan laughed. "Jesus... you're really asking me that?"

"Why not? We barely even know each other anymore. The last time I saw you we both had bum fluff on our chins." Simon raised his glass in a small salute.

"I thought you'd kept tabs on me? You seem to know enough about where I work."

Simon shook his head. "No... I've not kept tabs, not exactly. My Aunty Annie still lives in Near Grove. Whenever I call her, she mentions you – tells me what she's heard. She knows we used to be close." It was only partly a lie.

"Christ," said Brendan. "Good old Aunty Annie. I remember her – she always used to give us those old-fashioned sour sweets." He grinned. "I fucking hated them, but was always too polite to tell her."

Simon laughed softly. "Me, too, mate. They were bloody horrible."

They sat for a while in a silence that was almost companionable, or would have seemed so to a casual observer. They sipped their drinks slowly now, the initial nerves having dissipated. Someone put a song on the jukebox, an old number Simon didn't recognise; a woman singing the blues. Her voice was strained, almost painful to hear. It was beautiful.

"How's Jane?" He glanced at Brendan, wondering if he'd pushed too far.

Brendan's eyes flashed, but then he relaxed again. "Took you long enough to ask."

"Well," said Simon. "It's none of my business really, is it?"

Brendan licked his lips and blinked rapidly. "She's fine. *We're* fine, in case that was your next question. We're more than fine, actually."

"No, that wasn't my next question." Simon leaned back in his chair. "But I'm glad. I'm really glad that you're still together. It makes sense; the two of you, it's logical. Know what I mean?"

"Yes," said Brendan. "It does make sense. It makes a lot of sense. We were always close..."

Whatever was left unsaid, Simon felt it prudent not too push too hard to find out. Had the two of them slept together when he and Jane had been an item? They were only fifteen, barely old enough to know their own hearts, never mind anyone else's. That made sense, too: them sleeping together behind his back. He hoped that it *was* true; their infidelity would make him feel a lot better about the way he'd abandoned them.

Simon nodded. "Yeah. Yeah, I know. You have kids, now, don't you?"

"Aye," said Brendan. "Twins: Harry and Isobel. They're ten years old... the same age we were when, well, you know. When that shit happened to the three of us."

There was another short pause, when neither of them spoke, but this one was strained. Something sat between them now, something that had not been there before. It licked its lips and waited; it had all the time in the world.

"Are you still in touch with Marty?" Simon leaned forward; his back was aching. The bar seat was old and the cushion was too soft.

"No," said Brendan, shaking his head. "We lost touch years ago, when he went off the rails. Did you know about that?"

Simon nodded. "I know a little. Didn't he start boxing, and then some kind of injury cut his career short? Then he went... dodgy?"

"*Dodgy*'s the right word for what he is." Brendan pointed at his glass. "It's your round."

Simon got up and bought two more beers, then returned to the table.

"Marty Rivers," said Brendan. "What a fucking psycho he turned out to be."

Simon said nothing. He just let the other man speak.

"He used to train for hours: up at dawn for early runs, then in the gym every night for sparring sessions. He was intense; serious about his sport. Then he crashed his motorbike and his girlfriend was killed in the accident. He was a mess. His injuries never healed, not properly, and his career was over before it even began. A lot of people said that he might have been a great, that he would have gone places. But we'll never know."

Simon blew air though his lips. "Jesus, I didn't know he was ever that good. I remember he was always fit, and hard as nails, but I didn't realise he took the boxing that seriously. I thought it was just something he did because of his dad – you know, the cult of the hard man, and all that."

"No," said Brendan. "He was serious. He loved to box. When it all went tits-up, he had nothing else to fall back on. He wasn't academic; he wasn't driven, like you. He didn't have anyone special in his life, not after the bike accident. So he started working the doors on the roughest pubs in Newcastle. I heard a lot of rumours about illegal boxing contests in social club basements, maybe even bare knuckle bouts. Somebody told me Marty took on and beat the King of the Gypsies about ten years ago, but people tend to talk a lot of shit around here. You never know what to believe." He stood up quickly, then reached out and steadied himself by gripping the table. "I need a piss. I'll get a couple more pints on my way back." He belched and then headed off towards the gents at the other side of the room.

Simon was starting to feel drunk. He wasn't used to drinking this much during the day, just the occasional half-bottle of wine over a lunch meeting, or a cocktail with clients. The strong beer was making him dizzy; his vision was blurred.

Before Simon had time to properly register his absence, Brendan returned with more drinks. "Get that down your neck," he said, slamming down the glasses. "Our old mate Marty got involved with drugs, and he did a few jobs for a local gangster named Monty Bright. I'm not sure how much he was involved with that scumbag's affairs, but when Bright's gym burned down, with him in it, most people around here waved goodbye to bad rubbish."

Simon tried to focus on the words. "Yeah... I heard about that. Someone sent me the news item, a page from the paper. I don't know why, but whoever it is who sends me this stuff seems to think I'm still interested in what goes on in the Grove."

"Maybe it's Marty," said Brendan. "It might be his way of keeping in touch, of trying to cling to the memory of the Three Amigos."

Simon raised his head. "Hey, that's a good point. I never thought of that. All this time, I just assumed it was you. We were best friends."

Brendan put down his glass, gripping it tightly. "We were all best friends – the three of us. The fucking Three Amigos, remember? Best friends, until whatever happened that weekend tore us apart."

Simon wasn't sure how he felt about one of them speaking the thought aloud. It was true, of course it was, but he had not felt confident enough to vocalise what he thought. But clearly Brendan thought that way, too – and maybe Marty did, and that was why he'd been sending all that stuff, trying to keep the Amigos together, even in this small way.

"I need you to help me contact Marty," he said, leaning across the table. "Don't ask me how I know this, but I think it's important that the three of us at least get into a room together and talk about the past. Even if it's just for our own mental wellbeing, we need to sit down around a table and try to work through what happened back then."

Brendan clenched his teeth. His face was thin, the colour fading from his cheeks. "This isn't some Hollywood blockbuster, mate. We can't re-form our little gang and slay the monster before running off into the sunset. That's not how it works in the real world. The Three Amigos don't exist anymore. I'm a broken-down, drink-dependent security guard, you're a phoney little rich-boy with a chip on his shoulder, and Marty is a fucking maniac who'd probably break your neck if he ever saw you again..."

He bowed his head, letting go of his glass. "We're not heroes. We can't even stand the sight of each other."

Simon tried to counter his remarks, but could think of nothing to say. Brendan was right. This was stupid. What the hell had he been thinking to even come here? "Do you want to know why I bought that place – the Needle?"

Brendan nodded. "Tell me," he said, his voice low, a whisper.

"I bought it because I want to tear it down, brick by brick, timber by timber, bit by bit. I want to reduce that fucking building to its component parts, and then sift through them, looking for what we all lost. I want to find out what happened to us, so I can move on and put it behind me. I'm sick and tired of being haunted. I'm fed up of running away from my demons. Look at us – we've both been hamstrung by whatever happened twenty years ago, and neither of us has the slightest fucking idea what it was. What happened to us in there? What did we leave behind?" He felt hot tears running down his cheeks and wiped them away with the back of his hand. "What was taken from us?"

"I don't know." Brendan could not look him in the eye. He kept his head lowered, gazing at the stained tabletop. "I wish I did."

"This place," said Simon. His voice had taken on a strange hissing quality. He was speaking quietly, trying to make sure no one overhead him, but the rage had altered his tone. "It's the place – the Concrete Grove. Have you never noticed how there's always a strange atmosphere here, like a constant gas leak? And what about the streets? Even the layout of the estate is fucked. I mean, why is Grove Street West at the east end of the Grove? And why does Grove Drive West point north to south? It's like someone was playing games, or the place has been flipped over so many times that the compass has lost all meaning. I remember several times, drunk and walking home, I would end up in a part of the Grove that I shouldn't be in. Somehow, I'd get lost, even though I knew exactly where I was going..."

Brendan looked up. His eyes were filled with tears. "It's just... just the Grove. The whole place is fucked. It's like a town planner's worst nightmare, or something."

Simon pulled back; he'd already said too much. He could not risk pushing any harder, not yet. "I dunno, Brendan... really, I don't. Nothing feels right here. It's like confusion and anxiety is the natural mental state."

"Okay," said Brendan. "I'll help you. We'll go and see Marty. If it means that much to you, we can sort it out."

Simon did not know how to respond.

"You and me, we'll find out where he's living and we'll go round there, see if he's willing to talk. What harm could it do, right?"

As Simon gazed deeply into Brendan's eyes, he knew that his friend was lying. But for the life of him, he did not understand the nature of those lies, or what truths they were meant to hide.

CHAPTER EIGHT

"ARE YOU SURE you want to do this now?" Brendan's voice sounded dry and croaky, as if he'd smoked a whole packet of cigarettes in one sitting. "I mean, there's no real need to do it now. We could wait until the morning, if you like."

Simon shook his head. "I've waited twenty years to come back here and see this place again. If I don't go in there now, I probably never will. But I can't do it alone, not the first time anyway. We're both here, so why not?"

"Okay, if you're sure."

Simon increased his pace and drew level with Brendan. He'd been walking a couple of steps behind, taking in the gritty early evening atmosphere as he tried to sober up. "Yes, I'm sure."

Brendan turned his head. His mouth was a grim line. "I've been in there hundreds of times now, and there's nothing. I'm not sure what you're expecting to find, but the place is empty. Empty of everything. There are no ghosts, no memories clinging to the walls or ceilings like bats. Just a lot of dust and filth and old drug workings."

The two men walked a little way along the curve on the east side of Grove Road, and then crossed the road to enter a narrow, overgrown cut between gardens that led on to Grove Crescent. The east side of the estate was the roughest part; the worst kind of scumbags lived here. The west side was relatively peaceful, and many of the residents along the roads that skirted the Embankment – including Brendan's street – were honest, hard-working families. But here, on the opposite end of the Grove, the rules were not as clear cut.

Grove Street itself was wrapped in a kind of murky haze; the streetlight at the end of the short road had been vandalised. It was still early, and the sky offered some brightness, but the other lights around the estate were already coming on, illuminating the corners of this strange world in a frantic effort to beat the oncoming night. Simon had the strange thought that darkness always fell early on the estate. The lights always came on here before they did elsewhere. Maybe it was part of some plan by the council: they switched on the streetlights to try and fool the yobbos into thinking it was later that it really was, in an effort to send them home off the streets.

"Come on," said Brendan, taking the lead again. "Let's get this over with. I want to get back home to see my kids before I have to come back here and start my shift. I've barely seen them all day."

"Sorry," said Simon. "I didn't realise..."

"Don't worry about it." Brendan approached the gates of the compound and took a set of keys from his pocket. He rattled the keys as he selected the correct one and then slid it into the main lock. "So that was you last night – in the four-wheel drive?"

Simon nodded, then realised that Brendan couldn't see him because he had his back to him, and answered. "Yeah, that was me. I did a little drive-by."

"You should've come over. I would have put the kettle on."

Simon sensed more untruths, but he was unsure whether or not Brendan was simply being cautious, afraid to open up too much because of the dead weight of years that stood between them.

"Come on. Let's get this done." Brendan pushed open the gates and stepped inside.

Simon followed him into the enclosure, feeling as if he were walking into a prison – or perhaps a complex trap. He knew that he was being impulsive by coming here right now, but he also realised that he couldn't put off this confrontation indefinitely. It had to be done; he needed to face the past if he stood even a chance of unlocking its secrets.

The Needle glowered down at him. That was how it felt, as if the building were leaning over slightly and staring at the top of his head in silent rage. His skin itched; his vision swam. Simon considered himself a brave – and sometimes even reckless – man, but this was something different. This was madness. In his time, he had stood toe-to-toe with some of the most feared businessmen in London, negotiated with fierce adversaries over money, and once had even grabbed a renowned investor by the throat in a boardroom and threatened to break his nose... but those were safe battles. The numerous enemies he'd bested were made of flesh and blood, not brick and mortar and the essence of lost memory.

He had a flashback then, as he knew he would: a vision of oak trees, with soft, pale moonlight filtering like dust motes through the canopy of branches. Something moved beyond the perimeter of the circle of trees, slowly circling the three of them – Simon, Brendan, and Marty, whining and sitting with their backs to each other on the hard ground.

There was nothing more. That was it; all he was given.

"The trees," he said, not even realising until it was too late that he'd spoken the words out loud.

"I remember that, too." Brendan turned towards him, his face pale and devoid of any readable expression. "There was a circle of oaks... with us sitting terrified in the middle."

Simon nodded. He rubbed his cheeks with the palms of his hands and felt the tough stubble as it rasped against his flesh. "Yeah... I haven't thought about that for years. I'd forgotten about the trees. How could I ever forget something like that?"

Brendan smiled, and it seemed to split his face in two. "It's because you weren't here. You went away, and you broke a connection. The trees are one of the few memories I have. I dream about them. And I dream about being tied up by their branches." He broke off then, as if he wanted to say more but had changed his mind.

"What do you mean?"

"Nothing," said Brendan. "It's nothing."

They walked on, towards the towering form of the Needle. Its grey walls were impassive; its dingy presence was a glimpse into another time and place. Simon felt the present shiver, as if the very fabric of time and space was straining at the seams and attempting to transport him back in time twenty years. The sky stretched above him like a thin sheet, the ground threatened to shift beneath his feet, and the landscape around him seemed like it was poised on the cusp of a change.

The day's alcohol intake drained from him, leaving him cold and sober.

"This way." Brendan walked to the main doors. They'd been exposed; the wooden boards that had once protected them from vandalism now lay in pieces on the ground beside them. Brendan reached out and unlocked the doors, opened them slowly, and stepped aside. "Are you ready?"

"Yes." And Simon *was* ready. At last he was ready to enter the tower block and reclaim at least a fragment of his childhood. He clenched his hands into fists, as if preparing for a fight, and stepped forward, walking stiffly up the steps and into the building. His skin went cold, hot, and then cold again; it felt like he was passing through different rooms, each with its own temperature. He'd never been so detached yet so curiously involved in a single moment. The muscles in his neck tightened and his head ached.

The ground floor was in ruins. Graffiti, broken concrete, piles of rubbish all over the floor. It was nothing like what he'd expected. The interior was a tipping ground for broken things, and it was only fitting that he and Brendan should be here: two broken men looking for a way to fix themselves.

"How does it feel?" Brendan's voice sounded as if he were perched on Simon's shoulder, speaking directly into his ear.

"Weird. I thought... I expected to be more afraid, but all I feel is tired and reluctant. It's like a chore. Something I have to do. Does that even make sense?"

"No." Brendan's tepid laughter echoed, bouncing off the walls and giving it a false sense of vigour.

"Okay, okay... you know what I mean. It's like an anticlimax. I've built this up so much, and for so long, that it's almost disappointing now I've finally got here."

"Yes," said Brendan. "I do know what you mean – I had the same experience. I hadn't been back here for years. Then, when I was twenty-one, I just broke in through one of the first floor windows and took a look around. I wasn't afraid; it was just an empty building. Like I said, there are no ghosts here. You won't find our childhood selves waiting for you in a cramped little room."

Something scurried across the floor, and when Simon glanced in the direction of the movement he saw a mouse or a rat burrowing into a pile of old clothes.

"They're the only monsters you'll find here, mate. Plenty of vermin nesting in these old walls... they've made it their home."

Brendan's phrasing made Simon momentarily nervous, but he shrugged off the feeling. It was nothing; just words.

Then, gradually, he became aware of another sound – this one far off, coming from somewhere deep inside the building. It was like slow dragging footsteps, perhaps somebody moving lazily through the rooms, wandering aimlessly. He listened for a moment, trying to pick out the direction of the source of the noise, but he couldn't be certain of where it originated. The sound seemed to be coming from nowhere and everywhere at once.

"Is there somebody else here?"

Brendan took a step forward, in front of Simon. "Not that I'm aware of."

More lies. He'd always been able to tell when Brendan was lying; his voice lowered, he was unable to look whoever he was speaking to directly in the eye.

"This place is empty." Brendan stayed where he was, with his back to Simon.

"Don't lie to me," said Simon, moving forward and placing a hand on his friend's shoulder. "There's no need."

Brendan shrugged off the contact, but did not turn around. He kept staring ahead, into the dusty shadows and along a narrow hallway leading off from the main reception area. "There's nobody here. Or if there is, it's just some kid mucking about."

"Okay," said Simon, unwilling to force the issue. "Sorry – I didn't mean to get at you." The shuffling sound had stopped. In its place, Simon could just about make out a low, soft humming, like air forced quickly through narrow pipes.

Brendan sighed heavily. "Just like old times. You always were a bit of a bully, talking us into things, convincing us to get into trouble." His voice seemed to hold an element of humour, but it was only a sliver.

"That was then and this is now." Simon backed away. He didn't want to get into this, not now: not here. He'd lived with the guilt for twenty years, and it was too soon to bring it out into the open.

He'd been the one who'd cajoled the other two into coming here, and following... whatever it was Brendan said he had seen. The clicking figure: the beaked man with the stick. Captain Clickety. Simon had been the one to come up with the idea, and despite the other Amigos' reluctance, he'd forced the issue, calling them babies...

Back then, as now, he'd always kept pushing until he got his way.

Pushing... it was his major skill, the thing he was best at. That was how he'd made his first million; it was the one trait that had kept him going while others had fallen away, giving up when things got too difficult. But not him: no, not Simon Ridley. He just kept pushing and pushing until something gave, and then he pushed some more, just for the hell of it.

The curious humming sound waxed and waned; it was still audible, but only just. Was it an old boiler? Faulty air vents?

Simon had already decided that he would not push now. He'd pull back and rein that tendency in, because sometimes pushing was just a quick way to fall off the edge. That was the real key to his success – the knowledge that although brute force and focus could often get you places, there were times that called for a soft touch, situations in which a gentle nudge was more effective than a hard shove if you wanted to open a door.

The humming sound moved away, becoming fainter and quieter as it shifted deeper into the body of the building

Sometimes, Simon knew, a whisper could be louder than a scream.

TWENTY YEARS AGO, WHEN THE DAYS WERE MUCH BRIGHTER...

THE TREE HOUSE is coming along nicely. It will be the den of the Three Amigos, when it is finished, and each of the boys is prepared to do whatever it takes to get the job done.

The light is fading slowly from the day. Daytime animals are being replaced by their nocturnal counterparts in the dense shrubbery. The sky has taken on all the shades of evening; the clouds scatter and dark patches show like great bruises against the heavens, and the sun is poised coyly at the tip of the horizon.

Marty is sitting on a makeshift wooden joist, high up in the branches of the chosen tree, hammering in six-inch nails. His face is a study in concentration; his body moves fluidly, as if he was born to the task. Simon watches his friend work, feeling a shiver of pride, but also a slight tug of jealousy. Marty is physically strong, good-looking and a great fighter; he is popular among the girls, and most of the boys at school are terrified of him. Simon can only dream about commanding that kind of respect.

Brendan is dragging more wood from the pile they'd made earlier, his thin body struggling with the load. Simon walks over silently and begins to help. Brendan smiles, but at that exact moment the sky darkens a little more and the smile looks pained, almost fearful.

Brendan swore that he saw a figure earlier: a tall man wearing a beaked mask, and with things that must have been false legs hanging down past the hem of his Halloween coat. Having now recovered from the initial shock, the boy still seems fragile. He wears his fear like the badge of a pop band he is ashamed to like.

The two boys drag an old plywood wardrobe door over to the tree where Marty is still hammering. They position it below the partially-built platform, and stand looking up at their friend. After a short time, Marty stops hammering, runs the back of his hand across his forehead – it is a studied move, one he's probably seen in a film – and looks down at the others from his perch.

"You ready for this bit?" Simon peers upwards as his friend's shape becomes a dark outline against the darkening sky.

"Yeah." Marty nods. "I don't know how we'll get it up here, though."

"I do." Brendan takes a step closer to the base of the tree. "We can set up a pulley system. I saw it in a book. All we need is that load of old rope over there and some well-tied knots." He crosses the ground and bends over, sorting through the bits and pieces of rope they found in the tumbled remains of another den – this one abandoned, with its fabric door hanging in tatters and the old lino, used as a floor covering, all torn and coated with mud. "Yep," says Brendan, turning to glance at his friends. "This'll do fine. We can have the platform raised before we have to go home for dinner."

The lowering sun shivers behind him, causing a strange rippling effect in the sky. For a moment it seems to Simon that Brendan's form becomes unstable, that it might break in half at any moment and the two separate pieces – like conjoined twins suddenly given their freedom – will drift off into the landscape, becoming parts of the patchy sliver of nature in which the boys are standing.

The illusion lasts only a fraction of a second, but it resonates deep within Simon's consciousness. He feels that he has been given a glimpse of something, has looked through a window into another place that exists alongside this one. Perhaps even another world.

Marty drops from the branches above and lands gracefully at Simon's side. He is an athletic kid; he plays football for the school team and has never lost a fight in his life. Marty is a born battler. Everybody says so, even the boy himself. Fighting is all he knows. He has been battling his father, and his father's rages, since he was old enough to understand the true nature of violence. He learned young. They were lessons he learned in the cot.

Standing there, with his friends, Simon has another flash: a brief image of the three of them as grown men, standing hand-in-hand on the grass. They are bright, energetic boys, and in his mind this translates to success in the grown-up versions of the Three

Amigos. He smiles; the vision makes him happy, despite the questionable truth of what he sees. Then he notices that the adult Marty is clutching at his side, and the adult Brendan is wearing clothes that are covered in dark stains. His own grown-up counterpart stands at the centre of this fading frieze, his face lean and angry.

"Let's get cracking," says Marty, keen to keep active, as if labour enables him to forget about the rest of his life. His hands are bunched into fists and the muscles in his neck stand out like thick wires. His cheeks are flushed from the physical labour and his forehead gleams with sweat.

"Right," says Brendan, seeming older than his ten years. "I've seen this before. All we need to do is tie these ropes together and attach it to the wood, and then we loop one end over that fat branch there and tug on the other end so the wood gets lifted up. One of us can stay in the tree, and guide it onto the frame. The other two will need to pull on the rope as hard as they can."

"Sounds easy enough," says Marty.

"Yeah, if you're a gorilla." Simon smiles.

"No, really. It's easy-peasy. I saw it on a film. It worked in the film, so it'll work now."

The other two boys nod, convinced by the cinematic precedent. Whatever doubts Simon might have had are pushed aside by the thought of the three boys acting out their own little movie, right here on Beacon Green.

"Can anyone, like, tie a proper knot? A pirate knot or something?" Marty steps forward and picks up a short length of rope. "Some of these are a bit small. We'll have to tie them all together to make one long piece."

"Just tie them really, really tight. It'll be okay." Simon takes the length of rope from Marty's hands as he speaks. He pulls on the rope, testing it. "It's pretty strong. If we double and triple tie the knots, it should hold when we pull the wood up into the tree. Trust me. Brendan's idea's going to work."

And that is all they need to go ahead with the plan: Simon's word, his blessing. Despite the fact that there is no official leader of the Three Amigos, and each boy brings his own strength to the table, it is always Simon who has the last word. The other two members of the small gang look up to him in a way that can never be spoken of; they defer to his superior intellect, his quiet presence. It has always been this way, even when the boys were infants. Simon was always the silent leader; he is in command, whether or not he wants the job. He is the one who pushes the others forward, giving the group momentum.

They work in silence for a while as the day slips away and the long shadows crawl like living things around Beacon Green, clustering at the bases of the trees and in the dense foliage of the small overgrown area the boys have played in since they were first allowed out of the house alone. It is their place, where they feel most at ease. There is nothing to fear on the small patch of waste ground, and their parents would not even pause for thought at the prospect of giving the boys free rein, to come and go as they please on this part of the estate.

Before long the separate pieces of rope have begun to form a single long rope. The knots are firm;

overdone, if anything, but at least they will hold when the real work starts.

"So what do we do after?" Simon looks up at his friends. "I mean, when we've done this? If we leave it here, unguarded, some other kids will come along and wreck it."

There is a brief pause when the boys stop working, glance at each other, and wait for someone to say what they are all thinking.

Simon continues: "We need to guard the den," he says, once again assuming his role as the leader, the member of the group whose responsibility it is to say such things aloud, to give voice to the collective consciousness of the Three Amigos. "Like army blokes. Like soldiers, yeah? We need to stand guard and protect what we've built."

Marty nods. Brendan squints, blinks, and then finally nods his own assent.

"Me and Bren will go back to mine and tell my mum and dad that I'm sleeping at his. Then we'll go to his and say to his mum that we're sleeping at mine. They won't check. They never do. They don't care." Silence again, but this one tense and filled with things that can never be discussed: the unfeeling attitude of both sets of parents; the fact that even at ten years old, the boys know that their mothers and fathers should take more care with their offspring. They all know that Simon's mother and father will be caught up in their own private war, and that Brendan's mother will be so far into the bottle of gin she keeps in the magazine rack at the side of her chair that she won't even remember the conversation.

"I'll climb out of the window after I'm supposed to be in bed." Marty's eyes are hard, cold. Behind them, just about visible through the tears that he always manages to keep at bay, are the images of violence that dwell in his own home. The father that hates everyone, including himself, and takes out those feelings of rage and helplessness on his own son. The bruises hidden beneath Marty's shirt. The cigarette burns on his upper arms.

"We'll meet back here, then." Simon raises his left hand, palm facing outward, splays his fingers, and then slowly makes a fist, one finger at a time folding in towards the palm, little one first and the thumb last: the secret salute of the Three Amigos. The other two boys follow suit, making their own slow-motion fists. Brendan does it with his eyes closed. Marty stares at Simon's face, his jaw clenched tight and his cheekbones as sharp as blades.

Without another word on the subject, the boys continue their work, knotting the ropes, making their primitive pulley.

Soon the job is done. The boys stand and admire what they have made. Brendan holds the rope in his hands and tests the joints, pulling at them, trying to tug them apart. "This is good," he says. "This'll definitely work."

Brendan kneels beside the sheet of plywood. There are already holes drilled along one edge, perhaps construction joints for the piece of furniture the wooden panel was built to be part of. He threads one end of the rope through two of the holes, and then loops the rope over itself, securing it tightly. He tests this knot, too, second-guessing his own work. The knot holds.

"Who's going up there?" Simon looks up, at the rickety structure they've created across two sturdy branches.

Brendan drops the plywood onto the ground. "I think the strongest one should climb up there. Marty, you're easily stronger than us two, so you can go up. You'll need to grab the edge of the wood and try to push it into place on the frame. It'll be really hard, but me or Simon wouldn't have a chance of doing it." He holds out his skinny arms, as if to underline his point.

"Okay." Marty runs to the base of the tree and leaps up, catching hold of a low branch. He seems happy to be physical again.

"We've gotta be careful," says Simon. "We don't want to get hurt. This thing's got sharp edges."

Brendan glances at the wood, nods. "Yeah. Do it slowly."

"Okay, I'm ready. Throw one end of the rope up here!" Marty's arm is dangling, his fingers grasping. "Hurry up."

Brendan grabs the loose end of the rope, gathers in a good length, and then stands directly beneath the platform. He swings the rope, squints as he takes aim, and then throws the end upwards. It barely lifts above his head before falling back down to earth.

"Bugger," says Brendan, his body going loose and his bottom lip pushed out in a sulky half-pout.

"Don't be daft," says Simon, bending down to pick up a large stone. "We need to make the end heavy. Here... tie the rope around this."

Brendan takes the stone and forms the end of the rope into a tight knot around the heavy object. "It's a monkey's fist," he says, grinning. "Old sailors used them as weapons when they had fights. I read it in a book." He swings the rope, the heavy end whistling through the air. "God, I bet it would hurt if you got someone on the head with it."

"Throw it up!" Marty's arm is still dangling. It looks like the tail of some weird animal.

Still swinging the rope, Brendan takes a single step back and hurls the stone into the branches. Marty's hand clutches, misses, and then clutches again; the rope wraps around his forearm, and his fingers close quickly over the rough hemp. "Got it!" he shouts. "I'll sling it over this branch."

"Yay!" Brendan jumps up and down on the spot.

"Yes!" Even Simon is caught up in the moment, thrilled by this small success.

There's a pause while Marty removes the stone, and then it drops at Simon's feet. Then the end of the rope comes down out of the tree, twisting like a snake. Simon grabs the rope and guides it down. Then he and Brendan start to take up the slack.

"Okay," says Simon, loudly. "We're going to start pulling."

"*Tally-ho!*" Marty screams from his spot on the branch, his voice funny and high-pitched.

Laughing, the other two boys begin to pull on the rope. The plywood panel shifts, turns, spins, and then slowly begins to rise. The weight isn't as much as they'd guessed, but it's an awkward method of lifting a rectangular sheet, and the exertion starts to tell on them.

"It's coming! I can see it." Marty is excited. He is in his element.

Simon grits his teeth and concentrates on making his pulling action steady and rhythmical. He doesn't want the timber to jolt or judder. It needs to rise as smoothly as they can make it; and if they try to rush what whey are doing, somebody might get hurt.

The panel swings as it rises, and the two boys on the ground keep their heads down, staying low so that it won't take off the top of their skulls. As soon as it is hanging at a level far enough above them for safety, they straighten up, planting their feet and keeping a tight grip on the rope. Simon is at the rear, and he makes sure that he gathers the loose end as more of the rope is fed through his hands, forming a coil near his left foot.

"I've got it!" Marty sounds as if he is shouting through clenched teeth.

"Brace yourself." Simon sets his body, leaning backwards.

"This is working..." Brendan peers up into the branches, trying to get a good view.

"Careful," says Simon, as he feels the rope tighten in his hands. The panel drops a few inches, then, as he takes the weight, it is suspended for a moment above them. "Bren... I can't hold it... it's gonna drop!" But Brendan is staring at the plywood panel, as if he is seeing something magical.

Inevitably, the panel drops. The rope skids through Simon's fingers, burning his skin, and the panel plummets to the ground. He falls back, stumbling but not quite going down, and Brendan doesn't move. He just watches as the panel drops towards him, whistling as it moves through the space.

"Bren!"

Brendan begins to turn, and it is this which saves him from taking a blow to the head. Instead, the panel slices across his right forearm, taking off a swathe of skin and drawing blood, as it flashes past him. Brendan falls down, grabbing his wounded arm, and opens his mouth to scream.

Simon moves quickly, running to his friend. He goes down onto his knees and inspects the arm. Blood is running freely, and the skin has peeled away from wrist to elbow. The cut is not deep, but it is messy; Simon thinks he'll probably need stitches.

Brendan is wailing, but he's trying not to cry. His eyes are wide. His face is pale.

"Bloody hell," Marty is at Simon's side. "Bloody, bloody... bloody hell."

"Are you okay? Can you move?" Simon is afraid to touch his friend's arm, in case he makes things worse.

"Y-yeah... I can move." Brendan sits up. His arm is coated in blood. The blood looks bright, like movie blood. That's all Simon is able to think.

"You need to go home. Or to a hospital." Marty starts to move, bending down to help the injured boy to his feet.

"No!" Brendan shouts the word. It is enough to stop the other two boys in their tracks. For a moment, they can't move, can't breathe. They just stand there and stare down at the third Amigo.

"You're hurt, mate. This is finished." Simon feels a twinge of regret as he speaks. He doesn't want this to be over, not any of it: the day, the den-building, the summer. He wants to stay ten years old forever, staving off an uncertain future by playing in the trees on Beacon Green.

"No," says Brendan, but softer this time. "I'll be fine. It's just scraped off some skin. Once the bleeding stops, we can start again."

Simon feels a sense of admiration towards his friend. A choice has been made. Blood has been spilled. Like a sacrifice. Brendan's inner strength is revealed.

"We can't stop now. We have to finish what we started." Brendan's face is still pale, but his eyes are on fire. "We've gotta finish this."

For a second, perhaps even less, nobody knows what Brendan means. Then, like water flowing through a crack in a dam, reality pours in and they realise that he means the den, the work they have been doing all day.

Now that the moment is broken, the boys feel able to move again. Marty takes off his T-shirt. "Here," he says. "Use this as a bandage."

Simon turns around and stares at Marty's body. The boy already has muscles: his arms are hard; there is the vague suggestion of a future six-pack airbrushed across his stomach. There are fresh cigarette burns alongside the old, white scars on his upper arms and in the soft skin of his elbow joints.

He takes the shirt and slings it over one shoulder. He takes a handkerchief from his pocket – the one his grandmother bought him the Christmas before she died; he always carries it with him, but is never quite able to say why – and starts to scrub the blood off Brendan's arm. The bleeding has slowed, almost stopped.

Once the arm is relatively clean, Simon uses Marty's T-shirt to cover the wound, which under close inspection isn't as bad as it looks. He ties it tightly, remembering from a film or a book that pressure will stop a wound from bleeding. It was probably in a war film. He loves war films. So he pretends that this is a combat situation, and he is treating a fallen comrade. In order to continue with the fight, the soldier has to get back on his feet, and it is his responsibility to make sure that happens.

"Are you sure you're okay, soldier?" He stares into his friend's eyes, looking for the cracks in his wall of courage.

Brendan nods. That's all he does. He does not speak. Then, slowly, he gets back to his feet and walks over to the plywood panel, begins to inspect it for damage. "It's fine," he says without turning around. "Everything's fine."

But for some reason Simon doesn't believe that. Deep down inside, like a big bass drum sounding some terrible beat, he feels certain that nothing will ever be fine again.

PART TWO

LOCALISED NECROSIS

"But you're not going to be the one to save me."
– Marty Rivers

CHAPTER NINE

MARTY POURED HIMSELF a drink and waited for the phone to stop ringing. He glanced over, at the telephone table, and smiled. He knew who it was. It was her – Melanie. She wouldn't leave him alone.

He sipped his cold beer and crossed the room, stood by the phone. He reached out and laid a hand on the tabletop, only inches from the black plastic device. He wasn't going to pick it up, but this felt like teasing, so he allowed his hand to creep across the desk and tickle the edge of the phone.

The ringing finally stopped.

His recorded message kicked in: "It's me. I'm not here, or I can't be bothered to answer. Leave me a message." Then there was a short, high-pitched bleep.

"Hi, Marty. It's me. Again. I've tried you on your mobile and didn't get an answer, so thought you might be at home. Am I going to see you tonight? I mean, if I'm not, you could at least do me the favour of telling me. I'm sitting here wondering why the fuck I persist with you. I get nothing back, so why should I keep giving you all this attention?"

Marty took another mouthful of beer. He didn't feel a thing as he listened to Melanie's whining voice. He supposed that he ought to feel at least something – lust, irritation, interest, resignation. But, no; he was empty. The girl inspired no emotion. She was just another warm, keen body on a cold night, a name and number in his mobile phone contact list. Nothing more than that.

When she ended the call he reached out and pressed the button to delete the message. She was history, this girl – he never wanted to see her again. Even the promise of her trim body, and the things she liked to do when she'd had a few too many Bacardi Breezers, held little appeal.

There would always be another one just like her. Women like Melanie were drawn to men like him; they couldn't help themselves. It was a kind of self-abuse, the desperate way they clung to the kind of bloke who lifted heavy weights, took drugs, and battled in back alleys when the pubs were closed. Melanie and her ilk were addicted to Hard Men – they were like groupies following a famous rock band around the world, all too willing to lower their morals and spread their legs in return for the slightest crumb of attention, even if that attention was ultimately negative. He had never been able to understand the mentality, but had exploited it his entire life. He'd taken hundreds of these women to bed, and not one of them had ever touched him inside, where it mattered. None of them had inspired within him anything more than a blunt craving for sex.

Marty was not an evil man. He'd done many bad things, yes, but he told himself that he was not inherently a bad person. He was intelligent – unlike a lot of his peers – and he was self-aware enough to realise the error of his ways, but none of this insight had ever stopped him from doing what he did best.

It was too late for Marty to change; the world had moved on around him, but he'd been stuck here in one place for twenty years. His chances were all used up. There was nothing left for him but how things were now, how they'd always been, and how they would remain until the day he died.

"Sorry, Melanie," he whispered. "But you're not going to be the one to save me." He smiled; he drank; he turned away from the phone.

Marty walked over to the window and looked out at the Baltic Flour Mill and the river beyond. Gateshead had changed a lot since his youth, when he'd cross the river to buy drugs, fight in amateur boxing bouts in local working men's clubs, and crack skulls on a Saturday night in the rough pubs along Low Fell before heading off into Newcastle to catch a late club and score with some orange-tanned slapper from Walker or Byker, or perhaps a single mother from Fenham or Benwell.

Yes, things had changed a lot around here.

Redevelopment money had turned the old flour mill into a magnet for the region's artists, and people from all across the country came to visit the gallery and spend their money in the pubs and restaurants along the Quayside on both sides of the Tyne. All that cash, it meant good times for a lot of people – especially the criminal fraternity. And Marty had always been well enough connected to skim a lot off the top. His old friend Francis Boater had introduced him to a few people, and they'd vouched for him to others higher up the food chain, until Marty had become part of their world.

He'd fought for them, these people. He had entertained them by knocking men unconscious in social club boxing rings, and then, when he was unable to get a license because of his injuries, in abandoned warehouses after midnight. It made his wallet fat and his body hard; he was a born fighter, and there was always someone ready to exploit that in a man, and money to be made off the back of it.

He turned away from the window, the sound of skidding rubber tyres ringing in his ears. The soft thump of impact, the sound of breaking glass, a girl's screams... it had happened a long time ago, but the accident had changed his life. The girl – Sally – had died from her injuries, and he had been damaged enough that the British Boxing Board of Control had revoked his boxing licence on medical grounds.

His fists, however, did not recognise the board's authority. So he'd carried on fighting. It was all he knew, what he was. If he peeled back his skin, there'd be steel beneath. He was solid all the way through, and no man had ever put him down.

He stared at himself in the mirror above the fireplace. He was not wearing his shirt – he'd been ironing a clean one when the telephone rang. He looked at the muscles in his shoulders, the toughened pectorals, and the solid slab of his upper abdominals. He had avoided the crappy fashion tattoos that blighted the flesh of most of his peers. He didn't have a six-pack; didn't need one, in his game. Six-packs and absurdly defined guns were for gym bunnies. Fighters simply needed to be ironclad.

The old scars along the inside of his biceps were clearly visible in the lamplight. The ones on his wrists he saw every time he took off his watch. Faded burn marks, from the tips of lighted cigarettes. When he was younger, he had become fascinated with body conditioning. If he toughened his body to accept and absorb pain, then no one would ever hurt him. Not his father, not the men he fought for money, not the bastards he battled for fun.

Nobody.

"All the king's horses and all the king's men..." He whispered the old nursery rhyme, staring at his lips as they formed the words; "...couldn't put Humpty together again." It was his mantra, the way he summoned strength from the dismal depths of his rage. Memories bristled behind his eyes, threatening to spill out into the mirror. Fear pushed the glass, like a hand pressing against it from the other side.

He turned away from the mirror and went to the ironing board, forcing away his dark thoughts and the snippets of bitter recollections. He finished ironing his shirt, watching the muted television. There was some kind of talent show on, but he wasn't really interested. He just watched the bright, eager faces as they scrolled across the screen, mouths open, he supposed, in song, but they looked to Marty more like silent screams.

He switched off the iron and left it to cool, and then put on his shirt. Feeling calmer now, more in control, he enjoyed the feel of the warm material on his skin. He turned off the television and went over to the iPod docking station. He put on his favourite playlist and hit 'shuffle'. It was the one with all the old blues singers: Aretha, Billie, Ma Rainey and Bessie Smith. Most of the people he mixed with liked drum 'n' bass, techno, or stomping euro dance anthems, but not him. Marty liked the blues, especially when they were sung by a strong female voice. He knew the blues well.

Billie Holiday sang about Strange Fruit and Marty Rivers closed his eyes. He thought about those black bodies swinging from the trees, and then, as if a channel had been opened, his head filled with second-hand images of death: fleshless Jewish prisoners, liberated and staggering out through the sagging gates of Nazi death camps; the hacked-up victims of machete-wielding Rwandan death squads; a young Russian soldier beheaded by laughing Chechen rebels; nineteen-year-old British squaddies blown apart by Taliban devices in the deserts and mountains of Afghanistan. Bullets strafed the space inside his skull, and he accepted them, knowing that he had spent his entire life dodging the same shots. He lived below the line of gunfire, always ducking and moving, bobbing and weaving, trying to remain in one piece.

The Holiday song came to an end and was replaced by Janis Joplin. Her broken heart flooded the speakers.

Marty left the room and went into the master bedroom. He wasn't quite ready to treat this place as his own. He'd only been living here for a couple of months, and was due to move out when the owner returned from New York in another couple of months' time. He was house-sitting; none of this stuff was his. Even the iPod was borrowed, and he'd downloaded the music on his landlord's computer. Marty owned nothing, and in turn nothing owned him.

He went over to the bed and went down on his knees. The carpet was thick and soft; the bed linen was expensive. He reached beneath the bed and pulled out his suitcase, then stood and placed the case on the bed, opened it and stared at what was inside. The acorn had appeared a few weeks ago. He'd woken up still wearing his clothes, feeling hung-over and strung out way past his limit. He remembered that it had still been dark, probably the early hours of a Sunday morning. He put his hand in his jacket pocket to check if he had any money left, more out of habit than anything else, and his fingers had closed around a small, hard object.

The acorn. The acorn with his initials scratched into its surface.

He had no idea where it had come from; anyone could have slipped it into his pocket. He'd been all over the night before: working on a pub door in Jesmond, then to a house party in the Concrete Grove, and finally he'd staggered back here with some woman whose name he didn't even know. Glancing over at the other side of the bed, her memory was still there. The skin of Melanie's' bare shoulder glowed in the darkness. Her arms were thin and pale.

But now Melanie was gone and the acorn remained. It was a fair trade, he thought.

He didn't know what the acorn represented, or why his initials had been scratched into the flesh, but something inside him told him that it meant more than he was ready to confront. It had something to do with what had happened to him and his friends twenty years ago – of course it did. Marty wasn't stupid. He'd taken the tests; could even join MENSA if he wanted. But Marty had never been much of a joiner.

The acorn was from one of *those* trees, the oaks that had appeared inside the Needle... at least that's how it happened in his dreams, the ones he'd suffered back then and the ones that were still with him now, clinging to the inside of his skull like dirt. The trees that shouldn't have been there, but were there anyway, surrounding them like sentinels. Marty, and Brendan, and Simon: the Three Amigos.

He smiled. He had not thought of that name in years.

Was that what the acorn was meant to tell him? That the Three Amigos would ride again?

He closed the lid of the suitcase and slid it back under the bed, then straightened and glanced out of the bedroom window. The blinds were open; the river gleamed like a road of razorblades beyond the pane. A bird, tiny and fragile, hovered on the other side of the glass. Marty went over to the window and stared at it. It was a hummingbird.

There had been hummingbirds then, too: twenty years ago, darting above them, in the trees. Impossible creatures, they were not meant to be here in the cold, desolate north-east of England.

The hummingbird flew directly at the glass, colliding with the transparent surface. Then the bird backed up and tried again. Like an oversized bluebottle fly, it made several clumsy attempts to fly through the window, but each time its tiny body simply slammed into the glass, too light and insubstantial to break through.

Marty watched in slow-dawning horror. He didn't understand why he was so afraid, but the sight of the hummingbird slamming into the glass made him feel sick with anxiety. It was a sight that should not be real; an image from a dream that had invaded the waking world.

After a short while, the hummingbird gave up the fight. Its wings blurred as it flew slowly backwards, away from the window, an illusion of stillness hiding frantic activity. The bird kept moving that way, facing him, looking him in the eye, until it was swallowed by blackness. To Marty, it seemed like it had simply vanished into the enveloping night air.

He ran from the room, into the bathroom, bent over the toilet and threw up. Again and again, until there was nothing left in his stomach, and then he kept on retching and dry-heaving, until finally he slumped sideways onto the cool, tiled floor. His stomach ached; the pain was cyclic, wave upon small wave of cramps.

Marty realised that his fist was closed around something. He forced it open, as if the fingers belonged to someone else and were reluctant to budge. There, at the centre of his palm, was the acorn. He had not put it back in the suitcase. For some reason that was beyond him for the moment, he'd kept it with him, unwilling – or perhaps unable – to put it away.

He closed his eyes, closed his fist, and waited for the cramps to pass.

Once the pain had subsided, he was thirsty. He set down the acorn beside the sink and filled one glass after another with cold water straight from the tap, using it to wash out his mouth and his insides. Soon he felt a lot better. He was thankful for that. Tonight's work needed a clear head and a fit body. If he was to beat his opponent, he needed to remain focused, and his reactions would have to be perfect.

He stared at himself in the mirror. His long, lean face was mean; the skinhead haircut accentuated the look. His grandmother always said that he looked like the kind of man she should be afraid of, and then she'd throw her frail arms around him and beg for reassurance that he was okay, that he was living a decent life.

He lied to her every single time. He couldn't bear to tell her the truth – he was unable to admit to her that he was a bastard, just like his father. That he hurt people for fun and for money. He fought to find catharsis. Each punch he threw, and every kick that made contact with a stomach or a thigh or the side of a head, made him feel better about himself. These acts of violence allowed him to forget his own failings, if only for the length of time it took for his opponent to recover and retaliate.

He smiled in the mirror, but his face felt rigid.

He head-butted the mirror, hard, and cracked the glass without shattering it. When he pulled back his head, there was a tiny cut along the front of his brow, just beneath the hairline. A speck of blood glistened under the harsh bathroom light. He lifted a hand and used his finger to smear the blood across his forehead. Marty was unbreakable: even sharp glass did him no lasting damage. He gritted his teeth and raged silently at his own reflection, and at the face of his father crouched behind those tensed features.

Glancing down at the acorn, he began to feel dizzy, drunk on his own anger.

"Humpty Dumpty sat on a wall..."

He tasted the promise of battle on his tongue, like an electrical charge.

Tonight, he would make another man pay for his own sins, and for his father's sins before him. This night, just like many other nights, Marty Rivers would draw someone else's blood in his quest to understand what it meant to be a man.

"...Humpty fucking Dumpty had a great fall."

CHAPTER TEN

BANJO WAS LOST in the Needle. It happened to him all the time, especially lately. He would start wandering, going slowly from room to room, floor to floor, and eventually find himself standing in an area he did not recognise: a small, cramped hallway, or a large room with only one door and no windows. It was strange, like a prolonged dream. Sometimes he would sit down and wait to see if the interior would change again, this time with him watching. It never did, though; it never altered in front of his eyes, only when he wasn't looking.

He remembered the fire. The burning gym and the horrible men who'd died in the flames. He had no idea how he had managed to get there from the hospital, or why most of the skin of his face had been removed. When he slept, he dreamed of creatures emerging from the broken screens of old televisions, and voices in his head that told him to hurt himself.

His mind had been empty for so very long. Then, gradually, it began to fill with thoughts and images; vague recollections of a life that may or may not have been his. Drugs and parties and a nagging hunger. A few women, a few men: a lot of empty relationships. Then there was a room, a chair to which he'd been bound. And a bullish man who had been kind to him, and then led him into great harm...

There was not much else until he woke up in hospital, and then another blank spot which ended in him being in a room filled with flames. Following this there was the Needle.

And then, of course, there was the girl. The girl and the chores she'd asked him to carry out – the deliveries he'd made to three men on her behalf.

The pretty, pretty girl, with her pretty, pretty wings. She'd told him her name once, but he couldn't remember it right now. He forgot a lot of information this way, as if his thoughts were leaking out through holes in his head, like water from a colander.

He walked along a short hallway with an exposed concrete floor, his arms held out at his sides and his fingers scratching the walls. It was dark in here; the windows were covered with security shutters.

There was an open door at the end of the hallway, and he could not fight the urge to enter whatever room lay beyond. He knew that it might lead him into trouble, and that he would probably regret following the impulse, but he was too weak to turn around and walk away.

Something moved behind him. It sounded like a mouse or a rat scurrying across the floor. He pretended that he had not heard the sound, preferring instead to focus on the doorway up ahead. Now that he was closer, he saw that there was soft green light spilling from the rectangular frame. The door was open. He smelled burning.

Burning.

But no, it was not the same as before: this fire would not hurt him.

He studied the open doorway. On the other side, positioned along the far wall, was a row of televisions. Their screens had been removed and fires had been set in the guts of the appliances. The flames were bright green. A small pyre burned inside the shell of every set.

Unable to turn away, Banjo stepped into the room. He closed the door behind him, yet he had no reason to block his escape route. He was puzzled by his own actions; his hand seemed to move of its own accord.

Banjo moved to the centre of the room. The walls were bare: no paper, no plaster, and no paint. Just squares of bare concrete. Shadows clustered at the corners of the room, at floor and ceiling level. The fires shed little illumination, despite the healthy green flames. The weak, swampy light spilled across the floor for a foot or two, and then diminished, expired, as if eaten up by those shadows. The flames did not destroy, they simply burned. They burned perpetually.

Banjo sat down in the middle of the floor. The concrete was cold, even through the seat of his jeans. He reached out his hands, opened them, and tried to gain warmth from the flames. He felt nothing. Banjo moved closer, shuffling forward on his backside, but still he felt no heat. The fires were cold.

Something shifted up above him, at the apex of wall and ceiling, and when he looked up he saw a long vine or a creeper curling back like a tongue withdrawing into its mouth.

The ceiling was growing a thin layer of vegetation. He felt so close to that other place – the one the girl had told him about – that he could almost breathe its air. The cold green fires crackled and popped; the air moved with a draught; the vines moved like snakes across the ceiling.

Banjo felt as if he was standing on the border, just about to take a step across but somehow barred from doing so. It was over there; he could see the rim of a new horizon. But he was not allowed into those territories.

A shape drew itself together from the shadows and the vegetation, forming a long, narrow ovoid. It made no sound as it slowly detached itself from the ceiling, hanging down on trailing vines, to drop onto the floor to his right. The shape was upright; it resolved into a figure.

The girl.

"Hello, Banjo," she said, stepping out of the shadows. She was wearing the skin of an animal and her long black hair was knotted with leaves and twigs. Her bare legs were thin, the bones of her knees as prominent as her elbows. Her face was pale, narrow. She looked hungry.

Banjo smiled. She meant him no harm, this child of that other place.

"Thank you for your help." She took a few steps towards him and then stopped. She opened one hand and a tiny hummingbird flew out of her fist, circled his head, did a lap of the room, and then flew into the shadows from which she had emerged. "It's almost set now. Not long to go. All the pieces are in place, and we just need to wait for them to move closer together." She smiled. Her teeth were stained dark from the leaves and berries she ate in order to survive.

Banjo nodded. He tilted his head, eager as a hound for his mistress's affection.

"You remember me, don't you?"

He nodded again, excited this time. Keen to impress.

"That's right. It's me. It's Hailey." She covered the next few paces in an instant, and suddenly she stood right before him, reaching down to stroke the side of his bandaged face. "Don't worry," she said. "It's okay... I won't hurt you. Not me."

He realised that he was crying.

"Remember? I'm your friend. We help each other. We help each other hide from him – the other one. You remember him, too, don't you? The bad one."

Banjo pulled back, as if from the chill green fires in the television screens. He heard himself whining like a whipped cur.

"That's right. The other one: the Underthing. It's because of him you're the way you are, with your face all torn apart and your mind in pieces. The Underthing did this to you. The television things were his. The Slitten were mine, but they've gone now. All used up. We all make our own monsters over here, in the grove and the little place beyond the grove. Some of them are forever; some of them are temporary, not meant to last beyond the moment when they are needed."

He had no idea what she meant, but her words soothed him. They made him feel whole and happy and loved. He pushed his bandaged cheek into the palm of her hand, wishing that he could fly away, like the hummingbird.

"Here, let me help." She crouched down in front of him, her white features hovering like a vision in the gloom. Her eyes were dark, nearly all pupil, and her cheekbones were as sharp as blades. "Let me take a look." She smelled of fresh air and wild flowers and herbs – honeysuckle, jasmine and rosemary. Her sweat was nectar. "The doorway must be clean, unsullied."

Banjo smiled; he opened himself up to her, yielding to her touch.

The girl began to remove the wrappings from his face. She did so slowly, carefully, smiling all the while. Her hands moved slowly and easily, and he felt no pain. The bandages came apart, peeled away, and fell from his damaged face like shedding skin.

"Oh, you poor, poor baby," she said, and then she leaned forward and kissed his scarred cheek, keeping her lips there, cooling his maimed flesh.

Banjo was dribbling like a baby. She was his mother, this strange, sombre girl, and she loved him.

"It's looking better," she whispered. "Your face. It looks much better than before. Some of the power of the grove has touched you. I'm not sure how, or why, but it's helped a little." She removed her hands from his face. "Would you like to see?"

Banjo shrugged. He tilted his head again. Then, trusting the girl, as he always did, he slowly nodded his uncovered head.

The girl stood and walked across the room, then bent down to pick something up. The fires glinted on the reflective surface in her hand, and as she walked back towards him Banjo watched the play of the flames in the glass.

"Let's see... come on, don't be shy. Take a good look at yourself. Look at the doorway."

The girl raised the shard – not a mirror exactly, but a piece of broken glass that served just as well. She pressed it closer to Banjo's ruined face, and at first he twisted out of the way, trying not to see. But then, as she stroked his head with her free hand, he relented and waited for the looking-glass to show him what he had become.

The fires shimmered in the cloying, shut-in air. The girl said nothing. Banjo held his breath.

Then he stared into the glass.

The flesh had not grown back; his face still looked… *exposed*. It was raw and naked, like something denuded which should always have remained unseen. The bones were covered by a thin layer of tissue, but it was like paper. It wrinkled and threatened to tear apart when he tried to smile. And yet… madly, he *did* look better than he'd hoped. The girl had not lied about that. He could still see parts of his jaw through the holes in his sunken cheeks where flesh should have hidden them, but the ragged edges of his wounds were smoothing over, becoming less repellent. His eyelids looked odd, without any flesh to the sides of and beneath the eyes, but at least they made him look halfway human.

He opened his lipless mouth, licked his front teeth – upper and lower rows – and then bared them like a wolf.

"See," said the girl. "I told you so. You know you can always trust me. I'll never lie to you, Banjo. We need to be honest with each other, if we stand any chance at all of stopping the Underthing. We need a bond based on trust."

Banjo stared at the monster in the mirror, and thought that he wasn't so monstrous after all. Certainly not compared to the one the girl was talking about. Because, compared to the Underthing, he was nothing like a monster… nothing at all.

CHAPTER ELEVEN

SIMON WAS STANDING in the middle of the motorway looking up at the hill upon which he knew the Angel of the North should be standing. Light drizzle coated his skin like sweat, the sky yawned above him like some passageway into a cosmic room, and the sculpture was noticeable only by its absence.

The grass on the hill was long and unkempt, as if nobody had been here for years. A line of scrubbed dirt ran around the base of the rise, with trails springing off on either side of the hill – front and back. The path that led up to the sculpture was cracked and broken; huge portions of tarmac had been scoured away to reveal the uneven base course beneath. Ashen clouds lowered across the scene, unbroken by Gormley's great northern masterwork. The scene was apocalyptic. The world had somehow ended, or was just about to.

Simon turned around and glanced along the road. It was empty. No traffic moved along its length, but far off, in the distance, dark clouds gathered like harbingers of chaos. He stared into the heaving black mass, but could make out nothing solid. There seemed to be protean shapes moving within the black folds – figures that kept shifting between people and animals – but he could not be sure. Perhaps it was just air currents causing the illusion of form and substance.

He turned back towards the hill, and right at its top there was now a small figure. The figure stood motionless, with its arms outstretched in the same pose as the Angel. He watched for a few minutes, but still the figure did not move.

"Who are you?" He knew that whoever it was would not hear the question. He was too far away, the light breeze was blowing in the wrong direction, and the air was thick and turgid. "Tell me who you are."

The figure remained motionless. The sky darkened, turning the figure into a silhouette, or a black template carved out of the world, showing only darkness beyond.

Simon began walking towards the figure on the hill. He had no idea why he felt compelled to approach it, but something was calling him. His body responded to an impulse that was too subtle to explain, like the currents of the sea or the phases of the moon. He stepped onto the shattered footpath and dodged the worst of the damage. The stones were blackened, as if they'd been burned. He struggled to keep his footing; the path seemed to tilt and sway, but not in any way that his eye could discern.

He looked up, away from his shoes, and this time the figure *had* moved. It was standing in the same position, with arms outstretched like aeroplane wings, but it was now facing him. There was another difference, too: the figure was wearing a mask, with a long beak for a nose, and had about doubled in size. Simon knew that he should be running, to get away from the figure, but his legs refused to obey the command sent from his brain.

So instead he climbed the shattered footpath, up the hill, towards the beaked figure that stood so still and so silent in the darkness. He knew who it was; he had seen the figure before, in waking life as well as in dreams. It was Captain Clickety, the one who had taken their boyhood, the creature the three boys had followed to the Needle from Beacon Green twenty years ago. He was here; he had come back. But why had he returned, and for whom was he waiting up on the hill?

Simon felt only minimal danger. He suspected that Clickety had not come for him, but the one he wanted was linked to him. Was it one of the others – Brendan or Marty – and if so, why one of them and not him? There was a sudden pang of resentment then, of shameful envy, and he struggled to explain it. Like a knife in his gut, the feeling sliced him neatly and painlessly.

If there was horror to be had, why could he not be the one to experience it? After all this time, since running away and trying to build a life for himself, there was still a gap at his core, and that gap was the absence of horror. He knew that now; finally he could admit it, if only to himself.

The figure did not grow nearer as he approached it. "Come back," he whispered, tasting the night: it was cold and coppery, like blood but with an underlying bitterness.

When he reached the summit of the hill the figure was gone. Its mask lay on the ground at his feet, staring upwards: an invitation. Simon bent over and picked up the mask. It felt smooth, soft, like silk, and there was little weight to it. He lifted it towards his face, turned it around, and stared into the back of the mask. Looking through the eyes of Captain Clickety, he surveyed the land. Vast acres of the earth lay scorched before him, trees had been felled and hacked into pieces, and the earth itself was churned and broken. This was the monster's dream: it was how he saw the world in which Simon and his friends lived. Incapable of seeing beauty, it substituted a veneer of destruction.

Simon threw the mask away. He could not wear it, and he certainly did not want to view the landscape through its eyeholes for much longer. He could not bear the dreams of the damned. Because he knew that the thing which called itself Clickety was indeed damned – and that damnation had touched them all, twenty years ago. It touched them still, reaching across the years and travelling the blighted inner landscapes they held deep inside them. Damnation was a road he had built within himself, a route he did not want to take.

He became aware of a vibration, as if the ground beneath his feet were beginning to tremble. Slowly, he got down on the ground and placed his ear to the earth. Yes... there it was... a slow, rhythmic rumble, like vast machinery working somewhere deep beneath the planet's crust. He recalled the Morlock machines from *The Time Machine* – a story he'd loved as a boy. Was he hearing them now, the shambling Morlocks and their infernal machines?

No, that was fiction. He could not retreat into stories, not any more. He needed to confront reality, no matter what the cost.

The vibrations grew stronger and Simon stood, afraid of what they might represent. Was something tunnelling through the earth, heading for the surface right under his feet, on the spot where the Angel of the North had once stood – and should still be standing, casting its protective wingspan across the region?

He backed away, moving across the top of the rise, and then lost his footing. He tumbled down, turning and spinning and coming to rest on the footpath at the base of the earthen platform. This, too, had been torn up, perhaps by some kind of construction equipment, or perhaps by the hateful hands of a giant.

He began to move, running away from the now-barren site of the Angel. He ran across the long grass, careful not to lose his footing again, and made for the main road. Still there were no cars in sight; the road was empty for miles... except for those churning black clouds, which had now begun to coalesce, to pull together and form a single vast shape on the horizon.

Simon stared in mute horror – or was it just an echo of horror, a faint tremor of the feelings he had experienced so long ago?

The Angel of the North stormed out from those dark clouds, taking huge footsteps to cover the ground between them. Simon stood and he stared and he watched as its massive steel feet rose and plunged, making great dents in the road, cracking the blacktop, zigzags snaking from the impacts.

It was coming. The Angel was coming, and it was going to kill him, to stomp him, to flatten him into the road surface. Simon had never been so certain of anything in his life.

He turned and ran, heading away from the gigantic effigy, moving south, wishing that he could reach London at a sprint, without pausing for breath. He should never have returned here, to this godforsaken place. It was no longer his home; he was not welcome within its borders.

Glancing over his shoulder, and exposed by the light of the moon, he saw that the Angel had drawn closer. With each terrible step it took, the distance shrank by yards. Those steps were immense, and his were tiny, puny: he could never outrun this nightmare image. However fast he moved, and wherever he went, it would always be gaining on him, covering the ground faster than he ever could.

He was haunted by the north, and by the ghosts he had tried to leave behind.

The sculpture – always artfully rusted – looked as if it had been left unattended for generations, and the material had decayed. The steelwork had turned black in places, and there were human body parts wedged between the lattices of its framework. The spaces between the layers of metal were filled with raw meat; blood dripped down its flanks, its legs, and formed streaks on the dark road surface. Its mighty wings beat the air rigidly, pivoting at the shoulders. It would never fly, this thing, but it might just about manage to hover, or float, at least a few inches off the ground.

The dark Angel was close now. It must be only minutes before it was upon him, bearing down like a mountain, a living, sentient part of the landscape he had tried so hard to abandon...

* * *

HE WOKE WITH a scream lodged in his chest. The muscles were working, but no sound would come out. He felt like he was choking... his throat was stuffed with chunks of rancid flesh, like the offal decorating the oxidised exoskeleton of the Angel.

He sat up in bed, his hands clutching the sheets, and tried to breathe. After a short while, he realised that he was not dying; his airwaves had opened up again, and he sucked in air and attempted to shake off the nightmare.

That's all it was: a nightmare. The worst he had ever experienced.

His head throbbed, and he imagined his brain small and shrivelled, like a walnut, from the alcohol he'd consumed with Brendan. There was no clear memory of going to bed, just a hazy recollection of falling backwards onto the mattress and succumbing to blackness. Back in London, he didn't generally drink the kind of volume he'd knocked back today. It was a different kind of drinking he did back there, less deliberate and much more social. Even when he drank alone, he stuck to wine or spirits, so he wasn't used to the peculiar, heavy drunkenness brought on by quaffing so many pints of ale.

His phone was on the bedside cabinet. The display showed several unopened text messages. They would all be from Natasha. He knew this without even looking. He had no idea why he was ignoring her, but for some reason he wanted to keep his distance. Was it the idea that she might be polluted by whatever was happening in the Grove, and he wanted to keep her pure and untouched? It sounded plausible, but he had never before placed her on any kind of pedestal. That was one of the reasons she'd liked him so much to begin with: all of her other boyfriends had been in awe of her beauty, treating her like some kind of untouchable princess. Simon treated her like every other woman he'd been involved with – he kept her at arm's length, not allowing her into his life far enough for her to have an impact when she eventually left him. Because she would leave him, they always did. He made sure of that.

He got up and crossed to the window, reaching out to pull the curtains slightly apart. He looked out at the street and it was empty; he glanced behind him and the glowing digits on his travel alarm told him that it was after 2 AM, not quite late in the day-to-day life of the estate. But it was nice to see the place at ease for a change, with no gangs of youths or suspiciously parked cars to add to the threat.

Turning back to look out of the window, he saw a small shape darting through the air across the street. It was either a tiny bird or a large insect, and it moved at great speed, whipping out of sight before he could identify exactly what it was. Or perhaps it was simply a shadow, a shade: another slight fold in the fabric of the Concrete Grove...

Simon returned to the bed and sat down. The bare room closed in on him, its walls looming too close and the ceiling lowering by fractions. He closed his eyes, and behind the lids he once again saw the massive, implacable approach of the Angel... chunks of raw meat sliding around at its core, dark blood sheeting across its torso. The Angel threw back its head and roared, but silently. No sound came; its rage was muted.

What had that been about missing the horror, or the lack of horror causing a fault line in his life? Why the hell had he thought that, even in a dream? Real horror was not something he ever wanted to experience again.

He turned at the waist and opened the top drawer in the bedside cabinet – the only furniture in the room, other than the bed and a cheap flat-pack wardrobe. Rummaging around inside, passing over his watch and his wallet and some paperwork, his fingers closed around the acorn. It felt larger, but that could have been a trick of his imagination. He did not retrieve the acorn to find out; he just left his hand in the drawer, fisted around the object.

"Bring me your horror," he said, the theatrical language making him feel slightly absurd. "Bring it on, Clickety, you fucking bastard. I'll swallow it all and then come back for more."

But he was lying. He knew he was lying. Sitting there alone, in a small, spartan room in the town where he'd left his childhood, the lies piled up against the walls, like diseased corpses awaiting a decent burial.

CHAPTER TWELVE

It was 2:30 AM and Marty was ready to be let off the leash.

The crowd in the Barn would be small but select, with men in tailored suits or designer sportswear and women in expensive dresses. There was a lot of alcohol floating around, and most of the people in there were either drunk or well on their way. Bodies pressed close, couples fondled each other, and strangers flirted like it was the end of the world and all they wanted was to go out with a bang.

These people loved a bit of sexual tension to go along with their violence.

Marty was sitting in the back of an old Rover, wrapping his hands in protective tape: criss-cross, wrist, palm and knuckle. Even though these bouts were advertised as bare-knuckle fighting, he never fought without some kind of protection. He'd seen too many men break their knuckles, shatter the bones in their fingers, or smash their wrists in so-called 'pride fights'. Marty wasn't like them; he was clever. Yes, he was an idiot who fought for money, but he was a clever idiot who made sure he chose bouts where there was at least some kind of rule book.

He smiled, staring at his fists. He flexed the fingers. The wrappings were perfect: nice and tight. Some men had hands like glass, but Marty's were like steel rods covered in a thick layer of rubber.

"You okay back there, Rivers?" The man in the front passenger seat did not turn around. He just sat and stared through the windscreen. His big bald head sat on a neck as thick as a horse's thigh, and the expensive leather jacket he wore glistened like a beetle's back.

"Fine," said Marty. "Just take me to the fucker, and I'll put him down. Then we can all go home and count our money."

The man laughed. "Aye, you're a funny bastard. Has anyone ever told you that?" At last he turned around, and his small, squinty eyes looked as hard as stones beneath his curiously light eyebrows. His face was wrinkled, but it was difficult to tell how old he was. Even Erik Best's closest associates didn't know his true age; it was a well-kept secret, and the fact that he never told anyone betrayed the man's huge capacity for narcissism.

"Yeah," said Marty. "They tell me all the time. I'm a regular fucking stand-up comedian, me."

Best turned back to face the windscreen and the Barn beyond, the smile stuck to his face. Marty did not trust this man an inch. Erik Best was an ex-boxer, and a thoroughly old-school monster, who always played with a game face. Nobody knew what he was thinking; not one person could see beyond the façade. And that was the way Best liked it. No one got past his defences; not even women.

"This Polish boy – this Aleksi – he's a big lad. You sure you can handle him? I have a lot of money riding on you, and my friends have even more, so the last thing we want is for you to go down on your arse, marra."

Marty grinned. His cheekbones felt solid and unbreakable, like teak. "I've seen the tapes. I can handle this kid. He might be big, but he does the same thing every time. He feints with his left just before swinging that big right haymaker. He's strong, but he's clumsy and obvious. No proper training. I can take him."

The bald head nodded once. "Just make sure you fucking do, or you and me will have a little problem. And I doubt either of us wants that, eh, marra?"

Marty waited a beat, just to show that he wasn't scared (although he should be; Best was a bad bastard from way back, when hard men were genuinely hard). Then, quietly, he said, "No sweat, Erik. I'll even string it out a bit, just so your friends get their money's worth."

Best's laughter filled the car. It sounded genuine, but Marty knew that you could never be sure with a man like Erik Best.

The silent driver guided the car off the motorway and along the minor roads. They were several miles out of the city, where the countryside began to encroach and cancel out the manmade structures. Not too far away, the Scottish borders demarcated the ancient boundaries between the old tribes of the Britons and the Picts: it was a place of ruined castles and ley lines; of ancient stone cairns, secret underground waterways and the spirits of the marauding dead. The land was steeped in a history that Marty had only ever learned about in school. The real stories – the petty wars and the personal politics and the blood that had drenched the earth – were something of which he knew very little. But still it scared him. He feared these open spaces, seeing glimpses of an ancient world that he could never truly know. Strip away the urban glamour, the cars and the suits and the money, and all you had left was the bare earth... and the old bloodstains that would never truly fade.

The farmhouse loomed on the horizon. It was an old structure, all ancient timber beams and locally quarried stone, and as far as he knew nobody had lived here for decades. Erik Best ran a lot of his entertainments out of this place: dog fights, sex and drug parties, and of course the bare knuckle bouts upon which he'd built his reputation.

As they drew closer to the old building, Marty saw people milling about on the grass outside the Barn, located several yards away from the main building. The lights were on in the house, but the doors were open and the majority of the select guests had already begun to gather at the place of combat.

"They're all ready for you, me lad. Let's not let them down, eh?"

Marty said nothing. He checked the wrappings on his hands and did a few neck-stretching exercises. He was limber this evening, but there was always room for a little more flexibility. The key to this kind of gig, he knew from experience, was a combination of stamina and flexibility. With those two elements in place, you could easily outdo brute strength. If you knew what you were doing.

And Marty knew what he was doing.

They parked the car slightly away from the other vehicles – mostly four-wheel drive yummy-mummy school-run models, but with a couple of Mercs and Beamers parked alongside them. The driver stayed where he was, and Best climbed out, going round to the rear to open the door for his star attraction.

Marty nodded and got out of the car. "Thanks," he said, scanning the area. He'd been here before, a handful of times, so he already knew the layout. The last time he'd been at the farm, it had been for one of Best's infamous parties, but the time before that was for a bout in the Barn against a wiry gypsy blessed more with aggression than with ring sense.

"You ready, marra?" Best stood before him; the top of his head came up to Marty's chest. He was small, but he was deadly. Sometimes people forgot this fact, and they always came off the worse for it.

"Fuck, yes." Marty clapped his hands together and started to jump up and down on the spot, short, sharp movements meant to get his circulation going, to get his buzz on. The air was warm; the sky was strangely bright for this time of the night. He unzipped his tracksuit top, turned around, and threw it into the car. He was pumped; the muscles in his arms and shoulders felt tight, in a good way. He was *primed*.

Best walked over towards the infamous Barn and Marty followed. He threw some quick air punches, snapping them back just for show. He rolled his head on his neck and shrugged his shoulders. He made his face neutral; he wanted to give nothing beneath the surface away, he had to protect what was inside, behind the mask he always wore.

Humpty Dumpty, he thought. *Humpty fucking Dumpty...*

Fear surged through his body, starting in his belly and spreading out along his limbs. He bit down on the terror, swallowing it back down, consuming it and taking raw power from it. This was what he had cultivated, when he would condition his body as a teenager. All those small cuts, the burning cigarettes, and all the times he had held his forearm to the flame of the gas cooker in the kitchen. It was all done to summon this fear: the fear of Humpty Dumpty and the beatings his father had dished out in the name of discipline.

"Humpty Dumpty," he whispered, tasting the words, the regurgitated fear, the horror that had dogged him for twenty years and taken on the form of a nursery rhyme because that was the only way he could think of to deal with the cold, dark feelings that gnawed away at his insides.

He remembered the trees up along the edge of Beacon Green, and the small, fat thing that sat in the branches of his memory, gibbering and giggling and spitting as he watched it swinging its legs and slapping its egg-like torso. The thing that was never too far from his dreams, the creature that could simply not have existed... but it had; the monster was fact, not fiction.

Humpty Dumpty was real. He had seen it, twenty years ago, hours before he and his friends had followed the figure they'd christened Captain Clickety into the Needle and lost a slice of their summer, their lives, their fucking childhood.

Best spoke to a lot of people as they made their way to the Barn, but Marty ignored them all. The designer suits and the dresses, the leering, sweaty faces and the wet mouths that bayed for blood. They were worse than animals, these people; all they wanted was to see someone get hurt, anyone. It didn't even matter who got trashed, or how much money was lost in the process. As long as they got a glimpse of bloodshed, and heard the sound of bones cracking, they were happy. They would go home and they'd fuck each other senseless, thinking of the blood-stained combatants they'd seen, pretending that they were tough enough to get inside the ring and trade fists with a brutal stranger. Telling each other that they understood what it meant to be a man.

Marty knew that he was a stand-in, nothing but a rich couple's role-play: they barely even saw him as a real person, just an extension of the video games they played and the action films they watched as they snorted cocaine off the lid of a DVD case. He hated these people; he wanted to break them all into little pieces and piss on the remains. But instead, he'd be their show pony and take their money, and go back to the flat to patch up his injuries ready for the next time.

He knew his place, and they knew theirs. This was how the world worked: there were those who paid and those who played, and then there were those – like Erik Best – who *facilitated* the action. In many ways, this last role was the worst of all, because there was little honour in manipulating the pieces on the board. At least the actual players got their hands dirty, whether it was from the ink of printed money or the blood of the defeated.

Marty had once been present when Best had accepted a delivery of business cards. Small, neat font, good quality ivory card; they must have cost a lot of money.

The words stamped on the front had said: *Erik Best — Facilitator.*

Erik Best knew his place, too.

They entered the Barn, walking in through the open double doors. Everyone crowded in alongside them or behind them, being careful not to jostle in case they prompted some early violence. Marty smiled.

There must have been thirty or forty people present, but the noise was kept to a level that would not be heard from the road. Marty wasn't sure about the logistics of these bouts or how Best managed to organise them and keep the authorities away, but they were usually low-key affairs with the details and guest list kept secret until the last possible minute. It took a lot of money to buy your way in, and once you were there it still didn't mean you were guaranteed a return visit. Everything was at the whim of the organiser. Best kept a tight rein on things, and he enjoyed keeping people guessing. Nobody would ever take him for granted.

A crude ring had been set up at the centre of the barn, enclosing an area of approximately six metres square – near enough to regulation boxing ring size to suggest that somebody had at least taken the preparations seriously. There was straw scattered on the floor, long stakes had been driven into the ground at each corner, and sagging lengths of old climbing rope lashed it all together. Marty remembered this set-up from last time: it was surprisingly sturdy, and the stakes had held even when he'd thrown his last opponent against one of them, almost snapping his spine. There were lighting rigs strung across the ceiling, but the halogen bulbs were not quite powerful enough to dispel all the shadows. The interior of the Barn had a dusty atmosphere, as was fitting.

"Can you smell it?" Best turned to face him, raising his strange blond eyebrows. "Can you smell all that fucking middle-class cash?" His smile was wolfish, and his skin was moist with sweat. He looked... Marty struggled for the right word, and then settled on *hungry*. Erik Best looked ravenous.

Across the other side of the Barn, surrounded by four or five men dressed in gaudy sports casuals, there stood a tall, broad-shouldered man with cropped white hair and ugly tribal tattoos across his upper chest and shoulders. He was staring at Marty. His face was long and pale and his eyes were narrow; the muscles in his jaw were so tense that it looked like they might burst through the skin at any moment, like parasites escaping their host.

"That's him," said Best, nodding in the direction of the other fighter.

"I know," said Marty. "Not very pretty, is he?"

"He looks tough." Best glanced at Marty, as if judging his response.

"It's the ones who don't look tough you have to worry about. You know that. Blokes like this one, they're all image, all gym-bought muscles, cheap tattoos and a whole lot of front. Just look at you: a short-arse with a pot belly, and yet you're the most fearsome bastard I ever met." He smiled, letting Best know that he was at least half-joking. Nobody else could get away with talking to Erik Best like this. Marty knew that he was afforded certain privileges because he made the man a lot of money...

Best laughed softly, shook his head. "You're a cunt, Rivers. But that's why I like you." He slapped Marty on the right bicep – hard, with enough force to let him know that he was being favoured.

"Humpty Dumpty," said Marty, looking back at his opponent. The other man was having his shoulders massaged by a short, fat man in a comically dated Kappa tracksuit. His curly black hair was soaking wet, as if he'd been caught out in the rain.

"One of these days," said Best, moving away, "you're going to have to tell me what the fuck that means, marra."

Marty did not smile. He couldn't. He was entering the zone, the place where all bets were off and no prisoners were taken. He smelled phantom blood in the air and his head was filled with the distant sounds of battle: cries and screams and gunfire, women wailing in a litany of loss as their menfolk were slain in the streets. Towers falling. Planes crashing. Cities burning. He felt connected to an ancient source of warfare, a rich seam of death and destruction that raged constantly beneath the surface of the world. This, he knew, was the real face of humanity. Some people – those like him and the man across the Barn – were either born or created to fight. The difference was fractional; whether by design or birthright, they were warriors. The only thing that mattered now was who would walk away as the victor and who would remain there in the makeshift ring, face to the floor, bleeding into the dirt and the hay and suffering the ignobility of defeat.

"Okay, everyone, we all know why we're here." Best's raised voice silenced the gathered onlookers. He was that kind of man, one with a high level of natural charisma. Glasses and bottles clinked, somebody coughed, whispers hung in the air, but his voice rose above it all. "Give us a few minutes to have a chat with the fighters, and then we'll start the bout. Keep drinking, keep betting, and don't give me any fucking reason to not invite you back here." He grinned, but his eyes shone with barely repressed fury.

Marty followed Best across the room, towards the spot where the Polish kid was standing with his cronies. They were silent; all eyes were upon him as he stepped across the dim space. The Polish kid started to shadow box, but his gaze remained fixed on Marty. His technique wasn't bad, but Marty's was a lot better.

Marty nodded his head once and bared his teeth in a feral grin. The kid stopped his performance, realising that it was not having the desired effect.

"Okay," said Best once they had all gathered together. "You all know the rules, and as I've said before, if anyone tries anything funny, they're fucked. I have men who will pile in at a given signal and crack your skulls if you even look like you're messing about. I want a clean fight... but not *too* clean. Got that?"

Marty nodded.

"Yes," said the fat, curly-haired man in the Kappa, his English clipped but perfectly clear. "We know rules. We play by rules. It is the same everywhere. My man will win this, whatever rules may be."

The Polish fighter smiled. Marty noticed for the first time that his front two teeth were missing from the upper row. He probably wore dentures, and had taken them out for the fight. Rather than make him look tougher, it showed a potential weakness.

"Right then, retreat to your corners and get ready. Let's get this thing going and make some money." Best watched as the men walked around the ring and took up their positions at their allocated corners. The Polish fighter climbed in through the ropes, followed by the fat man, clearly his trainer and corner man. The others just stood there and practised looking shifty, like extras in a cheesy gangster flick.

"Where's Jock?" Marty scanned the barn, looking for Best's usual corner man.

"He's here... somewhere. Probably drinking my fucking whisky."

A small, lean man in a flat cap appeared at ringside, raising a hand in welcome.

Marty walked to his side of the ring and shook the man's hand. "Jock. How's it going?"

"Nae bad," said the wiry Scotsman. "You feeling fit?"

Marty nodded. "Fit as a butcher's dog."

"Good." Jock lifted the middle rope and stepped aside to allow Marty to climb through the gap. "You should take this kid easy. He's big, but he's slow as fuck and he telegraphs them big punches about half an hour afore they arrive."

Marty started moving, keeping his feet light. He'd been training for this bout for about a month, with early morning runs, sparring sessions at a friend's gym in Byker, and some work with heavy weights.

He was lucky in that he was naturally athletic, and his early boxing training had taught him his ring craft. Most of his opponents in these bouts were either Irish gypsies with no style and plenty of energy, or men like this one – immigrants who were fighting to feed their families, because they had no other saleable skills to offer this flattened economy.

Everybody feared the gypsies, but Marty was more cautious of the fighters who had more at stake than a campsite reputation. A man who fights for his children, for his wife, is a man who will not go down easily, and even when he does go down the odds are that he won't stay there for long unless he is put out cold.

A fight like this one was like a fight against himself: battling his own inner demons, but each with a different face and a different style than the last. Some of them were experienced martial artists; a few of them might even be champions of some obscure brand of cage fighting back in their own country. But they were all tough as steel, hard as iron nails. They never quit until they had no choice.

He looked at the small, exclusive crowd on the other side of the ropes, scanning their faces for anything other than a shallower version of the kind of hunger he'd seen breaking though Erik Best's features. But all he saw were shining eyes, open mouths, and a never-ending demand to be entertained.

Marty would entertain them. Hell, yes. He'd show them something they'd never forget.

He'd show them Humpty fucking Dumpty.

CHAPTER THIRTEEN

IT WAS NIGHT in the Concrete Grove. Clouds scudded overhead, clustering around the pyramidal tip of the Needle. Shapes moved within those clouds – birds or shadows, or perhaps something else, something more sinister. The sounds of the estate combined to create a song of sorrow: barking dogs, a distant car or house or shop alarm, an occasional raised voice, the tinny beat of somebody's stereo left to play dance music into the wee hours...

Brendan looked up from the book he was reading, feeling as if he were being watched. He experienced the sensation whenever he was alone, had grown up with it hounding his days and blighting his nights. He never felt safe, even when he was by himself – *especially* when he was by himself. It was as if something had stalked him across the years, keeping an eye on him, watching his progress. Whatever it was, this thing, it had been drawing closer, narrowing the distance between them as the years played out into decades.

Something was keeping a close eye on Brendan, and he knew in his heart that it had begun on the night that he and the other two Amigos had been trapped in the building outside the cabin in which he now sat.

He was reading a Stephen King novel and trying to pretend that fictional terrors were more frightening than real life, but he also knew that this was a lie. Real life was worse, always so much worse, than fiction... and hadn't his life become a fiction, like something from the books he liked to read?

How many times had he gone over the same page in the book he was holding? It felt like time had slowed down and he'd been there for hours, reading and re-reading the same passage. But still the story made little sense, and the intricacies of the plot eluded him.

He stood up and went to the door, opened it and looked out at the night. Darkness lay like a shroud across the landscape. He blinked, his eyes burning for a moment, and then he glanced left, then right, before stepping out of the security cabin. The Needle loomed above him, watching him, just like whatever he and his friends had disturbed had always watched him, and in the same way that he often examined himself, in the mirror. Filled with doubt and mistrust; not quite believing the image that he saw reflected there in the glass.

The acne on his back had calmed down earlier, but now it was beginning to itch. He resisted the urge to scratch at it, and clenched his hands into fists.

No, he thought. *Don't touch it.*

The thought of the telephone call he'd received from his boss only a couple of hours earlier filled him with a rage that felt like something sexual, a slow-building sensation demanding some kind of release. Brendan was nobody's gofer, but right now, wrapped up in the arms of an endless night – a night that had lasted for two decades – he felt like he was bound to his old friends like a horse strapped into an ill-fitting harness.

This time Simon had gone too far; his actions were offensive. Brendan knew that he was probably overreacting, and that Jane would talk him down in the morning, but when it came to Simon Ridley, and the way that bastard had left them all here to rot, he often found it difficult to rein in his emotions.

The skin on his back and shoulders itched madly. He tightened his fists and dug his fingernails into the palms of his hands. One pain to take away another, like for like, tit for tat: it was like old magic, and the spell never failed.

Grinding his fingernails into the soft flesh, he forgot about his acne, and imagined his fingers digging right down into the skin and gristle and tearing through his hands, emerging from the other side dripping in blood.

Sighing, he looked up, at the second, third, fourth floors, and saw a shadow flit across one of the intact windows. Was it Banjo, the junkie, making a night-time patrol of his own, or was it something much worse? He remembered a man with a stick and a beaked mask, a figure who made a sound like maracas but in slow motion. They had called him a name, Captain Clickety, but he knew now that the simple act of naming your demon does not banish it back under the bed or to the rear of the wardrobe... sometimes a demon will like its given name, and it will reach out to embrace those that named it.

Sometimes the monsters were real.

He turned around and went back inside the cabin. Glancing at the novel, he was unable to pick it back up and finish the chapter. Not now; not tonight.

Not when it was night in the Concrete Grove, and the memories were so close to the surface that they threatened to break through and hurt him.

Once again, the skin of his back and shoulders started to itch. This time, he knew, it would be even more difficult to resist scratching at the wounds. Maybe they'd open up and bleed anew, causing new pain to layer over the old.

CHAPTER FOURTEEN

"SHAKE HANDS," SAID the ref, pushing Marty and The Polish kid together at the centre of the ring. Marty stuck out his wrapped hand and the other man grabbed it, squeezed hard, and shook it once.

"*Zaraz cię zabiję,*" said the Polish kid – Aleksi. His name was Aleksi. Marty needed to remember that, if only to register who it was he had beaten.

The two men parted company, backing away towards their corners. The next time they came together, it would be all business.

There were as many variations of the rules in these bouts as there were fighters. This time, as was often the case with one of Erik Best's fights, it was old school: fists only, no feet, no chokeholds, no head butting; no biting or gouging or elbows. The ref – a big man himself, another ex-boxer – was there to ensure that nobody stepped across the line and the fight was, insomuch as any illegal bout could ever be, a fair one.

Unlike boxing, there were no rounds to speak of. This was a fight to the finish. The man who remained standing at the end was the winner and would receive the entire purse. The loser would depart empty-handed and no doubt suffering from worse injuries than wounded pride. Such was the way of these things, and Marty was as experienced as anyone else he knew on the small, secretive bare-knuckle circuit. He'd learned the hard way, after the accident that ended his boxing career. At the time, he'd felt that he had no other option than to fight. He was a born fighter, so he simply continued along that same path.

People were shouting and screaming. Men and women jostled for position, trying to get a good view. The Barn was now a place of gladiatorial combat. The air was thick and heavy with the expectation of violence, and the audience moved as one amorphous mass, heavy and swaying, their sweat mingling and rising in a thin, steaming cloud. Couples grabbed at each other beneath the poor lights, in some savage act of foreplay. Others stood and watched, generating an altogether different kind of energy.

Marty ignored it all and moved slowly forward, raising his guard. Aleksi kept his own guard low, just as he had done in the videos Erik had supplied for Marty's research. It was apparent that the kid relied on brute strength, but that was no match for speed, guile and ring craft. The two men circled each other like great beasts, each summing up the other, inspecting his opponent for weak points. The roar of the crowd was reduced to a whisper; Marty focused on the other fighter to such an extent that everything else faded away. His vision narrowed to a tunnel and he began to smell the other man's musk. Soon he would taste him, like a tang in the air. His senses would be so attuned to the task, and to his foe, that his body would have recognised him in a dark room filled with a hundred strangers.

"*No chodź staruchu*," said the kid, his Polish wasted on Marty. "*Dalej, dawaj*."

Marty waited, waited, waited... smiled, bobbed his head and weaved a little, throwing wide a few light jabs just to rile the other fighter. He said nothing, he never did. He was a silent enforcer, a man who let his fists speak with a language of their own.

The lights flickered overhead, but Marty was only dimly aware of the change in illumination. He did not take his eyes off Aleksi. To do so would break the spell.

The lights flickered again, and that was when the kid decided to strike. He moved in surprisingly fast, going low with a decent shot to the body. Marty turned to the side and bent at the waist, not enough to dodge the blow completely but more than enough to absorb its immediate power. He responded with a short left hook, which caught the kid on the side of the head. The kid staggered, his feet shuffled backwards, and Marty slammed a good straight right into the centre of his forehead. He felt the dull jolt of the impact through his fist and along his forearm.

The small crowd made even more noise at this point, but Marty barely registered their jeering. He went in fast, double-jabbing all the way, and pushed the kid back onto the ropes. He lost his footing for a second, his left leg buckling slightly in his stance, and it was enough for Aleksi to mount a spirited retaliation. Marty retreated, blocking a barrage of mostly wild blows, and tried to work out exactly how far he was from the ropes on his side of the ring. He couldn't risk grappling with this one; he was outweighed by at least two stone, and had less reach. He had to keep on the move, ducking and dodging and wearing the other guy out with combination shots.

They stood toe-to-toe for a moment, trading blows. Marty used his defence, and was pleased to see cuts opening up on the other man's face: a long gash across his brow over the left eye, a nick in his cheek beneath his right. Blood washed down his face, thinned by the adrenalin in his system.

Marty took too long admiring the damage. He felt a glancing blow to the temple and reeled; he was rocked immediately by another quick punch to the cheekbone, this time from the big right hand. Then, just as he was beginning to think he'd misjudged or underestimated the kid, he saw what he'd been expecting from the beginning. The Polish kid dropped his right shoulder an inch or so and feigned with a left, preparing to unleash his main shot: the big looping right. Marty struck before the kid had time to consider his next move: a straight right, catching Aleksi on the chin; he followed with a double-left jab, and then finished the combination by throwing all he had into a sweet right uppercut that he dragged right up from the floor.

Marty felt the bones in his hand compress as the blow made contact; it was a good one. The kid toppled to his right, his hands going down, the arms limp, and staggered backwards towards the ropes.

It was time to finish him. Most fights lasted only seconds, very few more than a couple of minutes. In the movies, they went on for a long time, but in real life they were scrappy affairs, consisting of brief bursts of energy and *longueurs* of heavy breathing and grappling. But there would be no close contact fighting tonight. That was not in the script.

Marty moved in for the kill.

Left, right, left, left, right... boxing all the way, not brawling, and using his training and experience to subdue the other man. The kid was flagging; he didn't know what to do. His big weapon had failed him, and he had no craft to fall back on. Blood was smeared across his face; the light in his eyes went out.

And then it happened.

Just as the kid slumped back onto the ropes, a strange transformation occurred. It did not last long, just a flash, like an echo of a memory, but suddenly the Polish fighter was no longer in the ring. Leaning against the ropes was a huge, oval torso with stubby little legs that ended in hands instead of feet. The face was made up of large, heavy-lidded eyes, two holes for a nose, and a lipless mouth that was more like a thin crack in the flesh-coloured shell.

This was no longer the Polish street fighter.

It was Marty's old friend Humpty Dumpty.

He threw one punch after another, laying into the image, trying to make it go away, to crack the shell. His vision blurred and then flickered, and the egg-shaped monstrosity changed back into a big loose-lipped Polish kid with blood on his face. But it was too late for Marty to do anything but continue his assault. He kept punching, his fists aching, his fingers crunching, and could do nothing but wait until his terrible rage was spent. Anger drove him on, fuelling his body and inuring it to the pain in his hands. He was once again the child whose father had beaten him for no other reason than to toughen him up, who grew into a teenager who burned and lacerated his own body so that nobody would ever cause him pain or beat him in a stand-up fight.

Just as Marty thought he might black out and enter the darkness where a bastardised kid's rhyme lay in wait, sung through a crack in the world, he became aware of many hands upon him, an arm wrapping around his throat, and people pulling him off the other fighter. Realising what was happening, he went limp, his arms hanging loose at his sides, and allowed himself to be dragged away without further protest.

His opponent lay on the ground, his young face a mask of red. He was not moving. He did not even seem to be breathing.

What have I done? thought Marty. *Who did I become?*

At last, the audience had fallen silent. This was too much, too harsh for them to process. They came here expecting violence, and they had faced absolute savagery. Marty realised that he was screaming, but the sound was nothing that could be described as words. It was just a long, wailing lament, a cry of rage at the things that had pushed him to this point and driven him to fight with a demon from the pages of a children's book.

"Get off me," he cried, shutting off that other noise – the one that made him sound as if he'd lost his mind. "Get the fuck off!"

Who the hell was I trying to hurt? Not him – not the kid.

As the figures released him and backed away to give him room, he got to his knees and stared at them all. The ref was shaking his head, Erik Best was smiling, and a few of Best's heavies were trying to stop the Polish corner crew from climbing into the ring. Marty held up his hands and stared at them. The white wrappings were coated with blood.

Nobody can hurt Marty, he thought, recalling the years of self-damage, of extreme body conditioning, and the insane physical tests he had put himself through before the age of thirty. *Nobody hurts Marty... not even Marty.*

Best stepped forward and bent down, trying to be heard above the clamour. "That was some fucking show, marra," he said, grabbing Marty's shoulder. "But I think we need to get you out of here before it all kicks off." He squeezed Marty's arm, earnestly.

Marty nodded. With Best's help, he stood, feeling shaky and ill. The egg-shaped creature was no longer in the ring, and when he glanced beyond the ropes, at the people being herded away from ringside, he caught no sight of it anywhere in the vicinity.

"Quickly. This way." Best guided him to the edge of the ring and lifted the top rope. Marty stumbled through, falling onto his knees as he hit the dirt on the other side. He looked up, staring at one of the ceiling lights. The bright spot held his gaze; it pierced his skull, burning into his brain, and once again he saw the terrible stunted image of a grinning Humpty Dumpty. He closed his eyes and twisted his head to the side, trying to rid himself of the horror.

Some kind of fracas was occurring off to his left. Marty could not hear clearly, just a dull roar, as if his ears had popped under pressure. He opened his eyes to see, and was just in time to catch the fat Polish man in the Kappa tracksuit forcing his way through the crowd. Marty blinked. His ears felt as if they were stuffed with cotton wool. He wasn't sure what was happening, but he realised that things were not right. Then, just before someone grabbed him by the back of the neck and dragged him away, the Polish man hit Marty hard in the side. The impact was dull, yet it burned briefly. Marty moved in slow motion, glancing down at his left side. There was a shock of red there: a stain. The stain was moving, blooming like a flower. Spreading across his left side…

That was when he realised that he had not been punched. He'd been stabbed.

Sound rushed back into his ears and he pressed his bandaged hand to the wound. The tips of his first two fingers slipped easily between the edges of the cut, and they went in deep. The blood was warm. He felt no pain.

"Jesus," he said. He looked back up, towards the hanging light fixture near the ceiling, but saw only the incandescence of the bulb. Then he looked back at his hand. His fingers were red and slick. There was a white halo around them, from staring too long at the light.

"Get him over here," said someone he'd never seen before. "Now!"

Erik Best was charging around the Barn like a bull, clearing out the rest of the crowd and directing his men to grab hold of the Polish contingent. The fat man was lying unconscious on the ground at the foot of a broad timber post. Someone had wrestled one of the other corner men onto his back and was slipping in a couple of punches to his kidney area. Two other men in suits had pinned the last Polish man to the wall, where they were taking turns to hit him in the gut.

Marty was being walked quickly by three men towards the opposite corner of the Barn. Doc, an old guy in a shabby grey suit, was laying out medical equipment on a plastic bench beside a low wooden table. He was smoking a cigarette and his hands were shaking. Carefully, he placed a scalpel, syringes, scissors and various dressings onto the flat top of the bench.

Marty was forced to lie down on the table, strong hands pushing down on his chest. He still could feel no pain – the rush of adrenalin was probably masking it, but he knew the numbness wouldn't last for long. Soon his left side would be in flames.

He opened his mouth. His lips were dry. "Is it deep?"

The doctor looked up from where he was inspecting the wound. "Yes, but it isn't fatal."

Erik Best appeared at the side of the table. "Can you fix him up, Doc?" His face was shiny with sweat.

Marty was drifting in and out of a dream. None of this was really happening; it was like a play or a movie. He'd fallen asleep in front of the television.

"Not a problem," said Doc, peeling off a pair of rubber gloves stained with blood and putting on a clean pair fresh from the sterile packet. "The wound's located far enough forward that it's missed his kidneys. Luckily, because it's on the left side where it *might* have happened, it doesn't seem to have hit the liver. Higher up, though, and it would have got his spleen." Doc grinned around his cigarette. "I should really make a larger incision to explore the wound, but I'm happy enough with my diagnosis that it won't be necessary. This is basically your textbook loin wound. I'll use lignocaine to anesthetise locally, clean it out, and then I'll chuck in some ethilon sutures to stitch him back up." He smiled again, a man happy with his work.

"Quit the shop talk," said Best, glancing around to look over his shoulder. "Just fucking patch him up, marra."

The Barn had grown quiet now, as most of the onlookers had been moved outside. They would be inside the house by now, quaffing Best's champagne and talking about how close they'd been to real violence, true bloodshed. There would be a lot of fucking going on afterwards, and Marty hoped they felt satisfied with his performance.

Marty watched in silence as Doc jabbed him with a needle, then, after what seemed like hours, the man began to apply the sutures. He was still smoking his cigarette – or had he lit up another? – and the entire process had taken on a surreal air.

So this is what it feels like? he thought. He'd often wondered, and had even known a couple of people who had been wounded by blades in the past. *It's not so bad. I've gone through worse.*

"You did good," said Erik Best, leaning down close to speak. "You gave them what they wanted. You entertained those fuckers." Marty felt a soft, hot gust of breath against his cheek. He smelled

Erik Best's halitosis. "And that's what it's all about – entertainment."

Best was grinning.

Marty nodded. He felt high, as if he were on heroin.

"And don't worry about those Polish fucks. We've taken them away, and they won't be coming back."

Marty nodded again. "Humpty Dumpty," he whispered.

"What?" Best's face loomed large in his vision, like yet another monstrous image from his butchered past. But, thank God, it was not oversized and egg-shaped; thank fuck it did not belong to a monster.

TWENTY YEARS AGO, BEFORE THE MONSTERS WERE REAL

MARTY SITS IN his room, listening to music. The volume is set low so that his father won't hear what he calls 'that stupid crap' and come in with his fists swinging. The tape is a recording of a Simple Minds album. Marty can't remember who gave him the cassette, but he likes the tunes... there's something about them that suggests the kind of freedom he yearns for but will probably never achieve.

Marty gets off the bed and walks to the window. He looks out over the estate, watching the slow movement of clouds above the Needle and the way the stars seem so far away, yet at the same time close enough that if he reaches out he could grab one. It's a feeling that echoes the way he feels inside: that weird distance that isn't really a distance, not a physical one. He struggles with the notion, and then puts it out of his mind.

He checks himself out in the mirror on the wardrobe door. He is wearing a pair of stretch Geordie Jeans and a thin woollen sweater. It was his birthday outfit, and already he is outgrowing the garments. He pulls a bodybuilder pose, bending his arms and tensing his biceps. Even at ten years old, he is aware of the changes taking place in his body. His father has not been as quick with his fists lately; he watches Marty with a new kind of awareness, especially when he is wearing just a T-shirt or wandering around in his skivvies.

Before long, Marty thinks he'll be strong enough to take on his old man. He has already begun to condition his body, like the fighters in the martial arts magazines he buys with his pocket money and smuggles into the house. But he has gone further than those guys; he causes himself real pain, genuine damage. He has a sharp penknife he uses to cut the flesh of his forearms, and he holds his fingers against the flame of a lit match.

It's not so much that his father hits him, but more about the way the bastard treats Marty's mother. He knows that his father beats her at least once every two weeks – sometimes more often, if he's been drinking a lot. He rarely leaves marks, but there was that time last summer when they had to tell everyone that his mother had fallen down the stairs. She had two black eyes and her top lip was split and swollen. The skin around her jaw was red and tender to the touch.

If his father does that again, he thinks that he might kill him. He could use the penknife. It would be hard work, because the blade is so small, but it's sharp, and Marty has taught himself how to use it.

Outside, someone lets off a firework. Marty turns back to the window, drawn by the sound, and he watches the brief flaring of red and blue lights in the sky. The lights splutter and die as they fall back to the ground. Their flight is over before it has even begun.

"I hate you," he whispers, not even knowing if he means his father, the estate where he feels so trapped, or even himself. Sometimes he even despises his mother for being so weak, for not running away from the man who so casually and regularly abuses her.

He thinks about the silly tree house he and his friends are building. The Three Amigos – the name was Simon's idea, after some film he read about in a magazine, a comedy about rubbish cowboys that's supposed to be coming out next year. Marty isn't really into funny films, but Simon said that Steve Martin is in this one, and Marty laughed himself ill at the one the American made about the mad brain surgeon, even though he only understood something like half of the jokes. He remembers they watched it on video one Sunday afternoon at Simon's place, when his parents were out at the pub. Simon likes movies; he knows an older kid who works on the local video van and gets him all the latest ones pirated for free.

Marty is more of a reader than a watcher. He loves his books. His father, of course, hates books. He thinks that only poofs read. So Marty keeps all of his novels and short story collections stashed away at the back of the cupboard, covered by some old blankets his mother was going to throw out. He loves fantasy – *The Hobbit* is his favourite, but he's managed to get most of the way through *The Fellowship of the Ring* and he's proud that he understands a lot of what's going on. Some of it's a bit tricky, and a lot of the words are new to him, but he's plodding on as best he can, making use of his dictionary if he gets really stuck on anything.

He likes Strider. He wants to be Strider, even though he knows that it's just a book and none of it is real. But inside his head, it's all real: in there, where nobody else can see him, he fights orcs and dragons and kicks the crap out of his dad on a regular basis.

He opens the wardrobe and takes out a light jacket, just in case it gets cold outside later on, during their all-night vigil. He doesn't really believe that anyone – bigger kids or roaming adults – is going to wreck what they've built, but that isn't the point, not really. The reason they're all meeting up when their parents have gone to bed is because they need to be with each other. There's a connection between the boys that goes deeper than friendship. They are like brothers, linked by blood. Their parents don't give a damn, so they each give a damn about the other. Together, as part of the gang, they are strong. No one can hurt them.

He sits back down on the bed and waits for his parents to stumble up to bed. They won't be late tonight because they've been drinking all day. His mother uses vodka to block out the pain and pointlessness of her life, and his father chugs down gallons of beer because he wants to drown what he is.

Marty is untroubled by these insights; he has them all the time. He's a bright boy – much more intelligent than the teachers at school are willing to believe, and probably as well-read as anyone five years older than him. But it isn't wise to put his brains on display, so he keeps them covered by an illusion show of brute force and disinterest. He plays the game, makes sure he never gets above average marks for his schoolwork, while all the time he is reading ahead, and filling his notebooks at home with the work he does on his own.

Marty knows that this won't get him anywhere. He is trapped here, in the Grove, just like his parents and their parents before them, but there is no reason why his mind cannot be allowed to roam free, exploring the boundaries of the world written down in books.

Before long he hears his parents climbing the stairs. His mother is giggling and his father is whispering too loudly. They're talking about sex – or, more specifically, his father is telling his mother that tonight he's going to 'take her up the shitter and make her squeal'. Marty feels like crying. He barely knows these people, and has nothing in common with them apart from that they all share a house together. He's a prisoner, like the Count of Monte Cristo. He is trapped here, in this hell, and outside the window is yet another, much larger hell. All he can see for miles and miles is variations on the same theme. Somewhere out there, the devil is waiting, and by reading and learning he is keeping him at bay.

His parents' bedroom door shuts softly, and then he hears the clicking of the lock as they shut themselves in for the night. He closes his eyes, trying to stem the flow of tears, and then opens them again. They feel wet, prickly. He grits his teeth and grinds them together, then bites the side of his cheek. The pain takes it all away, pushing it to the side. Pain is good; it always does that.

Marty waits another few minutes, until the sounds begin. At first it's like the grunting of pigs, and then, once the headboard starts slamming against the wall, it sounds like two animals fighting. There's a thin line between sex and violence in his parents' bed, and Marty knows more about the sexual act than any other ten-year-old he has ever met. He knows far too much; he knows it all. Once, when he was small, his father made Marty watch them at it. They were drunk – his mother objected at first, but a sharp punch to the kidneys put an end to that – and Marty was forced to stand there at the foot of the bed while his father pounded into his mother, smiling all the time. Smiling and grunting and repeating the words, "This is what it's like. This is what's it's like." At the time, Marty had no idea what those words meant, but now he realises that his old man was talking about the whole world. This, he was saying, is how the world works. Like it or not, it's the most basic truth of all: some fuck, some get fucked.

Too much truth for a ten-year-old, but Marty is thankful for the information. It will make it easier to hit his dad when the time comes, to put the man on the ground and stamp on his hideous grinning face.

He stands and crosses the room, opens the window. The night air is warm, but there is the hint of a breeze, and he smiles as he feels it move against his cheek. Like fingers, reaching out to caress his skin in a way that his mother never did, not once in all the years since his birth. Marty knows. He remembers. She has never shown him a moment of physical affection... which is why he hates the fact that he loves her.

He throws one leg over the windowsill and stares out into the darkness. Sodium light stains the sky, the streets, the parked cars and the walls and roofs of the houses. Marty changes position, twists around, and carries out a hang-and-drop. He bends his knees when he lands on the ground below the window, absorbing the impact. He saw that in an army film. *Kelly's Heroes. Von Ryan's Express.* One of those great old movies Simon told him to watch on TV.

The downstairs lights are out and the curtains are drawn. He keeps low, almost crouching, as he runs across the short width of lawn and hops over the garden wall, hitting the footpath with silent feet and running fast, running quiet, until he reaches the end of the street. Once there, he pauses for breath, watching the neighbourhood. A dog is barking; it never shuts up, even during the day. The sound of a police helicopter grows louder and then, after a few seconds, fades as the chopper moves away from him over the estate.

Up at the Arcade, a burglar alarm wails. Either someone has broken in to one of the shops or a circuit breaker has tripped the alarm; it happens three or four times a week, always at least once over the weekend. Burglar alarms, car alarms... it seems like there's always one going off somewhere on the estate, signalling to the uncaring residents of the Grove that something has happened. But no one ever comes, not one person turns the alarms off. They will, he thinks, go on forever, marking the passage of time until everyone alive now is dead.

And even then they'll continue, wailing into an uncertain future.

Marty walks, now. There's no need to run, and moving quickly through the Concrete Grove at this hour would only lead to suspicion of wrongdoing. If that police chopper came back, they'd follow him from above; a patrolling police car might start to chase him. He knows that any self-respecting policeman would stop a ten-year-old out walking alone this late at night anyway, but at least this way he doesn't look like he's up to no good.

But nobody accosts him as he makes his way towards the north end of the estate, cutting through onto Grove Crescent and circling the Needle. He watches the massive tower block as he walks the curve, never taking his eyes off the building. He doesn't trust it; never has. To Marty, the Needle has always possessed a personality, a mind of its own. It watches the estate, looking into the lives of the people who live here... it's a silly thought, a stupid kid's fantasy, but at the same time he cannot rid himself of the illusion that the building is watching over them all.

He walks along Grove Street, turns left on Grove Crescent, and then heads down Grove Alley. The streetlights are weak. The darkness seems syrupy, as if it is capable of smothering the light. Something moves behind him. He stops, slowly turns, and catches sight of a small, stumpy shape running across the head of the short alley running between two large back gardens.

Marty feels fear nipping at the back of his neck, like his father's hands clutching him. He reaches up and around and rubs at the skin there, trying to dispel the sensation. The shape moves again, crossing back the way it came. It is low to the ground, perhaps a foot and a half in height, and as wide as a beach ball. But, no, that isn't quite correct... it can't be a ball, because it isn't round. Whatever this thing might be, it is oval, egg-shaped.

And he thinks he knows what it is.

Marty stands and stares as the shape peeks out from behind the wall. Now, even in the poor light, he can see that it has hands, but they are bigger than they should be on such a small body. The fingers are long and pointed, with nails that look like claws. Those fingers grip the edge of the wall as if they are slowly dragging the body around into his eye line.

"Who's there?" His voice sounds tiny in all that night. It's a stupid question to ask, anyway. If someone is stalking him, they're hardly going to announce their name.

"Leave me alone." Another stupid thing to say. "Who are you?" He can't stop now: the idiotic words are coming thick and fast and unstoppable. Something twitches at the back of his mind: a memory, an image, something unpleasant from his childhood. He remembers that his father once bought him a book of fairy tales and nursery rhymes, but they were not the same as the ones he'd read in school. Marty thinks he might have been five or six, and that year the old man made a sudden and unexpected effort. He pretended to be interested in his boy, and would read to him at bedtime. This book – he can't even recall the title – was the worst of all. Rumpelstiltskin killed all the babies, the princess with the glass slipper started cutting the flesh off her foot to make it fit, and Little Jack Horner stuffed himself so full of pie that he exploded in his corner... but the most memorable one, the story that Marty stills dreams of, even now, was Humpty Dumpty.

The strange egg-shaped creature was drawn to look like a monster. Leathery hide, large, slanted eyes, no arms, and horrible stumpy legs with hands on the end of them instead of feet. He sat on his high wall and drank beer from a brown bottle, laughing and throwing stones with his hand-feet at everyone who walked past below. Then, one day, when he was too drunk to keep his balance, he fell off the wall and shattered, like an egg. Weird stuff oozed out of the cracks in his hide: ugly little critters that were more mouth and eyes than anything else, borne on a tide of filthy slime.

Marty has been terrified of the story ever since his father first read it, grinning and putting on a horrible deep voice.

He remembers the king's men on their horses arriving to try and put Humpty Dumpty back together, but Humpty didn't want their help. He lashed out at the men, killed some of the horses, and the little monsters that had come out of his shell nipped and bit at the soldiers' ankles. Finally, one brave soldier used the butt of his rifle to batter Humpty Dumpty to death... but next day, as a procession of the townsfolk went by his wall, the creature was back up there, with the cracks in his hide held together by metal clamps, throwing stones at those who had come to celebrate his destruction.

Where on earth had the book come from? He knows now that it clearly had not been written for children, and was probably meant to be funny... to the young Marty Rivers, lying shivering in his bed and listening to the sounds of his parents as they abused each other, the image of Humpty Dumpty could not have been less amusing. The creature from the book came to represent the thing that he was most afraid of – the fears he could never, ever name.

And here it is again, that improbable Humpty Dumpty monster, following him through the dark streets of the estate.

He turns and runs, heading for Beacon Green, where he knows his friends must already be waiting for him. He hears behind him the rapid slap of misshapen hand-feet on the concrete paving stones, and knows that if he turns to look over his shoulder he'll see the egg-shaped creature bounding along behind him, gaining with every step.

There is a short passageway between the chip shop and the off-licence on Grove Terrace, and Marty throws himself at its entrance. He runs faster, heading for the low metal barrier at the end of the passage, and when he gets there he hits it hard and high and scurries over the top, ripping the knee of his jeans and scraping the skin there deep enough to draw blood. He does not look back as he runs across the long grass, heading towards the row of trees bounding the Green. Then, once he is inside the clammy darkness, he darts west and makes his way towards the clearing where they've constructed the platform of their tree house.

When he sees his friends, he smiles and pretends that nothing has happened. It takes him a while before he can even bring himself to look behind him, along the pathway upon which he stumbled, but when he does so he sees no sign of an egg-shaped shadow, or even a misplaced rustle of greenery.

Friendship has banished the monster. It always does. Because friendship is the best – and only – weapon they have.

PART THREE

DEADLY BIRDS OF THE SOUL

"The good old bad old days..."

– Jane Cole

CHAPTER FIFTEEN

BRENDAN WOKE UP feeling as if he hadn't even been asleep. The blackout curtains – God bless Jane for buying them when he'd first started working nights – were still shut tight across the windows, barring all light, but his damned body clock knew that it was morning and had decided that it didn't want to shut down for any longer. He couldn't remember finishing his shift this morning, and regretted going in half-drunk. If he'd been sober, perhaps he would have taken the phone call from his boss in a more dignified manner.

Jane shifted in bed beside him, stretching out across the mattress and making a small whining sound.

"You awake?"

She didn't reply, but she threw one arm across his chest and bent her knees so they pressed up hard against his left thigh. She was sleeping naked again. She got hot while she slept, and even if she wore a nightdress to bed she would often take it off during the night. Her skin was soft and smooth, and her hair tickled the side of his face. He closed his eyes and inhaled deeply. Brendan had always loved the way his wife smelled, especially after a night in bed.

He lay there in the darkness, his vision sketching shapes in the air, and waited for Jane to wake up, or for her alarm to go off and rouse her. He didn't want to wake her, but nor did he want to be alone with his thoughts. He felt... aggressive. The kind of anger that had not touched him for a long time; the drink helped keep it at bay. So did the bondage DVDs and the specialist magazines.

He felt his erection twitching into life and reached down, beneath the covers, to cup his balls. His libido was weak these days, as far as Jane was concerned, but still he was prone to the occasional morning glory. He smiled, and then remembered that he was angry. He scratched the hard shaft of his penis, enjoying the sweet, sharp pain caused by his fingernails, and then Jane stirred again at his side. He took away his hand, bringing it back up from under the bed sheets, and turned his head to face her.

"Morning," she said, her voice slow with sleep. "What're you doing awake?"

"Rough night," he said, wishing that he could make out her face in the darkness.

She shifted, propping herself up on one elbow. He could feel her staring at the side of his face. "Did somebody try to break into the site?" Her voice was normal now; she was wide awake.

"No, no... nothing like that. Don't worry. I just had a phone call that I didn't enjoy."

"Who was it from?" She slid out of bed and crossed the room to the window. Brendan could make out the vague lines of her body as she walked past the foot of the bed, like a shadow moving within the shadows. A vertical line of light appeared as she opened the blackout curtains just enough to illuminate that part of the room. The light spread, throwing items into relief – the chair by the window, the wardrobes, the dressing table, his wife's naked body, heavier around the middle now that she was getting older but still a wonderful sight to behold.

"Thanks," he said.

"Sorry." She moved away from the window. "Should I close them again?"

"No, I wasn't being sarcastic. I meant that. Thanks. It's nice to see you like this... you know, with nothing on."

She smiled. "Oh, shut up." She made a show of trying to cover up, and then gave up and opened her arms, her hands shaking in a dancer's jazz-hands motion. She wriggled her hips. Her meaty thighs jiggled, but it was a sensual movement, something real and earthy and essential. "So," she said, walking back around to her side of the bed, still smiling. "Tell me about this nasty phone call."

He adjusted his position on the bed, turning his body so that he could look right at her. Jane's mouth was slightly open, the lips showing blackness instead of teeth in the dim light. It was a disconcerting image. He reached out and ran his hand along the side of her waist, and then on down to her thigh.

Jane giggled. "Come on then, mister. What's up?"

"Oh, it's probably a lot less than I'm making out, but it kind of pissed me off at the time." He stared into her blue eyes.

Jane raised her eyebrows but said nothing as she slid back into bed beside him.

Brendan sighed. His back started to itch, the acne flaring up again. It had been fine since that short outbreak last night, but now – as if following some kind of cue – it was starting to bother him again. "I got a call from my boss."

Jane nodded. "Lenny Campbell? Okay... what's so weird about that? Or do you not like him checking up on you?"

"He wasn't checking up on me." Brendan left his hand resting on the curve of Jane's thigh. He opened his fingers and pressed his palm flat against her hot skin. "He rang me to tell me not to come in tonight." He blinked, glanced at his hand, and then looked back at his wife's face.

"Oh, shit. You've been fired?" The smile vanished. Her eyes clouded over. She pulled the bedclothes upwards, covering her nakedness, as if in some kind of punishment.

Brendan moved his hand away. "No... no, I haven't been fired, or made redundant, or had my hours cut. He told me that I was still on the payroll but that somebody else was paying my salary. I've been hired as private security."

Jane shook her head. "I'm not following this. What did he mean, 'private security'? What's that all about?"

"It's him." Brendan looked away, his gaze roaming the walls and taking in the framed school photographs of the twins, a wedding photo on the dresser, and the cluttered surfaces in the bedroom. "It's Simon fucking Ridley, isn't it? He rang Campbell and brokered some kind of deal. I'm working directly for him now. That arrogant bastard is paying my wages, paying for the food I put on the table, the roof over our heads. He can't leave well alone; he has to interfere." He felt the rage building again inside him. Sitting up, he pressed his lower back against the headboard. His upper back was burning; a strip of lava spilled across his shoulders. The pustules were signalling to him, responding to his wayward emotions.

"Calm down, pet. Maybe it's not what you think. Perhaps he has a good reason – like, he's trying to help? He always was a clumsy, inappropriate shithead, and this is probably just another example of that. I bet he thinks he's helping us out."

"My shoulders hurt." Brendan had closed his eyes. He saw red fire behind the lids. It was like staring down into an active volcano. "My back's stinging."

"Take deep breaths." Jane sat up, the covers falling away to expose her breasts and her belly. Small pink rolls of flesh around her waist; she always called them her 'mummy-tummy'. "It's okay. Don't get yourself so worked up." She rubbed his arm with her hand, and then started to massage the back of his neck, just above the infected area.

"I hate this," he said, not opening his eyes. "I hate me."

"I love you," said Jane, still applying pressure to the nape of his neck. "So I guess you're screwed, aren't you?" The pressure increased; it was blissful. Nobody could calm him down quite like Jane.

"Thank you," he said, and opened his eyes.

"Listen, I have to get the twins up, get them ready and take them to school. Are you going to be okay?"

He nodded. "Aye, aye... Of course I am. Just a bit stressed, that's all. That idiot coming back here and trying to track down Marty... it's freaking me out. He wants to get the three of us back together, like the old days."

"The good old bad old days..." Jane's voice held not a trace of humour.

"Yeah." He reached up and grabbed her hand, squeezing it. "That's exactly what they were." Her fingers were hot, as if she'd been handling hot coals. "I'll be fine. You go and sort the twins out and I'll try to get some more sleep. If I don't, I'll be a nightmare later on."

Brendan yawned. Dimness shimmered at the edges of his vision.

Jane curled up her nose, an expression she sometimes made when she was thinking. "Invite Simon over for dinner. Tonight. We can talk like adults, get some stuff out into the open for a change."

"Aye," he said, not fully registering what she'd said. "Okay."

Jane left the bed and approached the window, where she shut the blackout curtains. Her body was diminished by the retreating light, like an oil painting being slowly erased by chemicals. She left the room without saying a word, grabbing her dressing gown from the back of the door. When he was on nights, she always kept the following day's clothes in the bathroom, so that she could get dressed without bothering him. She was good like that: thoughtful.

Brendan lay down on his belly. His back was causing him too much irritation to put any weight onto the affected area. The acne was no longer hurting, just making its presence felt. He kept the covers down around his waist just to let the air circulate across the broken flesh. He closed his eyes. He didn't even realise he was sleeping...

* * *

(...UNTIL HE WALKED across the room and opened the curtains, where he looked out of the window and down to the street. But the street was gone. In its place there stood a vast forest, a wall of trees whose trunks and branches reached up to form a canopy above the roof of the house, the roofs of all the houses. He could not see through the thick gathering of tree trunks; it was dark in there, the air black and dense and unwelcoming.

Even from here, this compromised vantage point, he could see that there were bulky things moving within the dense trees, flitting from trunk to trunk, hiding in the gloom. The sunlight did not reach them through the thick canopy; they were creatures of the dark, inhabiting the shadows.

He stared down at the bases of the trees, trying to pick out a pathway. The foliage there was bunched together, as if it had been left to grow for many years. There were no proper paths, no hacked trails through this undergrowth, and the trees were untouched by human hands.

All that lived there was whatever had always been there, hiding among the trees and the bushes and burrowing into the rich, loamy earth.

He opened his mouth to speak, but the trees began to shudder, silencing his voice before he could make a sound. A strong wind gusted through the forest, snaking between the tree trunks, and brought with it the stench of carrion. He could smell it even through the closed window. As he watched, the window glass began to stain, to darken, as if slowly tainted by smog. Just before he lost sight of the trees, he glimpsed something vast and ageless and shapeless surging towards him, causing the branches to quake and the trunks themselves to lean apart and uproot to make room for the gargantuan interloper...)

...HE DIDN'T REALISE he was sleeping until he woke up, still lying on his front, his mouth tasting like yesterday's stale beer. His eyes were sticky. He struggled to open them fully, and settled instead on peering through slits.

The house was silent. Jane must have taken the kids to school, and then she'd probably gone for her morning gym session – or did she have a class, dancing or spinning or circuit training, something like that? He couldn't remember. Everything was so hazy; his brain felt as heavy as a bowling ball as it shifted clumsily inside his skull.

He did remember her suggesting that he invite Simon to dinner, though, and right now it sounded like it might be a good idea. Meet on home turf; talk things through like adults. She was good like that, Jane. She always knew what he needed, even before he did.

He pulled his arms under him and straightened them, forcing his stomach off the bed. But there was something wrong – the action wasn't as smooth and easy as it should be. He felt heavier than he ever had before in his life, as if... as if there was someone sitting on his shoulders... his acne-ridden, pus-weeping shoulders.

"What?" He could say no more; it was too much of a strain to even attempt it. He blinked his crusty eyes.

Whatever was perched upon his shoulders shifted its weight, scratching at the already ravaged skin. He winced, holding back a scream, and then flopped back down onto his belly. Panicking now, he reached up and around and tried to grab whatever it was, to throw it off his body. The thing – small and hard and slippery – scuttled across his shoulder blades, dodging his anxious fingers and adjusting its riding position.

"Come here," he whispered. "Bastard." He grabbed for the shape, trying to get a grip on its elusive form, but the thing moved further down his back, tracing the line of his spine. In the unnatural darkness, lying flat on his belly, Brendan began to suspect that he was going to die. Nobody would ever know what happened here, in this room, and he became convinced that this was an attack by a sliver of whatever power they had confronted that day twenty years ago, when they were held captive inside the Needle.

Something about this situation felt so familiar, as if he had been here before. Not here, in this room, but in this position, with something crawling across his back and tearing at his flesh. Infecting him... polluting the skin of his back and shoulders with a poison that would harm him for the rest of his life. Driving its fingers beneath his skin, probing his orifices, his most private parts.

Acting out of desperation now, he flipped over onto his back, ignoring the pain as his acne burst against the sheets, and let out the scream he had been holding on to since waking, hoping that it might break the spell.

Something small and fast darted across the mattress, dropped onto the floor at the foot of the bed, and scurried into a corner of the room. Brendan struggled to his feet and made his way to the window, pulling back the heavy blackout curtains to let in the light. He was blinded for a moment, bright sunlight taking away his vision. When he was able to open his eyes, he spun around and inspected the room. Nothing was out of place. Everything looked as it should: the books on the shelves, the photos, the pictures on the walls, the furniture. It was all so depressingly normal.

Had he still been dreaming? It was possible; it had happened before. If he was honest, it happened all the time. He would wake up, unsure if he was still trapped inside a dream or a nightmare, and everything around him would take on a sinister slant. Sometimes he would even see things, strange visions that he could not explain.

But no, that couldn't be right. He knew that this time he had been awake, and there had been something inside the room with him, pestering him, harassing him.

He walked across to the wardrobe, reached up and opened the door at the top, near the ceiling. Fumbling through the DVD cases and the curled pages of magazines, he grabbed hold of what he thought was the acorn but it felt too big... much bigger than before. He used both hands to bring it down, and when he looked at the thing in his hands he was shocked to see how much it had grown.

The acorn was now the size of an Easter egg and covered in faint cracks, some were beginning to open up and give a glimpse of something fibrous, like dense webbing, inside. He turned the acorn around in his hands, and at the back, where he'd been unable to see, there was one crack that was much larger than the others. It was big enough, in fact, for something to have crawled out. An insect, perhaps, or a small mammal – something like a field mouse...

He held the acorn in his hands, peering into the crack. From what he could make out, the acorn was hollow, and it was empty. Whatever had emerged from this cocoon was still out there, in the world. Like a living bad dream hatched from inside a human skull, released to create mischief.

CHAPTER SIXTEEN

SIMON WAS DOING push-ups on the floor when his phone rang. He jumped up and grabbed the handset; it was Brendan's home number, rather than Natasha trying to track him down again. For reasons he couldn't even begin to think about, not until he had everything else squared away, he still did not want to speak to his girlfriend – no matter how badly she wanted to speak to him.

He knew that Brendan would have been told by now about the new arrangement he'd made with his boss at Nightjar Security Services, and he had the feeling he might have pushed things too far by taking control in such a way. Pushing, he was always pushing. It was like he was unable to resist forcing people's hands.

"Hi Brendan. How's tricks?"

There was a slight pause, and then Brendan's voice filled the airspace. "Yeah, okay. Actually, no, I'm tired and pissed off."

Simon blew air out of his mouth, making his lips flap. "Listen, I'm assuming you had a call from your boss last night."

"Aye." Brendan said nothing more.

"I know I should've spoken to you first, but I did it on the spur of the moment. I thought it might help us both out. I mean, you can hardly help me track down Marty while you're working nights, can you? Also, it frees up your evenings to spend with your family. I thought it was a win-win situation... you know?" His reasons sounded feeble, but he wasn't lying. He had not been completely selfish in organising the situation with the maudlin supervisor at Nightjar... only a little.

"Jesus, Simon. You always used to do this. Take control. I was fucking raging at you last night, but now that I've slept on it – well, for a couple of hours, anyway – I've calmed down. I'm still pissed off at you; I just don't want to hit you right now."

Simon smiled. "Thank Christ for that. I always suspected you might be able to take me in a fight and don't really fancy finding out."

"Fuck off," said Brendan. "Listen; let me get this out of the way before we continue. Jane's invited you over to dinner this evening. It was nothing to do with me – her idea. She thought it might be good for us to sit down over a civilised meal and talk."

Simon wasn't sure about this. It felt like somebody else was doing the pushing. "Oh... okay. Maybe that's a good idea."

"Maybe. And maybe not," said Brendan. "But it's done now. She's expecting you over – come for around seven-thirty. Dress fucking casual."

Simon found himself laughing again, softly, as if the years were falling away like layers of dead skin. "Don't worry; I left my good tux at home. I'll just throw on my Armani suit and be done with it."

"And again, I say fuck you, matey."

This brief exchange made Simon feel a lot better about interfering with Brendan's job, and with his life. He wasn't sure that he'd be so calm about the situation if the roles were reversed, but then he remembered that Brendan was having trouble sleeping. He was probably glad that he'd be able to rest his head on his own pillow at night, next to the woman he loved – a woman both of them had shared time with, at certain points in their lives.

Shit. Why did he keep thinking about that? He had a beautiful girlfriend, an emotional safety net in case everything else failed... so why did he keep thinking about a relationship that had ended before it had even had the time to begin? It was harmful, almost a form of self-abuse. Was he using the memory to punish himself, for leaving them all here to face the things he could not?

"Remember I told you about Marty's grandmother? How she still lives here on the estate?"

He had no idea. He could remember no such conversation. "Yeah, of course." He had to regain focus, to concentrate on the moment rather than all the moments he had lost, discarded like empty food wrappers. "What about her?"

"Well, I've had a strange morning, so I spoke to her about ten minutes ago, just before I called you. She's willing to see us. She's old, but her mind's still more or less intact. She remembers who we were – when we were boys. She said she always liked us, and wondered what had happened to make us go away."

Simon said nothing. He couldn't work out if the comment was some kind of rebuke, or even if it was aimed at him. He kept thinking about Jane, and the time they'd spent together. Her soft lips, the curve of her thighs in her skin-tight jeans, the way she'd worn her hair – long and dyed white-blonde – and the sweet words she'd used to try and convince him to stay.

"Okay," he said, shaking it off. "What time?"

"She said to go round for midday. She's going to make a pot of tea."

"God," said Simon. "Old women around the country, they're all the bloody same. Tea, biscuits, and a nice bit of gossip."

"I'll come for you at quarter to. Be ready." Then Brendan hung up the phone.

Simon got back down on the floor and finished his push-up routine – it was helping to clear his hangover. Then he did some abdominal work – crunches, scissors, and a few minutes of trunk twists – before a feeling of nausea stopped him.

He always tried to keep himself in shape. Natasha didn't like it when he got porky, and he had always put on weight easily, even as a child. He'd been carrying an extra few pounds that summer, when it happened... when they went into the Needle and gained access to another world.

"Like Narnia," he said, staring at a patch of peeling wallpaper and studying the plaster beneath. "Through the back of the fucking wardrobe..."

He picked up his phone and re-read the last few text messages Natasha had sent him.

Luv u
call me
somethin rong?

Jesus, sometimes she acted like a lovesick teenager. He couldn't handle that kind of (badly spelled) emotional clinginess. It scared him and made him instinctively back away – that was why he was reluctant to call her, to speak to her. She was being needy and that was scaring him off, just like it always did.

He relented and replied to her last message:

I'm fine. Very busy. Will call you when I can. x.

He switched off the phone in case she responded by calling him back immediately. The kind of mood she seemed to be in, that was entirely possible, and then he'd be forced to talk to her. In his current state of mind, that would be a bad thing.

A very bad thing.

He took a shower, got dressed, and left the flat, stepping out into flat, bright sunlight. Looking up at the sky, the clouds seemed frighteningly distant, as if the lid was peeling off the top of the world. He did not want to see what lay beyond; the thought of eternity terrified him, even now, as an adult. He remembered lying in his bed at night as a small child, looking through the window and trying to imagine what was at the end of the universe. It used to hurt his head, and he would often cry himself to sleep after trying to calculate the dimensions of infinity.

Simon set off towards the Arcade, where there was a greasy spoon café called Grove Grub. He passed a group of teenagers at the corner of Grove Side and they all stopped mid-conversation to turn and stare at him, following him with their surly gazes.

It had been a long time since he'd experienced this kind of casual antipathy. Even in London it was rare to be examined by strangers in such a direct manner, certainly where he lived. Simon's old senses began to bristle, returning to life after years of neglect. He clenched his fists and maintained eye contact. He knew that any sign of weakness would be leapt upon, used against him.

The group continued to stare. There were two boys and three girls, and they all wore similar cheap sports clothes – no-name running shoes, tracksuit bottoms, hooded sweatshirts, and baseball caps. One of the boys – the biggest one, who was wearing a cap with a motif of a cartoon dog smoking a joint – spat on the ground near Simon's feet. He smiled. Simon kept up his pace, not speeding up or slowing down to avoid the spittle on the pavement, and gritted his teeth.

Once he'd turned the corner, he heard mocking laughter. They'd done nothing, said nothing, in his presence, but now that he was out of sight they were full of bravado. Nothing much had changed in the years since Simon had walked these streets. Nobody had any balls; they all waited until your back was turned, or your attention was elsewhere, before sticking in the knife.

A hundred yards along Grove Crescent was the Arcade. The row of shops had always been here, ever since Simon could remember. The retail outlets renting the premises had changed, of course, but these were minor adaptations to the demands of the economy rather than any kind of improvement in consumer choice. The people round here did not want quality goods; they wanted cheap and cheerful products that would do for the time being. These days, the shops were tenanted by a DVD rental outlet, a pizza and kebab takeaway service, Grove Grub (which was the only constant factor in the Arcade, having been there since Simon was a boy), a flower shop, a betting shop, a butchers-and-grocers, a small hardware store, a hairdressers with a solarium place in the flat above, and a grimy newsagent with faded advertisements for chocolate bars and comics in the chicken-wire-covered windows.

More local kids in sports apparel hung around on the steps outside, mums stood smoking and chatting over prams, shady-looking men ducked in and out of the betting shop doorway, clutching or dropping onto the pavement creased slips of paper.

Simon entered the café, looking for an empty table. There were still a couple of hours to kill until lunchtime, so the place was not what he would describe as busy. Just a few old geezers drinking tea, a couple of grey-haired women eating a late fried breakfast, and a solemn-looking young man reading a red-top newspaper in the corner.

Simon sat at a table by the window. The plastic seat moved across the tiled floor with difficulty. The table was covered with a paper tablecloth depicting birds in flight. The salt and pepper shakers were glass, but they were old and chipped and the salt had hardened to a crust in the bottom of its receptacle. An enamel sugar bowl sat at the centre of the table, next to a plastic rose in a narrow vase. There was something black in the sugar. Simon thought it might be a dead fly, but he hoped it was just a piece of fluff or even cigarette ash.

"Getcha?"

He glanced up. Standing at his side was a young girl with her hair tied back into a ponytail that was so tight it made her face shine. She held a stubby betting shop pen in one hand and a tiny notebook in the other. She too was wearing tracksuit bottoms, but she had on a stained white apron over the top of her grey sweatshirt to identify her as a member of staff.

"Hi. Could I have a black coffee, no sugar? And, erm, how about a couple of poached eggs? On brown toast? No butter."

She frowned, nodded, and snapped her chewing gum between her teeth. "Yeah, we can do that for you." She scribbled on her pad. "That all?"

Simon smiled, but it fell short of reaching her. "Thanks."

She nodded again, as if agreeing with something, and then headed back to the counter at the back of the café, where she proceeded to repeat his order at great volume through an opening to the back of the premises, where the kitchen staff was hiding.

Simon sat and watched the people walking by on the other side of the plate glass window: single mothers, absent fathers, pensioners holding hands, young couples shambling behind prams, the occasional overweight man or woman piloting a motorised shopping cart. It was a typical weekday in an urban shopping precinct, filled with those too old, too infirm, too lazy, too uneducated, or simply too defeated by their circumstances to hold down a day job.

Dirty sunlight glanced off the grey concrete paving stones, the sky looked wide and bright, yet curiously lacking in dimension, like a matte painting in an old film. Simon felt anxiety tightening across his chest, like a straightjacket binding him into the past. He thought again of his old friends, and the short journey they'd made from Beacon Green to the Needle. Still, after all this time, he struggled to remember why they had really gone to the tower block that night. They were following someone, he was certain of that; but he had no idea who that person might have been, or even if it had been a person at all. Maybe it was an animal: a stray dog, or a badger leaving its sett on the Green. But no, he had a definite image of them trailing a figure – following from a distance, like spies.

He also knew that it had been his idea. He had convinced the other two to take part in the plan, to leave the den they'd made and pursue whoever it was had been abroad that night. The memories were so close, yet still they remained out of reach. He was like a shipwrecked man swimming towards a shore that never seemed to get any closer, no matter how far and how hard he swam.

"Here's your coffee."

Simon turned around and smiled at the waitress. She didn't smile back. Her hand was still on the handle of the coffee cup, and she snatched it away as if she were afraid he might touch her.

"Thanks," he said.

She took a step back, away from the table, but did not move away. Curling up one side of her mouth, she folded her arms across her small breasts. "Can I ask you a question?"

Simon picked up his cup, took a mouthful of coffee and put it back down again. The coffee was bitter, but at least it was hot. "Yeah, sure. Why not?"

"You're one of them, aren't you?"

Simon shook his head. "I'm sorry... what do you mean?"

She glanced down at her feet and then back up again, looking at his face but not quite at his eyes. He realised that she had not made direct eye contact with him since he'd sat down. "You're one of them three lads – the ones who went missing all those years ago."

"How do you know about that, then? You must be – what, all of eighteen? You weren't even born when it happened."

She sighed, shrugged her narrow shoulders. "My mam used to know Marty Rivers. She went to school with you, a couple of years above. She talks about it when she's drunk. She even kept the newspaper: the report about how the three of you went into the Needle and didn't come out again for a whole weekend. She says that something bad happened to you in there. She used to tell us – me and my brother – to keep us away from that place." She tilted her head in the direction of the tower block, just in case he was under any illusion as to where she meant.

"Yes, my name's Simon. I was one of the boys. I'm surprised anyone even remembers us... what's your mum's name?"

"Sheila Dyson."

The name rang a bell. He had an image of a mousey older girl with hair that looked as if it was never washed, a pale complexion, and heavy shoes. "Yes, I think I remember her. Didn't she go out with Marty for a while, before you were born?"

"Dunno," said the girl, losing interest now that his big secret was out. "Maybe. She screwed around back then."

Simon laughed softly. "That's very candid of you."

The girl shrugged again. "She's a slut, my mam. And a drunk. Always was."

"Fair enough." He took another mouthful of coffee.

"There's something I've always wanted to know... I never dared ask either of the other two whenever I saw them around. They're too scary."

"And I'm not? Scary, I mean?"

She grinned. "Leave it out. You're about as threatening as a plastic doll, mate."

"Okay. I'll try not to be offended by that. What is it you always wanted to ask?"

She licked her lips and flicked hair away from her face with her hand. She was pretty, in a weary kind of way, like a lot of the girls around here. Her features were arranged nicely, but she lacked the spark that transformed mere pleasantness into beauty. She'd missed being conventionally attractive by a hair's breadth that seemed more like a mile.

"Well? Now's your chance. Ask me. I might even answer." He smiled.

The girl chewed on her bottom lip, and then finally said the words. "What happened to the three of you, in there?"

Simon leaned back in his chair and rubbed his cheek with the fingers of one hand. "That's exactly what I've always wanted to know, too."

"Suit yourself, mate," she said, walking away.

"Wait a minute," he said, as an afterthought. "Have you seen Marty Rivers lately? I've been looking for him."

The girl shook her head. "Nah. Not for ages."

Simon watched her as she went to the counter. His food was waiting when she arrived, but she walked past it and into the room behind the counter. Shortly, a large man wearing a white chef's apron, the sleeves rolled up to show his badly tattooed forearms, emerged from the doorway and picked up the plate. He carried it over and put it down in front of Simon without saying a word.

Simon smiled. Then he ate his breakfast.

After he'd paid the bill he left the café, feeling obscurely and belatedly offended by the girl's behaviour. On the one hand, he was amazed that she even knew who he was, but on the other he felt as if she'd dealt him some kind of blow. He was unable to pinpoint his exact feelings on the matter, but he did know that he felt disturbed.

Perhaps that's what led him to alter his course and head for the Needle, or perhaps he had always intended to go there again that day, ever since waking up in a strange bed. Whatever the reason, he picked up his pace and walked towards the daunting shape of the tower, trying to stare it down.

When he reached the security compound, he took out his keys and opened the gate, walked in, and locked up again. He didn't want anyone coming in after him, and his strange confrontation with the waitress had made it clear that some people still remembered and drew dark associations with the place.

There was no watchman on patrol during daylight

hours, so he walked past the security cabin and right up to the main entrance. He let himself in with his set of keys without even pausing at the threshold, thinking that momentum might give him strength. He didn't want to think about why he might need to be strong, or what kind of courage he was looking for within himself. An echo of the waitress's words mocked him: *You're about as threatening as a plastic doll, mate.*

Did he really come across as so weak? In business terms, he knew that he was a man to be reckoned with, but here, on the tough streets of his youth, he was just another skinny twat in a nice suit. The girl had suggested that Brendan scared her as much as a real hard man like Marty, and the fact that Simon barely even registered on her threat-radar bothered him for reasons that he could not explain. He kicked a cardboard box, sending it skidding across the reception area and into a pile of old blankets.

"Wow," he muttered. "That's really tough." He smiled, his anger dissipating as he relaxed. What the hell was wrong with him lately? Had this entire trip been nothing more than a big mistake, a journey into a past darkness the nature of which he would never understand? He wondered if he should have brought Natasha with him after all, if only to keep him sane. Then he remembered all over again that she was the one who unbalanced him, and that her constant demands on his affections were probably sending him slowly mad.

The faint odours of stale urine and old smoke drifted into his nostrils. He walked a few paces across the reception, dodging piles of rubbish, and stopped at the foot of the stairs. The doors had been removed; shattered glass covered a small area below the bottom step, rough diamonds on the concrete floor.

"What's hiding in here?" His voice sounded small and weak, as if he'd regressed by coming in here again. Sometimes, when the nightmares dogged his sleep, he would imagine that his younger self was still trapped here, running between the rooms and wailing in the hallways and corridors, begging to be let out. Then, when the black dog of depression really bit deep and sleep eluded him completely, he would wonder if it was actually his *future self* that had been lost here, in this place. Was an older version of Simon Ridley, crippled and beaten by the flow of time, even now roaming the spaces above him, trying to reconnect with all the versions of his self that he had never been allowed to experience?

"What are you?" His voice was his own again, the adult he pretended to be. "Show yourself, you bastard." Such tough words; empty bravado. There was nothing here, not really. Just dust and shadows and whatever remained of the memories that he could never quite grab hold of.

He placed his foot on the first step and peered up the staircase, watching the dust motes as they danced in the air, trying to make sense of the dimness that hung there like a light mist. The walls of the stairwell seemed to change colour as he watched, running from white to grey and then to brown. They changed shape, too, rippling softly, as if something moved beneath the plaster. Simon knew that he should turn away, leave the building, but curiosity held him there. Curiosity and something else:

perhaps the promise of revelation. Because wasn't that why he was here, to have something revealed to him? Was not that the whole point of his idiotic journey north? He had come here to discover what was missing from his life, to find out what had been removed to create the hole at his core.

The plaster began to crack, pieces of it falling away to drop silently onto the stairs. He knew there should be sounds accompanying the destruction, but was not surprised when there were none. The whole scene was being played out in silence, like an old film, and all he could do was stand and stare.

Simon watched, fascinated, as the small branches squirmed out from beneath the plaster, popping through the degraded joints in the brickwork. They moved as if they were alive, like snakes, lazy creatures waking from sleep to stick their heads out of the nest. The thin branches – like a sapling's – writhed and stretched and wavered in the stairwell, daring him to pass. He grabbed hold of the handrail and prepared to take another step, to start climbing the stairs, but something held him back. He had a strong feeling of dread; the certainty that if he went up there, he would not come back down. Perhaps he would even meet that mythical version of himself, and they would embrace like brothers before dying. Was that it? Had he always been meant to die here, but had somehow escaped? Was it his own demise that waited for him here, within these cold concrete walls?

The branches danced before his eyes, reaching for him, grasping in the air. They slipped gently around his wrists, binding him in a way that he remembered from before. Pulling away, he managed to break their grip, snapping them. And then, as he moved backwards, shifting just out of their reach, the thin branches began to wither. They turned grey, black, as if singed by unseen flames, and exploded into little clouds of ash. The plaster repaired itself, like a film reel running backwards, and before long the walls were exactly as they had been. There was no evidence of the strange growths, the struggling saplings. There was nothing there.

He felt rejected. Whatever power resided here had turned its back on him, folding its arms and tapping its foot until he left the premises.

"Soon," he said, moving back through the reception area. "I'll come back soon… and I'll have them with me. My friends. The Three Amigos."

Upstairs, from several floors above him, he heard the sound of laughter. It sounded like a girl, and it was familiar. He strained to remember where and when he had heard the childish sound before, but nothing came to mind.

The laughter had died, replaced by a sharp clicking sound, like cards being slowly shuffled. This, too, sounded familiar, and it filled Simon with such a sense of dread that he felt like crying. He was a child again; he was terrified. The bad man was coming, Captain Clickety was on the loose… and he was coming for Simon.

A familiar emptiness yawned within him, threatening to consume him, so he left the Needle and headed back towards the sounds of the present.

"Soon," he said again, but this time it was a promise he made only to himself.

CHAPTER SEVENTEEN

BANJO CROUCHED AT the top of the stairs, trying to peer all the way down to the bottom floor. He saw a pale shape flicker through the murk, and then he heard the main doors slam shut. He stood up straight, turned around, and looked at the girl who called herself Hailey.

"Don't worry," she said. "He's gone. He wasn't here to hurt you... none of them are. They're here for something else. It has nothing to do with you. You're safe now, as long as you stay close to me. The Underthing can't touch you. He's afraid of me, you see." She smiled and to Banjo it was like the sun coming up in that other place, the one he had only ever glimpsed. Behind her, he could see the outlines of trees; they shimmered like a mirage, but he knew that they were real. They had always been real. Soon he would be able to touch them. Before long, he would enter that old grove of oak trees and sit at the heart of the magic that nested here, within this tower. He would find himself in a place that was both ancient and ageless, a land where the dreams of men became living things, and where myth was reality.

"It won't be long, now." Hailey smiled; her face shone golden, like the wavering shapes of the trees over her shoulder. "He's coming out. We're luring him, like a fish with a baited line. Not long now until the Underthing shows himself and we can be rid of his pollution. He's already making mistakes, showing his cards."

Banjo stood and approached her, drawn by the sight of her unfolding wings. He reached out, but he did not touch them, not yet. He wasn't allowed. All he could do was watch, and yearn, and wait.

Hailey rose a few inches off the floor and hovered there, her beautiful, multi-hued hummingbird wings glowing in the dusty air.

CHAPTER EIGHTEEN

THEY WERE WAITING for Simon when he went outside.

He locked the gates, checked that they were secure, and turned around. The three boys were standing there, at the edge of the Roundpath, watching him in silence. He recognised one of them from earlier at the Arcade – the big lad with the trippy Scooby Doo baseball cap.

"Can I help you?" The words made him sound more confident than he felt. He clenched his fists, holding on to the bulky set of keys – a good weapon in a pinch, he recalled from somewhere – and waited for a response.

"Who the fuck are you, like?" The biggest of the three – Scooby – stepped forward, spat on the ground after he spoke. Like the others, he was wearing jeans, trainers, and a hooded top. The sweatshirts were all the same style; the one the leader wore – if that's what he was – was red, and the other two were blue and green.

"Well?" repeated Scooby, his arms loose, ready for combat.

Shit, thought Simon. *I'm out of my depth.*

"I own this place. Why, what business is it of yours?"

"Ooooh!" Green Hoody began to laugh. "What a fucking prick."

Scooby smiled, rolled his shoulders like a boxer. "I'll ask you one more time, and then I'll fuck you over. Who are you? I saw you talking to my lass in the café." He pronounced the word 'cafee'.

"Listen son," said Simon, stepping away from the fence. "I'm nobody you want to be messing with – okay? I was just talking to the girl, that's all. I didn't know she was your girlfriend. In fact, she was the one who spoke to me." He stood his ground, shaking. He hoped that the boys couldn't tell, but he felt his entire body flooding with adrenalin.

"Funny cunt, in't he?" Blue Hoody had found his voice. It wasn't worth the effort: weak, high-pitched, as if his balls were yet to drop. Green Hoody just stood there, his face a blank mask, not even capable of a proper expression.

"You trying to say that my lass was chatting you up?" Scooby turned to his cohorts, opening his hands in a questioning gesture. "Is that what he's saying, lads? Eh? That my lass wanted his cock?"

Simon said nothing.

"Aye," said Blue Hoody, nodding. "Aye, that's what he said. I heard him."

"For fuck's sake..." Simon had run out of things to say. Debate was not an option. These kids wanted blood, and nothing else would satisfy them. Years ago, when he was a teenager, he would have been able to handle this situation – in fact, it probably wouldn't have happened. Back then, he was an insider, this was his patch. But now he was a stranger, an outsider, and considered fair game by the local beasts.

"Give us your wallet." Scooby had stopped smiling. He held his hands at waist level and flexed his fingers.

He must have been, what, fifteen years old? "Now." He bared his teeth. His cheeks were pockmarked, and his front teeth yellow, probably tobacco stained.

"Listen, lads–"

"No, you listen." The boys each took a single step forward, like one entity composed of three parts. "Do what I said, and empty your pockets. If you do, we might not hurt you."

Jesus Christ, was this really happening, in broad daylight?

Suddenly Simon was no longer afraid, he was angry. This was good; he could use it. He let the rage flood through him, filling him up from the inside, like a tap being turned on somewhere in his gut. "Fuck off, son."

He'd barely finished his sentence when the boys struck.

Scooby moved forward and threw a punch, which landed sweetly on the side of Simon's face. He reeled backwards, his own hands coming up, and he was pushed further back by the advancing boys. He lashed out, feeling his fist connect with bone, and started screaming abuse as he tried to pummel his attackers.

His energetic defence did not last. He went down after a few seconds, taking more blows to the face, and a hard one to the stomach. His breath came in thick, jagged bursts; his kidneys ached; he felt his head go down. Then, before he even had a chance to attempt any more punches, he felt the solid connection of a foot to his temple.

He stayed down, unable to fight gravity. The ground grabbed him, held him, and refused to let him go, while darkness inched in from the corners of his vision.

He was aware of the boys – Scooby, Blue Hoody, Green Hoody – going through his pockets, and then they dragged off his suit jacket. There was laughter, yelling, and the sounds diminished as they ran away, leaving him there on the ground.

The only reason he did not black out was because he vomited, bringing up his bland breakfast in the dirt.

After several minutes he stopped heaving. There was nothing left in his stomach to come up, and his throat felt raw. He struggled to his knees and inspected himself for damage. A few bruises on his face, a sore side, no blood. As far as beatings went, this one was mild. They were amateurs. He'd suffered worse when he was mugged by one man in London, four years ago as he stumbled drunk through the streets behind King's Cross.

But the bastards had taken his jacket, and his wallet and mobile phone had been in the pocket. "Shit," he said, looking upwards. He had no memory for numbers, not these days when everything was stored on a SIM card, so he would not be able to call Natasha, or Mike at The Halo. "Shit, shit, shit..." Nobody would be able to contact him, either.

He struggled to his feet, taking it slowly as the blood rushed to his head and made him dizzy, and then headed back towards the flat. He had a few loose notes in his trouser pocket, but his debit and credit cards had been in the wallet. He needed to get to a phone and make a few calls, stop the cards and order some new ones. He checked the ground for his keys; they were still there, near his foot. Okay, this could have been much worse. Yet still he felt angry. This was his birthplace, where he was from – how dare those little fuckers do this to him!

Beneath the anger, buried away in a place where he rarely looked, there was also shame. He was a grown man, a successful property developer, and he had been unable to handle a bunch of kids. They'd kicked his arse and hung him out to dry, and he was embarrassed at the pathetic effort he'd made at defending himself.

Next time, he thought, I won't go down so easily. But, in that same quiet spot in his gut, he knew that he would. He always would, because despite the lies he told himself, he was not a real fighter. He was a survivor, but not a warrior. Experience had already taught him that.

Simon let himself into the flat and inspected himself in the mirror. His face was already bruising – the right side was slightly swollen, a lump developing along the side of his jaw and across his cheek. He was hardly turning into the Elephant Man, but the swelling would be noticeable.

He took a shower, dressed in some clean clothes, and then rang directory enquiries on the landline to get the number of his bank. He cancelled all of his cards, and because he was a priority customer, with large sums in his accounts, he was told that a new set of cards would be couriered to him within twenty-four hours. Again, he felt ashamed. Money got you what you wanted, the things you needed, and it got them to you faster than it did to anyone else. He took some notes and loose change from the drawer by the bed. He always split his money in this way; it was an old habit he'd not lost.

As an afterthought, he rang the emergency services number and was put through to the local police station. He told the officer on the other end of the line what had happened. They asked if he was hurt. When he told them it was nothing serious, and he did not need medical care, they gave him a crime number to quote in the instance of any insurance claim and asked him to call into the station when he could to give a statement. He hung up the phone, wondering if there had been any point in calling them.

Simon went downstairs and into the pub on the corner of Grove Court and Grove Road. The Dropped Penny had become, by default, his temporary local. He needed a pint, and perhaps a whisky chaser. The day had started badly, and unless Brendan delivered the goods with Marty Rivers' grandmother, it was bound to get a lot worse.

He drank his first pint of bitter down in one, savouring the brief bloated feeling in his gut, and then ordered another. He took the second pint and the double malt to a table in the corner, where he sat and glared at the television above the bar, waiting for the alcohol to do its job. He drank the second pint slowly, alternating each mouthful with a sip of the whisky. Some of the other patrons glanced at him, but they did not stare. In pubs like this, on estates like these, a man with minor facial injuries was nothing out of the ordinary, and was often the last person you'd want to make eye contact with.

Simon enjoyed the aura of danger around him. He wondered if those little bastards would come in here to spend some of his money... the thought shattered his fragile machismo. He didn't want to see them again, certainly not this soon after the attack, and not without someone to back him up.

He remembered what the girl in the café had said about Brendan, and how she'd seemed wary of him. That was the kind of company he needed. He hoped his old friend would find him soon, so that he could ignore the quiet, taunting voices in his head, the ones that were mocking him for being so easily defeated.

The Dropped Penny was quiet. Men drank in pairs; an old woman sat at the bar, her legs crossed to stop herself from falling off the stool. The young barman watched a football programme on the television, trying to lip-read as muted managers and players were interviewed outside stadium dressing rooms.

There was an air of desperation about this place, but Simon felt comfortable around these people. They might be alcoholics, wife beaters, petty criminals, or they might be high court judges slumming on a daytime session. Nobody cared; they were only here to drink, not to cause trouble or to ask any awkward questions. They each existed in their own little world, shut off from everyone else.

Brendan walked in just after noon. He stood in the doorway, not quite coming fully inside, and peered into the gloomy interior. The fruit-machine made a few noises, somebody laughed more loudly than a joke deserved, and finally Brendan's gaze came to rest on Simon. He nodded, walked in, and crossed the room to the bar.

Simon watched his friend as he ordered two pints. He was staring straight ahead, as if concentrating on something. Then, when the glasses were placed before him, he paid his money and turned away, strolling over to Simon's table.

"What happened to you?" His face did not change as he said the words. He looked unmoved, unconcerned: he'd only asked the question because it would have been peculiar not to. He didn't really care about the answer.

"I was mugged. Three kids. They took my phone and my wallet."

Brendan smiled; the expression was smug rather than amused. "You're not the man you used to be, mate. Back in the day, you would've outrun them easily."

"Thanks for all the sympathy. You really are spoiling me."

The two men sat in silence for a while, drinking their beer. The atmosphere in the pub remained subdued. The Dropped Penny was not an establishment where people gathered for lunch, discussing business proposals over a nice Caesar salad. The clientele of this pub was more likely to grab a quick bag of pork scratchings between pints, if anything at all, and their debates and discussions revolved around football, horse racing, and possibly the state of the nation.

"Fancy another before we head off?" Simon's face had stopped hurting, the pain dulled by the alcohol.

"Yeah, why not. I don't have work tonight, thanks to you, so I can do whatever the hell I like."

Simon stood and walked across to the bar, ordered two more pints, paid for them, and returned to the table. It felt right. This mechanical process – drink, forage, drink – was something that he could understand and rely on when everything else in his life seemed so unreliable.

"Sorry," said Brendan, relaxing now that he'd had a

drink. "I didn't mean to make light of what happened to you. At least it doesn't look too bad."

"No worries. I probably had it coming. Walking around in designer togs, flashing my money... they must have been watching me since breakfast. I've forgotten how to act around here."

Simon glanced around the room, not looking for anything in particular, just watching. "It's not like it was when we were kids, you know. We had a fight, it was fists and feet and a lot of huffing and puffing. These little bastards will pull a knife on you, maybe even a gun if it's after dark and you pose a threat to their drug deals." Bitterness made his voice seem heavy, as if the words weighed more than his mouth could carry. There was sorrow, too, and regret: a sort of grief for the way things had been long ago, when life on the estate had seemed so much simpler.

He put down his pint glass but did not let go. He stared at his hand, at the fingers wrapped around the glass. "Tell me, Brendan. What do you remember from that night? The night we... went missing." He did not look up. He didn't want to look into his friend's eyes.

Missing... and they still were, all of them, when it came right down it.

Brendan sighed. Then he spoke. "I remember us making the den in the trees, and then I saw something. Somebody. A man in a mask... like a bird's face, or something."

"Captain Clickety?" said Simon, finally raising his eyes.

Brendan nodded. "Yes." He exhaled loudly. "Remember, it was something Marty told us. Back in the seventies, a couple of kids – twins – who lived in the Needle were tormented by a poltergeist. They called him Captain Clickety, because they kept hearing a clicking sound, like castanets. I've read about it since... most of the rumours are false. Nobody seems to want to talk about it these days, but one of the twins died of a heart attack. At least that's what the records say. Natural causes, anyway. Probably shock-related."

Brendan leaned forward in his chair, his chest almost touching the top of the table. His face was sombre, his eyes narrow. "Captain Clickety," he whispered in a singsong voice.

"Captain Clickety
He's coming your way
Captain Clickety
He'll make you pay
Once in the morning
Twice in the night
Three times Clickety
Will give you a fright"

Simon felt cold. The old rhyme had chilled him, bringing back snippets of memory, torn and tattered visions, like a shredded sheet: the inside of the Needle, all dark and damp and empty; a figure moving through the darkness, rustling in the low-hanging branches of trees; a girl, her skin shedding light as she came towards them, smiling... movement, like huge wings, curling around her back and shoulders.

Brendan spoke again, as if he had not broken off from his account: "I remember the platform falling, cutting my arm – I still have the scar." He glanced down, at his arm. "And we went back that night, sneaked out of our houses, and met up there, to guard the den. What a bunch of babies – acting like cowboys." He smiled, despite the solemnity of his tone. "We saw someone again – possibly the same figure – and we decided to follow him, to spy on him. It was just a game, a bit of fun... that was all. A fucking kids' game." His eyes were shining with tears. "Then... then... we were in there, inside the Needle, and we were so fucking scared. We were terrified."

Simon reached out and grabbed Brendan's hand, clutching it. He didn't care who saw them; he didn't give a damn what it looked like. "But how did we get in there? That's what I can't remember. I didn't even see the figure, although it was my idea to follow him. I don't remember how the hell we got inside that place."

Brendan looked deep into his eyes. "Me neither."

Simon pulled his hand away, suddenly embarrassed by the contact. He glanced around the room, but nobody was taking any notice of their exchange. In The Dropped Penny, nobody eavesdropped on your conversation; nobody gave a damn about your business, whatever it was.

Brendan took a large swallow of his beer. He licked his lips.

"I went in there earlier," said Simon. "I went in there again, by myself this time. That's when I got mugged, as I came back out. They were waiting for me. But while I was in there, something happened. I saw things, things that shouldn't have been there."

Brendan pressed his lips together.

"I saw twigs, skinny little branches coming out of the walls and moving around like snakes, like they were trying to grow. They wrapped around my wrists, trying to bind me, like we were before. I heard a clicking sound, up on the higher levels. Clicking, like the sounds I remember from twenty years ago." He had run out of steam, losing the rush that had forced the words out of him in a torrent. "I think I did. I'm not sure of anything anymore. I have these dreams... strange dreams."

"I do, too," said Brendan. "Nightmares, but they always seem so real at the time. It doesn't even feel like I'm dreaming. Feels like... like real life, but flipped over, messed about with, shaken up into weird forms."

Simon nodded. "That's it. That's exactly it."

Brendan slammed one hand down onto the table, not too hard, but enough to make a loud, hollow sound. "You're right. We have to find Marty."

Simon listened to his old friend. For the first time, he seemed to be truly on board, to be taking all of this seriously.

"We need to find him and ask him if he's been dreaming like this too. If he feels like something's reaching for him, trying to pull him back, towards the past."

Simon's blood was racing through his veins. His skin felt hot. He was no longer cold: he was burning. "Is that how you feel?"

Brendan nodded. "Aye."

"So do I, mate. So do I..."

Brendan closed his eyes and began to speak. "*Captain Clickety*

He's coming your way..."

"Stop it," said Simon. "Just cut that shit out, right now. You're acting like a fucking child. We need to focus, we have to keep a grip on the situation."

"What situation is that, then?" Brendan picked up his glass, but it was empty. He placed it gently back on the table. "How exactly do you describe what's happening to us, if in fact there is anything happening to us and we're not just going mad? Or always were mad, ever since some bastard locked us up in the Needle and abused us for a weekend."

"A weekend that felt like an hour," said Simon. "Remember that little fact? I do. When we came out of there, it seemed like we'd only been inside for an hour, but it had been two days. Two whole fucking days. I still don't have that time back – do you?"

Brendan shook his head. "Okay, yes. I do remember that. It's the thing that scares me most about the whole thing, those lost days. Where did it go? I mean, what the hell did we do for all that time? What did he do to us?"

"And who, or what, is he?" Simon pushed away from the table, suddenly uncomfortable within the walls of the old pub. "Let's get out of here. The quicker we find out where Marty might be, the better for us all. Having that tough bastard with us will make everything seem a bit less oppressive."

"Yeah, okay." Brendan stood, pushing back his chair. "Let's go. We have an appointment to keep with an old lady and a pot of tea. She might even have cake." He smiled, and it almost reached his eyes.

Almost.

CHAPTER NINETEEN

Marty sat on his sofa with the blinds closed. The noise of the city – the busy quayside traffic, the lunchtime crowds surging towards pubs and cafes for their salads and panini and plates of antipasto – dimmed to nothing but background noise.

The television was on, tuned to a twenty-four-hour news channel, but he had the sound turned right down. A woman with shiny blonde hair and impressive bone structure mouthed banalities that he had no desire to hear. He stared at her face, at her flawless skin, and imagined it peeling back to show the bone beneath. For some reason, that made him smile.

Marty was stretched out, with his legs trailing on the floor, and he was wearing only a pair of baggy gym shorts. His torso was bare. He was sweating; his skin glistened, as if he had been sprayed with water. In one hand he held a whisky bottle, and in the other he had the acorn. He was rubbing the surface of the nut with his fingers, polishing it, making it shine. It was a reflexive action, something to use up his nervous energy.

He took a long swig directly from the bottle. The whisky was good stuff: Talisker, his favourite. The liquor burned all the way down his throat, a golden trail of soft pain that sliced right through him.

His stab wound was aching.

He had taken off the dressing to give it some air. The stitches had already started to come loose, fraying like the hem of an old shirt, and he had been bleeding again. There were balled up paper tissues on the floor near his feet, stained red. The bleeding seemed to have stopped for the time being, but the place where he'd been stabbed felt raw, as if it might burst open at any minute. That bastard Doc; he didn't have a clue, had done a botch job when he'd stitched up the cut. But Marty couldn't go to a hospital, because they'd ask awkward questions. Stab wounds had to be reported to the police – it was the law. And that would create all kinds of problems.

He rolled the acorn around with his fingers, and dropped it onto his tight stomach.

With his other hand, he put the whisky bottle down on the sofa, leaning it against a cushion, and grabbed the remote control. He flicked through the channels, but saw nothing to interest him. Daytime television was appalling; it made him angry. Sensationalist intervention shows with career-choice chavs taking lie-detector tests to prove if they were the fathers of grasping brats to appease women who were aged before their time and desperate to hang onto something, however vulgar. Property programmes with smug middle-class city-types renovating old houses they'd snapped up in repossession auctions. Quizzes made by and for the mentally subnormal. Panel shows featuring faded soap stars and ex-cruise ship singers scrabbling at the foot of the broadcasting table for the scraps of one final meal before they were carted off like old horses, to have their sagging tits and prolapsed vaginas turned into glue.

"Jesus," he said, surprised at the anger in his thoughts, the absolute venom coming through from somewhere. He knew that he was furious because of the stabbing, and the way the fight had ended, but this was something different. He had not felt this kind of pure, incandescent rage for a long time – not since the accident that had cut short his dreams of a career in boxing. It made him light-headed. The anger was so uncut, so undiluted, that it felt like the prelude to some kind of sexual thrill.

He closed his eyes and saw her face. Sally: the girl who'd been killed all those years ago, when he was nineteen. He had loved her, or at least he'd thought so then, when everything was so uncertain, especially his feelings. But she had been young and pretty, and knew how to handle him. She had possessed the softest hands he'd ever known.

Sally had been riding pillion on the Suzuki, her arms wrapped around his stomach, her chin resting against the back of his shoulder. They'd been racing out into the Northumbrian countryside, just looking for a space to call their own for a while, a quiet spot to lie down on the grass and cuddle. Night was gathering in the sky, chasing the lowering sun, but there was still enough light to see clearly. The road had been straight, and lined with low dry stone walls on either side. They had an unobstructed view of flat green fields, and in the distance craggy outcroppings rose like the backbone of some half-buried beast. It was all so beautiful... just like the girl, like Sally.

Marty had not been driving too fast, not really: possibly a few miles per hour over the speed limit, but it was nothing that he couldn't handle. He felt in complete control of the Suzuki; its master. It was just another part of the beauty of that early evening.

Then, without warning, he'd seen it come stumbling out from the right, padding along on those ghastly oversized hand-feet into the middle of the road, where it turned to face him, its awful mouth growing wider and wider as it waited for him to arrive....

Humpty Dumpty.

The same hideous figure he'd dreamt of when he was a kid, and then seen for real the night he and his three friends had lost all those hours inside the Needle. It was a part of his life that he'd tried to block out, and Sally was helping with that. She helped him see light beyond the darkness, a faint glimmer that grew stronger every day that they spent with each other.

She *was* the light. It was part of her purpose, to make him see the candle she held out for him.

Even now, years after the event, he had no idea why he'd tried to turn the wheel. The rational side of him said that he must have been trying to turn into the path of the thing, to mow it down and kill it. But another part of him, the side that was and would forever remain a rotten coward, told him that he was trying to turn away, to dodge a collision with the creature from his nightmares in case it managed to grab hold of him.

He lost control of the bike. It skidded off the road, hitting a fallen section of wall, the victim of bad weather and escapee sheep. The tumbled, moss-coated stones acted as a ramp, and the bike took flight. They landed badly on the other side, at the bottom of a slope. Sally's injuries were fatal: she took a short time to die, and was barely conscious all the while. Marty lay pinned beneath the Suzuki and the corpse of the girl he could have loved forever, until somebody came along and noticed them there.

"Sally," he whispered now, in the soft, false darkness of the room. "I'm so, so sorry." He grabbed the whisky and took a hit. He blamed the heat of the drink for the tears that dampened his cheeks.

And how many women had there been since Sally, ones that could never live up to her ghost, no matter how hard they tried? Indeed, the fact that they tried counted against them, because Sally never had. She'd just trusted in the fact that he cared for her, and never pushed, never forced anything. Or was that just him glorifying her memory, romanticising her?

There had been scores of such women. Of that he *could* be certain. He'd never counted – he wasn't that vain – but he did know that he'd long passed the century mark. Over a hundred pairs of open legs, smooth, taut bellies, open mouths, needy eyes, and hands that were never quite as soft as the ones he sometimes dreamt about. That meant over a hundred minds that he'd barely taken the time to get to know, and it was his loss, because some of them had been good people, intelligent women who were drawn to him for reasons of their own. He'd just never been emotionally invested enough to care. There'd been the slags and sluts, of course: empty one-night stands used as a way of beating back the darkness, but only a few. There had also been women who, if he were not so damaged, he could have fallen in love with. Like Melanie, the girl he'd dumped the other day. She was good-looking, interesting, had an incisive wit... but still he had started ignoring her calls, wishing her away. Stepping back from whatever it was she had to offer.

None of these women had held a candle, lighting his way along the dark path. Only Sally had ever done that.

He was absently rolling the acorn between his palm and his stomach, moving it across his belly. It was smooth and cold, like a cold compress. The pressure, when he applied it close to his wound, eased the pain. It felt good, like a balm. He pressed it against the stitches, rolling it over the area where the knife had torn through his skin and penetrated his body.

The motion of the acorn, and the pressure it produced, also took away his rage, the dark thoughts of a past that could not be changed. His mind began to feel empty; the bad stuff was being siphoned off, like blood through a catheter.

A soft humming sound grew in his ears, and Marty looked up, at the window, but no shadows moved beyond the drawn shades. The humming turned gradually into another sound, something that made him feel uneasy all over again, despite the acorn's movement across his belly. A quiet clicking noise, like hard nails drumming against plastic or playing cards flicked right beside his ear. Marty rolled onto his side and stumbled off the sofa, falling to his knees and then rising to his feet, adopting a defensive stance. His fists were clenched; his hands were raised. He was ready to fight... always, always ready to fight, whenever the need arose.

The sound faded, as if it were moving away from him, perhaps along a dark, deserted corridor inside a ruined tower block. Briefly he smelled the sap of summer trees, felt a light breeze blowing against his naked torso, and heard distant cries, like twisted birdsong.

He was safe. He wasn't there, inside the Needle. He was safe and sound and prepared for action, within walls that were concrete, yes, but much newer, and not as haunted as the ones from before – the old, grey concrete walls that still surrounded his soul, cutting it off from daylight. Making it so that he could not see Sally's candle; would never see it again, even in dreams.

Marty relaxed, letting his hands drop to his sides. He had to coax his fists to open, but they obeyed him. He sat back down on the sofa and picked up the bottle. Took a large swallow.

He felt around on the sofa for the acorn, experiencing a sudden desire for the security it had provided. He could not find it anywhere, not on the surface of the cushions, or down the back or sides of the cushions. He raised his hands to his head and scratched his scalp, rubbing his temples as he moved his hands across his skull. Looking down, wondering if the acorn had in fact dropped onto the floor, he noticed a small lump in his abdomen.

Time slowed down, stopped. The image of the television seemed to freeze, but when he glanced at it the picture began to move again, as if mocking him.

He looked down again, at his body.

His torso.

At the lump. In his belly.

The lump was positioned to the left of his navel, not too far from the knife wound (what had that fume-stinking old sawbones called it, a loin wound?). The lump was large, almost the size of a golf ball but more oval in shape. It stretched the skin around it taut, making it pale and thin-looking.

Marty reached down and patted the area around the lump. There was no pain, not even minor discomfort. It was as if the area had gone numb from some kind of anaesthetic. The kind you might receive before minor surgery, given to you by a heavy-breathing medic in a face mask.

He knew what it was, of course. Marty was a lot of things, but he wasn't stupid.

It was the acorn.

Somehow the acorn had got... *inside* him. It had entered his body.

He looked at the wound. The stitches had come undone. There was no blood; the wound was perfectly dry. To him, in that moment, its inner edges looked like the labia of some mutant vagina; the pink inside was the interior of a woman's genitals. He had no idea why he was thinking this way, but the image would not shift. He was stuck with it.

Suddenly, as he watched, the acorn began to move. Inching its way along inside his torso, towards his navel, it rolled like a slow-witted dung beetle. Again, there was no pain. He felt nothing, nothing at all. It was as if he had been cut off from all the nerves in his body below the shoulders and above the pelvis:

everything between these points was vague, like something that didn't quite belong to him. It was like dreaming awake, caught in that idle moment between sleeping and waking, when the two states bleed into each other to become something entirely different. It wasn't unpleasant... not really. He found himself fascinated by the slow-rolling movement beneath his skin, and the way the skin itself stretched like elastic to accommodate the travelling seed.

The acorn stopped moving.

Marty felt bereft. He realised that he'd enjoyed the sight of it shifting across his abdomen. He reached down and flicked it gently, and just the once, to encourage it to move again.

The acorn responded.

It rolled across his stomach, causing his navel to protrude as it passed beneath the recessed pink knot (he was always so oddly proud of being an 'outy' rather than an 'inny'), and round towards his opposite flank. The acorn disappeared then, under his body, but he was aware of its presence under the skin of his back. He still could not feel the acorn, but he knew that it was still in motion, as if some previously hidden sense was tracking it around his body.

Marty knew that he should be worried, perhaps even frightened, by what was happening to him, but he could not summon the energy to react in this way. He watched as the acorn completed its slow circuit, passing under the wound – making those labial folds purse and open like a kiss – and then back to its starting point to the left of his navel.

"Wow," he said, feeling drunk on the experience. "Fucking hell."

He reached down again and placed the end of his index finger against the conical top of the acorn. Then, without even considering what kind of damage he might be doing to his insides, Marty pressed down on the seed.

The acorn sank into his belly, vanishing into the yielding flesh. The skin popped back to its natural shape, and there was no evidence of the acorn ever having been there, beneath the surface of Marty Rivers, under his demented skin.

He blinked and looked up at the window. The blind was glowing white, like a screen, from the sunlight behind. What was happening to him? He felt like he'd just woken up from a long sleep. Had he been dreaming? Surely what he thought he'd experienced could not be real. It was impossible. A hallucination.

He looked down at his flat belly, and then at the dry wound. Everything looked fine.

But deep down, despite the fact that he did not want to listen, a small, scared voice – his ten-year-old self – was whispering: *It wasn't a dream. You were awake. This is really happening. Clickety-clickety-click.*

CHAPTER TWENTY

THE OLD WOMAN lived on Grove Terrace, in a house that backed onto Beacon Green. Simon could remember Marty going there for lunch every Sunday – a big roast, with Yorkshire puddings and all the trimmings. His parents would never have made such a meal. In Marty's house, it was always whatever came out of a can served with bread – French toast on a weekend, as a little treat.

Brendan knocked on the door, rapping three times with his knuckles. There did not seem to be a doorbell, or even a knocker. The front garden was small and neat, with well-tended borders and a lawn that was cropped as short as a football pitch. The house number was painted on the wall to the left of the door in white emulsion.

"I hope she's home." Simon glanced at Brendan.

"She said she would be," said Brendan, fidgeting with the buttons at the neck of his shirt. He looked uncomfortable, as if he were in pain, or perhaps his clothes didn't quite fit him properly. Whatever the cause of his consternation, it was making him fidget in a way that looked exhausting.

"You okay?"

Brendan stopped fidgeting. "Aye, I'm fine. Why?" He didn't make eye contact.

Simon sensed something, a kind of reluctance on

Brendan's part to reveal what was wrong with him. "It's just, well, you seem a little off. You know, like you're hurting or something. You keep wincing, and you're pulling at your clothes. The shirt, the jacket."

Brendan shook his head. "No, mate. It's nothing. I have a rash, that's all. Jane started using some new kind of washing powder – it was on sale. I think I'm allergic." Still he did not meet Simon's gaze.

"Oh. Right. That explains it." Simon shrugged, took a step back, and glanced along the road, then back at the front door. "Where is she?"

As if on cue, the door opened. A small, well-dressed old woman stood in the hallway, peering over the rims of her spectacles. "Hello," she said. "You must be... Marty's old friends?"

"Yes," said Brendan. "We spoke on the phone earlier. I'm Brendan, and this is Simon. Thanks again for sparing us some of your time." He smiled but it looked like he was grimacing.

The old woman grinned, showing her gleaming dentures. Her face was weathered, crosshatched with creases and wrinkles, but she had the demeanour of someone a lot younger. "Oh, when you get to my age all you have is time. It might be nice to spend some of it today with a couple of good-looking young men." Clearly she still had a sharp mind.

Still smiling, she stepped aside, turned, and walked down the hallway.

Simon stepped over the threshold and entered the house, and Brendan followed, closing the door behind him. The house smelled of cinnamon, with a hint of fresh lemon. It was a nice smell; homely and welcoming.

The woman had turned left and they followed her into a room. The first thing Simon saw was a small bird cage on a stand. Inside the cage was a tiny green budgie. When he and Brendan entered the room, the budgie hopped from its perch and grabbed the side of the cage, where it hung by its claws next to a portion of dried cuttlefish and watched them.

"That's Percy," said the old woman. "He's mute. He can't sing, can't talk. He can't make a sound at all, if I'm honest. But he's good company." She sat down on an overstuffed sofa, stretched out her short, thin legs on the carpet. "And I'm Hilda. Marty's Nan." Her smile never seemed to waver. It just hung there on her wizened face, displaying those too-white dentures and hiding her thoughts.

"Thanks for seeing us," said Simon. He sat on a chair opposite the bird cage, taking another quick look at the silent bird. The budgie was watching him, its beady, unblinking eyes never moving from his face.

"I've made tea... if one of you lads wouldn't mind getting the pot from the kitchen there." Hilda tilted her head towards the door.

"I'll go," said Simon. He jumped up and walked out of the room, leaving Brendan to the small talk. The bird was making him nervous. The neatness of the room, the way all the pictures and photographs formed geometrical patterns on the walls, didn't sit right with him. It was all too ordered. Simon had never trusted people whose homes were too tidy; he needed at least a small amount of mess around him to feel comfortable.

The kitchen was spotless. He imagined Hilda using all her free time to clean the place, every day, top to bottom. His mother had done the same, keeping a tidy home to hide the darkness at the centre of her marriage. He'd never realised before, but that was why he always created a mess, why he never felt at home unless things were in slight disorder. It counteracted the way his mother had kept things too prim and proper, her mask of domesticity.

The teapot was on the bench beside the sink, the tea brewing. It was on a little tray, alongside three cups and a plate of garibaldi biscuits. He picked up the tray and went back to the living room, where it seemed as if the budgie had been staring at the empty doorway, awaiting his return.

"Here we go," he said, setting down the tray on a small occasional table near the gas fire.

"Thank you, son," said Hilda, sitting upright and pushing herself forward on the sofa. "How do you take it?"

"Just black," said Simon. "One sugar, please."

"White with two," said Brendan, shuffling on the seat, looking less comfortable as time went by.

"So," said Hilda, after they'd all had a mouthful of tea. "You want to know where Marty's been living. Is that right?"

Simon waited for Brendan to answer, but the other man remained silent, staring at the wall. His lips were pressed together, as if he were holding something back. He didn't look comfortable in his own skin.

"Erm, yes," said Simon, taking the initiative. "We're old friends... I don't know if you remember us, but we all used to hang around together. The three of us, we were best mates, when we were younger."

"I'm not daft, you know." Hilda put down her cup and ran the palms of her hands over her thighs, straightening her dress. "You were the other two, the ones that went missing with Marty. Of course I remember. You were nice lads back then, all of you. Good lads. That was a terrible thing." She leaned back, pressing her spine against the sofa cushions, and briefly closed her eyes. She was still baring her teeth. "Whatever happened to you boys in there, it changed you all. I know that. I've seen it, with Marty, and with you, Brendan."

Brendan flinched at the sound of his name. "I'm sorry?"

"I used to see you a lot around the Grove, but I started seeing you less and less. You always seemed to work nights, and it's always that lovely wife of yours who takes the kids to school. I haven't seen you in years, son. Considering we live around the corner from each other, that tells its own story."

Brendan grimaced. It was probably meant to be a smile, but it wasn't quite there. Clearly he felt uncomfortable being the focus of the conversation, but for some reason he did nothing to deflect the old woman's attention. He just sat there, saying nothing.

"So, can you tell us about Marty?" Simon took a bite of biscuit. "These are nice." He smiled, crumbs on his lips.

"Like I said, I'm not daft. I suppose you know all about the things he's been doing to make a living. Illegal boxing matches, working on pub doors, and God knows what else. Everybody knows about our Marty, and about the kind of person they think he is. Hired muscle. A bruiser."

"We're not here to judge him, Hilda. We just want to talk to him. It's something about... about what happened to us back then, when we were ten." He'd taken a risk telling her this much, but as far as he could tell, there was no other option. This wasn't some cracked old crone, sitting rocking in her front room waiting to die. She was a sharp lady; there could be no fooling her, even if he could be bothered to try.

"Well, that's good to hear. I know he's done some bad things, but he's my grandson and I love him." She paused, picked up her cup and took a sip, and then cradled the cup in one hand, like a small animal. "He was in a bad smash-up, years ago, on his motorcycle. His girlfriend, Sally, was killed, and Marty was unconscious in hospital for twenty-four hours. I sat by his bedside, holding his hand, waiting for him to either die or wake up. Nobody seemed sure which it would be." She licked her lips. She was wearing lip-gloss; it made them shine. "When he did wake up, the first thing he said was 'Humpty Dumpty'. It sounds silly, I know, but he said it with such fear in his voice that I never mentioned it to him. I don't even think he knows he said that, or that I heard it. Not even now." Her eyes were as shiny as her lips. She was lost in the memory.

"I'm sorry to hear that."

She nodded. "Aye, it ruined his dreams of boxing. That's why he started having those other fights, the ones that happen late at night in warehouses and basements... he thinks I don't know about them, but I do. I always knew."

"I bet you know a lot more than anyone, Hilda." Simon glanced at Brendan, but his friend failed to notice.

"Oh, aye. Us oldies, we see a lot. We see it all. There's nothing much else to do expect watch, you know.

Watch and remember what we've seen, just in case it turns out to be important."

Brendan was scratching vigorously at his back, knotting up his jacket at the nape of his neck. His face was pale. He seemed to be somewhere else, not here in the room. It was as if he were miles away, not even aware of the exchange taking place beside him. Simon willed him to turn around, to regain his focus, but Brendan just kept scratching away at his upper back.

Jesus, he thought. *What's his fucking problem?*

"So, Hilda... Do you have an address or a telephone number for Marty?" Thankfully, she had not noticed Brendan's weird contortions on the chair. She was distracted by her memories.

The budgie hopped around inside its cage, restless.

"I have his mobile number, but he doesn't answer unless he knows who's calling." She reached across to a sideboard on her right and grabbed a ring-bound notebook and pen. Her stick-like fingers scribbled down the number. She tore off the page and reached across the table, handing it to Simon.

"Thanks," he said. "All we can do is to try our best, I suppose."

"I'm not sure where he's been living. He's always moved around a lot, you see. Never stays in one place long enough to settle in or give me an address. I even have to send his Christmas card to a post office box. The last I heard he was in Newcastle or Gateshead, looking after someone's flat while they're working away. He has a lot of acquaintances, does our Marty, but not many friends. None at all that I've met, anyway."

Simon smiled. "*We're* his friends," he said, folding up the sheet of paper and slipping it into his trouser pocket. "If he still wants us, that is."

"That's nice," said Hilda. "The past is important. Memories are the ties that bind us to each other. If he does call me, I'll tell him you're looking for him. I'll vouch for you, too. Tell him that you're still nice lads and he should make the effort to see you."

Brendan stood suddenly. He was jittery; unease bled from him like a fine mist. "Sorry," he said. "Could I use your bathroom?" His eyes were huge. He was standing in such a way that Simon felt he was trying to hold something inside, like a man with chronic diarrhoea who's been struck by sudden stomach cramps.

"Top of the stairs. First door on the left." Hilda raised a hand and pointed vaguely at the door. The budgie, stuck behind narrow bars, skittered on the cage floor. Brendan hurried from the room.

"Sorry about that. I don't know what's wrong with Brendan. He's been ill, something he ate." Simon leaned back and crossed one ankle over the other, pretending to be at ease in this too-neat home with its floral-patterned curtains and mute bird in a tiny cage.

"I suspect there's more wrong with him than that." Hilda nodded, as if agreeing with her own statement. "He's never been right, that one. Even before you lads came out of that tower block, he was a bit strange. Distant, like: always off with his head in the clouds."

"He's fine," said Simon, feeling the need to protect his old friend. "Just a bit quiet. He always was the shy one." Lies, all lies; Brendan had always been outgoing, at least in the years before the Needle.

"Listen, son." Hilda shuffled forward again.

"Marty's been seeing a girl. Melanie Sallis. She works part-time in the betting shop on the Arcade: three days a week. He never sees anyone for long – never has, not since poor Sally and that motorbike accident – but as far as I know, they're still an item. She's a decent girl, Melanie. Tells me stuff about my grandson. Go and see her today; tell her I sent you. She might be able to help you get in touch with Marty. Christ knows, I've done all I can – the little sod barely even calls me these days. Sends me text messages. Can you believe that? Text messages to his old Nan! The cheeky bugger." Her anger was faked; the tone of her voice suggested only compassion.

"Thank you, Hilda. You've been a great help."

Her smile was gone now. The lines and wrinkles on her face seemed to have deepened, become filled with shadows. Her dentures looked huge. "Just promise me that you won't go stirring up bad things from the past – things that are best left alone."

Simon leaned forward. He placed a hand on her knee. "I just want us – all three of us – to be able to move on with our lives. That's all. I want us healed. I want all that stuff, whatever it is, put away in a box for good. I want... I want us to be friends again, just like we were back then, before everything got so damned dark."

She placed her hand over his and squeezed. Her bones felt tiny, like a bird's. He glanced at the budgie; it was immobile, and staring at him through the bars.

Brendan chose that moment to come back into the room. His hairline was damp, as if he'd washed his face; his eyes and cheeks were red, as if he'd been rubbing them. He looked more tired than Simon had seen him since their reunion. He looked... wasted.

"We'd better go. Thanks again."

"Let yourself out, lads. These old legs of mine are playing up again, and I'd rather not stand, if that's okay." She wriggled her feet, as if to demonstrate what she meant.

"Don't worry, we can find our way out. Bye, Percy." Simon stood and approached Brendan, ushered him out of the door.

"What the hell was wrong with you in there?" They were standing outside, on the footpath next to the gate to Hilda's place. "I thought you were going to do all the talking? You left me high and dry. It's a fucking good job she liked me, or we would've got nothing."

Brendan was leaning against the privet bush next door. He rubbed his cheeks, licked his lips. "Sorry... I just. I didn't feel well. I have this rash... on my back. It's been bothering me."

"Okay, okay." Slowly, Simon started walking backwards along the street, in the direction of the Arcade. "I'll see you tonight, for dinner. Just get yourself home and have some rest. We can talk again then. I'll bring some wine for the table. We can get pissed and go through all this new information."

Brendan looked up. His cheeks were pale now, but there were thin red lines, like scratch marks, running from just under his eyes to a point level with his mouth. "Where are you going?" The marks faded to white as Simon watched.

Simon turned around and increased his pace. He glanced over his shoulder but did not alter his stride. "Me? I'm off to put a bet on."

CHAPTER TWENTY-ONE

Jane was out when Brendan got home. She was always out these days, as if the walls of the house were no longer able to hold her. He staggered through the door and into the hall, feeling giddy, light-headed. His back and shoulders ached. He leaned sideways against the wall, out of breath. His vision was swimming; he waited for it to clear.

He turned and stared at his reflection in the mirror mounted in the hallway. His face was damp with sweat, and his eyes were bloodshot. Behind him, hanging on the wall, he could see a family photograph: him, Jane, the twins. It was like a catalogue shot, deliberately posed to sell him something he didn't need. As with every family shot in the house, he had the sense that something was missing.

"What's happening to me?"

After a few seconds he turned away, disgusted with himself. He felt weak, absent, as if he was barely making an impact on the world. The safe existence he'd created over the years was being threatened. Everything was changing.

Carefully, Brendan took off his coat and hung it on the hook at the bottom of the stairs. He grabbed the banister and started to climb, heading up to the first floor. His legs ached; his back was burning. His other hand groped along the wall, feeling the ridges of the cheap wallpaper.

When he reached the top of the stairs he was breathless. He shoved open the bathroom door and turned on the light. Despite the sunshine, the small room never got much natural light. It was always dim in there. He looked again at his reflection in the mirror and did not recognise it from the one downstairs. His features looked different, as if he'd transformed somehow on the journey up to this level. He shook his head, trying to dispel the idiotic thoughts.

Pull yourself together. Get a fucking grip.

Slowly, he peeled off his shirt.

He'd deliberately worn a shirt that was two sizes too big, just to give the acne some breathing space. He wasn't sure if it had made any difference, but it was all he could think of. Back at the old lady's place, when he'd got up to use her bathroom, he'd taken off his jacket and seen specks of blood on the shirt collar. Since his strange experience early that morning, when he'd felt pinned to the bed by some angry force, he'd become convinced that the spots on his back had begun to change. He was almost afraid to inspect them and see what they looked like now.

Brendan dropped the shirt on the bathroom floor.

He turned slowly to the side and started picking at the plasters that held the dressing in place. There were small spots of blood on the white cotton gauze. It wasn't much, but it was there, like a warning. He pulled at the plasters and removed them, wincing as they pulled out tiny hairs, and then lifted the dressing to reveal his lacerated flesh.

Turning around to present his back to the mirror, he strained to look at the reflection of his rear side. Despite the presence of the blood, the pustules looked dry – drier than they had in a while. No fluids glistened on his body; no vile-coloured ichors had been spilled. The acne was more like a patch of damaged skin than individual wounds. It looked as if someone had laid a sheet, or several sheets, of treated rubber over his upper back – like a TV special effect in a hospital soap opera. He flexed the muscles there, testing it. The pain flared briefly and then died.

But then something strange happened.

When he stopped moving, the wounds continued to stir. The damaged skin shuddered, as if from an electric current being passed through it. The skin clenched, like the backs of hands making fists, and as he watched, parts of it rose, like flaps – or like two eyelids.

Beneath each of these thin lids, there was a small, dark eye. For some reason Brendan was not shocked. He knew that he should be – he realised that eyes opening up in a person's back was not a normal or natural occurrence, and he should be screaming in horror – but instead he experienced a strange overwhelming sense of calm.

The eyelids blinked, fluttering like a cheap whore's on a neon-soaked boardwalk. The eyes weren't human, he could see that clearly. They were yellow, rather than white, around the outside, and the pupils were strange... black and horizontal, like rectangular slots at the centre of the iris. They reminded him of something and he struggled to grab hold of an image. Then, suddenly, it came to him. Those weird eyes... they were the eyes of a goat.

The eyelids blinked again. Brendan had the feeling that they were waiting for something – perhaps for him, to acknowledge them.

"I'm not afraid," he said. "I know I should be, but I'm not. I was afraid of you twenty years ago, when you locked us up in the dark, but that was a lifetime ago. You don't scare me, you fucker. You make me angry, not afraid." He curled his hands into fists.

The eyelids widened; the black, slotted pupils contracted. From somewhere in the small bathroom – the ends of the taps, the bath plug, the toilet bowl – came a familiar clicking sound. It started slowly, gaining speed as he listened, but remained at a constant volume.

"It's just a trick," said Brendan. "You can't hurt me. If you could, you'd have done it by now. You've had twenty fucking years to kill me, but I'm still alive. I'm still here. So do your worst. I dare you."

The two eyelids blinked again. And then they closed.

Brendan was shaking. He had not felt so alive in years. There was fire in his belly, his blood was molten lava, and he felt as if he could take on anyone and win. "*Do your fucking worst*," he whispered.

He filled the sink with cold water and washed his face, then dabbed at his back with a wet cloth. The infected skin looked the same as it had done before, before those weird eyes opening. Oddly, it seemed as if the acne was healing, the badness leaking out, draining off. He pressed his fingertips against the spots, but they did not burst; the skin didn't break.

Bending down, he picked up his shirt. When he straightened up he looked again at his face in the mirror. This time his own eyes were like a goat's, with dull yellow irises and slotted black pupils. He stepped backwards, stumbling, and fell sideways, almost into the bath, slamming his arm against the edge of the tub as he did so. Breathing heavily, he pulled himself upright, using the sink for leverage, and looked directly into the mirror.

His eyes were normal again.

"More cheap tricks," he said, leaning forward, pressing his nose against the glass. "They won't work now. We're all grown up and we don't scare easy." He smiled. In the mirror, his face looked sweaty and manic. "We're not little kids."

Brendan threw the damp shirt in the direction of the washing basket and then took off his jeans, socks and underpants and sent them the same way. He walked naked along the landing and went into the bedroom, where he picked out some clean clothes. He also selected another outfit for later that evening – dark dress trousers, the black silk shirt Jane had bought him last Christmas, and his best pair of shoes.

He sat down on the bed and began to polish the shoes with a duster. The methodical task calmed his mind, helped him to relax.

Why am I no longer afraid? he thought. *What's happened to me? I should be terrified.*

He buffed the black shoes with the soft yellow cloth, pausing occasionally to breathe onto the leather upper, misting it.

I'm not the strong one. I'm the weak member of the group, the one who would die first if this was a horror film.

He smiled.

Exhaled.

Buffed.

If this were a film, he would not be sitting naked on the bed, shining his shoes. He'd be buying some obscure book on demonology from a backstreet dealer, or hiring an exorcist. But real life wasn't like the movies; reality was something you had to go through to fully understand the complexities, a series of obstacles that were meant to be endured. Sometimes passivity was the only option, and not everyone could be a hero. In real life, the monsters were often defeated by common sense and a blunt acceptance of the reality they presented. You didn't always have to fight, to confront the thing in the closet, the leering face under the bed.

Some battles were fought in the mind. Some wars lasted forever.

He examined his shoes. They were as shiny as he would ever get them. He could almost see his face in the polished surface. As far as he could tell, his eyes were the same as always.

Brendan put away the cloth and set down his shoes at the side of the bed. He laid out the clothes he intended to wear to dinner and dressed in the others, tucking his T-shirt into the waistband of his jeans. Jane hated that; she said it wasn't trendy. But Brendan had never been a fashionable man. Sometimes – more often than not, if he were honest – he wondered what the hell she ever saw in him. He had never been her type. But maybe that was part of the appeal?

Simon had been her type, and he'd dumped her.

Crossing the room, he went to the wardrobe and stood on his tiptoes. He couldn't be bothered to retrieve the box from under the bed, so he struggled on his tiptoes to reach the thing he was looking for. The acorn, when he brought it out, was dusty, its skin peeling back in thin, dry folds. It looked old, rotten and decayed: an empty husk, devoid even of terror. He held it between the palms of his hands and pushed the hands inwards. The acorn held at first, but as he pressed it began to burst, the sides caving in as he forced his palms together.

The acorn turned to dust in his hands.

The skin of his back twitched, just once.

Brendan clapped his hands together, rubbing and cleaning off the greyish dust. He splayed his fingers and stared at his palms. They were pale, bloodless. The lines looked faded, as if his hands were smoothing out, becoming babyish.

At last his fear began to show itself. He closed his eyes, closed his hands. His back crawled, as if a million tiny insects were marching from shoulder to shoulder.

Brendan wished he knew how he felt, or how he was supposed to feel. Perhaps if he could translate his emotions into words, he might stand a chance of surviving this season in hell. Or at least he'd die knowing what was happening to him.

CHAPTER TWENTY-TWO

SIMON APPROACHED THE Arcade with caution, wary that the kids who'd mugged him might be hanging around, laughing and still going through his wallet. He looked around, checking out the area, and moved slowly, like a man with something to hide. He was ashamed of his cowardice, but at the same time he knew that he'd been outnumbered. One on one, it would have been a different matter – he would have fought harder, better – but confronted by three young men, overpowered by the force of numbers, he hadn't stood a chance.

He'd tried calling the mobile number Marty's grandmother had given him, but it had led nowhere. All it did was ring out, an endless, monotonous tone. He'd even sent a text, identifying himself and asking Marty to get in touch, but had the feeling that any initial contact would need to be face-to-face, man-to-man. He got the impression that Marty was that kind of guy.

Shoppers slow-danced in and out of shop doorways. Middle-aged men in loose jogging bottoms hung around smoking and staring belligerently at passers-by. Simon sidled up to the front of the betting shop, trying to act as if he belonged here.

The large windows were covered with posters advertising races, fights and football matches, with betting odds listed in their alien language. He pushed open the door and stepped inside, feeling an oppressive atmosphere wrap its fingers around his body. He hated betting shops. His sports-obsessed father had spent a lot of time in this one, and others just like it, so Simon had a near-physical reaction whenever he was in the proximity of one of these places. He felt nauseous; his head began to pound.

Rows of flat-screen televisions lined the top of the walls near the ceiling, padlocked into metal frames. Other screens, smaller and lower down, showed a constant scroll of betting odds. Along the walls, between the lower television screens, were booths at which men stood writing out their bets on small slips of paper. Most of them looked deep in thought, a few of them looked wary, fewer still looked afraid.

Simon took a deep breath and held it for a couple of seconds. Then he moved to the back of the shop, towards the counter. There were three separate windows where people could place a bet, protected by bullet-proof glass screens. Behind the one on the left was a thin, pale-faced young man who kept biting his fingernails. The middle screen housed an obese old woman with frizzy brown hair, her spectacles too small for her swollen face. The final booth, on the right, was the one he needed. The woman behind the glass was young, slim, and rather beautiful. She looked out of place in these surroundings, like a pedigree dog stuck in a kennel for strays. Her black hair was held back in a loose ponytail, she wore too much make-up, and the skin of her face sported a familiar orangey fake tan... yet still, despite all of this, she was gorgeous. Scrape off that muck, allow the shop-bought tan to fade, and Simon had no doubt that she could pass for a model.

He walked to the window, taking the opportunity to approach her while everyone else inside the shop watched the numbers and horse names scroll down the screens.

She smiled.

"Hi."

She nodded. "Yeah."

"I... listen; I don't want to put on a bet. I just want to talk to you."

She smiled again. "I'm flattered, mate. Really I am. But do you know how many blokes ask me out every day, how many phone numbers get written on the back of spent betting slips, how many sad losers just come straight out and ask to see my tits?" Her face hardened; the smile slipped away. "I'm not interested."

"No... no, you've got it wrong. I'm not trying to pick you up. I'm a friend of Marty Rivers."

Her entire attitude changed. Her posture straightened; the muscles in her face and neck tensed, making her look older, less attractive, and she leaned forward, towards the glass. "Marty? Did he send you?"

"Not exactly."

She began to move away, her lips curling into a silent snarl. This wasn't the kind of reaction he'd hoped for.

"But I have a message from him." It was the first thing that came into his head. Simon knew that he was asking for trouble by lying to this woman, but what else could he do? "You are Melanie, aren't you? Melanie Sallis?" He tried his final gambit: "Marty's grandmother told me to come and see you. She said you were his girlfriend."

She laughed softly. "That's my name, yes. As for the other part... well, I'm not so sure. Maybe you should ask him." Her eyes shone, with anger rather than sorrow.

"My name's Simon Ridley. Could I speak with you, Melanie? Not here – somewhere else, where we can sit and have a proper talk. It's important, I promise you. I won't waste your time."

She glanced over his shoulder, at the interior of the betting shop, and then her eyes took him in again. "Marty didn't send you at all, did he?"

"No. No, he didn't. But I really do need to talk to you, and it is about Marty. I promise."

Her eyes flicked left, then right. She pursued her lips, and then opened them slightly. Her teeth were remarkably clean and white, unlike anyone's he'd ever seen outside modelling or television. He wondered how much she'd paid for all that dental work.

"Okay," she said. "I'll give you fifteen minutes. I'm due a break, anyway." She looked right, at the obese woman. "I'm off for a fag break, Denise. I'll be back shortly."

Denise shrugged and turned away.

"Come on," said Melanie. "I have the flat upstairs. We can talk in peace up there." She grabbed a leather jacket from the back of her chair and opened the side door of the cubicle. There was a combination lock, and she spun the numbers without looking.

She walked past him, towards the betting shop door. Her waist was narrow, her hips thin; she had long legs, and the short skirt she was wearing showed them off. Simon followed her outside, and then along a narrow alley at the side of the betting shop. She stepped up onto a metal stairway, took a key out of her pocket, and opened the door there.

Simon waited to be invited up.

"Come on, then," she said, shaking her head. "I haven't got all day."

He followed her inside.

They went up a stairwell, Melanie's high heels echoing like gunshots in the enclosed concrete space. At the top of the stairs was another door, clearly the main door to a flat. She used another key and unlocked the door, and then pushed it open.

He climbed the last couple of concrete stairs and followed her into the flat, closing the door behind him. He was standing in a narrow hallway. There were two doors in the wall on each side. Up ahead, he could see Melanie moving around in a small living room, putting her coat down on the arm of a sofa, brushing something off the front of her skirt.

Simon walked along the hall. There were framed prints of Paris, Barcelona and New York on the walls. "You travel a lot?"

She turned as he entered the room. "No, but I wish I did. That's what those pictures are – wishful thinking. One day, I might even get to see those places." Her smile was small and sad. "Drink?"

"No thanks. I'm already full up with tea and if I have anything alcoholic I might collapse from exhaustion."

"Suit yourself," she said, sitting down heavily on the patterned sofa. She slid off her shoes and flexed her stockinged feet. "You now have ten minutes to explain yourself," she said. "And if this isn't as important as you claimed downstairs, I'll fucking Mace you." She smiled, but it was devoid of humour. She pointed at the small, cluttered coffee table under which she'd rested her feet. There was indeed a can of Mace on the tabletop.

"Really, I am a friend of Marty's." Simon kept his distance. "An old friend. We haven't seen each other for a long time, but I need to see him, to speak to him about something important."

"You aren't impressing me yet," said Melanie, curling up her legs on the sofa. "Sit down. I was joking about the Mace. It isn't even real – it's a novelty cigarette lighter." This time the smile was mellower, tinged with humour. "If I thought you were a threat, do you think I'd have invited you up here?"

Again, Simon felt obscurely insulted. Did he present a threat to nobody around here? Was he really so harmless?

"I've seen your photo," she said. "I saw it at Marty's place."

Simon shook his head. "When we were kids, you mean? A school photo?"

"Nope. In his wallet – a clipping from a London newspaper. He showed me, bragged about how one of his old mates was a millionaire." Her legs squirmed on the sofa.

"He keeps a photo of me in his wallet?"

"Weird, eh? But Marty Rivers is one strange dude." She stretched out those long, slender legs, making herself comfortable. Simon wasn't sure if this was the preamble to some sort of seduction. She certainly looked as if she were limbering up for something.

"I don't understand." He sat down on the chair opposite, sinking into the soft cushion.

"That makes two of us. He seems really proud of the fact that you got away from here, though. I mean, he doesn't talk much about you – but that one time, when he showed me the photo, he was, like, beaming with pride." She blinked slowly.

Simon could barely believe what he was being told. All this time, he'd thought that his old friends had forgotten about him, perhaps even hated him for managing to get away while they'd stayed behind. The truth was, at least one of them had wished him well, silently supporting his escape. A welter of emotions surged though him – pity, regret, hatred, despair, and even what he thought might be affection.

"So what do you want to talk to me about? Surely you can just call Marty on the phone?" She feigned disinterest, examining her nails. They were long, and painted deep red.

"No, I can't. I was telling the truth when I said that we hadn't seen each other. I got out of the Grove not long after leaving school, and we haven't even spoken since then." He breathed heavily, feeling tired all of a sudden, as if by taking a breather here, in the small, cramped flat, he had allowed everything to catch up with him.

"Oh. I see. So now you want to know where he is? Maybe get an address?"

Simon nodded. "His grandmother told us that he doesn't answer his phone unless he knows who's calling, so we struck out there. I tried calling him earlier, on the way here, but only got his voicemail."

Melanie laughed. "Marty is a paranoid man – the most paranoid man I've ever known, to be honest. He doesn't trust anyone. The circles he moves in, the people he knows... well, let's just say that it pays him to be suspicious of people's motives."

Simon sat up straight and rested his hands on his knees. He felt awkward, displaced, as if he had no business being here, with this woman. "Yes, I've heard that he's into some dodgy stuff. Criminal stuff. How deep is he involved?"

Melanie bent her legs at the knee and sat up; it was a graceful movement, like something a dancer might do. "He doesn't really talk to me that much. He doesn't talk to anyone, really. All I know is that he's always out at night, and he often comes home with bruised knuckles and blood on his shirt. He's a violent man, but only if you cross him." Her face changed again, then, becoming cold and hard and bitter. "I suppose that's the attraction with a man like Marty Rivers – that sense of danger, and the fact that you know he'll protect you. That counts for a lot in a place like this, doing a job like I do." She tilted her head, indicating the betting shop downstairs, then shrugged, stood and walked across to the window. "He's stopped calling me. I haven't seen him for days. I guess he's dumped me." Her shoulders tensed as she looked out of the window, across the estate. "He doesn't like to get too close to people."

Sunlight flared, creating a soft halo around her head as she turned to face the room. Simon squinted against the glare, feeling as if, for a second, he had been transported elsewhere, to another place that existed alongside the reality he knew.

"I suppose I can give you his address," she said, moving towards him, out of the light. "I don't owe him anything, not now. He thinks he can pick people up, use them for a while, and then throw them away. What do I care if you know where he's staying?" The light faded behind her. Simon felt the absurd urge to get up and run towards it, try to prevent it from going away.

"Thanks," he said. "I appreciate it."

Melanie picked up a pad and a pencil and started to write down the address. "It's on the other side of the river – Gateshead. A penthouse flat on one of those nice new riverside developments that keep popping up along the quayside up these days."

Simon smiled. "I remember when Gateshead was a shithole."

Melanie looked up from the notebook. "It still is," she said. "People just pretend that it's changed. Isn't that what we all do? We pretend that things aren't what they really are?"

Simon wasn't sure what she meant, but it sounded like her words had taken on a meaning that she had not intended, as if they were talking about something else.

She tore the page from the notebook and handed it to him. She looked pensive, as if this was the end of something that she was reluctant to finish. "Don't tell him you saw me. I've had enough of his crap. He had his chance and now it's gone. I want to get on with my life, and if that means leaving him behind, then I'm cool with that."

Simon nodded. "I won't mention you. And thanks again... this really does mean a lot. Could I ask you something else?"

Melanie returned to the sofa, where she sat and began putting on her shoes. "Time's up, mister, so make it fast."

Simon folded up the piece of paper and slipped it into the back pocket of his trousers. "Did Marty ever mention anything about what happened to us when we were kids?"

Melanie looked up as she struggled with the strap on her right shoe. "What do you mean? What happened when you were kids? Is that what this is all about? Some kind of closure for a falling-out you all had when you were younger? I thought it might be something more exciting than that." Some of the hair had fallen out of her ponytail, and slid down over her eyes. She didn't bother moving it out of the way, just peered through the dangling fringe.

"Yes," said Simon. "It's about unfinished business. I just wondered if he'd ever spoken to you about any of it, that's all."

She shook her head. "'fraid not. Like I said, Marty's an insular bastard. He doesn't give much away."

"Thanks again, then. I'll let you get back to work."

When she did not respond, Simon took it as his cue to leave. He walked back through the flat and opened the door, then stepped out onto the shabby little landing. Once he was outside, in the open air, he felt like he'd been released from confinement. But he looked around, and realised that all he'd done was pass from one cell into another.

He moved along the alleyway between the shops and turned right, walking once again past the betting shop. He did not look in the window. If Melanie had gone back inside through some other door, maybe one that linked the upstairs flat with the rear of the shop, he didn't want to be seen checking her out. She was an attractive woman, but she had an aura of melancholy that he had found difficult to bear. He couldn't imagine staying with such a woman, where every movement, each tiny gesture, seemed like it was hiding another meaning.

He walked along the Arcade, lost in his own thoughts, and only when he was level with the butchers at the end of the row did he see the boy. It was Scooby, from earlier that day – the cocky ringleader of the group who'd taken Simon's wallet. This time the kid was on his own, walking up ahead with oversized earphones clamped to his head.

A surge of rage travelled the length of Simon's body, originating in his chest and moving through his torso, to end up in his fists. Here, he felt, was a chance for redemption, an opportunity to bolster his self-image and dispel the cowardice he'd experienced before. If he could get back his phone or his wallet, or at least scare the kid, then he could once again feel like a man. He realised how shallow the thought was, and how it diminished him in some way, yet the part of him that was always pushing overcame his doubts.

The boy turned right, into Grove Street West. Simon followed, keeping his distance but increasing his pace so he could see if the boy ducked into a ginnel or an alleyway. The boy continued along the street.

On either side of them, many of the properties were boarded up. The burnt-out shell of an old gymnasium – Simon remembered the newspaper report he'd been sent – cast a dark stain on the footpath.

Scooby stopped outside the burnt building, stuck his hand into the pocket of his tracksuit top and produced a key. Moving quickly, he unlocked the heavy-duty security door and began to enter the building.

Simon moved fast, without really giving much thought to what he was doing. He had no plan; he just sprinted across the road, knowing that the boy couldn't hear him through his headphones, and barrelled straight into Scooby's back, sending him sprawling inside. He slammed the door without looking back and went for the kid, kicking him in the side.

"Fuck!" Scooby's cries were too loud; he was compensating for still wearing the headphones.

Simon knelt down and grabbed the headphones, wrenching them off the kid's ears. The walls around him were scorched and blackened. To his left, half a staircase hung suspended in mid-air, the ends of the treads seared away. The place smelled of old flames.

"What the fuck?"

"You don't recognise me, do you?" Simon grabbed the kid's face with both hands, letting his fingers sink into his stubbly cheeks. "Where's my fucking wallet, you chav vermin?"

Realisation dawned; the kid's eyes took on a panicked look. His mouth started to work but he said nothing.

"My wallet. Now!"

Scooby shook his head. "That's gone, mate. We cleaned it out and stuck it in the post box in Near

Grove, by the community centre. You should get it back in a few weeks." There was a cocky little half-smile on his face.

Despite the situation, Simon did not feel as if the boy was afraid enough of him. Still, he wasn't threatening, the people he met did not respect his aggression.

"You little bastard." He pulled back his right fist and punched the kid in the face, just below his right eye.

Scooby cried out. He tried to fight back, but Simon held him down, shifting his body weight so that he was kneeling on Scooby's shoulders, pinning him down.

"Fear me," he said. "Be fucking afraid of me." He started punching again, and he did not stop until Scooby lay still, his eyelids flickering and his lips slack and bloodied.

Simon stood up and backed away, pressing his back against the wall. What the hell was he doing, beating the kid senseless? What had come over him to make him act this way? He rubbed his face with his hands, and then wiped them on his trousers. He glanced over at Scooby, sprawled on the dirty floor, his face damp with blood.

He looked at the palms of his hands, and then at his fists. His knuckles were red and angry. He rubbed them on his trousers.

Simon went to the door, opened it, and peeked outside. The street was empty. Nobody came along here unless they were up to no good – he suspected that Scooby had come inside the burnt-out gym to smoke some weed or perhaps even to make a drugs drop.

Shit, he thought. *That means someone else might be on their way here to pick up the merchandise.*

He returned to Scooby's body. The kid was stirring. He made moaning sounds as his legs twitched. Simon hadn't killed him; that was good news, at least.

He checked Scooby's pockets and found a large plastic baggy filled with white powder in the left hand pocket of his tracksuit bottoms. A drugs drop, then. He put the bag back in Scooby's pocket and returned to the door. He slipped outside, closing the door behind him, and then jogged to the end of the street, where he turned back towards the Arcade. Nobody paid any attention to him, despite the fact that his jacket was dusty from where he'd leaned against the wall. He hoped that there was no blood on his face, from when he'd touched it with his hands.

As he walked, heading towards the relative safety and security of the Grove Court flats, Simon felt better about himself than he had in quite some time. That exultant moment of opportunist violence, the way he'd handled the scruffy little upstart back at the ruined and abandoned gym, had served its purpose: right now, at least until the shame and the guilt kicked in, he felt like a man again.

CHAPTER TWENTY-THREE

It was already growing dark when Marty arrived at Doc's house. He couldn't believe it was summer; it was only seven o'clock. The darkness was creeping in early, as if trying to get a head start on the season and usher in the short days of autumn.

He looked up, at the churning sky, and realised that the light was being blocked by a dense layer of dark clouds. The day was still there; he just couldn't see it.

Marty had a few enemies in this part of Jesmond, mostly from the days when he'd worked regularly as a pub doorman, so he didn't come around here often. He'd learned long ago to walk away from possible friction; life was too short to risk making it shorter in a kerbside brawl. A younger Marty – maybe even the Marty from five or six years ago – would have laughed at that and called his older self a coward. But these days, he knew the score. He realised that his life had been lived far too long in the line of fire and sometimes it's better to dodge a bullet than to try and catch it in your teeth.

Doc's place was a three-storey Victorian terrace with a large garden and an outbuilding. There was a greenhouse tucked along by the fence. This had surprised Marty in the past; he hadn't figured Doc for a gardener. He'd been to the house on a couple of previous occasions, having various knocks and bumps treated, but had never before turned up on such short notice.

Nobody knew the old medic's real name. Or if they did, they hadn't bothered to remember it. He was simply Doc, and the old man never complained about it. According to local legend, he'd been a popular ringside doctor at pro bouts back in the day, but the drink and an ex-wife with expensive tastes had wrecked him, leaving him to scrape a living by less conventional means. Marty had once been told that Doc was struck off by the Medical Council, but nobody seemed to know why.

He knocked on the door and waited. A few seconds later a light went on in the hallway, shining through the decorative glass panels in the door. A small shape shuffled towards the other side of the door and opened it.

"Thanks for seeing me," said Marty.

"It's no bother," said Doc, turning to the side. "Please, come in. You know the way through, don't you?"

"Yes. I've been here before, remember?"

Doc nodded, but clearly had no idea. "Come on in, then, and let's take a look at that stab wound."

The house was filled with old things. Expensive things. The ex-wife must not have been fully successful in her endeavours to ruin the man, if he'd managed to hold on to this house and all the possessions crammed between its walls. There was clutter everywhere; the walls were covered with paintings (real paintings, not prints), and every piece of furniture – even those in the wide hallway – looked antique.

"Nice place," said Marty, walking through into the huge reception room.

"Thanks. I've lived here for a long time. It probably needs renovating, but I haven't the heart. I enjoy age; even in myself. I was never happy as a young man." He smiled.

There was a leather medical table with wooden drawers in the sides set up at one end of the room. Marty remembered it from his previous visits, and guessed that it was always set up for business, ready and waiting for paying customers. He knew that Doc had a little sideline tending the stab and bullet wounds of gang members and drug dealers, and was paid handsomely for his services. The wounds sustained in the kind of fights Marty took part in were probably light relief compared with that.

"Take off your shirt, Marty. Lie down over there, on the table." Doc was scrubbing his hands at the sink against the opposite wall. He did not look up, just stared closely at his hands as he slathered them in blue fluid beneath the hot tap.

Marty did as he was told. The pain had returned, and the dressing he'd applied to the wound was coming loose. He folded his shirt and set it down on a chair, and then climbed up onto the table. He lay flat on his back, with his arms crossed over his chest. It was a death pose, and it made him feel uncomfortable. He moved his arms to rest by his sides and stared at the ceiling, the sculpted plaster rose at its centre, and the bright light that hung from it.

"So what's the trouble?" Doc stood over him, his pale arms pink and hairless in the harsh light.

"Is it infected? That's what you suggested over the phone." He leant over Marty's torso. His breath smelled of whisky and ginger.

"God, man, how much gauze did you use?" He peeled back the dressing and cleaned out the wound. "What happened to the stitches? Have you been picking at these?"

"No... they just came out, on their own. Maybe I knocked it against something, I can't remember."

"You fucking guys... you're all the same. With your cheap gold rings and your tribal tattoos, thinking you're real tough guys. You can't hurry nature, son. Healing – every kind of healing – takes time and care. You can't hurry it along like a slut on a first date." His hands were soft and gentle, unlike when he'd worked at ringside. Here, on his own turf, the man became the skilled doctor he must once have been, before life broke him.

"Doc, this might sound a bit funny, but I need you to inspect inside the wound. I think I got something in there."

Doc stopped working. He straightened his back and stared at Marty's face. "Are you high, son?"

Marty shook his head. "No. I just have this... this *feeling*. It feels like there's something moving around in there, under my skin." He looked away, unable to meet the old man's gaze.

"Jesus Christ on a bike. You people... drugged up, fucked up, and walking around like you're masters of the universe. Don't you realise what kind of mess you're making of your life?" He shook his head, talking to himself now. "I don't know; some folk just never know when to quit the game."

Doc grabbed some stainless steel pincers and a scalpel off a tray and paused. "I'll try to make sure this doesn't hurt much, but I'm not making any promises."

"Okay. Just have a look... check around in there, would you?"

"Aye. Don't worry. If there's anything in there, I'll have it out in a minute." He bent back to his work, his eyes widening, his lips pressing together.

Doc was as good as his word. The examination did not hurt too much. Marty gritted his teeth a couple of times, but the mild pain was tolerable, much less than he'd expected.

"I'll put in a few more loose stitches," said Doc, when he'd finished. "There's fuck-all in there, son, so please leave it alone this time. If you have any discomfort, just give me another call. Don't start imagining symptoms – that's my job." He winked.

"Thanks," said Marty, closing his eyes.

When Doc had finished, Marty handed him an envelope of used bills. Doc didn't bother counting the money; he simply nodded, smiled, and walked Marty to the door.

"Remember," he said. "Just leave it alone... let it heal."

"I will," said Marty, but the door was already closing in his face.

He went back to his car and sat behind the wheel with the engine running. Aretha Franklin was singing on the radio. He listened until the song ended, and then switched it off. He drove away from the kerb, watching the street, wondering what was happening to him. None of this seemed real. It was like a dream he'd once had, when he was a much younger man. The acorn he'd imagined burrowing under his skin was a metaphor, but he did not have enough information to understand what it meant.

Back at the flat, he poured himself a whisky and took out his phone, ignoring the voicemail and text prompts. He dialled Erik Best's mobile number. The call went through to voicemail, as he'd expected. Erik screened all of his calls.

"Erik, it's me. Marty Rivers. I have something important I need to tell you. Call me back." He ended the call and drained his glass, then got up and poured a double. Then he sat back down and waited.

He grabbed the remote control and turned on the stereo. Muddy Waters sang about a Mannish Boy. Marty closed his eyes and enjoyed the music, letting it infect him with its melancholy. His mobile must have buzzed for thirty seconds before he realised he had a call.

"Hello. Erik?" He'd answered without looking at the display. He only hoped that it wasn't Melanie.

"What is it, Marty?"

No preamble: just get straight to the point. "I quit. No more fights for me. That last one... it wasn't right. The game's changed."

There was a pause during which Marty thought he might have said the wrong thing, or at least picked the wrong time to say it. Then Best began to speak. "I won't try to talk you out of it, Marty. Actually, I've been expecting this for a while. Just do me one favour, yeah?"

Marty swallowed a mouthful of whisky. "What's that?"

"Go away and have a proper think. Sleep on it; run everything though your mind. Then, in a few days, a week, if you still feel the same, we'll have this chat again. There'll be no hard feelings from me. If you really want to chuck in the towel, I'll respect your decision. I will call on you for other favours, though, just like before. Just a bit of heavy work here and there, or maybe the occasional stint on the doors. A man still needs to make a few dollars, mate, and I'll always need a battler like you on my team."

Marty relaxed. "That seems fair enough to me, Erik. I'll speak to you in a few days. But I doubt anything will change. I've made my decision."

"Okay, marra. Speak to you soon." The phone went dead.

Marty was about to hit the 'off' button on the handset when he remembered that he had a text message and a couple of voicemails. He'd ignored them before, assuming that it was Melanie, but this time he checked, just in case. Both messages were from the same person: Simon Ridley.

"Fuck me," he whispered, listening to them again. "Fuck me, Simon Ridley." The messages were short and to the point:

"*Listen Marty, this is Simon Ridley, from years ago. Please give me a call. I need to speak to you about something.*"

Later, "*It's me again, Simon. Call me. It's important; very important. Have you been having dreams? Dreams about a grove of trees and that time we spent in the Needle?*"

He opened the text message and it gave the same information in fewer words.

Marty stored the number and put down his phone. Then he picked it up again and switched it off. He did not want to speak to anyone else this evening. He needed to think.

He struggled to control his breathing.

His side ached. Something moved sluggishly beneath his skin. The world turned; the remains of the day moved briskly towards night; his life passed in a succession of moments, each a layer of his self being peeled away by the things that had happened to him.

CHAPTER TWENTY-FOUR

BRENDAN WAS NERVOUS. He was drinking too much, far too quickly, his clothes felt uncomfortable, and whenever he looked at the clock on the shelf, time seemed to have moved quicker than the laws of physics allowed.

Jane was in the kitchen, cooking the meal. He could tell that she was on edge, too, but she would not tell him why. He suspected it was simply the fact that she hadn't seen Simon since he'd left the Grove, but his habitual paranoia kept trying to make more out of the situation. Did she still harbour feelings for her ex-lover? Would she look at him in the same way that she used to look at Brendan, all those years ago when they first got together?

He finished his can, crushed it in his fist (an old habit, one he'd picked up from watching *Jaws* in his teens: Robert Shaw, Quint, the old sea dog). He bent down and grabbed the fresh can resting on the floor between his feet, popped it open, and took a mouthful of cold ale.

"What time is it?" Jane's voice carried through from the kitchen. The twins were banging on the floor upstairs, running around from room to room, playing catch, or indoor football, or simply running because they could.

"Seven-forty!" He took another swig of his beer and stood, moving across to the window. Typical Simon: late as always.

"Have you checked your phone? I'd hate to think that he might have called to cancel and we didn't get the message." Jane moved up to him from behind, slipping her arms around his waist. She kissed him on the side of the neck. Her breath was warm; her lips were wet from the wine she'd been drinking.

"He'll be here. He just likes to make an entrance." He stared out of the window, at the empty street. The sky was darkening, the clouds were low, and lights had already come on in some of his neighbours' front rooms. He'd never noticed before just how early they came on, and for some reason the thought unnerved him.

Jane rubbed his stomach with her hand. She pressed her lips against the back of his head. "Don't worry," she murmured. "He's probably more nervous than we are." Then she was away, back to the kitchen to keep an eye on the preparations. She'd kept the menu simple: a prawn cocktail starter, chicken and tomato with penne pasta for main, and a cheesecake bought from the bakers on the Arcade for dessert. Simon would probably think it was cheap, working class; no doubt he was used to eating out every night in classy London restaurants where they served small bowls of sorbet between courses.

Suddenly Brendan felt like a fool. Standing there in his cheap trousers and badly ironed shirt, he knew he was a fraud, a pretender. Why had he bothered to try and be something he was not? He should have sat around waiting in his work jeans and a T-shirt.

Simon-fucking-Ridley wasn't worth all this trouble. All they were doing was feeding his ego, making him think that he was something special.

He gulped from his can, trying to stem the sudden flow of hatred. He had no idea where it was coming from, and didn't see any reason why he should be thinking these things, or why Simon's imminent arrival should be affecting him in this way.

He turned away from the window and sat back down on the sofa, facing the television. The kids were still clattering about upstairs, causing a lot of sound and fury, and he expected Mrs. Broadly from next door to start banging on the wall. She hated children, and never missed an opportunity to complain.

There was a knock on the front door, followed by the chime of the doorbell. Simon was here. He had sneaked along the street, down the path, and onto the front step while Brendan had been occupied, lost in his own banal thoughts. He stood, straightened his shirt (hating himself for doing so), and went to answer the door.

"Brendan!" Jane's voice, loud and slightly panicked.

"Aye... I've got it. It's him."

He could see Simon's outline through the textured glass panel in the door, a slim, elegant shape. He waited motionlessly, as if he were a statue and not a real person.

Brendan paused for a moment, waited for a lull in the commotion on the first floor, and then opened the door.

The man on the doorstep was Simon, as expected, but he looked different... somehow *less* than he had done before. The bruising on his face had already faded, but his skin looked discoloured, slightly jaundiced. He seemed thinner than earlier that day, his garments less fitted, and when he smiled it didn't quite reach his eyes.

"Are you okay?" He stepped back and opened the door fully, making room for Simon to enter.

"Yeah. Yes, I'm fine. Just feeling a bit tired, that's all." Simon held out a bottle of red and a bottle of white, one in each hand. "I didn't know what we were having, so I brought both." He smiled again, and this time it was better, healthier... but still there was something missing. "Anyway, I'm here. Thanks for the invite." He stepped slowly across the threshold.

"Thanks for coming. You know the way through, yeah? I'll just grab you a beer from the kitchen." Brendan shut the door behind his guest and watched him walk along the hallway and enter the living room. He went to the kitchen and opened the fridge, taking out two cold beers.

"This won't be long," said Jane. Her cheeks were flushed. The kitchen was warm. "I'll go and get the twins down and we can all say our hellos." She reached out as he straightened from the fridge, her hand lightly brushing the collar of his shirt. "Nice shirt. Didn't I buy you that?" She winked. He smiled. It was a rare moment of solidarity, one that felt like it lay outside of their roles as parents, even as husband and wife. In that moment they were friends, and they were allies.

Brendan took the beers back into the living room. Simon was sitting on the sofa, perched on the edge of the seat and watching the television. His eyes were small and hard; his face was tense.

"There you go." Brendan handed him a can. "Get that down you, bruiser."

Simon opened the can, smiled weakly, and took a long swallow. "Why is it that beer always makes things better? They should give it out on the NHS."

"Let's turn this shit over. I'll put some music on." Brendan picked up the remote control and switched the channel. One of the music channels was playing big-hair rock anthems from the 1980s. "That's better... might cheer us up."

Sounds of movement came from upstairs. Jane was herding the kids, trying to get them under control. He could hear her raised voice, the twins giggling, and then Jane joining in the laughter. He loved his family. They were all he had. Everything he needed.

Footsteps across the ceiling, then down the stairs.

"Here they come," he said, turning towards the door.

Jane walked in first. She looked gorgeous. Her hair was in disarray, but slight dishevelment had always looked good on her. Brendan turned to face Simon, and saw him staring at Jane, too, his eyes wide, his face twitching into a smile.

Brendan turned back to his wife, clenching the beer can in his fist. He didn't understand why he felt so anxious.

"Hello, Simon Ridley." Jane seemed to float into the room. With both men's eyes upon her, she became more graceful than ever. "Long time no see." The twins entered behind her, silent for once.

Simon stood and walked to the middle of the room, where he halted, as if he didn't know what to do. He stuck out a hand. Jane laughed, took the hand, and shook it, then she bent towards him and kissed him on both of his cheeks, left, then right: celebrity style.

"This," she said, turning to address the twins, "is Simon. Say hello, kids. Simon, this is Harry and Isobel. Our children." She was beaming; that was the only word Brendan could think of to describe the way she looked. At first he suspected that she might be trying to flirt with her old flame, but then it hit him. She was proud. She was glowing with pride, showing off her husband and her children. Her family. She was telling Simon, without words, how good things were for her now, and that she hadn't missed him one bit, not one tiny bit since he went away.

The kids started to laugh, now at ease. They went to Simon and started babbling information: telling him about school, about their bikes, their friends and teachers. Simon started to relax. Brendan wasn't sure why his old friend had been so tense when he first walked through the door, but all that was gone now. He became the perfect guest: interesting, interested, charming, and funny.

Brendan felt himself relax, too. He'd been worrying for nothing. Simon wasn't a threat; he never had been. If anything, it had always been him, Brendan, who was the real threat. Hadn't he taken Simon's girlfriend off him all those years ago, and given her everything she needed?

For the first time in his life, he felt equal to Simon-fucking-Ridley. And in doing so, he opened a door inside himself that allowed all the old, suppressed feelings of friendship to emerge, returning to the light. This wasn't so bad; he could even get used to it. Maybe he and Simon could be buddies again, after all, and once they managed to speak to Marty it might even be possible for the Three Amigos to mount up and make a triumphant return. Perhaps Simon was right after all, and they could band together to slay the monsters of their youth.

Simon played cards at the dining table with the twins while Brendan helped Jane in the kitchen. He was spooning the prawns and Marie Rose sauce into wine glasses crammed with lettuce leaves while she took their best china dinner set from the display cupboard and wiped it down with a tea towel.

"See," she said. "It's going okay, isn't it?"

Brendan smiled. "Yeah, I suppose it is. The kids seem to like him."

"I'll just put them to bed, so we can eat in peace."

Brendan nodded. "Yeah, okay. I'll get me and Simon some more beers. Wine?"

"Hell, yes," she said as she walked out through the door and into the hall.

Brendan heard Jane say something to the kids – probably telling them to say good night to the visitor – and then the three of them trooped upstairs, making as much racket as humanly possible. He pulled two fresh beers out of the fridge, tore off the ring-pulls and then took them through into the living room.

Simon looked much more relaxed. He was crouching on the floor, picking up pieces of Lego and smiling. "They're great kids, mate," he said, raising a hand and pointing in the direction of the door. "*Really* great kids..."

"Thanks." Brendan dropped into a crouch and helped him tidy up the toys. Then, when they were all neatly put back in their box, the two men started on the fresh beers. "I suppose you'd say they're the centre of my life, those two. I can't imagine not having them."

"Cheers to that," said Simon, lifting his can and taking a long hit of the beer.

The two men moved over to the dining table. It was already set with cutlery, and a candle – as yet unlit – placed as a centrepiece. "Do you have a lighter?" Simon took hold of the candle and teased the wick between his finger and thumb so that it stood upright.

"Here," said Brendan, handing over a box of kitchen matches.

Simon struck a match and lit the candle. Neither of the men spoke, and the act seemed to take on a kind of symbolic significance. Simon held the candle aloft; the light from the flame caressed the contours of his face. He smiled – at nothing, at everything – and then he placed the candle back on the table.

"Should we, like, say a little prayer?" Brendan put down his can and belched.

They laughed.

"Okay," said Jane, from the doorway. "What did I miss?"

"Nothing," said Simon, shaking his head.

"Nowt much," agreed Brendan.

"Hmm. Well, is someone going to give me a hand setting out the food?"

"Aren't I supposed to be the guest?" Simon winked, took a long swallow of his beer, and let out a loud "Aah..."

"Twat," said Brendan, standing and following Jane into the kitchen.

They ate the starter in a comfortable silence. Brendan

opened the white wine Simon had brought, and it was finished before the main course. "I'll get another from the fridge," said Brendan, standing.

While Brendan was in the kitchen he heard Simon and Jane talking in low voices, but this time he didn't feel threatened by them. The beer and the wine, the food, the fact that they had all relaxed in each other's company, had quietened his paranoia. Even his back felt soothed, as if the calm had extended to envelope his body.

After the main course, Jane cleared the table and then popped her head back into the room. "I'll just be a minute. There's something I want Simon to see."

Simon glanced at Brendan and raised his eyebrows. Brendan shrugged. "You've got me, mate. She didn't mention anything earlier."

Jane returned in less than a minute, carrying a large cardboard box from Argos. Brendan recognised it as the packaging from a DVD player they'd bought the kids a few Christmases ago.

Jane set down the box at the centre of the table, pushing away the coasters and the placemats and moving her glass so that she didn't spill her wine.

"Okay," she said, glancing at the two men, one by one: first Brendan, then Simon. "This is going to seem weird, but bear with me. Okay, Brendan?" Her eyes flicked to her husband. Brendan felt the skin of his shoulders tighten, the rash flaring as if in warning. But he said nothing; he just nodded and took a mouthful of wine.

Jane closed her eyes for a few seconds, and then opened them again. She lifted the flaps on the box and took out two black box files. "This," she said, "is sort of a collection." She opened the top box file and took out an old newspaper, folded over to a report about strange birds seen gathered about the tip of the Needle. It was a recent edition; the incident had occurred only a few weeks ago. "It's an unofficial history of the Concrete Grove. For years now, I've been keeping anything that you might describe as odd or offbeat – news clippings, photographs, even a few hand-written stories people have told me about events they found hard to explain."

"What is this, Jane?" Brendan went to stand, but she put out her hand to stop him. "Jane?"

"I'm sorry. I know I should've told you about this, but once I'd started keeping it a secret, it was easier to keep on going. I'm not even sure why I started collecting this stuff in the first place – initially, I think it was a way of keeping Simon in the loop, or maybe making sure he never forgot us." She glanced at Simon.

Brendan looked at him too, across the table.

"So it was you? It was you all along?"

Jane nodded.

Brendan felt the anger surging through him. He didn't understand what was happening, but it seemed that his wife and her old boyfriend had secrets between them after all. He'd been right to be paranoid. It was true, all of it. They'd been running around behind his back... Somehow, they'd managed to keep some kind of long distance affair going without him noticing.

"Brendan... Look at me, Brendan."

He turned to face his wife. She was shaking her head.

"What is this?" His voice sounded whiny; thin and reedy and childlike.

"Ever since Simon left, I've been sending him reminders of what he left behind. Reminders of you, and the hell he left you to carry on your own. That's how it started, I suppose: as a form of revenge. I might as well admit that now. Then, as time passed, it turned into a habit. I just kept sending them. Whenever he moved, I did a little research and located a new address. I wasn't even sure if they were correct, those addresses – not until now, anyway."

"Oh, yes." Simon exhaled a long breath. "Yes, I've been getting this stuff for years. Emails, too."

"Emails?" Brendan leaned back in his chair, pushing it away from the table. He felt a little better about the situation, yet still he knew that somehow he had been betrayed. He just could not figure out how, or why.

"The emails were a lot easier," said Jane. "Google is your friend." She smiled, nervously. "I'm just glad you never replied."

"Shit, mate, remember I told you about this? I thought it was Marty, sending me all that stuff. But it was Jane." He turned to face her. "It was you!"

"Should I be angry about this?" Brendan grabbed his wine glass and gripped the stem. "I mean, you've been keeping secrets from me. Both of you."

"No," said Jane, walking around the table and sitting on his knee. She stroked his face with the palm of her hand. She tilted her head close to his. "Just me: me and nobody else. And I'm sorry. I don't know why I didn't tell you. I think at the start it was because I didn't want to upset you. Remember, it took you a long time before you could actually talk about your feelings, how you felt deserted by your old friends." She kissed the side of his face. "I would never do anything to hurt you." Her smile was warm; her words were like fire.

"I know," he said. "I know you wouldn't, but this feels strange. As if I should feel hurt." He kissed the tip of her nose.

"Okay," said Simon, pouring more wine. "So you're not going to punch me?"

"I should. But I won't." Brendan picked up Jane's glass and handed it to her.

"Let's call this a clean slate," said Jane, standing. "No more secrets. You two need to work together to get Marty involved in all this, and then the three of you need to sit down and talk – *really* talk, about everything. All of it."

"Yes," said Simon, raising his glass.

"Aye," said Brendan, mimicking the gesture.

"And I'll stop interfering. I shouldn't have done that." Jane lifted her own glass high into the air.

"It worked, though," said Simon. "I could never forget. The Grove was always in my mind. No matter how hard I tried, I could never get this place, or all of you, out of my mind." He paused, nodded. "Hell, yes, it worked."

"Daddy..."

They all looked over towards the door. Isobel was standing in the open doorway, in her white nightdress. Her face was damp with tears. "Daddy... something's wrong, Daddy."

Brendan got to his feet and ran across the room, scooping her up in his arms. She was cold. Her body was shaking. "What is it, baby? What's wrong? Are you poorly?"

The little girl shook her head. Her blonde hair was

moist. "It's Harry. There's something wrong with Harry. He's being sick."

He handed Isobel to Jane and headed for the stairs, taking them two at a time. When he reached the first floor, he moved quickly to the kids' room. He pushed open the door and saw Harry kneeling on the floor at the end of the bed, his arms ramrod straight, his shoulders hunched. He was retching, dry-heaving, his little body jerking and spasming as his stomach muscles worked overtime.

"Oh, God... Harry. What is it, son?"

"Daddy!" Harry screamed the word and then went into another convulsion. There was dull yellow vomit on the floor, inches from his face. He turned his head to the side, and in that moment Brendan saw that his son's throat was swollen. His neck was actually bulging, already twice its normal size; his cheeks were puffed out, as if they were filled with hot air. He tried to speak again, but his voice could no longer get past the constriction.

"Harry!" He went down on his knees and grabbed the boy's shoulders. Harry's skin was hot and his pyjamas were soaking wet. "Oh, God..."

"What is it?" Jane was behind him, standing in the doorway. He looked back and saw Simon there, too, holding Isobel's hand. His daughter's face was pale, almost white. She looked like a ghost.

"Harry!" He turned back to his boy just in time to witness another convulsion, and this time Harry was bringing something up, a small, lumpen mass that Brendan could make out rising in his throat. The boy's neck fluttered; his eyes rolled back in his head, and his mouth opened, opened...

The soggy object was forced out between his wet lips, and dropped onto the floor, right into the pile of fresh vomit. Harry slumped sideways, possibly in a faint. The small lump began to twitch. Brendan thought it was a giant moth, ready to break out of its sticky pupa.

Nobody moved. For a moment – and that was all it took – none of the three adults could even speak. They all remained locked into position, bound by their fears.

The object rolled on the floor, and then it began to transform. Tiny wings twitched outwards, unfolding from the body, and a tiny head emerged from beneath one of them. The thing made no sound; it just started flapping its wings, slowly at first, and then fast, faster, until they were nothing but a blur of motion. And the hummingbird floated up from the floor, soundless and graceful and totally out of place, an alien object in Harry and Isobel's bedroom.

Brendan turned his head to follow the bird's progress, and watched as it flew past Simon and Jane – both of them stepping back from the doorway to allow it out of the room – and into the rest of the house. The sight of the thing triggered a chain of detonations, submerged memories exploding at random inside Brendan's head, but they went up in smoke before he could grab them.

Then, snapping back into the moment, he bent down and cradled Harry in his arms, moaning and stroking the boy's sweat-damp head. "Call an ambulance," he said. "Do it, quickly."

Outside the bedroom, on the cramped landing, Isobel began to weep.

CHAPTER TWENTY-FIVE

SIMON SAT DOWN on the bed and tried to make sense of everything that had taken place this evening. He was tired and his head throbbed, yet he still felt drunk. Things were changing so fast. Everything was fluid; he could not lock his thoughts in place, not even long enough to examine what they meant.

When he'd first arrived at the Cole house, things had been tense. He had been unable to settle down after the violence he'd perpetrated upon the kid in the burnt-out building, and it seemed to him that Brendan had something of an attitude – which was understandable, really, the way that Simon had been pushing the man.

Jane's presence, however, had made all the difference: she had calmed the situation simply by being there, and they had all slowly relaxed into an almost pleasant groove. When she had made her revelation regarding all the stuff she'd sent him over the years, things had threatened to become tense all over again, but she'd handled it beautifully.

He still couldn't understand why she'd been sending him those updates – not fully. Yes, it was a way of anchoring him to the Grove, of forcing him to remember – or, rather, not to forget – that he'd left the other two Amigos behind to live with the mess they'd all made, but somehow he felt that there was something more to it. She did not know what had happened when the boys were ten years old; nobody did, not even the boys themselves. So why would she put her marriage at risk to keep her claws in his life?

It was all too complex, an emotional assault course that he was nowhere near fit to complete. He was out of shape; his stamina was gone. The truth was, he had not been in good enough shape for this kind of onslaught for years.

He lay back and kicked off his shoes, wriggling on the sheets until he found a comfortable position. Outside, a dog barked, children laughed, a distant siren made a tune to which the city danced. The darkness behind his eyelids writhed.

Jane. He could see her now, emerging from that darkness.

He would be lying to himself if he thought that he did not still find her attractive. Her youth had faded, there were lines and blemishes where once her skin had been smooth and flawless, but still there was something about the woman that drew him, sent his blood pumping too quickly around his body. There was a homely quality to her beauty that intrigued him. Natasha didn't have that. She was too perfect, too model-like: zero body fat; a flat chest; porcelain skin; a way of carrying herself that suggested she was always aware of people watching her. Whereas Jane moved naturally, with an almost slovenly gait. She didn't give a damn who was watching, or if nobody was. She was her own woman; nobody could own or rent her image. She was real. She was a beating pulse under the skin of life.

When he'd first seen her this evening, his initial reaction had been base: he wanted to fuck her. He felt ashamed of himself for having these thoughts, but that didn't negate them. Jane was his one regret: back in the day, they'd never made it past the heavy petting stage – a feel of her tit through her lacy bra cup, a hand on her warm, moist pudenda, but only over the top of her knickers. Once she had grabbed his crotch when they were kissing in the back of somebody's car. He remembered it now; he had been breathless, his chest hitching and his legs shaking. She had never done it again.

He wondered how often she and Brendan made love. He tried to imagine what her body looked like beneath the baggy, unflattering clothes she wore. Was it full, voluptuous, like a real woman, rather than thin and scrawny, with the bones jutting through her paper-thin flesh, like Natasha?

He realised that he was rubbing his cock. He was hard as steel.

He stopped and turned onto his side, feeling obscurely guilty, like a schoolboy fantasising about his best friend's mother.

She had kids. *They* had kids – Brendan and Jane. They were a family, a solid unit; he could not come between them, even if he tried. It was all just make-believe, another way of trying to hold on to a past that he had never really owned in the first place. Of trying to identify what was missing, what had been taken from him when he was ten years old and the world had seemed so large and filled with promise.

Kids...

What on earth was going on with those two kids?

The ambulance had arrived in five minutes, and two paramedics had inspected Harry's throat for blockages, massaged his tiny chest, and pushed an oxygen mask over his face. By that time, the worst of it was over. The hummingbird – had it really been a hummingbird? – had flown, and the boy was breathing easier, but they had not taken any chances. Jane had gone with them in the ambulance and Simon had called a taxi for Brendan, insisting that he pay the fare when it arrived.

It had all happened so quickly; the whole scene had played out faster than he could recall. He barely even had time to register how he felt, what it all might mean in terms of the reasons for him being in the area. It was all linked – he knew that, could not deny it – but he didn't understand how, or why. The dots were there, all over the page, but he was unable to connect them.

A hummingbird...

Small, silent, and forcing its way out of the boy's throat, being born into the world.

A hummingbird...

Just like the ones he could remember from the Needle, when he and his friends had been imprisoned there. With his eyes closed, he could remember the sound of their wings beating: a hushed whisper in the darkness. He could see the colours of their feathers, the multi-hued blurs they had become as they darted across the room, emerging from conical nests high up in the branches of the old trees.

There had been a forest in there: inside the Needle. There was a forest indoors, but he could not imagine how that might be true. It was impossible, a child's daydream. Trees growing indoors; one world enveloped by another; wheels within wheels; stories within stories. A fairytale...

Other, darker memories remained out of reach, backing off from him, not allowing him access to the secrets they might reveal. All he had, all that he could recall, were the trees and the hummingbirds... and the girl. The girl called Hailey: the same girl from the newspaper report, the girl who had gone missing last year on the estate, along with her mother. The girl with the hummingbird wings.

But how could they be the same person? How could that girl – the one who had lived on the Grove so recently – be the same as the winged phantom he had seen inside the Needle twenty years ago? It made no sense. They must be two different people. Perhaps they were related.

Surely that was it. Mother and daughter, or aunt and niece, perhaps they were even grandmother and granddaughter. But then, it seemed, time was somehow elastic inside the Needle; it looped back on itself, creating cracks and fissures where bad things might scuttle through. Perhaps their childhood selves were still in there now, going through the same nightmare he'd already experienced twenty years before...

Sleep stole over him, moving across his body and carrying him away. When he opened his eyes he was in another place, yet he knew that he was still somewhere in the Concrete Grove, lost in a fold in the fabric of the place, paused at a point where all things converged and time lost all meaning.

Time lost all meaning...

The low, fat clouds were dark brown, the colour of old bloodstains, and the sky beyond them was black. There were graduations in the blackness, but he could see no stars: just an endlessly folding darkness, an overpowering sense of nothingness.

The Grove was a wasteland: buildings had fallen, roads were shattered, chunks of tarmac lay strewn across the dirt, and broken paving stones littered the scene like the forgotten building blocks in a child's game. Something had happened here – something devastating. An apocalypse had taken place, and as far as Simon could see, there were no survivors. The houses had all been flattened, taken apart, and the burnt-out shells of vehicles resembled the abandoned carapaces of giant dead beetles.

Up ahead, the Needle was in ruins. It had fallen like some mighty citadel, an ancient fortress from a storybook battle. The concrete looked like old stone, and had taken on less modern forms. Like ruined castle ramparts, the concrete walls and lobbies had been destroyed and reshaped.

Upon a pile of rubble he saw a familiar giant figure. The Angel of the North sat like a chastised schoolboy, its legs drawn up against its chest, its arms down by its sides and its hands resting on the concrete block upon which it was perched. There were manacles at its wrists; it had been bound and left to die.

Simon walked closer, drawn to this curious sight. He was afraid, but his curiosity compelled him to get a closer look, now that he was certain the creature could not harm him.

The Angel's head was bowed, the cold steel face hidden between its knees. The mighty wings were folded back; rust had broken away from the lattice framework, settling like strange dandruff onto its broad shoulders.

A woman sat at the Angel's side. She was tall, a giant, but not quite as large as the Angel. She was naked, and across her thighs were draped the bodies of two children, a boy and a girl.

As Simon drew closer to the group, he saw that the dead children were twins: they had the same dark curly hair, pale flesh, and each had a trio of acorns tattooed across his or her narrow back. The boy lay looking up into the woman's face, staring into her eyes. The girl was draped face-down across the woman's legs, her buttocks sallow and flaccid.

"What is this?" Simon's voice sounded strange. The intonation was flat; the words bounced back at him, as if he was bounded by thick walls. "What does it mean?"

The woman turned slowly to face him. Her hair was long and dark. Her breasts were saggy, empty bags laid across her ribcage. Her nipples had been removed. There was no blood, just flat, cauterised flesh. Her body was young, but it was battered, and her face was so very old. She mouthed words to Simon, but he could not hear. He stood and watched the silent mummer's performance, wishing that he could help, that he could take on at least a fraction of the woman's burden. If he could help her, he thought, then might not he also be able to help himself? It was an odd thought, based on nothing but intuition, but it felt like the truth.

The woman was crying soundlessly. Tears of blood ran down her lined, wrinkled face. She did not wipe them away. She just clutched her children, her poor dead children, and tried to convey a message he would never understand, no matter how long he remained here.

The Angel did not move.

The Angel was broken.

Simon looked to his right, his gaze drawn by a subtle movement, a flicker at the edge of his vision. The dark earth began to rise and fall, and then to churn. Like the woman's weeping, the motion was soundless. He watched as the ground shuddered and was torn apart, and something broke the surface. What rolled into view was not unlike the back of a whale, or perhaps the flank of an elephant wallowing in cool mud, and it appeared only for a moment. Then, his mind clear at last, Simon thought it had resembled more the segmented flank of a giant maggot burrowing through the topsoil. Now that the shape was gone, he had the impression of boils and tumours on its hide, splits and cuts in the thick flesh which had oozed yellow fluids...

He turned again to the woman, the bereft woman and her dead twins.

She was mouthing a word – the same word, over and over again. Simon glanced back over to where the earth had been disturbed, but this time there was nothing to be seen. He looked back at the woman. She was still mouthing the word.

He stepped forward, approaching her. Her eyes were white, with no pupils, and her lips were thin, like blades. Silently, she repeated the same word, again and again and again... the same single word.

Doors swung open inside Simon's memory, and a wind gusted through the empty halls of his mind. It was coming; something was on its way now. So he waited. Bracing himself against this alien earth, watching a giant woman as she repeated a silent warning, and wishing that the Angel would move, just an inch, he waited for whatever was coming.

Underthing.

He heard the word as if it had been spoken, but not by the woman. By someone else, twenty years ago... a girl, a young girl called Hailey.

Underthing.

This was the thing that had taken him, taken them all, the foul creature that had stolen their youth, tainted their future, and torn apart the foundations of their friendship. This was what had called him back to the estate, and finally, after all these years, he recognised the monster they had followed into the Needle, the beast with no name, just a description:

The Underthing.

Simon knew that this was a dream, but if he allowed it to happen, and the events whose aftermath he could see took place, nothing would ever be the same again.

The doors in his mind stayed open, and his worst fears came lumbering through, wearing so many masks that he could not help but realise they were still hiding, still concealing themselves. One mask at a time, piece by piece, Simon began to discover what had been hiding in his darkness.

TWENTY YEARS AGO, WHEN THE DAMAGE WAS DONE

THEY ARE WAITING on the platform, huddled beneath an old tarpaulin they discovered folded under some bushes not far from the old Beacon Hill railway platform. The sheet smells of piss and alcohol; when they found it, Marty said it must have been used as a tramp's bedding. They all laughed at that, but still they hauled the sheet back to their base camp to use as a cover.

The night is clear. Thin clouds are just about visible, high up in the seamless black of the sky. The moon is somewhere between half and full, and it shines down like a spotlight upon the area where the boys have made their den.

Night birds sing in the dense undergrowth, or hop between tree branches. When they close their eyes and keep quiet, not making a sound apart from their breathing, the boys can almost fool themselves that they are not on the outskirts of a grey conurbation, but somewhere out in the countryside. For a moment, anyway, before the sounds of distant engines and alarms intrude upon their reverie and spoil the lie. Then reality comes flooding back, and something inside them dies.

"Can you hear something?" Brendan's voice is low, timid. He does not move.

"Like what?" Even Marty sounds cautious. "I didn't hear a thing."

"Shush..." Simon pulls the tarpaulin down and peers over its edge, scanning the ground below the tree.

Something rustles in the bushes to the right of their position, making them shake. Then, softly, a low clicking sound begins to build, rising gradually from near silence to a soft, low, ratcheting noise.

"What is it?" Brendan tenses beneath the sheet; they all feel it, the fear that has crept up on them, taking them by surprise. Like the arms of a drunken parent, it clumsily envelopes them, making them feel unsafe.

"I dunno. Sounds like a rattlesnake." Simon moves slowly across the platform, towards the edge of the plywood base. He lies down on his belly and gently pulls himself towards the platform's roughened lip, staring down at the ground. Low branches shudder; the sound builds, dies down, and then builds again.

"Captain Clickety," says Brendan, his voice now not much above a whisper.

"What's that?" Marty shifts, making the platform creak.

"I dunno. It's just a name... something from an old nursery rhyme or summat. I remember it from infant school. I think it's something we used to sing in class. That's who I saw earlier: Captain Clickety."

The movement down below ceases but the sound continues, as if once begun it might never stop.

Then, softly and in a childish sing-song voice, Brendan begins to chant:

"*Captain Clickety*
He's coming your way
Captain Clickety
He'll make you pay
Once in the morning
Twice in the night
Three times Clickety
Will give you a fright"

Simon glances over at his friends. "Shut up," he says. "Just shut up. That's creepy." He feels his eyes blinking rapidly, and doesn't seem able to stop them.

Brendan smiles, but there is no humour in the expression. As young as he is, Simon realises that the smile is one of desperation. What he doesn't know is what to do about it, how to put things right and make the world feel safe again. Perhaps when he is older he can be that kind of hero, but now all he can do is endure the confusion.

"There's somebody down there." Simon hears his voice before he even knows what he is going to say. "Right under us. Hiding in the trees. I don't think he knows we're up here."

The platform creaks again.

"Don't move," says Simon. "He's there." He doesn't understand how he knows the presence is male, but that's how it feels: like there's a man down there, peering up at them from the shadows.

There is nobody there, beneath the platform on which they are huddled, but for some reason he feels the need to push his friends, to coerce them into action in the only way he knows how. On the surface, he believes that he is trying to allay their fears by confirming them – by giving the boys something they can turn their attention towards, they might stop being so afraid of the things that don't matter. But under this, where the part of himself he can never understand holds sway, he realises that he is simply pushing for pushing's sake. He has always done this, ever since he was an infant: at nursery, at school, at home. It was the only way for him to get noticed, to command attention. Otherwise, he would have blended into the background, becoming unimportant.

So he pushes, just like he has always pushed.

The lies trip from his tongue.

"He's moving away now... he's in the trees and he's moving. It's some guy in a funny costume. I think it's the same guy Brendan saw earlier: the one in the bird mask with the walking stick, the weirdo. That one. The creepy one. Captain Clickety."

He watches the unmoving bushes, the unambiguous trunks and boughs of the trees, the dancing shadows as they skim across the ground – and that's all they are, trees and bushes and shadows. It feels good to push, but he knows that it shouldn't. He knows it should feel bad.

He knows that he should be terrified. But he isn't; he's excited.

"Let's follow him," he says, clamping down on the smile before turning again to face his friends. "Let's spy on him. He might be a robber. We could find his treasure. Like Tom Sawyer, in the caves. Remember?"

Marty says nothing, he just stares out into the darkness, his face thin and pale and unreadable.

Brendan shakes his head, but Simon knows that he can change his mind. All it will take is the right kind of pushing, the application of pressure from a certain angle. That's all it ever takes, with anyone, and Simon has the gift of finding those angles, picking them out and exploiting them for his own purposes.

"Come on," says Simon, goading the others. Then, smiling, he says the magical words that are guaranteed to get a response, asks the question that can be answered in only one way by a couple of ten-year-old boys:

"What, are you too scared to come with me?"

It doesn't take long for them to climb down out of the tree, leaving the half-built den behind, the loose tarpaulin fluttering gently in a slight night-time breeze.

Each boy's actions confirm the actions of the other two: they are a team, a unit, acting as one entity, each permitting the others to behave in a certain way. They walk slowly through the trees and head towards the lonely lane of Beacon Grove Rise. Right will take them to the derelict railway platform, where older kids go to take drugs, drink beer, and muck about. They turn left towards the centre of the Grove, and eventually the Needle.

A tall figure moves up ahead, heading towards the cut-through formed by Grove Nook. Simon glimpses it for but a moment, and it might just be shadow play, but he convinces the others that it is the one they need to follow – the creature that will now forever be known as Captain Clickety, just like the character in that creepy old rhyme. A shape without an identity, a fear with no real purpose... a nameless, faceless entity that will haunt them all until the day they die.

"It's him, isn't it?" Brendan's question hangs in the air; neither of the other boys even needs to provide an answer.

"Come on," says Marty, assuming the dominant role in the group. Simon has sown the seeds; the others are simply falling into their natural grooves, taking up their allotted positions in the simple structure of the small gang.

They walk along the street in single file, turning left as they reach Grove Terrace. There are no cars on the road at this hour. The house lights closest to the boys are all turned off, the windows dark. Even the usual urban sounds seem to have been suspended for a little while – no barking dogs, no distant alarms or revving engines. A pocket of stillness exists in the night, and they have entered, crossing its borders to stand at the edge of a new place.

The boys cross the road, walk along Grove Street and step onto the Roundpath, the narrow walk-around circling the Needle. The large building hovers above them, as if cast adrift from its concrete foundations. It seems to totter and sway, and as they approach the place they feel a sense of dislocation, as if they have ruptured something, broken through an invisible wall. The upright tower of the Needle straightens like a snake discovering it has a backbone after all, and the few unbroken windows on the upper floors seem to collect all the available light in the area, transforming into small, bright screens.

Simon looks up, at those grim windows, and upon them he sees played out, like a movie, scenes from his own life: his mother and father shouting, his much younger self hiding in the bedroom wardrobe and weeping, an endless queue of wine bottles lined up along the skirting board in his parents' room... all the hurt and the frustration, the pointlessness of his existence is summed up in those scant few images, and he knows that he is not going to turn away. He is going to enter the building and find out what has gone inside there before him, and perhaps even discover something miraculous within its walls.

For a long time, Simon felt like he was nothing, just a speck. His parents did not love him; his teachers thought he was a waste of space. Then he found that he could manipulate those people into noticing him, and he focused his energy on making that happen.

But this is something different. The situation in which he finds himself, poised at the edge of revelation, makes him feel that the world is ready to notice – not just his family and friends, not even all the other people who live on the estate. The world. The planet. The very earth itself might look at him as he strides across its surface, making footprints in the muck and the filth and the squalor.

This might just be his chance to be somebody.

"I'm going in there," he says, moving forward, his body moving with a sense of great ease, even of inevitability. "I'm going to see what's happening." He feels no fear, only a sense of what he will years later recognise as longing. For his entire young life, Simon has only ever been shown the banal, the prosaic, but here is something that could elevate his experience. Here is evidence of the sublime.

"Me, too," whispers Marty, gripped by the same spell, the same dark magic.

"Wait for me," says Brendan, as he catches up with the other two boys. "I'm coming, too." But the he does not sound as convinced as his friends.

The tower does not move an inch.

The earth beneath their feet is stiff and unyielding.

The night closes like a fist around them.

PART FOUR

THE THREE AMIGOS RIDE AGAIN

"It's not what I expected."

– Simon Ridley

CHAPTER TWENTY-SIX

SIMON AND BRENDAN stood outside the low-rise apartment complex in Gateshead, in view of the Baltic Flour Mill and not too far from the banks of the River Tyne. They could hear traffic in the distance, and somewhere nearby loud music was playing – in a public park or a local beer garden – and it drifted on the still air, bringing with it a sense of subdued frivolity.

"Jesus," said Simon. "It hasn't half changed round here."

Brendan nodded, but he did not speak. He looked exhausted. Simon reached out and touched his arm, rubbing the sleeve of his jacket like a concerned mother. "We don't have to do this now, mate. You can go home, be with your family."

Brendan turned to face him. "No," he said, smiling lightly. "It's fine. Let's do this. There's nothing to be gained from my going back. I told you, the kids are fine. Harry's home and Jane's coping. I'd only make things more stressful if I was hanging around at the house."

Simon squeezed Brendan's arm. His friend had been through a lot the previous night – Harry throwing up, and what could only have been a small bird erupting from his throat. Then the boy going into some kind of convulsive fit. The ambulance.

The hospital. That was a lot to deal with, for anyone... especially a neurotic night owl with serious attachment issues.

Simon's new mobile phone was yet to turn up from the distributor, although his new credit and debit cards had arrived by courier that morning, at the break of dawn. So when he'd got out of bed Simon had called the Coles from the payphone on the corner (which was miraculously still working) to find out how the kid was doing, and Jane had told him that Harry had finally been sent home to rest about an hour ago, feeling restless but more or less comfortable. They'd taken samples of his blood, done some tests, and little Harry had sat up in the hospital bed smiling and chatting and asking for food. He didn't seem to realise what was going on, and had no memory of what had happened back at home the night before.

The doctors had taken plenty of time to convince themselves that Harry was in good health, apart from a sore throat and a minor headache, and then told the family that he could be taken home. He was prescribed infant aspirin for his aches and pains, a week off school to recuperate, and plenty of pampering from his parents.

"Come on, then," he said, turning to face the apartment block. "Let's get up there and see if he's at home."

The two men walked along the path at the side of the residents' car park, looking at the expensive vehicles lined up in their private spaces: Jeeps and Land Rovers, sports models and coupés. There was a lot of money in those white-painted parking spaces.

"Looks like Marty's landed on his feet." Brendan seemed calmer now, more focused, if exhausted. "I always knew he would, eventually."

"He's only flat-sitting. It isn't his. None of this belongs to him." Simon felt a pang of envy, or perhaps it was more like bitterness, swelling in his stomach. He didn't want anybody thinking that one of his old gang members had been more successful than him. He'd spent a long time, and given up a lot of personal involvement, to get where he was today, and he needed everyone to know that he'd earned it and that he was the top man. He didn't like feeling this way, but he *did* feel it. Simon guarded his success closely, like a private stash of wealth; he hated feeling inferior to anyone, especially the people he'd left behind.

They approached the main entrance and Simon examined the neatly hand-written name cards above the buzzers. He wasn't sure why he was doing this, because he already knew that Marty was staying in flat seven, the penthouse. But he was nosey; he liked to know things, even if they weren't important. Just the knowing itself represented some kind of control, and it made him feel good to gather details towards himself like a child collecting shells on a lonely beach. It was not so much that knowledge was power, but that it gave him an edge over other people when it came time to push.

He glanced at Brendan, who was looking around furtively, like a criminal keeping an eye out for trouble. He smiled. Then, turning away, he pressed the buzzer for flat number seven.

There was no audible sound from where they were standing when he buzzed, so the two men just stood on the step for a while, waiting for something to happen. When nothing did, Simon reached out and pressed the small metal button again, and then leant forward and peered through the thickened glass panel, trying to make out any kind of movement in the entryway. He saw closed doors on the ground floor level, and a concrete staircase leading up to the floors above. There was nobody there; the place seemed deserted. Potted plants stood at intervals around the ground floor, like sentinels guarding the doors of each flat. He guessed that everyone who lived there was probably out at work – all the office workers, the bankers and solicitors, who could afford these high-spec dwellings no doubt put in long hours to meet the mortgage payments. There was no evidence of any children – no bikes or buggies or mislaid toys. These places were designed for young, upwardly-mobile people: professional couples and post-graduate flat-sharers. They were empty, even when everyone was at home. He could see how easily Marty Rivers might fit in with a set-up like this, making no mark, casting no shadow; moving through the rooms and corridors like a ghost.

"Nobody home," he said, redundantly.

"Well, that's a bit fucking anticlimactic." Brendan sounded angry. He turned around and walked a few steps away from the entrance, kicking at the concrete flagstones. "I left my sick child at home for this?"

"Hey, it's fine. It'll be okay. Let's go for a drink somewhere and come back later. In fact, I'll tell you what... let's leave a note." He took out a piece of paper from his jacket pocket and started to look for a pen.

"Here," said Brendan, handing him a blue biro with a chewed end and no lid.

Simon flattened the paper against the glass of the door and scribbled out a quick note: *We came to see you. We'll be back*. Then he folded the paper in half and in half again, before writing Marty's name on the sheet and sliding the note under the door.

"Think it'll do any good?" Brendan's eyes were wide. He looked afraid. He must be more tired than Simon could even imagine.

Simon shrugged. "Fuck knows, but we have to try. What else can we do?"

They turned back to the apartment complex and stared up at the top floor. The windows were tinted; no interior light could be seen behind the dark glass. The sun, high above them, was more a promise of warmth that failed to deliver. Simon wondered if they were being watched. It certainly felt that way; as if Marty were up there, hiding, and examining their every move. Without even thinking about what he was doing, Simon raised his right hand, turned it so that the palm was directed towards the window, and opened the fingers. He made a slow fist, one finger at a time: the secret salute of the Three Amigos.

Come and see, he mouthed silently, his lips forming words that he held deep inside. *Come and help us*.

MARTY WATCHED THEM leave from the living room, standing before the large window in his old jeans and a torn T-shirt. He had not bathed this morning, and his mouth tasted stale. He idly rubbed the side of his stomach with the palm of his hand, feeling the lump there. It was like a growth, a tumour, and occasionally it moved – a slight twitching motion, like a dog makes while it is sleeping.

It was strange seeing his old friends again, especially together like that. They'd both changed quite a bit, but he would have recognised them anywhere. There was something about the way they moved, some trace of the children they'd been. Simon's swagger, Brendan's reticence... the boys had become men, and yet something vital had been left behind.

And there was the way that Simon had saluted him, just the way they used to when they were kids.

He knew why they were here. He'd picked up Simon's messages on his voicemail. At the sound of his old friend's voice, whatever was hiding within him – and he knew what it was; he just had trouble naming it now, because he suspected it could hear his thoughts – had turned right around inside him, hurting him. Doc had claimed that the wound was clean, that there was nothing inside, but Marty didn't believe that. He could feel it, curling around his abdomen: a small, squat invader, using his body as a home. Part of him knew that none of this could possibly be real, but another part of him – the part that had been stunted as a child, not allowed to develop properly – knew that it *was* real, and he was being possessed, or haunted, or both, by something from a childhood nursery rhyme. The infant Marty Rivers' deepest fears were manifesting inside the adult version; he was a cocoon, and soon that fear would hatch out, the egg within the egg, the horror coiled up within a nest of horrors. Soon it would return to the outside world, and Marty had no idea what might happen afterwards.

He turned away from the window and grabbed his drink. Whisky for breakfast again: this was becoming a habit. He took a sip and went through into the bedroom, where he stripped off his T-shirt and stood before the mirror. His body was smooth, the muscles visible beneath his skin. At first glance, it looked like he had a bit of a belly, like the unfit farts who hung around on the old estate. Then, upon further investigation, it was clear that the bulge in his abdomen was irregular; it wasn't formed by layers of fat. There was something... unnatural, weird and disturbing about it.

He laid a hand on the bulge and felt it shiver. It was like being pregnant, he supposed, and the thought was almost amusing.

Almost.

He recalled a newspaper report from a few years ago about a man who'd gone through breast implant surgery after a drunken bet. There was full-spread story in one of the red-top newspapers, with photos showing the man proudly displaying his new breasts in a low-cut shirt, the top buttons undone to show off his cleavage. At the time the images had repelled Marty; they had made him afraid in a way that he didn't understand, and this had quickly turned to disgust. Right now, standing before the mirror and examining his own altered form, he realised that it was the notion of invasion, of something foreign being present inside a person's body that had caused him such grief. That was why he'd never liked women with fake breasts; the thought of something underneath their skin, nestling there, had always made him feel slightly afraid.

The shape slithered around inside him, coiling around his innards. It wasn't painful. The sensation was even mildly pleasant. But the feelings it provoked were deeply disturbing, at levels he'd not even been aware of before. When he closed his eyes, he saw three boys bound by leaves and twigs in a secluded grove, and shadows moving, patrolling the boundaries like jailors.

"What do you want?" he said, speaking to the mirror. His silent invader tightened its grip and his heart began to pound harder. He thought of Simon and Brendan out there in the car park; he saw once again Simon's splayed fingers making a fist as he waved up at the window, mouthing words that Marty had been unable to lip-read.

He knew what they wanted. They wanted his help. They wanted him to join forces and help fight something. Just like he'd been fighting his whole life, but alone, standing apart from the crowd. Now it was time to forget about being the lone wolf and reach out, take hold of someone else's hand. Maybe he would feel another hand gripping his own, and whoever it belonged to would lead him out of the darkness in which he had always been lost.

Marty put on his jacket and left the room, then the flat. It was time to get things done.

CHAPTER TWENTY-SEVEN

THEY WERE SITTING at a table in the window, looking down at the river, drinking slowly, not speaking much; just waiting. Hoping for something to happen, waiting for the momentum to kick in and move them.

The bar – The Mill on the River – was new, with shiny tables and chairs and up-market clientele stopping off for a few drinks or a spot of lunch after viewing the paintings in the Baltic galleries. The bar (it was a *bar*, not a pub; to people like Simon and Brendan, there was a crucial difference) sat in the shadow of the old Art Deco style building, and benefited from its new status as one of the North's top art venues.

Brendan wasn't comfortable in places like this. He felt more at home in dingy drinking dens on impoverished estates, sharing space with drunken old men, youngsters already on their way down the slippery slope of drink-dependency, and broken-down single mothers looking for a brief window out of the hole they'd made for themselves. People in nice suits bothered him. He felt uneasy around them, as if he were an interloper and they knew it.

He sat opposite Simon sipping his pint – an expensive round; almost a tenner for two beers – and staring over his friend's shoulder. The river was the same one he'd known all his life, but from this angle it looked different. The colour was lighter, the slight waves less threatening, the current moving at a slower pace that might not tug you under if you fell in. The river he knew and loved – and sometimes hated – would pull you down and kill you within seconds.

"Just relax," said Simon. His face looked somehow loose on his skull, as if the last few days had tired him beyond anything he'd ever expected. Brendan knew the feeling. It wasn't just Harry's episode, the trip to the hospital and the night without sleep; there was a lot more going on than that. Like the river, his life had developed a weird current, and he was being dragged along by forces he would not have dreamed of months before. Even his own body was rebelling, taking on a life of its own. The skin of his back was trying to tear away from his frame, seeking a freedom that during darker moments he suspected might benefit him.

When he'd returned from the hospital in the early hours of the morning, he'd made sure his family were asleep and then gone into the bathroom. Stripping off his clothes, he'd been presented with a hideous sight: the flesh from the nape of his neck down to the base of his spine, just above his backside, was infected again. The skin had torn and split; viscous yellow fluid was slathered all over him. He was polluted; his body could no longer accept what was being done, the badness that he had held inside him for so long. His system was rejecting the filth; or was the filth simply coming out to play?

"I need to go to the bathroom." He slid his pint glass across the table and staggered across the room, following the signs to the gents. As he pushed through the door he bumped into a man coming the other way, and snarled. The man – who was talking loudly into a mobile phone – stumbled aside, letting Brendan pass, and there was such a look of pity in his eyes that Brendan wanted to smash the guy's face in.

He walked along a narrow hallway, bouncing off the walls, and came to the toilets. He pushed open the door to the gents and leaned against it, breathing heavily. His back felt soft, yielding more than it should against the wooden door, but there was no pain.

"Oh, fuck..." He looked around the small room. There was nobody else in there. He kicked open the four cubicle doors, but they were also empty. Then he grabbed a tall litter bin from the corner and pushed it over onto its side on the floor at the base of the door. Dirty paper towels spilled from the bin. It was a flimsy barricade, but at least it would warn him if someone was coming. He would have time to duck inside a cubicle and out of the way.

Brendan approached the wall-length mirror set above the row of stainless steel sinks. The sinks were pristine. In fact, the entire room was spotless – no piss on the floor tiles, no shit stains on the back of the cubicle doors, no graffiti scrawled on the walls.

He stared at himself in the mirror. His eyes were sunken, as if his skull was swallowing them, and his cheeks were dark, hollow. His hair had never looked so thin; he could see patches of pink scalp beneath the greasy filaments. He ran the cold tap and ducked his head to the sink, scooped cold water onto his brow. It did no good; he could not cool down. Something was boiling inside him, and it wasn't anger or resentment, not any more. It was pollution. He was polluted by whatever had happened to the three of them, tainted by the influence of that weekend.

He leaned forward, his hands gripping the sides of the sink, and stared into his own dead eyes. Red-rimmed, yellow at the edges, as shallow as glass. He looked wasted, defeated; the fight was already done, and they had lost.

His back crawled.

"Leave me alone..."

He thought of goat eyes and hummingbird wings.

As if in answer to his plea, a clicking sound started up behind him, inside one of the cubicles. It was soft at first, like someone snapping their fingers to low music, but as he turned to face the sound it intensified, growing stronger and faster.

Brendan walked slowly across the room, his feet whispering on the floor tiles. When he reached the open cubicle door he halted, listening. The sound was emanating from the toilet bowl. He took another step forward, so that he was standing over the bowl, as if preparing to unzip his pants and take a leak. The clicking sound continued. Brendan went down on his knees, grasping the sides of the porcelain bowl, and stared down into the clean, still water. Only his reflection stared back up at him, but it looked thin, ghostly: the face of a man who was haunting himself.

He pulled back from the image, a gag reflex causing his own throat to echo the sounds coming from the bowl. He fell backwards, onto his arse, and pushed with his feet against the bottom of the bowl. Sliding backwards across the tiles, he closed his eyes and wished that all of this would just stop, that everything would go away and leave him alone.

The clicking sound ceased.

Slowly, Brendan got to his feet and returned to his spot before the mirror. Scrawled across the glass in what looked like grease – perhaps oil and sweat wiped off human skin – was a word he'd never encountered before:

Loculus.

Brendan peered at the strange word, unsure of what it meant. Was it a name, a place, a person? What the fuck did it mean?

The word faded, as if drawn in mist. He reached out and rubbed the mirror clean, and saw a fleeting, jerky movement behind him. He spun around, but of course there was nothing there. He was spooked, seeing things. He could no longer trust even his own senses. Sight, sound, smell, touch... liars, all of them. He doubted now that he had even seen the word written on the glass.

He took off his jacket and laid it on the next sink along, draping the collar over the taps so that it wouldn't fall onto the floor. Then, without looking down, he began to unbutton his shirt. He did it slowly, methodically, not wanting to rush. Still there was no pain; no feeling at all. His entire back was numb, as if the nerves had been stripped away, the meat cleaved off the bone.

He placed his shirt on top of his jacket.

Even facing forward, looking at himself in the mirror, he could see the red blotches as they crept around his sides beneath his arms, caressing his small love handles. He turned to the left, looking at his right side, and the first of the boils came into view. Whatever had entered him – possessed him? – that night, when the acorn had disgorged its occupant, had done this to him. It had crawled inside him, letting out the twenty-year-old pollution but also bringing its own toxins, mingling them, stirring them up.

He turned the rest of the way around, craning his neck so that he could keep an eye on the damage in the mirror. Last night he had noticed the suggestion of something within the mass of ruptured tissue, something with eyes. Today that formation was clearer, the picture taking shape.

A rudimentary face was forming out of the chaos across his back, the marks and striations, the ruined flesh. A face that was at once familiar: features that somehow resembled his own.

The face sat between his shoulder blades, its eyelids level with the centre of his back. Its nose stuck out of the skin, the nostrils perfectly formed, and he could even make out the bone structure he'd stared at every morning in the mirror, the cheeks he'd spent years shaving every other day, the lips with which he had kissed his wife and his children countless times.

Brendan tried not to think about his dead twin often, but right now he was unable to think of anything else.

He'd heard the story many times as a child, and even researched the facts when he was older. He had not thought about it in any great depth since his own children were born, but now the memories surged forward from the darkness at the back of his brain.

He recalled the doctor's description by rote; it was like a fairy tale, an old story told to ensure his good behaviour. An old story about how, when he was in the womb, still an egg, more or less, he had been one of a set of twins. His egg had absorbed the other egg.

The process was called Vanishing Twin Syndrome. It was a quaint term, and he supposed it was named that way to lessen the blow, but it added to the fairytale quality of the account, making it into a story rather than a statement of fact.

Brendan, in his own pragmatic way, preferred to call it a case of *in utero* cannibalism.

He recalled what he had read in books and online. During the first trimester of pregnancy, a foetus would spontaneously abort and the foetal tissue would be absorbed, by the other twin, the placenta, or the mother. It was more common than people might think. The latest figures estimated that Vanishing Twin Syndrome occurred in 21-30% of all multiple pregnancies.

A common thing, then: one twin consuming the other.

At least it had not happened to Jane. They had been blessed with their own twins, and because of no genetic history of multiple births in her family, they supposed that his genes were responsible for the happy result. He was a twin. And his twin's face had now appeared on his back, like Jesus in a bowl of cornflakes or Elvis on a cheeseburger bun.

No sweat.

Nothing wrong with that.

He stared at the face in the mirror. When it opened its goat-like eyes, he was not even shocked or surprised. It seemed so natural, so perfectly natural, that the face on his back would open its eyes and smile. There were no teeth in its mouth – not yet, anyway – so the smile was rather crude, unformed, but it was friendly enough in its way.

The bathroom floor tilted sideways and Brendan set his feet apart to ride out the movement. Then, when the room settled down and stillness was restored, he said, "What do you want from me?"

The eyes in his back closed; the face sunk into the pus-lathered spots and pustules. Brendan felt dampness on his cheeks. He reached up and brushed away the tears. *How strange*, he thought. *How strange it is to mourn someone who has never really lived*.

The bathroom door opened an inch or two before hitting the bin. "Hey," said a voice. "What's going on? I need to use the bog."

"Just a minute," said Brendan, rushing over to lean against the door, to prevent it from opening any further and allowing an outsider to intrude upon this family business. "There's a bit of a mess in here... just cleaning it up. Could you use the ladies instead?"

The man grunted, huffed and puffed, and then went away.

Brendan went to the cubicle and wiped at his shoulders with paper tissues. Then he layered them over his back, like a second skin, before he put back on his shirt and his jacket and moved the bin away from the door.

He took one last look in the mirror before leaving. The smile he presented looked odd, disjointed. It made him look as if he'd lost his mind.

"Loculus," he said to his retreating reflection, wondering again what it meant, and if he was even pronouncing it correctly.

CHAPTER TWENTY-EIGHT

BRENDAN LOOKED ILL when he sat back down at the table. His hands shook as he gripped his glass, and he slopped beer down the front of his shirt.

This time Simon did not ask if he was okay; he was beginning to feel like a mother hen, clucking around the favourite chick. He felt bad for thinking it, but Brendan was still putting up walls, keeping him out, and if that was the way he wanted to operate, there was little to be done about it for now. He could only push so hard before breaking something, and that had never been his aim.

Simon finished his beer and began to stand. "Same again?" he said, pushing the chair back from the table.

"I'll get them." The voice came from slightly behind him and off to his right.

Across the table, Brendan's eyes widened.

Simon turned slowly. He knew exactly who would be standing there, but still it came as a shock to see Marty Rivers scowling at him, his broad shoulders blocking out a substantial amount of daylight from the window.

"Jesus," said Simon, brushing against the table and making the glasses wobble. The moment stretched, becoming elastic.

"No. It's just me. Marty. I believe you two characters have been looking for me."

"You were there, weren't you? Inside the flat when we came round."

Marty nodded.

"Why didn't you come out?"

Marty shrugged. His shoulders were huge. His entire frame was massive: wide chest, squared-off waist, thick arms. He looked exactly like what he was: a fighter. "I like to come to people on my terms. Even old friends. Now... what can I get you?"

Simon told him the round and as the enormous man walked across to the bar, he glanced at Brendan. "You're fucking quiet," he said.

Brendan nodded. "Aye, sorry. I'm distracted. Just let me get my breath back – yeah?"

Marty returned with the drinks, setting them down on the table. He pulled up a chair and sat alongside Simon, so that the two of them were facing Brendan across the table. Somebody chose that moment to turn on a CD player behind the bar. Low music stalked them through the tables and chairs – a female vocalist singing a bluesy tune.

"Well, well, well. This is nice." Marty had a pint of lager and a whisky chaser. He sipped the lager, his eyes unmoving, seemingly unblinking. His face was unreadable. "All of us here like this, having a friendly drink."

"It's good to see you," said Brendan. It was a feeble opening gambit, but it was better than saying nothing. "I mean, after all this time... I was never quite sure if you were dead or alive, or if you were even still based in the northeast."

Marty swallowed. "Yeah, this is a regular fucking reunion, isn't it? Just like in the movies. Like *The Big Chill*, only with added psychological damage."

Simon smiled. He couldn't help it. Marty's comment wasn't exactly funny, not really, but in that instant it seemed it. "So you're a film buff, then?"

Marty winked over the rim of his pint glass. "I love films, me. I'm a regular cinephile. Odds are, if I haven't seen the film I'll have at least read the book."

Simon was taken aback by the distance between the three of them. There were years separating the three men, yes, and lifestyle choices too, but there was also some uncommon kind of magic that had kept them apart – and right now, as they sat and drank in a riverside bar, that magic was weakening. He was aware of walls coming down, of barriers tumbling, and for the first time in longer than he could calculate, he felt at home in his own skin.

"So you got my messages?"

Marty smiled. "Yes, I did. I suppose we can dispense with the social niceties and get right to it."

Simon nodded. "So you know why I'm here, and why we need you?"

"I can make an educated guess." Marty took a long pull from his beer and then a small sip of whisky.

"Go on, then," said Simon. "Be my guest."

"So much for the tearful reunion... Okay." Marty put down his glass. "You've got it into your head that you can change the way you feel, the way you've always felt, if we all get together and talk about the past. If we can come to some kind of conclusion regarding what went on back then, you hope that

it'll free you and allow you to have a better future."
He paused, licked his lips. "I'm guessing there's a
woman involved. Maybe someone you think you
should love but you can't... and you blame the past
for this. You think that if you can sever all ties with
what may or may not have happened to the three of
us, it'll let you feel about this woman the way you
believe you should." He stopped, leaned back in his
chair, rubbing at his stomach. "So, am I right or am
I right?"

"Very insightful," said Simon. "But you're only
half right. I do believe that the three of us need to
confront our shared past, but I think we need to do
it more literally."

Brendan shuffled on his chair. He picked up his
drink and held it, not moving it anywhere near his
mouth.

Simon rubbed his chin, feeling the stubble growth.
"I think we need to go in there together – the
Needle. We need to make like it's twenty years ago
and march right the fuck in there, then shout and
scream and force whatever the fuck held us in there
to make an appearance."

Marty sat forward again, his arms flexing and
pulling his shirt tight. "And then what? Kick the shit
out of it?"

"In a manner of speaking," said Simon. "At first
I thought we were going to have to pull down the
place, brick by brick, so I bought it from the council.
Took me ages to convince them, and I paid well over
the odds. Now I realise that won't be necessary.
Simply by coming back here, I seem to have triggered
something. Whatever's been hiding here, making its

nest under the streets of the Grove, it's waking up... it's waking from a long sleep. Can't you feel it?"

Marty did not reply.

"You've been having dreams, haven't you?"

Marty nodded, but still he did not speak.

"Weird dreams that feel just like reality, but fucked-up, messed around. Apocalyptic visions, monsters from the past chasing you, things keeping pace with you in the dark?"

"Yes," said Brendan, joining in at last. He was gripping his glass too tight; his knuckles were white. "Yes, that's it. All of us... the three of us... we've been dreaming about the same things, the same place. Haven't we?"

"Yes," said Marty.

"Yes," said Simon.

"Another drink?" Brendan slammed down his glass.

Marty laughed softly.

Simon shook his head. "Is that all you guys do around here, drink? I've not drunk so fucking much in my life since I've come back."

"You're out of practice," said Marty. "And I'll have the same again, thanks." He glanced at Brendan, smiled, and let out another soft chuckle.

"It really is good to see you," said Brendan. "Both of you." When Simon looked over, he saw how pale Brendan's face had become, and he felt such a great wave of pity that it pressed him down into his chair, pinning him there.

Before he could say anything, Brendan stood and went to the bar, fishing nervously inside his jeans pocket for his wallet.

"Is he okay?" Marty leaned in close. He smelled of whisky and expensive aftershave. And beneath that, a deep, musky odour that made Simon think of violence: of punches thrown and threats made, of kicked heads and split skin and spilled blood.

"I'm not sure. His kid's ill. Last night, something strange happened. He went into some odd kind of shock, like a trance or something. Threw up and something... well, something really weird came out. A bird."

Marty closed his eyes. "A hummingbird," he said.

"How did you know? How the hell did you know about that?" Simon's hand made a fist on the tabletop; his nails scratched against the damp wood.

"I don't know. I... I just knew. When you said it, an image came into my head. Like a dream I once had but couldn't remember until now. The hummingbirds are important – we saw them back then, too. Can you feel it?" His eyes were wide, the pupils dilated. "It's like doors are opening inside me. Connections are being made, loose ends tying themselves together in neat little knots. Something's happening..."

Simon shook his head. "I wish I could say the same. It's what I wanted, why I'm here. But I don't... I don't feel any of that. My brain feels like when you push your knuckles into your eyes to fight sleep: that same kind of bunched-up pressure, when the darkness behind your eyelids starts to spark. That's all. I get nothing else."

Brendan had returned with the drinks. He set them down on the table, beer spilling over the rims. "I feel it," he said. "Just like Marty said. Cogs are turning; they're moving together, starting up some kind of motion. It's slow – very, very slow – but it's happening. What happened to Harry is only part of it. We can stop it, if we try. We can put an end to this shit."

Simon felt empty. Why was he the only one who could not feel the energies massing, the world reconfiguring and taking on a new shape around them? It wasn't fair; it was not right. He felt cheated, as if he were the victim of a con or a grift. He, Simon, should be the one to feel it first, the man to set off the reaction. After all, it was he who had come back here, in search of the truth, so it was only fitting that he was the one who acted as a catalyst for whatever would take place when the Three Amigos banded together for a fight.

The music on the stereo had changed to soft rock, a power ballad. The volume was still low, but one of the barmaids was singing along quietly as she worked. Simon watched her as she glided the length of the bar, picking up glasses, washing them, rubbing them dry, and mouthing the words of the song.

"Listen," he said. "Why don't we try something? How about this: each of us talks about what we can remember from that time, when we were held in the Needle? I know it isn't much, but maybe if we piece our memories together we might start to see a picture forming. It might help me to feel everything you're feeling."

Brendan looked nervous. He was biting his lower lip. "Do you think it's worth it? I mean, will it actually achieve anything?"

Marty leaned forward again, his big arms pressing against the table. "Is this, like, our *Rashomon* moment?" He smiled, shook his head. "Actually, I think it's a good idea. If nothing else, it might prompt something, press a button in one of our heads and free up other memories, images, feelings... whatever."

"Exactly," said Simon. "Are you in, Brendan?"

Brendan stared at the two of them, and then finally he nodded. "Okay." He took a drink. "So who goes first?"

There was a slight pause, a silence within the greater silence that had surrounded each of them for two decades, and then Marty spoke: "I went back there, you know. To that grove of trees. After I had my bike accident. You know about that?"

The other two nodded.

"Well," continued Marty. "I was in a coma for a while – not long, and it wasn't too deep. But while I was unconscious I went back there, and I stood enclosed within that grove of old oaks. I remember..." – he closed his eyes – "I remember it was night, and the stars looked miles away, too high to be much more than pinpricks. I could hear that same clicking sound – Captain Clickety's voice – but it was too far away to scare me. In fact, now that I think about it, the clicking sound was moving away, leaving me behind, and for a moment I felt abandoned. Then the trees and the bushes began to rustle. I felt that something was stalking me, or at least watching me from the undergrowth. I think it wanted me to follow it."

The barmaid was still singing. The bar had emptied out; there were not many people left drinking, other than the three men at the table in the window. Sunlight lanced through the glass, making a dagger shape on the table.

"It was weird," said Marty, "but I think I was looking for that girl – the one who spoke to us when we were tied up with branches in the middle of the grove of trees. I think... I think she saved us."

"Hailey," said Brendan in a whisper.

"Yeah, Hailey. The hummingbird girl. That was it. I could never quite remember her name. I was looking for her. I'm not sure why, but I needed to see her, perhaps to tell her something. Maybe to thank her. Other than that, all I could remember about actually being there the first time was that it was dark, I was scared, and that fucking bird-faced cunt was tormenting us. I think he probably tortured us – abused us, or something."

Brendan was nodding. "Yeah, yeah... that's what I remember most: the torture." He looked paler than ever, and his neck was scrawny, like that of a chicken. "It fucked me up, that torture. I don't remember any specifics, but it left me with..." He glanced at the others, his eyes wet, on the verge of tears.

"Go on," said Simon. "We won't judge you. Not us."

Brendan nodded. "Okay. Here goes. It left me with a kind of kink; a fetish, I suppose you'd call it. I read a lot of bondage magazines, watch the videos. I like to watch it happen to other people, to see them tied up and... and abused. Nothing bad, not real violence. Consensual stuff, light spanking, and that. I just like to watch." The colour came back to his cheeks; he was blushing. "Jesus, it left me liking bondage..."

Marty turned to Simon. "What about you? What are your memories?"

Simon's head dropped. He stared at a damp patch on the tabletop. "Not much. Not much at all. Just the grove of trees... and that's about it. I remember everything before that, when we made that stupid den, and thinking we were heroes that night, tracking down some kind of beast. But afterward, when we went in there... there's nothing. Nothing but the trees. The fucking trees."

A silence elbowed its way between them at the table. None of them spoke for a moment or two, as if they were each afraid to shatter the quiet that had fallen across them. Background sounds swelled: the music, the chatter of the handful of people left in the bar, the barmaid's soft, lilting voice as she continued to sing.

Then, finally, Marty spoke.

"Let me ask you something," he said, clasping his hands together on the table in front of him. "Does this – any of this – feel weird to you, or does it feel... well, normal? Does it feel natural?"

"You mean us?" Simon glanced at the other two men, one at a time. "Meeting here again, after all this time?"

Marty nodded.

"Not weird to me," said Brendan. "Not any more. I thought it did, at first, when it was just me and Simon. But now it's just like you say – it feels natural, as if we never parted."

"Yeah," said Simon. "Yes, that's exactly how it feels. It feels like–"

Marty butted in before he could finish: "It feels like we left each other yesterday, as children, and then met up again today as adults. It feels like no fucking time has passed at all."

The quiet fell once again around their shoulders, covering their heads, their mouths. They all stared at each other, eyes flicking from face to face, seeing beyond the masks of age. For all intents and purposes, the men sitting around the table were once again little boys. They were young again. But this time they were not afraid.

"You know," continued Marty, "I've always lived my life on the edge of glory. Never quite got there, just prowled around on the wrong side of the ropes, trying to fight my way in. Now I finally realise that'll never happen. I'm not going to make it. But maybe with you guys I can still make a difference, even if it's just to us. To the rest of our lives."

The barmaid's singing built to a small crescendo. The song was a sad one, and she knew the words by heart.

CHAPTER TWENTY-NINE

"We have to go back," said Simon, breaking the spell. "The three of us, all together... We have to go back in there and kick-start the whole thing, make it happen again. But this time we need to fight it, and beat it. This time, we stop it dead in its tracks."

The other two Amigos said nothing, but the mutual consent was evident in their faces, the posture of their bodies, the way they each sat forward in their chairs, as if eager to meet something head-on.

"We have to go there now, before we change our minds. We can't wait, not any longer."

He could see in their eyes that they agreed, despite remaining silent. Their features were old, worn, and tired, but those eyes – they were young boys, peering out from behind the broken-down faces of men.

CHAPTER THIRTY

JANE WAS WORRIED. Brendan had called her half an hour ago and filled her in on the latest news.

They'd met up with Marty and they were going inside the Needle; all three of them, together again, to see what memories they could stir up. Jane was put in mind of three boys poking a wasp's nest with sticks, and the wasps going crazy, their stingers dripping with poison. It was a stupid image, really – a ridiculous comparison – but nonetheless, she felt that her husband and his old friends were about to disturb things that might just be best left to rest in peace.

She moved around the house like a Prozac phantom, her mind in a haze, her eyes roaming across every surface, her gaze unable to settle in one place. She felt simultaneously energised and exhausted. It was a strange sensation, like running through treacle.

Harry was fine. The boy was sleeping soundly, oblivious to the concern he'd caused.

But she couldn't stop checking on him; she'd been up there three times in the past hour and was, even now, turning to climb the stairs again. She grabbed the handrail and began to ascend, her mind floating ahead of her. *He's okay*, she thought, not knowing if she meant Brendan or their son. *We're all okay*.

At the top of the stairs she turned and walked along the landing. The bathroom door was open. She could see the mirror through the gap; it was greyed-out, steamy with condensation. Had she taken a bath earlier? She must have done, but could not remember anything about it. Perhaps she'd bathed the twins – or maybe just Isobel, while Harry rested.

"Jesus," she whispered. "I'm losing the plot."

Written in the condensation was a nonsense word: *Loculus*. What was that, the name of a cartoon character or a TV show? Maybe Harry had been up and about...

Jane stopped outside the twins' room and waited. She didn't know what it was she was waiting for, but the pause felt right. It seemed like the thing to do. She pressed the palms of both of her hands against the door, and then leaned in close, pushing the side of her face against the wood. She listened, but could hear nothing. Of course she couldn't. Harry was asleep. Isobel was at school, and then later she was going to a hastily arranged sleepover at a friend's house on Far Grove Way.

The twins used to share a room when they were very young. She'd tried to separate them when they got older, and it had caused an uproar, with stamping feet and infant tantrums. She'd relented, but eventually they'd have to be separated again, and she knew that it would cause more trouble. They hated being apart, even when they were asleep. All the things you hear about twins had proved to be true.

Not for the first time she wondered about the origin of the twins; how Brendan had almost been a twin, so the genetic makeup was there, in his DNA, that someone on his side of the family could produce a multiple birth. But wasn't it meant to skip a generation? She supposed it had, in a way, because Brendan's twin had died *in utero*, not even given the chance to form into a proper foetus. It had been just the size of a thumbnail, probably even smaller. No eyes, no nose, no features of any kind. A floating being, without even a soul...

But Jane didn't believe in the soul. She was an atheist. The lure of religion had not drawn her to its flame, not in the way that it had her mother. Jane's mum had seen God as a way out of an abusive marriage; Jane had seen God as a convenient crutch for the weak to lean on. Where had God been when her father had beaten her, trying so hard not to touch her in the same way that he'd touched her sister? Where was the Holy Ghost when she'd lain awake at night, listening to his footsteps as he roamed the house, drinking and muttering and talking himself out of raping his own daughter? Some might say that it was God who had kept him away from her, but Jane preferred to think that it was the threat of going back to prison; he'd served three years for sexual assault when he was in his early twenties, and the experience had scarred him enough that he could not ever face another visit.

She pushed open the bedroom door and stepped inside. The curtains were closed, but dim light penetrated the cheap material. The room looked as if it were filled with dust; the air shuddered as she moved through the space. Harry was a motionless mound in his red plastic Lightning McQueen bed with the *Ben 10* quilt pulled over his head. His toys were dotted around his side of the room, on shelves and cupboard tops, and scattered across the floor. Isobel's side was much tidier; she had inherited her mother's eye for neatness and formality.

Harry didn't seem to be moving at all. She was worried that he'd stopped breathing. She knew that she was being silly, that the doctors had given him a clean bill of health, but still... when you were a parent, it paid to be just a little bit paranoid.

Slowly she crossed the room and stood at the side of the bed. She reached down and pulled back the quilt, revealing the sweaty top of Harry's head. His hair was soaking. She tugged the quilt down past the back of his knees (he was sleeping on his belly, as always). Still Harry did not move.

"Hey, kidda. You okay?"

He did not even stir.

Jane's heart felt as if it were gradually climbing her chest, inch by inch, making its way towards her throat. She swallowed; her throat ached. She heard a strange humming sound, but it was only inside her head.

"Harry?" Her voice was croaky.

She reached down and nudged his shoulder, just a little, barely hard enough to move his little body. Then she did it again – harder this time, applying more pressure, easily enough to wake him.

Harry was still.

"Harry... baby... wake up for Mummy."

She dropped down onto her knees at the side of the bed. Her hands ran over his back, feeling beneath his armpits to see if he had a temperature. His skin was cold; too cold. Not icy, not quite, but cold enough to be of concern. She rolled him over, onto his back.

"Harry!"

His face was pale. His lips were a light shade of blue. His eyelids did not flutter; the muscles in his face were loose, relaxed. She shook him, hard, trying to wake him. "Harry! Time to get up!" Her voice had become shrill, the tone rising as the panic set in. She fought hard to keep herself under control, to keep calm, but she recalled the hummingbird that had erupted from his throat, and the convulsions on the bedroom floor. Nobody seemed to want to talk about the hummingbird, at the hospital. They ignored it in the hope that it would go away, much like the bird itself had flown out of the room. The convulsions, though, fascinated them. They'd loved the fucking convulsions: they were normal, regular symptoms that could be studied and explained away. They were nothing at all like the insane image of a tiny American bird being expelled from a little boy's throat.

She picked up her son and ran for the door, cradling his head in the same way she'd done when he was a baby. She hurried downstairs – not too fast, just in case she fell and broke both of their necks – and made her way to the phone. She called an ambulance first, quietly amazed at how calmly she was able to handle the conversation.

She hung up the phone and pressed her fingers against Harry's neck. There was a pulse; it was strong, regular. He wasn't dead. That was good. It was something she could hang on to, a rope to cling to in the darkness, which was rising slowly from the floor like a thick mist to consume her.

Then she called Brendan, to tell him what was happening – even though she didn't have a fucking clue what was happening. She needed him here, with her, not on some stupid wild goose chase with a couple of blokes who had never really been his friends, not since childhood, and perhaps not even then, because they'd all been too young and far too selfish to know what friendship really meant.

She punched his number into the phone and listened to the ringtone, holding her boy against her breathless chest and wondering if she still had the strength to speak.

It was only when she got the recorded message, saying that his phone could not be reached, that she began to cry.

CHAPTER THIRTY-ONE

As they approached the Needle, Marty couldn't help but think of a scene from *The Good, the Bad and the Ugly*, Sergio Leone's spaghetti western about three criminals in search of Civil War treasure. The familiar theme tune filled his head; voices chanted, the warbling score sent a thrill – somewhere between delight and dread – through the channels of his body.

The Three Amigos were back in town, and this time they wouldn't go down without a fight.

"What's so funny?" Brendan stared at him, his brow creased and his eyebrows slanted.

"Nothing," said Marty. "Just a daft thought, that's all."

What the hell am I doing here? he thought. *How did they get me to agree to this? Two strangers in a bar, reminding me of old times I'd rather forget.*

He stared up at the tower block, feeling a strange sense of black-tinted nostalgia. The last time they'd all been here together, something monstrous had occurred. None of them could recall the details, but the act had spread a rancid shadow across the rest of their lives. It seemed melodramatic to think in those terms, but it was true. No other language could do the thought justice: there was nothing subtle about what had happened to them here, and he only wished that he could remember what it had been.

Or did he?

That was the big question, wasn't it? Did he really want to know what had gone on inside those tall concrete walls? Was he so eager to find out what had been done to them, when the sturdy upright panels had been so readily shunted aside to reveal a dark grove of trees and whatever waited beyond them, its intentions darker still?

Even now, standing before the building, he was unable to answer his own questions.

The sides of the tower looked black in the odd afternoon light, as if they were covered in oil. The blackness had a metallic sheen, and it shimmered. The illusion did not last; it was gone in moments, but it was long enough for Marty to realise whatever they had come to confront knew they were here. His stomach lurched; the thing within him shifted slowly, deliberately, chafing up against his internal organs and rattling like a prisoner at the bars of his ribcage. He was convinced that he felt a tiny hand-foot clutching his liver, and his chest took another knock from the wrong side... the inside.

He clutched at his side, gritting his teeth against the pain.

Whatever Doc said, he was convinced that he was carrying around inside him some kind of cartoon demon, a hand-drawn phantom from his childhood, a monster that had leapt from the pages of a book he should never have been allowed to read.

"So," said Simon. "Are we going to do this? Now, in broad daylight?"

Brendan nodded, quiet again.

"If this was a horror film, we'd wait till after dark before coming snooping around in a derelict tower block."

Brendan giggled, but it didn't sound quite right, like a pressure valve, a release of pent-up tension.

"Fuck it," said Marty, tensing his body, trying to ignore the tenant inside his gut. "What have we got to lose?"

"Everything," said Brendan. Now he was deadly serious; there was no hint of humour in his voice.

"Nothing," said Simon, moving forward and fumbling with his keys as he approached the gate in the hoardings. "Nothing at all." He waited a moment, looking up at the sky. Then he glanced back down at the ground, as if establishing his position in the universe. "This isn't exactly going as I'd planned," he said. "Not at all, if I'm honest."

Marty tried not to sigh. He was growing impatient, but he didn't want to let the others see. "How do you mean?"

Brendan placed his hands on the gate, as if trying to divine something of the atmosphere on the other side simply by touching it.

"Well," said Simon, "I thought we'd have a few drinks, catch up on each other's lives, and then slowly work our way up to this point."

"Why waste time?" said Marty. "Now that we're back together, it doesn't feel like any time has passed. We agree on this, don't we?"

Simon nodded. Brendan said nothing; just kept his silent vigil by the gate.

Marty rubbed his left cheek with his right hand. He felt the stubble rasping against his fingers. "It's as if our lives got stuck in a groove when we were ten, and nothing really moved on. Yes, you have your wealth and businesses, and Brendan has his family, but despite these things, we were frozen inside. Our hearts stopped beating; the blood was stilled in our veins. I know I'm not exactly explaining this very well, but..."

"Yeah." Simon closed his eyes. "Frozen... that's a good way of putting it. We moved on, lived our lives, but everything inside us was frozen in place. Speaking for myself, it's held me back in every relationship I ever had, made it so that I can barely relate to anyone in my life."

"So why the fuck do we even need to mess about, to dance around this moment? Let's just do it. We're here now, anyway, so we're all agreed. This is it; the time's come to defrost."

Even as he spoke, Marty felt his insides stirring as whatever monster he now carried within him responded to his words. He gritted his teeth, trying not to scream, and waited it out. Soon the movement died down, and eventually stopped. He thought this must be what it was like to be pregnant: to feel the existence of another inside the fragile envelope of your body.

"So we're all agreed, then? We're doing this now. Right now." Brendan had turned around to face them. He looked ill. His eyes were bright and feverish.

Simon stepped forward, brandishing the keys. He unlocked the gate with a steady hand and stepped aside to let the others through. When they were all on the other side of the barrier, he locked the gate behind him. Marty felt that there was something final about the action. He was unable to shake the feeling that all of them might not be coming back out, and those who did make it would be changed in more ways than he could imagine.

The last time they'd all been here together, time itself had behaved strangely: they thought they'd been inside the Needle for only a short time, but when finally they emerged from its shadow an entire weekend had passed. He wished he'd taken the time to tell someone where he was going today, but then he remembered that he had no one to tell. His friends from the fight game were merely acquaintances, and the only other significant person in his life was Melanie, but he'd already cut his ties with her. He could never tell his grandmother; she would worry too much, even about something she did not understand.

There was nobody. He was truly alone. It was a sad indictment of his life that the only two people who cared where he was right now were here with him, and he had not spoken to either of them in twenty years before this day.

"So this is what it all comes down to," said Brendan, suddenly, breaking into Marty's thoughts as if he were attempting to echo them and add his own spin. "These last few days of tracking Marty down. It all comes down to this: three strangers standing outside an old, empty building."

"No," said Simon. "Not the last few days, the last twenty years. This is it. This is what we've been waiting for, but didn't even realise. This is where we face down our fears."

"You're right," said Marty. "Both of you. All we are is three strangers who were once, for a brief moment in another lifetime, friends. It's taken us two decades to get back here, and we've had our own little adventures along the way. I've spent my time fighting. You, Simon, have spent yours in another kind of battle – but still fighting yourself, I'd guess, just the same as me. And Brendan. What about you?" He nodded towards Brendan, who was standing stiffly, as if awaiting some kind of verdict. "In many ways you were the best of us. You at least managed to have some kind of real life, and you've brought children into the world. You're the part of us that worked; the part that matters. Simon and me, we represent all the other stuff: the shit that went bad."

There was nothing else to say, nothing to add. The three of them stood there, renewing old bonds, waiting for some kind of energy to throb through their veins and pull them closer together.

Marty felt stronger than he ever had before in his life. But he also felt a weakness within him, a fracture that had always been there and that might yet prove to be his undoing. His hidden passenger – the fairytale nightmare hitching a ride in his belly – was reaching out, seeking that fissure, with the aim of making it wider and letting out whatever darkness it found there.

"Let's go," said Simon, striding towards the main doors of the tower block and brandishing his keys like a weapon. "Let's get this thing done."

The door opened onto blackness. Not a dim area or a room without light, but utter, perfect darkness. When they stepped inside, Marty felt like he was walking into water; it flowed over and around and into him, filling his lungs and making his eyes sting.

Fathoms deep, he stood there blinking and trying to get his bearings. He heard the doors close behind them, and the breathing of his companions. Then, struggling against the tide of darkness, he shuffled his feet along the floor and tried to move forward, deeper into the building that now felt like a wide open space.

Groping blindly at his side, he felt a small, cold hand grip his own.

Whose hand is this? he thought, as it squeezed his fingers, the grip tight and unwilling to let go.

"Keep hold of each other," said Simon. "Somebody grab my hand. I'm moving it around, by my side. Try to grab it."

"Don't I have hold of you?" Marty felt panic welling up inside him; he wanted to run, but there was nowhere to go. Every direction was just another pathway deeper into this pitch blackness.

"No, that's me," said Brendan, close to his ear. "You have my hand." The grip slackened; the fingers twitched.

Thank God, thought Marty, feeling slightly more relaxed.

"Okay, then. Do you have my hand, too?" Simon's voice sounded slightly farther away, as if he'd moved along a passage of some sort.

"No," said Brendan.

Voices: this was all they had in the dark.

"Me neither." Marty sounded hoarse; his throat was dry.

"Fucking hell... then whose fucking hand am I holding?" Simon's voice sounded weak, as if he were struggling to contain his terror.

Then, in answer, there was a soft clicking noise in the darkness, and a short burst of childish laughter.

"It's gone," said Simon. "It's fucking gone... my hand... it had hold of my hand... and its fingers were hot." Footsteps grated on the concrete floor, everyone's breathing was heavy, laboured, as if they were climbing an incline.

"Let's just... move forward." Simon again, sounding breathless.

"But which way is forward?" said Marty.

"This way." Brendan was taking charge. "Just follow my voice, Simon. I have your hand, Marty. Come with me. I think I can see light up ahead. I know the layout of this place. I think I have my bearings."

The clicking sound was still audible, but only just. Marty couldn't tell if it was behind them, up ahead, or off to the left or the right. Space had taken on alarming new qualities; the dimensions of this room were meaningless, a strange geometry had taken over. He could be inside a tiny room or lost in a vast, endless void. He wasn't sure; it all felt the same, limited and limitless.

This is how it feels to be lost, he thought. *Truly lost. Cut off even from yourself. This must be how it feels all the time... that thing. The Underthing.*

He wasn't quite sure where the word had sprung from, but with it came a suggestion of pity. He felt emotionally wrong-footed, shoved off centre. Was it even possible to feel sorry for a monster?

Brendan tugged on his hand and Marty allowed himself to be pulled slowly in one direction, trusting that it was the right way to go. The air was thick and heavy, like damp towels laid across his face, and that clicking sound kept waxing and waning in and out of the range of audibility, as if it kept crossing a threshold of some kind and then rushing back, just to remind them that it was still there, keeping track of them. He smelled burnt rubber and Parma violet candies: aromas from childhood, which produced within him a longing for things lost or left behind. The sweet, harsh taste of the sweets – like perfumed soap – was on his tongue, making his mouth water.

"This way," said Brendan, tugging harder on his hand. "We're almost there."

Almost where? The statement felt bigger than had been intended, as if it encompassed something beyond words: the time they'd spent wandering in their own darkness since the last time they'd been here together, the roads they had taken, the wrong turnings they'd made, the people they'd left behind.

Almost there...

They were almost somewhere, that was true enough. But was it somewhere they wanted to be? Whatever the answer to that question, Marty knew that it was probably where they *needed* to be, if any of them was to stand a chance of moving on from here and salvaging their lives.

He became aware of a light source up ahead, glimmering softly, like an underwater lamp. The light was greenish, swamp-like, and it did not look comforting. It was, however, more promising than this massive darkness through which they were currently trawling, like deep-sea divers cut off from their rope tethers.

They pushed on, and as the light became closer – that's how it felt; like the light was drawing near to them, rather than the other way round – he felt Simon's hand flailing at his own before grappling with his fingers and gripping him tightly.

"It's okay, mate," he said, not feeling okay at all. "I've got you." Yes, he had. Simon and Brendan had him... but who the hell had Brendan? Was he also holding somebody's hand? Someone who was not one of them? Was he being dragged towards the green light, trusting in some spectre to lead them to safety?

The three men stumbled into the green light, as if they'd entered a doorway and emerged from the sea onto dry land. Marty expected to be dripping wet. He even ran a hand across his shaved head, as if he were drying his scalp.

"Where are we?" Simon voiced the question for the three of them, much as he'd been the self-appointed mouthpiece of the gang in his youth.

Around them, all they could see were trees. A thick, dense screen of leaves and interlocking branches, through which was filtered that odd green light. Marty glanced around him; the patch of concrete they were standing on was surrounded on all sides by mirrors, reflecting trees that were not there: ghost trees, a phantom forest, a wilderness of the imagination.

"This can't be real." Brendan sounded as if he were trying to convince himself. "It's not... it's a dream."

"I can't speak for you two," said Marty, "but I'm wide awake."

As Marty watched, a shape flitted through the

trees. Or, more precisely, it moved quickly through the open space beyond the trees. He could not make out what it was, but the shape was small and agile. When he saw it again, he became convinced that it was standing upright, on two legs. Yet it did not seem entirely human.

Almost there...

"Jesus." He was afraid, yes, but beneath the fear was a sort of relief: they'd come a long way for this, and if they had encountered something normal, something natural, it would have been anticlimactic. To confront the weird, the magical, made sense. This was what they'd all expected, after their nightmares had gradually worn away at their sense of reality over the past few days.

"Where are we?" This time it was Brendan, and he sounded like a child, a little boy lost in the woods.

The clicking sound had stopped as soon as they'd entered the green light, and it had not resumed. Perhaps this was a place of safety, somewhere they could regroup and think about what they should do next. The light shimmered, as if the branches shifted in a breeze, and despite the feeling of being shut in, and the mirrored screens, Marty felt certain that they were near a portal that would allow them to enter another place, a place that was outside.

But how can that be? he thought. *How can we be outside and inside at the same time?*

The light flickered through the gaps in the greenery. The shape – the figure, because that's surely what it was – moved at the periphery of his vision, more slowly this time, as if it wanted to be seen.

"What is that?" Simon moved a couple of paces to

his left and raised his hand. The green light dappled his skin. "There's somebody there."

Brendan moved, too: he turned and faced the two of them. "It's a girl," he said, his face reflecting green. "It's the girl. It's Hailey."

The space in which they stood seemed to surge and swell, as if the revelation had triggered some kind of response. The area grew larger, its boundaries pushed away to allow them more room to manoeuvre. The darkness was forced back where it could not reach them.

The girl's face manifested in the leaves, becoming clearer as Marty stared. It was as if her features were forming from the vegetation, her eyes and nose, her small, curved mouth, her hair, all coming together organically from the life around her. She was smiling. Her eyes were green, like tiny round leaves.

"Hello again," said Simon. His hand – still raised – hovered in the air like a bird: a pale, pink hummingbird.

The girl's smile grew wider.

"It's been a long time." Simon sounded relaxed. It seemed that he was taking all this in his stride, simply accepting the weirdness in a way that Marty could only envy. He clutched at his side. His passenger was moving again, straining at the envelope of his skin.

"Hello, boys," said the girl. Her voice held the traces of a faint buzzing sound. Again, Marty thought about the sound of hummingbird wings – a light rasping quality which was not at all unpleasant. He'd definitely heard that voice before; the same words had come from her mouth twenty years ago, when she'd appeared at their side, holding back the darkness just as she was doing now, but by less sophisticated means.

"What are we supposed to do?" Marty said.

"I'm afraid you're stuck there." She smiled again.

"Stuck where? Where exactly are we?" Brendan said.

"Where you are isn't where I am. I'm here on one side, and you're on the other. But the place you're standing is in between. It's not one place or another. It's no place, really." She moved backwards, and only then did Marty realise that the soft buzzing sound was not in her voice: it came from her wings. The girl – Hailey – was hovering in place on oversized hummingbird wings, but they were the same colour and texture as the trees behind her.

"How can we get where you are? We have business over there, you see." Again Simon's voice was calm; he must have detached himself from the moment in order to deal with the situation.

"You need a doorway. The last time, you *were* the doorway – all three of you. Your hurt and your pain, the fact that you all yearned for something more than what you had, something better, allowed you to set foot here." She was still smiling. It was beautiful. "But that doesn't work this time. It needs something more."

"And where is 'here'?"

She shook her head. "Oh, where I am has many names. I suppose the best way to explain is to tell you a little story." She moved closer towards them, away from the screen of trees – which, Marty now realised, was thin, only two-dimensional. "Are you all listening?"

Marty nodded. His friends did not speak, so he assumed they'd done the same. They were all hypnotised by this beautiful girl, and her wondrous smile, and her amazing wings...

"Listen," she said. Then she told them her tale:

"When the first man dreamed, this place was born. It has no name, yet mankind has called it many things. We who dwell here call it *Loculus* – 'little place'. There are no other places, not really. There is only here.

"Loculus. The little place.

"This place is a container for dreams, a burial niche for them when they have nowhere else to go. Whenever you have a dream, or an idea, and nothing comes of it, that energy comes here. All energy is neutral in Loculus, and for a long time a sense of balance was achieved. Then human dreams turned sour; as Man evolved, became stronger, his dreams turned grander, and more foolish, and more easily spoiled. A lot of them went sour, like a vat of milk left out in the sun."

Marty felt a small, empty part of him fill up with this knowledge. He knew that the girl's story was true.

"Who, or what, is the Underthing?" His mouth was still dry, but he made himself heard. He had to know. "Is it Captain Clickety?"

The girl's smile was sadder now; it contained a capacity for misery.

"All energy is neutral in Loculus, and for a long time balance was achieved." Her smile faltered, fell away. "Then human dreams turned bad; as Man evolved, became stronger, his dreams turned sour.

Pollution entered this place; all this became tainted." She hovered backwards, raising her arms. "That's what the Underthing represents. *He* is the result of that pollution.

"Loculus is Heaven to some and Hell to others; freedom to one, a prison cell to another. It is nothing and it is everything.

"The Underthing is, in many ways, a prisoner of paradise. He wants to escape to the hell of the world in which you men live – a world I used to know. Loculus is held together by balance, two halves operating as a whole. The Underthing collects twins, clutching them to him in the hope that he can upset the balance – separate the two halves, split the two worlds and sneak in through the gaps. Not many twins are born in the Grove. In here, in Loculus, if there is the possibility of a set being conceived, he smells it through the fabric of the place, and he is drawn to it."

Twins.

Marty glanced at Brendan, who had clearly come to his own conclusions.

"He wanted me all along... because of the twins. He knew I could have twins. He smelled them on me when I was ten years old..." Brendan was crying. Tears streaked his long, pale face.

Hailey spoke again, through the trees: "Captain Clickety is an avatar. The Underthing cannot leave this place, so he sends out tendrils. Once there was a man who tried to enter Loculus... a plague doctor, a man who hid his lusts behind the mask of medicine. The Underthing uses him occasionally, to walk abroad out there, in the Concrete Grove. Like a tentacle reaching for something shiny, Captain Clickety goes out looking for ways to upset the balance."

"How do we get over there?" said Simon. "How do we get into this 'Loculus'? You mentioned that before, when we were kids, we were doorways. What about now?"

She shook her head. "I'm afraid that time is gone. This time I have sent you a new doorway. I can't do anything more. Last time I made myself known to the Underthing, and he's been aware of my presence ever since. I have no special power. I'm just a mediator – all I can do is show you the way to go."

At that moment something moved to Marty's right. He spun around, adopting a defensive stance – guard up, covering his face, feet pointing forward, knees bent – and saw a small, thin man with a white mask over his face walk out of the tree-screen.

"This," said Hailey, "is Banjo. He is your doorway. It's why he's here, what has kept him alive. He has this one job to do before he can be free of his nagging body and escape the demands of the world."

Banjo stood there, in his stained clothes, his white mask – which Marty now saw was made of bandages – shockingly bright under the strange, diffuse green light.

"Go ahead, Banjo." Hailey's voice had adopted a gentle, motherly tone. "You know what to do."

Banjo reached up and took hold of a loose flap of bandage, and then he proceeded to unwind the wrappings, turning the bandages round and round his head and gathering them in his fist. He kept on going, revealing yet more layers of white, until finally he uncovered what was hidden beneath.

The man's face was badly scarred. The scars were old, shiny, and reflected the green light like plastic. His eyes were open, and the lids were thin and tattered, like paper. He had no lips, just nubs across the top and bottom of his mouth opening. He looked like he was grinning: he was the man who grinned forever, but who never quite got the joke.

His raised arm moved around his face with mechanical regularity, removing the remaining bandages. Marty expected the movement to stop when his ruined face was fully exposed, but it continued after that.

In fact, when Banjo reached the end of the gauze dressings, he kept on going, unwrapping strips of his damaged skin in the same long, loose coiling motion. It was like peeling an orange: the flesh came away easily, like rind, and fell to the ground. Next was the bone, which was stripped away in the same manner. And beneath that, inside the man's skull, was a cluster of leaves. The dried leaves fell, falling to earth in a slow, spinning drift, and as Marty and the other men watched, something strange happened... Banjo was no longer there, and in his place there appeared an opening in the trees.

The screen had vanished; this was here, real.

Real trees; a real wood, and on the other side, a small, open space: a peaceful grove, within which they had once been bound and had pain inflicted upon their ten-year-old bodies.

All at once, and without hesitation, the Three Amigos stepped back into the ancient oak grove. There was no longer any doubt; each man wanted to be here, to settle old scores and put his ghosts to rest.

CHAPTER THIRTY-TWO

JANE SAT BY Harry's bedside, crying into her fists. She had been unable to contact Brendan. She felt helpless, a useless part in a machine that had gone spinning out of control.

The doctors – the same ones who'd sent him home – didn't have a clue what was wrong with Harry. His vital signs were all strong; the tests they'd run had come back negative. All the apparatus of modern medicine seemed to agree on the same result: Harry was fine, he was fit and healthy and should not be lying in a hospital bed in what was, for all intents and purposes, a coma.

"I need you," she said, not sure if she meant her son or her absent husband. "Please come back."

The heart monitor at the side of her son's bed beeped rhythmically and steadily.

Jane closed her eyes and wished: she wished that Simon-fucking-Ridley had not come back into their lives; she wished that Brendan had never been friends with those other two boys; she wished that she could do something to save her son, her family, her very existence.

The machine continued to beep.

Harry did not move. His face was serene above the bed sheets. His hair was neatly combed into a side parting – she'd done it earlier, just to occupy some time and get rid of the nervous energy rushing through her body.

The hospital ward was busy. The nurses had pulled the curtains around on their rail to give her and Harry some privacy, but this was still a public ward. The family had no private health care; they had to accept whatever they were given. She could hear the hushed voices of other visitors, the soft-soled nurses' shoes as they brushed across the tiled floor, the frightening sounds of other medical machinery. Somebody was speaking on the phone at the nurses' station. They laughed, and then remembered where they were and began to whisper.

Jane reached out and took Harry's small hand in her own, above the covers. There was no response from his body; his muscles did not even twitch. She felt empty, as if he'd turned his back on her, ignoring her show of affection. She knew this wasn't true, that she was being silly, but it did not help. Her son didn't even know she was here, at his side, crying for him.

"I need you to come back," she said, this time speaking to them both – Harry and Brendan. Isobel was still at a friends' house gearing up for the sleepover, ignorant of the hell Jane was going through. How did you tell a ten-year-old that her twin brother might die, and nobody could do a thing about it because they had no idea what was happening to him?

She closed her eyes, and for a moment – a second, at most – she thought that she heard Harry making a strange clicking sound, as if he were pressing his tongue against the side of his mouth the way he did whenever he saw a dog on the street or in a neighbours' garden.

She opened her eyes, but of course Harry was just the same: he had not made a sound.

Jane let go of his hand and stood. She took out her mobile phone and checked it for messages. There were none. She went to the nurses' station and told them that she was stepping outside to make a call, to see if she could contact her husband. The nurses smiled and nodded, and their eyes were filled with pity. Poor soul, they were probably thinking. He's probably out at the pub, or in the betting shop.

Jane went outside. When she made the call, and there was no answer, she felt like smashing the phone. She leant back against the wall and wished again: but this time she wished her husband dead... and instantly regretted the thought, tried to take it back.

CHAPTER THIRTY-THREE

IT WAS A seamless transition from standing in that small, cramped, green-lit place to being here, beyond the screen of oak trees, just inside the grove. Simon accepted the passage with an unfamiliar calmness. It felt like some kind of Zen moment: his mind and body acted as one, unified against the strangeness that was showing more of itself to him at every twist and turn of this journey. He'd gone beyond fear. He wanted to embrace horror – the horror he'd always felt should belong to him.

Hailey was nowhere to be seen. Now that Banjo, their doorway, had helped them enter the place she'd called Loculus, she had fled the scene, leaving them to their own devices. She did not seem to have any power here. He wondered if she'd exhausted her energies that first time, when she'd helped them escape.

He glanced at the two boys he'd known back then, who had become men he barely knew at all, and wondered what it was they were meant to do – why they were here. They were all present to face their fears, he knew that. But at a deeper level, unknown forces were warring. The three had become pieces in a game that none of them could understand.

He recalled his most recent dream, when the Angel of the North had been bowed and broken, and a weeping woman had cradled the body of her children

– her twin babies. It all made sense now, in a grim kind of way. That dream, he realised, was a prophecy, a glimpse of how things might be if they failed here.

Twins.

Two parts of a whole.

Yin and Yang: opposing forces.

Comedy and tragedy. Darkness and light.

This place, he thought, must exist in a state of turmoil: the balance shifting, constantly moving back and forth between opposing points. The Underthing – whatever it was – had sniffed out that Brendan was capable of producing twins and tried to claim him early, to tip the balance in its favour. That was why they'd been brought here twenty years ago; that was why they'd been examined by uncaring hands. It had not been sexual abuse, but a sort of medical examination, meant to find out which one was the future twin-maker. Then, before things had reached their terrible conclusion, Hailey had stepped in and helped them to get away.

He remembered, now; he recalled more than he ever had before.

Standing here, in the grove where they'd been tormented, he had a mental flash: Hailey standing between them and some huge, shapeless shadow, waving her arms, flapping her weird wings, and shouting, screaming, distracting it to give them a chance to get away. He could not remember who had managed to struggle free from the leafy bonds first, but after that, they'd acted together to break out and run free.

They had acted *together*. As a single unit... three separate parts, joining together to form a whole.

That was important to remember.

And that was all. He could recall nothing more. He probably never would. But at least, for now, he had his horror to hold – the sordid excuse for a life that he'd led could be traced back to an actual event, rather than the scattered fragments of shattered memory.

"Look." Marty was pointing with one hand while he gripped his side with the other. He seemed to be in pain. His face was pale, his mouth twisted into something that came as close to a snarl as Simon had ever seen on a human being.

"It's come back. It still wants us..." Simon watched as a great shadow roiled in the space beyond the trees, moving away from them like a mobile stain across the land. "Let's go and give it what it wants."

Simon led the way out of the grove of ancient oaks and into an open area. The sun hung miles above them, as still as a picture, and the hills rolled away to other patches of woodland, most of them burned and blasted. To the west, across a vale of green and grey, he could see the ruins of some kind of city. Cradled between two hills, in a shallow valley, the blackened buildings waited like a ghost of shelter. "What the hell is this place?"

It was all from his dream: a possible future, where everything was ruined.

Brendan turned in a slow circle, surveying their surroundings. "I don't know, but we've been here before. This land – it knows us. It can sense that we're here. Can't you feel it?"

"Yes," said Marty, still clutching his side. "It feels like we never really left."

Simon nodded. The truth of his friend's words dug

deep, piercing his heart; and in a way, they never *had* left this place, not really. All they'd done was peek outside the boundaries of a prison and pretend that their lives were part of another world, a place where people killed each other for money, fucked each other for company, and bobbed and weaved like fighters inside a ring, never stopping, not even pausing for breath before they reached the grave.

Ahead of them, at the base of the slope on top of which they stood, the earth began to heave. Above them, the sky turned dark, as if a huge shadow was passing above them.

Simon looked up, and what he saw there scared him more than anything else he'd seen since returning to the Grove. The sky was filled with hummingbirds. There were millions of them, just hanging there, hovering in the air about a mile above the three men, waiting for something to happen. They stretched out like a patterned sheet, covering the sky for mile upon mile – so far, in fact, that he could barely see the blue edges.

This had happened twenty years ago, too. He was certain.

"What do they want?" Brendan's voice was tiny; he sounded like a child.

"I think they want to watch us. Or maybe watch *over* us."

There were no sounds other than those caused by the men.

The air was still.

The birds were silent.

Even that incessant churning of the earth was soundless, like a film clip with the volume set to mute. They all turned to watch the chaos of soil, shifting and turning as if a huge invisible shovel were digging there. Something erupted from the muddy surface, its segmented back breaking through the soft crust and rolling like the body of a withered serpent. Its hide was dark and wet, yet covered with a fine mesh, like old teabags. There were bright yellow boils along the ridge of its spine, and as it lurched upwards and forwards, thrusting itself out of the hole in the earth, Simon thought that he saw what might have been a face amid the mass of waste that had been compressed to form its long, thick neck. Then he realised that it was *all* neck. Like a snake, or an old-fashioned image of a sea monster, it arched its body and slammed back into the earth, sending showers of mulch flying.

The creature did not move any closer. It kept its distance, toying with them from afar, coy as a lover. Simon had seen this thing before. He knew what it was called, if not what it was.

He had seen it in his dream.

"The Underthing," he said. "That's it. That's the Underthing. This time it's showing itself."

He glanced up, at the hummingbird sky, and saw that every tiny beak, every black eye, was turned in their direction. Whatever was happening here, it was larger than their experience. This meeting signalled a stage in the evolution of Loculus, and he was too dim, or too inconsequential, to be given insight into what form it might take.

"This isn't how I had it planned..." He turned to the others, his eyes moist, his mouth open. "It's not what I expected."

A loud clicking sound broke the silence, splitting the air and causing the birds above them to shiver. It was the call of Captain Clickety, the damned and damning song of their childhood nightmares. If the vision of waste and corruption before them was the Underthing, then the avatar, the tentacle they'd named Clickety, was now to make an appearance in the endgame that was unfolding around them.

"He's coming now. The Plague Doctor. Captain Clickety. He's here." Hailey stood beside them, her voice a whisper.

Simon wasn't sure where she'd come from, but he felt glad that she was here, if only for moral support. Her wings were folded down, plastered to her back like a weird cloak. Her hair was as black as a raven's wing; her leafy eyes were solemn. "The Underthing won't come near you... he's afraid. He can't touch you, because if he does, he'll fall apart. So much spiritual pollution can only hold itself together, in one piece, if it isn't subject to human contact. It's fragile, like an eggshell; too much pressure and it will break. That's why it always sends in an avatar to do its dirty work."

Pressure... the thought filled Simon's head, as if the space there had been waiting to enclose that one word.

Pressure...

Pushing...

Wasn't that the one thing he was best at – pushing, applying pressure? He'd done it all his life, to get what he wanted, and now he was faced with a real test of his talent. If he could push this thing, coerce it into doing his bidding, he might be able to save them all. The past would be shut out; the darkness would lift; the hummingbirds would move on and the sky would clear, letting back in the sun.

It was time to push.

*   *   *

BRENDAN COULD FEEL his unnamed brother on his back, like an unwanted passenger. The face that had haunted him from the inside without him even knowing, the familiar features he had never even laid eyes on until yesterday, was speaking to him silently. He could feel the lips moving between his shoulder blades, the frown forming on its brow, the diseased cheeks puffing in and out as they sucked at the air of this place.

He reached behind him and tried to slap at the face through his clothing, but it did no good. He graspéd at his back, attempting to still those lips, to stop that unforgiving toothless mouth from moving.

But the face – the terrible face formed of ruined, besmirched flesh – mocked him; it taunted him with one word, repeated over and over again:

Loculus.

He could feel the word forming on the lips of his back, tearing from his own rancid flesh, and almost hear it spoken aloud inside his mind. His brother, his never-lived, never-really-died twin, was chanting the word like a prayer.

"No," he whispered, "Stop it." He grabbed a handful of the material of his jacket and pulled; he felt the face laughing. He reached behind and battered at the top of his spine, hurting himself. He beat at the edge of the face, hitting, slapping, and punching.

Then he began to scratch – he had not been able to scratch there, on his back, for years, and the pain felt good. Even as the skin split beneath his clothes, even as the blood seeped from the wounds...

*   *   *

THE CLICKING SOUND was deafening.

It filled the air like helium in a balloon, forcing it close to bursting point. Simon could feel it worming its way beneath his skin, entering his bloodstream, forcing aside his bones and vital organs to aid its passage.

The music was inside him, and it was hideous.

He looked at his friends and saw that they were experiencing the same discomfort. Brendan was scratching at his back, pulling at his clothing. He took off his jacket and threw it onto the floor, and then began to tear at his shirt, flaying it from his body.

MARTY'S SIDE WAS on fire. He clutched at the wound, feeling the stitches fray and the dressing come loose. Humpty – that awful, terrible creature from his childhood's darkest nightmares – was moving around, picking at the wound from the inside, and trying to get out. This was where it wanted to be; it could smell the earth beneath Marty's feet and feel the breeze of this place on its ugly, chubby cheeks.

He could feel its deformed hand-feet scrabbling, tearing away at his flesh. His side felt warm; blood was being spilled. He looked down and saw his abdomen blowing up like a balloon, doubling, tripling in size...

He went down onto his knees, crippled by the pain. He pressed the palm of his hand into his beltline, trying to push the thing back inside. Was it trying to exit through his navel?

Then, wriggling, the thing began to shift around, turning itself like a breech birth. Its head was close to the opening; he could feel the lips of the wound begin to pucker and open, like a mouth preparing for a long, deep, loving kiss. His body was preparing to vomit out the interloper.

Humpty-fucking-Dumpty was coming out to play. And all the king's horses and all the king's men wouldn't be able to put Marty together again...

SIMON WAS ALONE, now; he had no back-up. Marty was writhing on the ground, clutching at his abdomen – which was swelling as Simon watched, as if the unholy clicking sound was filling it, bloating the man's stomach like a pregnancy. His swollen belly undulated, bursting the buttons on his shirt, and Simon saw that it was taking on the shape of a giant egg: a tight, pale oval.

"What's happening?"

"Look," said Hailey, pointing towards the trees at the bottom of the slope.

About a mile away, like some kind of border, was a stand of undamaged oak trees, not unlike the ones from which they'd emerged. As he watched, a figure stepped forward from the tree line, using a short cane to walk. Even at this distance, he could make out the dark floppy hat, the dark clothes and the white beaked mask.

"Captain Clickety," he said, the sound of the entity's voice invading his mind. Like the frantic beating of castanets, it played out a surreal soundtrack, ushering the figure into view. Clickety moved without moving;

he walked in place, as if exercising on a treadmill, and yet still he loomed closer, covering the distance in jinks and jerks.

Simon looked back at his friends. Brendan was hugging himself, but violently, as if he were trying to squeeze himself to death. If anything could be heard over the sound of clicking, then it would have been Brendan's screams. His mouth was open wide, his teeth bared, and he was wailing like a penitent monk, flagellating himself before a statue of the Saviour.

Marty was rolling on the ground, wrestling with what looked like a large, pink, gelatinous egg. He was beating at it with his hands, gnawing at it with his teeth. The thing was rudimentary, only partially formed, still attached to his stomach by strands and threads of bloody flesh.

"What can I do?" Simon turned to Hailey, but she was no longer there. She had deserted him just when he needed her most.

Her voice came to him, between clicks, and he heard her say: "Do what you must. Do what you do best. Just push."

Then it came to him: the way he could do this, how he could defeat whatever it was that had set itself against them.

Just push...

He had always pushed people, towards what he wanted them to do or away from himself. It was his skill, his only real talent.

He turned and looked at his friends, locked in their personal battles, and started to piece things together. He was the go-between here; he always had been. It was his role in life: to help others make things happen.

Just push...

He was the pusher. So he did what came naturally: he pushed.

"Get up," he said slowly and calmly. "Get the fuck up and join me." He stepped over to Brendan, who was still clawing at his own shoulders, tearing away the rags of his shirt. "Get up. Now. Leave the fucking spots alone and climb onto your feet. Help me now, or so help me, when I get back there, to where we live, I'll take Jane away from you..."

Just push...

"I'll take her to bed, and then I'll take her away from everything she's ever known. I'll show her all the things she's been missing, the life she should've had. I'll take her and I'll keep her and you'll never see her again."

It was working. Brendan staggered to his feet, his face contorted in pain and rage and bitterness.

"Stand with me... or you'll never get to hold your wife again." Simon raised his left hand, the palm facing outward. He splayed his fingers, and then slowly drew them into a fist, one finger at a time folding in towards the palm, little one first and the thumb last: the long-ago salute of the Three Amigos.

Brendan grabbed Simon's arm, but rather than a gesture of violence it was one of love; a bond, once broken, was being remade. Brendan realised what Simon was doing. They both looked down, at the old scar on Brendan's right forearm, and Simon remembered the time when they had built the den. A good time, a happy time, just before the darkness arrived.

Brendan smiled and nodded; he understood what was required.

"And you," he said, turning to Marty. "You fucking pussy. Call yourself a fighter? Call yourself a man? Look at you, rolling around in the dirt wrestling with yourself. Get the fuck up or get the fuck out. You're nothing; you're useless. Your father was right about you. You'll never be a real man." Tears clouded Simon's vision, but he kept up the assault. "Get up and be a man or just lie there like a little boy." It hurt him to say these things, but he hoped that Marty, too, would get what he was doing. "Just lie there, like you did when Sally died!"

Marty screamed: a roar of rage. He gritted his teeth, stood and faced Simon.

"Be a man." Simon squared up to his friend. This was it: do or die. "Okay, soldier?" His voice was an echo from a time before darkness; from the days when monsters were just things they read about in books or saw in films on TV.

Marty nodded.

Then, back together again – *truly* together, for the first time – the Three Amigos turned as one to face their enemy. Simon moved his hands away from his body and opened his fingers. The other two men took his outstretched hands, one each, and they held on as if they were afraid to let go.

Simon smiled.

Then he pushed again.

Three separate parts joined together to create a whole. He could feel the energy thrumming in his hands, spreading up along his arms to pool inside his chest, forming a hard little shell around his heart.

Captain Clickety stood before them, a nightmare in black. He stood with his weight on his left foot, supporting himself with the cane. His black hat was tipped at a rakish angle and his white beak pointed straight forward, like a stubby accusing finger. In his free hand – the one without the cane – he was holding out a photograph: a portrait of a young boy. It only took Simon a second to recognise the face.

The photograph was of Harry. It was old, tattered, taken a few years ago, but it was definitely Brendan and Jane's boy.

He felt Brendan sway at his side, as if he were about to pass out. Simon clenched his fingers around Brendan's palm, pushing his brotherhood, his love, towards his friend.

"Push with me," he said.

Captain Clickety nodded.

"You can't have him."

Captain Clickety nodded again.

Behind him, down the slope, the Underthing was writhing in a paroxysm of fury or excitement – it could have been either: anger at being faced down, or delight that the game was almost over and the twin was within its grasp. Everything hung on the cusp in this moment.

"No," said Simon. "I'm not afraid of you. Not anymore. I'll fight you. *We'll* fight you."

His friends were effectively hobbled by their own fears. Brendan was silent and swaying; Marty was repeatedly whispering the words "Humpty Dumpty" under his breath. It would have been a comical sight, under other circumstances, but now, in this situation, it was simply horrific.

Simon could smell burning shit and vomit and Parma violets. He gagged, the stench reaching the back of his throat.

Captain Clickety flipped the photograph over, showing him the reverse side.

There was another image forming on the white paper, a shot of Harry in a hospital bed, his face slack, the features blurred yet still recognisable. Jane sat at his side, holding one of his hands on the clean, white bedclothes. On her face was a look of anguish, so intense it almost burned through the page.

Suddenly Simon knew what he must do. He realised why he was here, what his role was meant to be. He'd spent twenty years envying the others their horror, and wondering why it was that he retained no horror of his own. Now he knew why that was; the knowledge came to him in a flash, like a migraine.

This was the horror he'd always been looking for, the terror that he'd spent his life tracking down without even knowing it. The dreams of the Angel; the prophecies of apocalypse. The Angel, he now realised, was meant to be him.

He was the Angel of the North...

And what was it that angels did? What was their great purpose?

Angels, like the hummingbirds hovering above him, were messengers. They had sacrificed their humanity to serve at the shoulder of their god.

Sacrifice.

This was his purpose; it was the reason he was here, the mission he'd come back to accomplish.

Sacrifice.

He smiled. "Take me instead. Leave the boy and take me."

Pushing... pushing hard... pushing for something he did not quite understand...

Hummingbirds began to fall from the sky.

At first they plummeted one by one, and then in clumps, like debris from a volcanic eruption. They fell around him, missing him by inches, but not one of them came into contact with him.

Captain Clickety was crippled beneath the deluge, his arms raised uselessly to protect his head. The clicking sound was by now cataclysmic; it was the sound of tectonic plates shifting in this strange, symbolic dream-world, of great stones grating together on the ocean bed.

Here was Simon's horror. This was his terrible prize.

Captain Clickety's lenses and mask were knocked off his face, and beneath these was another, smaller mask exactly like the first.

He straightened, stretching to his full height, reached up and removed this mask, too. There was yet another one underneath. He was a being made entirely of masks; a walking lie, a deception. One mask after another was torn from his face, and the hummingbirds continued to fall.

This, Simon realised, was the birds' own sacrifice, their way of confirming his thoughts, telling him that he had been right.

"Take me," he whispered, opening his hands and letting go of his friends – perhaps relinquishing his grip on those childhood friendships forever. The two men fell to the ground at his sides, kneeling like tired suitors before a prospective bride.

Gradually, the rain of birds ceased. The sky cleared. The surviving hummingbirds flew off in groups, letting back in the daylight.

Captain Clickety shuffled forward. He was broken, spent; a thing past its use-by date. His arms and legs hung from their sockets like a marionette's. The Underthing was no longer raging in the ground behind him. It had returned to whatever sewers or underground conduits served as its home, fleeing in the face of defeat, not wanting to watch as its plans were torn down.

Captain Clickety sniffed, like a dog, inhaling Simon's scent. His hat had come off and his head was bald and white, an extension of the beaked mask. He kept sniffing and sniffing, and then, finally, he stopped and slowly nodded.

Yes.

The sacrifice had been accepted. Perhaps this had been required from the start; there was a chance that Brendan had never been the one, that it had always been Simon, and only now was the truth being told.

Simon reached out and took the final mask from the face of his nemesis, his childhood fear. He crumpled it easily in his fist. This stagnant puppet of deception, this last bedraggled lie, wore nothing but a paper face. Beneath the final mask was nothing but a broken mirror. Simon stared into his shattered reflection, wondering what all of this could possibly mean. He studied his empty eyes, his sunken cheeks, his dry lips.

He barely even recognised himself.

Captain Clickety fell into a heap of greasy sticks and rags on the ground. The avatar was no more; he had been torn apart by the simple act of sacrifice, a show of friendship that monsters like him would never, ever understand. To love was human, not divine; to hate was simply monstrous.

The Three Amigos would live to ride another day, and everything that came after this would be different, cast in a new and uncertain light. Rather than a band of three, each would set off into his own sunset as his own man, liberated, freed at last from the terrible bondage of a shared past.

"What happened?" Brendan rose from his knees, topless, his shirt cast aside, his skin scratched and torn by his own fingernails. "Has it gone?"

"I'm not sure," said Simon. "I'm not sure about anything."

Marty staggered upright, to complete the group. He was bleeding from a gash in his side, stitches pulled free and dangling like threads. "Did you see it?" His face was ashen. He was crying openly, unconcerned by his show of what he usually saw as weakness. "Did you see Humpty-fucking-Dumpty?"

Simon shook his head. "I don't know what I saw... or what I'm seeing now." He looked up, at the brightening sky. A few straggling hummingbirds flew in circles above them, watching over these final few moments. "But I want to go home."

They turned around and walked towards the grove of oak trees, no longer afraid of what they would find at its centre: just the shadows of forgotten youth, frayed lengths of rope, and husks of memories that even now were losing their power over them.

For a moment, he thought he saw a ghostly outline of three small boys, holding hands as they stood in a row before the trees. Their outlines shimmered and they were gone; he had seen nothing, after all.

CHAPTER THIRTY-FOUR

"WHAT THE FUCK happened in there?"

They were standing on the Roundpath, outside the Needle. Simon had locked the gates and was returning the keys to his pocket.

"What the fuck happened?" Marty was clutching the remains of Brendan's shirt to his side. The blood was still flowing, but slowly.

"Would you do me a favour?" Brendan, still topless, turned around and presented his back to the group. "Tell me what you see there, on my back?" He still sounded afraid, but it was fear of a different kind.

Simon stared at his friend's back. It was scratched and bloody, but nothing more. "Just a few scratches."

"You sure? I mean really sure? I've suffered horrendous back acne my whole life. If what you're telling me is correct, I'm cured."

Simon walked over and touched Brendan's back. His skin was hot and damp, but apart from a few old acne scars, it was clear of any kind of blemish other than the ones caused by the man's own hands. "I promise," he said. "The only marks on your back are either very old or the scratches you gave yourself."

Marty hobbled over. "I still don't understand any of this. What did you do in there? Did you defeat the... the monster? Is it dead?"

Simon shook his head. "No. I don't think so. I think we just sent it away for a little while. How do you kill something that was never alive in the first place? It won't bother us again, though. It's done with us. We have nothing else that it can take."

"It... it *sniffed* you. Hailey said that it could smell twins. Are you a twin?"

Again, Simon shook his head. "There are no twins in our family. I was an only child. Whatever the hell it smelled on me, it wasn't that... maybe it just caught a whiff of my spirit, and decided that the fight was no longer one it could win? Who knows? I don't have a fucking clue."

The sky was dark. Night had fallen. He wasn't sure how long they'd been inside the tower, but it felt like days had passed in the outside world. He remembered that time had no meaning in there; in the place Hailey had called Loculus – the little place, where dreams went to die.

"Let's go home. Back to Brendan's place, check on Jane and the kids. I have a feeling they'll have their own story to tell, and it'll make as much sense as ours."

Brendan's head snapped up. "What do you mean? You think they're in trouble?"

"Not any more," said Simon. "While we were fighting our demons, they had to contend with one of their own. But I'm certain they're all okay, now. We won, didn't we?"

The three men went silent for a moment.

"Did we? Did we win, I mean?" Marty looked like he might collapse at any minute.

"Let's get you both seen to, eh? Then we can either talk about this until dawn and try to figure out what we just did, or fucking forget about the whole thing and move on with our lives. It's your call. I'm too tired to even think about it."

They moved off, away from the Needle, with Simon in the lead, Marty in the middle, and Brendan bringing up the rear, dragging his mobile phone from his pocket and checking the messages. He stopped in his tracks, the phone held against his ear.

"Oh, shit..." He listened to every message before allowing them to move off again.

"It's Harry. He's been ill again. But... well, according to the last message, he's okay now. Jane's still at the hospital, but she says he's fine. They just want to keep him in a couple of days to keep an eye on him."

Simon smiled. "He's fine. The boy's fine."

Marty said nothing.

Brendan called Jane's mobile and asked a lot of questions as he walked, promising her that he'd go right to the hospital once he'd cleaned himself up. He seemed a lot happier when he hung up, although he was crying. He even smiled.

"Yes, he is fine. He's eating fucking ice cream and flirting with the nurses."

Simon laughed, and turned back round, to look where he was going. He saw the figure only briefly, as it darted out from a ginnel that led to Back Grove Crescent.

Just before he felt a sharp punching sensation in his stomach, and fell to the ground, he recognised the baseball cap with the Scooby Doo badge on the front. The hat fell from the kid's head as he ran back into the ginnel, palming the bloodied knife.

Simon smiled. What else could he do?

He realised now that they'd never really escaped when they were children. Time had no meaning in Loculus; twenty years in the real world might be a few days in the little place. Captain Clickety, and by extension the Underthing, had simply let them leave. Because it knew – it had always known – that they'd come back.

Take me, he thought. *Take me back home, to a time when the world was smaller, the days were brighter, before the monsters were real and the damage was done...*

Simon died with that ironic smile still on his lips. He tried to speak. To tell Marty something, perhaps even to explain the joke, as the other man cradled him in his arms. But he didn't have the strength. He closed his eyes and accepted the onrushing darkness. Somewhere within it – from deep inside all of that vast black night – he heard a faint clicking sound, as if something approved of his passing.

The sacrifice had been accepted.

And still he did not know the reason why, or the full extent of what he had offered to save his friends.

WHAT COMES AFTER, WHEN THE SILENCE HAS BEEN BROKEN

Two DAYS AFTER Simon's death, Marty is on a train to King's Cross. Brendan badly wanted to make the journey with him, but Marty told his friend to stay at home and look after his wife and kids. Harry is fighting fit, but he still needs a father's attention. Jane needs some attention too, and even a woman that brave must be close to breaking point after everything she's gone through.

If he is honest, he also doesn't think Brendan's in the right frame of mind. He is stronger than he looks, but Marty is stronger. Marty has always been proud to call himself a bastard, and it is a bastard's errand upon which he finds himself.

The train pulls into the station. Marty disembarks, throwing his rucksack over his shoulder, and makes his way along the platform. The jostling hordes remind him of some of the crowds at the fights he's been in, and it makes him feel slightly nauseous to be surrounded by so many people.

He has only vague memories of the mutant Humpty Dumpty creature emerging from the wound in his side, and of fighting it on the ground in that... *other* place. The place he now knows as Loculus. He tries not to think of it, but he knows that it will return to him always, in dreams. Loculus is a defective storage pen for such dreams; it is like a leaking battery, and the energy of dreams runs both ways, in and out of its borders.

He knows this now. It makes things easier to deal with.

He also knows that Simon Ridley somehow managed to save them all. The details aren't clear, but the feeling that Simon has been a hero is embedded deep inside him, like a seed in fertile ground. And he hopes one day that seed will produce the flowers of memory. Then he can pay proper tribute to his friend, his saviour: the boy he wishes he could have known better as a man.

Marty turns left outside of the station, and follows the route he has memorised from Google Maps. The address was in Simon's notebook back at the flat on Grove Court. Marty was forced to break in to salvage Simon's belongings, because he had not been able to find the keys on the body.

The kid who murdered Simon is still out there somewhere. When he returns from this short trip to London, Marty has plans to track down the bastard himself. He's already spoken to Erik Best, and there are a couple of good lads on the case. Hopefully, by the time he gets back to the Concrete Grove, they will have found him.

Then it will be Marty's turn to play Humpty-fucking-Dumpty...

He finds The Halo easily. It is on a street corner, and the sign outside the pub is pretty hard to miss – a tiny transvestite angel with a big glowing circle around its head. He smiles as he glances up at the sign. Then he steps inside and heads straight for the bar.

"Excuse me," he says to the man standing behind the bar reading a paperback thriller. "Are you Mike?"

"Depends on who's asking," says the man, grinning.

Marty decides that he likes this man. He can see already why he was Simon's best – only – friend. "I'm Marty. We spoke on the phone."

The grin falls away. "Shit, yeah. Fuck... Marty. Good to meet you." He sticks out his hand and Marty takes it, gives it a quick shake.

"I'm sorry I had to break the news to you that way. How's Natasha taking it?"

Mike shrugs his narrow shoulders. "Not good. I'll go and get her. Like I said on the phone, she's been staying upstairs, in my spare room, for a few days. She hasn't had any visitors, or even spoken to anyone she works with. She needs to get her head together before the funeral. We both do."

Marty sits at a table and looks at his hands. His scars are livid today; his knuckles look like conkers in a bag.

"Hello..."

When he glances up from the table, she is there, standing at his side. He was not even aware of her as she moved across the room. Perhaps it is part of her training as a model, that ability to *glide* rather than walk.

"I'm sorry," he says again. It is something he finds himself saying a lot lately. "I tried to help him... but... but he died."

"In your arms." Her face is thin and pale, the skin of her cheeks as delicate as paper, fluttering as she speaks. Her pronunciation is slow and deliberate, as if she is trying desperately not to stumble over the words. Marty likes her accent.

"In my arms," he says, trying not to cry. "This is why I came here. To tell you face-to-face that... that I tried to save him. And that he saved me."

He stares at her impassive face for a little while longer, and then his gaze wanders down to her belly. She isn't showing, not yet; but Mike told him the news when Marty telephoned the previous day and arranged to come over and see her.

"How many months are you gone?" He nods at her stomach.

"Not long. Just eight weeks. I was going to tell him when he got back. I could not tell him something like that over the phone. That's why I was so desperate to see him. I almost came up there, to the northeast. I nearly came to see him before... well, you know." Her eyes are shining. Tears look good on her; she wears her grief well. Natasha is a true model; a natural.

Marty doesn't know what else to say, so he falls back on small talk, hoping that some day he can speak to this woman properly, tell her the truth – or at least as much of it as he can understand. "Do you know what you're having?" He flexes his hands on the table. They're stiff; his fingers ache. "I mean, would he have been the father of a boy or a girl?"

Natasha licks her lips. Her left eye twitches slightly. Not much, but it is a crack in the façade, a gap through which the depth of her grief can be glimpsed, like fire, if only briefly.

"Both," she says, her voice as low as a whisper. "I'm having twins. There are twins on my mother's side of the family, and it seems I got them, too."

Marty closes his eyes. Darkness floods in, drowning him.

Now, at last, he realises what Captain Clickety must have sniffed out on Simon, and what had happened right at the end, when a deal was struck.

He knows why the sacrifice was accepted, and how it might now be claimed.

"Twins," he whispers, and in that black moment the word becomes forever associated with absolute horror.